Mary Stanley was born in England and educated in Ireland. A graduate of Trinity College Dublin, she has worked in England, Italy and Germany. She now lives in Dublin. *Retreat* is her first novel.

Retreat

Mary Stanley

HEADLINE

First published in Great Britain in 2001 by
HEADLINE BOOK PUBLISHING

10 9 8 7 6 5 4 3 2

ISBN 0 7472 6736 7

Typeset by Palimpsest Book Production Limited,
Polmont, Stirlingshire
Printed and bound in Great Britain by
Clays Ltd, St Ives plc

HEADLINE BOOK PUBLISHING
A division of Hodder Headline
338 Euston Road
London NW1 3BH

www.headline.co.uk
www.hodderheadline.com

*For my dearest and
most outlandish friend.
For Ingrid Nachstern
who held my foot.*

Once upon a midnight dreary, while I pondered, weak and weary,
Over many a quaint and curious volume of forgotten lore –
While I nodded, nearly napping, suddenly there came a tapping,
As of some one gently rapping, rapping at my chamber door.
''Tis some visitor,' I muttered, 'tapping at my chamber door –
Only this and nothing more.'

From *The Raven*, by Edgar Allan Poe

Traditionally, Mother Immaculata addressed the girls on the Friday prior to the Easter holidays. This was no exception.

'Girls of St Martin's.' In full-length robes, Mother Immaculata, known as The Raven to her charges, glided into the hall in her wimple and full head regalia. She gave the impression of being on roller skates, as no actual leg or foot movement was discernible. 'On Sunday evening after Easter, all the girls of Fourth, Fifth and Sixth Year will move into the school as boarders, while the girls of First, Second and Third Year will return from their holidays a week later as they have already completed their annual Retreat.'

Most of the pupils were boarders anyway, so this would not make a noticeable difference in the dormitories.

'You will have the evening to settle down and acclimatise. Having said that, come Monday morning after breakfast, silence will commence. There will be no talking whatsoever until the following Saturday morning. That gives you five full days of contemplation and prayer.

'Contemplate on the indulgences you can amass both for yourselves and your dead relatives. With sufficient prayer you may be able to release many from the torment of Purgatory and send them on their way to the ultimate Happiness. You will all pray to God for a Vocation. He may call you to become a nun during the Retreat. You must be vigilant and prepared for the Calling. Each morning you will walk to the Sister Chapel where you will remain for the day, praying, reading and in contemplation. The Blessed Sacraments of Confession and Holy Communion will be available throughout the week and you should avail yourselves of Holy Communion on a daily basis.

'As usual, leaving the Sister Chapel and its grounds is forbidden, and of course Sutherland Square is expressly out of bounds.'

3

Then methought the air grew denser, perfumed from an unseen censer
Swung by Seraphim whose foot-falls tinkled on the wooden floor
'Child,' he cried, 'My God has sent me – to these angels he has sent me,
Confess, repent, be contrite of thy sins and crimes of yore
In nomine Domine repent, confess thy sins to me some more.'
                She shall confess, ah, nevermore.

Chapter One

Kitty O'Dowd sat on a bench in Sutherland Square.

Feck you, Andrew MacDonald, she thought to herself as she took a last drag from the cigarette which she was holding between the first two fingers of her left hand.

Known for communicating in what Mother Immaculata referred to as 'inappropriate language', Kitty O'Dowd now contemplated the nun in question. And feck you too, Mother Immaculata. She scowled as she nonchalantly flicked the cigarette onto the pathway where it glowed gently just beyond the reach of her foot.

Glancing at her watch she thought, well, he's not coming now, and shook her long, dark brown hair back off her shoulders and lifted her pale heart-shaped face to the spring sun.

Jayzus, she thought, as the time shown on her watch penetrated her mind. Ten to four. I'd better be getting back. She grimaced as she thought of what the rest of the afternoon held for her.

She scattered the ash on her tunic down onto the skirt with a disinterested sweep of her hand, and stood up, yawned and stretched.

She checked the path both left and right; she could see no one approaching. Her school tunic was already six inches above her knees. She hiked it up slightly further by lifting it above her belt, and adjusted her stocking tops. She thought about Andrew MacDonald. He was all right to look at, and good fun. And he would have been a preferable alternative to what was on offer in the Sister Chapel.

Kitty O'Dowd was not given to in-depth thought, but she was aware of Andrew's ability to focus on a person and to give them his full attention.

It was both interesting and flattering. Added to that, he had surprised her three weeks earlier with some of his observations at a birthday party, which is where she had first met him. And it wasn't often that Kitty O'Dowd was surprised. So when he had suggested that she slip out from the Retreat on a daily basis, and that he would endeavour to escape from his school to meet her, she had readily agreed.

Ah well, she thought. Sitting here waiting for him was still better than kneeling in that place pondering on purity, and whether or not I'm likely to be smitten by a vocation.

The idea of going back to the chapel, of slipping in through the basement window and joining her peers for prayer, prayer and more prayer, hovered in her mind. The sheer boredom of what was ahead of her appalled her. She hurried up the path and out of the gate at the south end. Two more hours of chapel and cloisters and bugger all, she thought.

She walked with her back very straight, her neck elongated and her long dark hair swinging loosely down her back. Her pointed chin was lifted high, giving her a slightly supercilious air.

Kitty O'Dowd was working on her walk. Because she had shortened her already short tunic and was wearing stockings, she could not afford to slouch at all. She also felt it would help her in her future career, a career not yet outlined either to her parents or to the nuns. So she walked with her shoulders completely still, and just moved from her hips.

Before crossing the road, she pulled a tiny mirror from her pocket and ran a wetted finger over her artfully plucked eyebrows and checked her perfectly parted hair. Putting the mirror away, she smoothed her hair with both hands, and then keeping her face totally impassive she hastened up the street in the direction of the chapel.

In the chapel, Mary Oliver, her dark brown hair cut in a bob which seemed to extend her neck, knelt holding two nails in her right hand. Her real name was Mary Olivier.

'*Moi, je suis* Mary Olivier,' she had said in French class three Septembers earlier.

'*Non*,' replied Sister Rodriguez. '*Tu t'appelles* Mary Oliver, and don't argue.'

The nuns felt there was a pretentiousness and an affectation in the pronunciation of her name and had insisted that both the 'i' and the French sound were dropped within the confines of the convent.

The nails she held in her hand were not fingernails, but two metal nails which she had acquired from the toolbox in the neighbour's shed at half-term. Her sallow skin looked pale in the shadowy lighting in the chapel, the hollows in her cheeks more pronounced. She looked up at the crucifix on the pillar to the right of the altar and slipped one of the nails into her other palm. She squeezed her hands tightly so that she could feel the points pressing on her skin.

If I were a nun, thought Mary Oliver (whose daughter, some twenty years later, would look at her in horror and say, 'Mummy, whatever you do, don't look up,'), I would sneak into this chapel in the dead of night, and I would lower the cross from the wall and dismantle Christ. I would bury him . . . I would . . . I would give him a decent burial. (Her daughter, a dark-haired child with olive skin and brown eyes just like her mother, would say, 'Mummy, Mummy, there is the most terrible thing on the wall, don't look, don't look.')

Mary Oliver glanced briefly to her right. Across the aisle she saw Bernadette O'Higgins turning the page of a copy of *Lives of the Saints*. She was mildly surprised to see Bernadette so absorbed in such reading matter on day one. But then, as she knew from three years' experience, day one of the Retreat was always an interesting day. There were those who approached the time of prayer and contemplation with the attitude 'well, let's give it a go', and those who thought 'I'll give it my all', and those like Kitty O'Dowd who would never give it a chance.

She ran the nails up and down her palms.

Sister Rodriguez came up the aisle. Mary Oliver heard the clickety-click of Sister Rodriguez long before she saw her. Her rosary beads clicked. So did her heels.

> *Gentle smiles have gentle nuns*
> *But their jaws are firmly set*
> *Through clenched teeth they rule their flock*
> *And every girl must pay her debt*

Mary Oliver sighed quietly. She hoped that Bernadette was not up to mischief. She glanced quickly sideways again. Bernadette turned the page of her book and nodded her head several times as though in agreement with her reading matter.

Mary Oliver looked back at the crucifix, not knowing that in twenty years' time her daughter would try to protect her from just such an image.

'Dear God,' prayed Mary Oliver with her sallow skin and her overly thin body. 'Dear, dear God, how could you allow such a thing to happen to your child? Dear, dear God, if I were a nun, I would take Him down for you and give Him a decent burial.'

(Her daughter, aged eight, would hold her knuckles in front of her mouth and, shaking her head in shocked disbelief, would say, 'Mummy, Mummy, close your eyes. You mustn't look.' And this being the first time Mary had been in a church in almost twenty years, she would look up and see a man hanging on a cross, and seeing it through her daughter's eyes, it would be all she could do to suppress a scream.)

With her long fair hair neatly braided into one thick plait which hung down her back, and her navy blue eyes following her reading matter, Bernadette O'Higgins heard the clickety-click of Sister Rodriguez coming up the aisle. Inside her head she grinned. Moment of truth, she thought.

As Sister Rodriguez passed her on the aisle, Bernadette turned another page and read slowly and carefully. She looked up towards the altar as if for reassurance, then her navy blue eyes returned to the book, and she bowed her head.

Don't overdo it, she said to herself. Her reputation was not for piety and she was bright enough to know it. But she also knew that she had surpassed herself this time.

The previous weekend, during the Easter holidays, while her parents had been at a dinner dance in the Shelbourne Hotel, she had headed for the family bookshelves. There she had chosen a leatherbound copy of *The Lives of the Saints, Complete and Unabridged With Emphasis on the Virgin Martyrs* (including illustrations of their deaths), better known among her siblings as *Lives of the Saints, Completely Gory*. With a blade, removed from her father's razor, she had sliced the cover off the book at the spine. She had made good use of a brand new tube of Bostik to glue the leather cover onto her recently acquired *Scrumptious Sex* (including seven hundred and twenty photographs and sketches to illustrate in detail what made it scrumptious). The denuded *Lives of the Saints*, complete, gory and unabridged, now lay under her mattress at home. At the end of term her plan was to replace the illustrated version of *Scrumptious Sex* under her brother's mattress and do a repair job on the *Saints* and its cover, and return it to the family bookshelves.

She had it well planned. She had even considered the possibility that her brother's book might not be in perfect condition by the time she returned it. But so what? Bernadette asked herself. He can't say or do anything about it. After all, he shouldn't have had it in the first place.

Meanwhile, in the church, Sister Rodriguez paused as she passed Bernadette's pew. She eyed the reading girl with a certain amount of interest. Must be growing up at last, she thought. We certainly know how to turn out young ladies at St Martin's, as Mother Immaculata says. She smiled and nodded at the neatly plaited Bernadette and went on up to the altar.

Bernadette (navy blue eyes laughing) caught Mary Oliver's eye and winked at her before returning to her perusal of the purloined book. She was about to turn the book upside down to see a certain picture from a different angle, but she restrained herself just in time.

I'd like to try that, she thought as she looked at the picture. She even looks a bit like me, she mused.

Glancing up at the altar, she watched the prostrate Sister Rodriguez and wondered, as she often did, what Sister Rodriguez's hair was like.

Kitty O'Dowd said she had no hair. That she had encountered the devil at the gates of hell and had had her hair burnt off, before the devil sent her to St Martin's to make the girls' lives a hell on earth.

Bernadette was fourteen when Kitty shared that thought with her. They had both giggled so hard that she had nearly wet herself. Now aged seventeen, she began to wonder if Kitty might have been right.

Grinny too, she thought, thinking about their Irish teacher, Miss Ní Ghrian. Only I suspect she *is* the devil incarnate.

Miss Ní Ghrian was hurrying across Sutherland Square, returning to the convent to supervise the girls for their last two hours of Mass and prayers before walking them back to the Mother House where they boarded.

She was moving at a furious pace and her tight checked skirt kept rising. She knew she was late but she would slip in at the back of the chapel and seat herself near the door. Her lateness should not be noticed. Ahead of her she thought she momentarily glimpsed Kitty O'Dowd with her too short uniform and her new walk, which all the nuns and even Miss Maple had commented on. This new walk was such that Kitty appeared only to move her hips, and her slender body and long legs irritated Miss Ní Ghrian beyond belief. She pursed her pinched lips even tighter. But when she looked again there was no sign of any girl on the street.

The first thing she did on entering the chapel was to see if she could spot Kitty. She glanced up and down the pews trying to identify her. Kitty stood out as a rule, both because of her height, and the way she held her head. The pews were now full of kneeling girls with mantilla donned heads. There was no sign of her.

Got you now, my girl, she thought with a smile. Got you now.

She stayed standing just inside the door so that she could nab Kitty when she appeared.

The altar boys were waving the incense burners and the smell wafted down the small chapel. The ten-year-old boys from the local national school had naïveté and dedication written all over their young and cherubic faces.

The organ started playing and the choir in the balcony above began singing. The Latin words filled the nave of the church and lifted with the organ, strong and pure. The girls in the body of the church joined in. The place was full of a serenity and a purity as they praised their God.

'*Laudamus*,' they sang.

Mary Oliver rolled the nails between her joined hands and thought, *Agnus Dei*, I am the Lamb of God.

Bernadette O'Higgins (navy blue eyes now thoughtful), kneeling on her *Lives of the Saints* so as to protect it from prying neighbours, listened to the words and felt momentarily uplifted by them. In the balcony, Kitty O'Dowd (pretending to be a chorister because it was the only way she had been able to get into the church unnoticed) opened and closed her mouth like a fish, in case Miss Maple should turn round.

Treasa O'Donoghue, whose bottom stuck out so that the pleats of her tunic did not fall evenly over it, passed her sheet music to Kitty in a gesture of friendship. Kitty took it and nodded slightly in appreciation.

Miss Maple turned and looked at her choir girls in approval. She noticed Kitty among them. She let her eyes move evenly over all the choristers, before looking down onto the kneeling girls in the body of the church below.

She wondered what Kitty had been up to that she had ended up hiding out among the singers. She had no doubt that Kitty was hiding out. Well, she thought. She's not doing any harm. She's singing along, in a manner of speaking. Why, she's even managed to acquire the music. Treasa's, no doubt.

She looked at the altar boys, and noted their concentrated faces and their childlike innocence.

They were carefully selected, she reasoned.

'Amen,' sang the girls. Over and over. 'A . . . a . . . a . . . men.' The incense wafted up so that the choir could smell it. The priest raised his hand in blessing.

'In nomine Patris, et filii, et spiritui sancto.'

'Amen,' replied the kneeling girls.

The girls stood as the priest and his altar boys departed. Then Sister Rodriguez turned and motioned the girls to return to a kneeling position. There was to be a further half-hour's silent prayer before they would return to the Mother House for tea.

Bernadette wondered if she could continue her reading of the illustrated *Scrumptious Sex*. After all, the girls on either side of her, who had only come into the chapel when the bell rang at four, would surely not care what she did. She pondered on this for a minute or two.

No, she thought, better play safe. She had a whole week to read her 'Saints'.

In later years when being interviewed for various science programmes on both radio and television, she always gave credit where it was due. 'My interest in biology really only started while I was on Retreat,' she would say carefully. When asked to elucidate, she would reply, 'The silence in church was beneficial to progressive thought.'

Further up the pew knelt Anna McBride, known as Bridie to her friends, one of whom was Bernadette. Bridie's thick, dark red hair fell to her shoulders in a mass of waves, her green eyes were closed, and the smattering of tiny freckles on her nose and cheeks were scarcely visible in the shadowy lighting in the church.

At the very moment that Bernadette decided not to continue reading her book, red-haired Bridie was involved in an intricate conversation in the theatre of her imagination. This particular conversation had been going on all day. Bridie was planning her elopement with Jean Jacques Versailles, a fictitious character whom she had created about a year earlier during her last Retreat. He spoke with a French accent, very similar to that of Mary Oliver's father whom she, Bridie, had not yet met (and whom Mary had not seen in about fourteen years). Bridie had put Jean Jacques on ice for the previous twelve months, bar the occasional interlude. Because of her fierce concentration and her dedication to doing well, she feared his company would distract her during her Leaving Certificate year. So, with her customary self-discipline, she had only allowed him to keep her company in prep when she was terribly lonely, or had permitted him on rare occasions to pop into the dormitory late at night to continue a conversation or to keep a tryst.

'But how shall we escape?' Bridie asked the dark-haired Jean Jacques.

'I'm working on it,' was his reply.

'But time is running out, my loved one,' she whispered in the shadows of her mind.

He stroked her dark red hair, and then lifting it with one hand he ran his fingertips down the back of her neck. She shivered.

'So little time,' she said, in the dank dark prison cell whence she had been brought that very morning in chains.

'I know, my sweet,' he replied, keeping his hands through the bars on the door so that he could continue to caress his most precious and beloved—

'Anna McBride!' The sibilant whisper penetrated the depths of Bridie's innermost thoughts. Bridie jumped and opened her green eyes wide. Sister Rodriguez was standing beside her, looking at her.

'Vanity is a sin,' the nun hissed.

Bridie looked bemused. What the . . . ? she wondered.

'Don't you dare run your hands through your hair like that,' hissed the nun.

Bridie both looked and felt startled. She had had no idea that she had been running her hands through her hair, and anyway, she thought, it wasn't me, it was Jean Jacques.

She nodded penitently to the irate nun and returned to the French Revolution and Jean Jacques' midnight caresses, forcing herself to join her hands in a pretence of prayer.

Mary Oliver, sallow-skinned and far too thin, slipped her nails into her pocket and, getting up, she joined the queue of girls who were going to confession on the first day. All girls were expected to go at some stage during the week. There were several different approaches to this compulsory confessional. A few of the girls went on day one to get it out of the way; a few left it until the last minute possible. Some went when the queue looked at its shortest, some when it looked at its longest because it was not supervised and there was the opportunity for whispered conversation. Mary Oliver went on day one because she planned on going again during the week, and by going on day one there was a better chance that she would have something else to confess five days later before the Retreat ended.

'Bless me, Father, for I have sinned.'

'Yes, my child.'

'It is two weeks since my last confession,' whispered Mary Oliver, not knowing that this was in fact the last time she would kneel in a confession box to confess and look for absolution.

'Yes, my child.'

'I have thoughts,' she said. 'Terrible thoughts.'

'Yes, my child. Tell me about them.'

She hesitated. The missionary priests who did the Retreats were known for their understanding; surely she could tell him everything.

'Are they impure thoughts?' he asked.

She could see his profile. The well-fed cheeks, the small eyes. It was the same priest who had said Mass that morning, not the ascetic evening prayer priest. She had heard one of the girls refer to him as a magpie. She didn't know why. Magpies thieve, she thought.

'No, Father. Not impure thoughts,' she said. 'Well, I have had impure thoughts, but those aren't what I wanted to tell you about.'

'Well, tell me about the impure thoughts first,' he said.

But I don't want to, she thought to herself. They are not why I am here in this box talking through a grid to you. I was going to confess them, but they are irrelevant. I need to talk about how I want to change things from the inside and how that is all I can think about.

'The impure thoughts,' he repeated. 'You were saying . . .'

The items in her head were listed according to how she had placed them there. Her normal confession told of irritation, the odd lie, impure thoughts, losing her temper; sins which she had committed and had then placed in order. Sometimes this was the order in which she had committed them, sometimes the sequence reflected the severity of the sin, and sometimes she tagged a particularly shameful one onto the end in the hope that it would not be noticed, or buried it in the middle of a litany of 'crimes'.

'I'm sorry, Father,' she said, her mind caught by what she really wanted to talk about.

'You see, Father, I want to be a nun and—'

'I want to hear your impure thoughts,' he said. 'I told you that. Tell me them first.'

High up in the church, Miss Maple nodded to her praying choir and gestured to them that they could leave the church by the spiral staircase which led to the porch of the church, and on down to the basement which is the way Kitty O'Dowd had joined the choristers earlier.

The girls trooped down the stairs in single file and out through the porch into the chapel grounds. They were not allowed to speak.

Miss Maple told them to start the quarter-mile walk back to the Mother House.

'Kitty,' she said with her most genial look. 'I'm so pleased you decided to join the choir.'

Kitty stood tall and straight in front of her. It was rare that a teacher addressed her without telling her to take 'that look' off her face, or to lengthen her school tunic.

'I will expect you up there with the choir every day of the Retreat.'

Kitty nodded. Hoisted with my own petard, she thought.

Miss Ní Ghrian appeared in the forecourt. 'Kitty O'Dowd,' she said, 'you are in big trouble, my girl.'

'The girls are on silence,' Miss Maple said. 'Is there a problem?'

'This is between Kitty and me,' retorted the irate Irish teacher.

'Well, as she's on silence and is one of my choir, perhaps you could bring the issue up with me,' replied Miss Maple.

Silence. Kitty watched Grinny's face and it was all she could do to restrain herself from grinning. The long-running battle between Miss Maple and the Irish teacher was well known among the girls, and Kitty's desire to smirk was almost overpowering. Miss Maple caught her eye and Kitty looked at the ground. She knew she had just been rescued and that it should be left at that.

'Go ahead, girls,' said Miss Maple. 'I will catch you up. Now Áine, what has Kitty done?'

'I didn't know she was in the choir,' came from the gritted teeth of the Irish teacher.

'Yes,' said Miss Maple. 'She is one of my true successes. I've been at her for a long time to join us, all year in fact, and I'm very proud of her.'

Kitty moved on and joined the others. She was taken aback both by the venom of Grinny's attack and by the strength of Miss Maple's support and the kind way she spoke about her.

Proud, she thought. Proud! That is a first.

In the confessional, Mary Oliver shifted on her bony knees on the wooden step. She was aware that they were sore. What does he want of me? she wondered. She did not understand. He seemed to be wanting to look at her impure thoughts in depth, which did not make sense as there was an unwritten rule that you could confess to impure thoughts and that this phrase covered a multitude; details were not required.

Her distress about seeing herself as a nun with a mission faded as she focused on her immediate problem. She had no idea how to answer the question. She thought quickly. There had not been any impure thoughts since her confession the previous fortnight. At least, she could not think of any. Perhaps her desire to remove Christ from the cross could be considered impure.

'Father . . .' She hesitated.

The girls in the pew outside shuffled on their seats and fell silent as they strained to hear what was going on in the box. Mary Oliver was taking an extraordinarily long time.

Miss Ní Ghrian approached the pew to herd the girls out for the walk home. 'Time to leave, girls. You can go to confession tomorrow.'

One of the girls pointed at the box and gestured that there was someone in there.

Inside the box, feeling constricted and trapped, Mary said that she did not think there had been impure thoughts after all.

She thought of Christ on his cross, and the smell of the incense lingering in the air outside the box penetrated through the cracks above and below the hinges on the door, and the walls of the box moved in on her and she thought of Christ buried in a box. She separated her hands, which had been clasped together and, retrieving the nails from her pocket, she grasped at the tiny shelf before the criss-cross latticework that separated her from the morning Mass priest. The box seemed very small.

Years later she underwent therapy to help her deal with the confined space on an aircraft, because debilitating claustrophobia meant she could no longer travel by air to visit her father. In a hypnotic trance, Mary Oliver told the doctor that the priest, while delving further into her impure thoughts, asked her did she often think about penises.

At the time, though, she just heard words pounding against the walls of the small confessional, and as the blood drained from her head, her thin hands fell away from the wooden shelf she was holding and she slipped in a dead faint against the door, which opened, and out she fell into the church.

In the horrified silence which followed her tumble, the girls, momentarily shocked rigid, jumped to their feet. Miss Ní Ghrian pushed past them and waved her hands frantically over Mary's white face. The priest pulled the curtain back on the window of his box and whispered, 'Next please.'

Afterwards in the dormitory, the girls whispered about what had

18

happened, some in a subdued way, some in an excited way. They were not brought up to criticise or to find fault in a priest in any way. But none of those waiting girls was left untouched by what they saw but could not identify as the callousness of this man. Whatever had gone on between him and Mary Oliver, at the end of the day it was Mary who lay unconscious on the floor of the church. Even Miss Ní Ghrian, not known for compassion towards any of the girls other than her favourites, was startled, to say the least.

'Would that be normal?' she asked Sister Rodriguez and Mother Immaculata later. 'I mean, for Father to continue the confessions just like that?'

'His Work is of Our Lord,' Mother Immaculata reassured her and poured her a cup of tea. Mother Immaculata had the ability to speak in capitals.

'Lots of sugar, Miss Ní Ghrian?' Sister Rodriguez inquired. 'I'm sure you've had a bit of a shock.'

Mary Oliver, on the floor of the chapel, slowly regaining consciousness, had more than a bit of a shock. She was aware of Miss Ní Ghrian flapping her hands over her face. She could not at first feel her own hands or her feet, and then she saw the faces of the girls peering at her. The last traces of incense wafted on the air.

'I didn't know how to get her back here,' Áine Ní Ghrian said later as she sipped her heavily sweetened tea. She was aware that in some way she had not perhaps handled the situation all that well.

'You did fine,' said Sister Rodriguez. 'But why is Mary's face marked . . . well, marked the way it is?' She was referring to what looked remarkably like handprints on Mary's pale skin.

'First of all she banged her head when she fainted. And then, when I got the Chapel Sisters, one of them slapped her face to assist her to recover.' Miss Ní Ghrian did not add that, having slapped Mary's face repeatedly, the Chapel Sister had hissed at the girl to get up immediately, that she was in the house of Our Lord and that she was letting her school down.

In the sickbay, Mary Oliver lay still, looking out into the night sky. The Sickbay Sister (known as Sister Sick to the girls) said, 'If you don't feel well in the morning, we'll get the doctor.'

Mary Oliver said nothing.

19

Treasa O'Donoghue, whose bottom stuck out so that the pleats of her tunic did not fall neatly over it, lay on her bed in the dormitory, on her stomach, and whispered to the Downey twins, 'But what did you hear? I mean just before she fell out of the box?'

'Nothing really,' they replied together. 'There was a silence. It seemed to have gone on for a bit.'

Treasa thought about that. Mary was one of her friends, but because it was Retreat, she was not allowed to visit her in sickbay. But even if she had not been a friend, her natural curiosity (for which she was famous) would have got the better of her.

'How long do you think she was in there?' she asked.

Downeyone said, 'A good seven or eight minutes.' Downeytwo nodded.

'And you heard nothing? Was there someone in the other box who might have heard?'

'No,' replied Downeyone. 'We were using the single confessional – you know, the one on the left of the church. The double one on the right wasn't being used.'

One bed up from Treasa O'Donoghue, Kitty O'Dowd snorted. Holding one long slender hand out in front of her, she was carefully painting her well-manicured nails with clear polish.

'Poor old Mary,' she said. 'They'll beat it out of her.'

'Sssssshhhhh,' went both Downey twins together.

The door opened and Mother Immaculata appeared. Every girl in the dormitory got to her feet and stood beside her bed.

Mother Immaculata stood looking at them for several long seconds.

'I hope you are all Adhering to the Spirit of Our Retreat, girls,' she said. In later years, when Father Ted appeared regularly on the television, every girl from that year thought that Mother Immaculata said 'girls' just the way Father Jack did. This made some of them laugh. It made others shiver.

Kitty O'Dowd, whose clear nail polish had got smeared when she leapt to her feet, stood very erect but scowling. The Downey twins, who had been lying on the same bed, had automatically jumped off on either side of the bed. They were both aware of the other's discomfort. Treasa O'Donoghue glared at Mother Immaculata. She, more than any of them, was acutely aware of the extreme isolation of Mary Oliver in sickbay. She knew that Mary would assume that the silence of Retreat was required even though she was not well. Eyeing Mother Immaculata, she wondered what had happened. Although she lacked Kitty O'Dowd's brazen approach to convent life, she was actually very astute and far more cynical. But although mentally rebellious, Treasa was also a pragmatist unless pushed.

Bridie in the next dormitory was already in her bed, dark red hair like a heavy bush of fire on her white pillow. She had tried to gain access to Mary Oliver in sickbay, but Sister Sick had said Mary was asleep. Bridie turned under the bedclothes to embrace Jean Jacques Versailles who had managed to pay the prison guard to let him visit his true, his only, his beloved.

'Jean Jacques,' she whispered to him, green eyes beseeching. 'Is tonight the night?'

'*Non*, my beloved Anna.' He never called her Bridie. When he had first appeared he had called her Mademoiselle. 'We cannot break for freedom tonight. There are double guards on every door.'

'Hold me,' she begged him.

'*Pas de problème*,' he replied and scooped her small fourteen-year-old body up into his manly arms.

In the next dormitory Mother Immaculata was continuing to address the 'girls'.

'It's been a long day, girls. Day one is always the Hardest but you're coming through it well. You only have five minutes until lights out and very few of you are ready for bed. I want you in your nightclothes and kneeling by your beds in two minutes flat. Kitty O'Dowd, your tunic is too short. If you don't lengthen it, you will be severely dealt with. Take that look off your face. Goodnight, girls. Sister Stanislaus will be in to do lights in five minutes.' She turned on her heel with a final glare at Kitty's legs and with a swish she was gone as if on roller skates.

'Effing cow,' muttered Kitty O'Dowd as she started to search for her nail polish remover.

The Downey twins, already in their pyjamas, pulled the dividing curtains between the beds so that they were separated from the other beds but could see each other. Treasa O'Donoghue grabbed her washbag and headed for the bathroom.

On the train heading south for leafy suburbia, Miss Maple met her father.

'Hi, Dad.'

'Hello, darling. How was it?' He moved his briefcase to make room for her.

She sighed.

'Uphill battle?' he asked as he patted her hand.

'All the way,' she answered him. 'All the way.'

They were silent for a while and she closed her eyes as the train's wheels lulled her to a peaceful place as they journeyed home. During dinner she filled her parents in on the general progress of the day.

'Kitty O'Dowd joined the choir.'

They both expressed their approval.

'Although I think it was more by default than by design.'

'Can you hold on to her?' asked her mother.

'I think so. I think she'll have to turn up in the gallery at least for the rest of the week.'

'I think you will work wonders with her,' her father said. 'As long as you can hold onto her.'

'That's the problem,' Maeve Maple said. 'You know I can't blame her, not one little bit. Some girls just never get a chance.'

'Well, in some ways she is lucky,' replied her mother. 'After all, there she is in a good school having already been expelled from two others. Not every girl gets that chance.'

'There are schools and there are schools,' said her father gently, 'and there are families and there are families.'

The three were silent. Their house was less than a mile away from the seaside hotel which Kitty's parents owned.

Mary Oliver (born Olivier), sallow skin paler than usual, watched the moon move through the sky as the hours ticked by. Her brown eyes watched it. Her mind did nothing. It was floating somewhere outside her body. Later, when she reconnected, she would wonder what had happened to the two nails she had been holding in her hands. Later, she would wonder what the priest had said that had tipped the balance. Later, she would wonder how she could go to confession again without going into the box. For the time being her eyes tracked the moon. Sickbay Sister, popping her head round the door and seeing that Mary Oliver was to all intents and purposes awake, spoke to her. The following day Sickbay Sister told Mother Immaculata that although Mary Oliver had appeared to be awake during the night, she had, in fact, not appeared to hear when she was addressed. But that was for the morrow.

Two in the morning and Kitty O'Dowd, unable to sleep, was having a smoke in the toilets on the second landing. She was contemplating the next day and whether Andrew MacDonald was likely to turn up in Sutherland Square and whether she could risk slipping out again. She was quite certain that the Maple would not tolerate her turning up late to the choir. But between lunch and four, provided I'm not late, and provided I've left a good enough trail, I should be able to get out, she thought.

She did not want to give Andrew MacDonald the idea that she might be interested, but she was interested. He was different. He had thought a few things out. She did not usually bother to think anything out. In fact it had never really occurred to her to think things out, at least not to the extent that he had. She had thought how to get expelled from the convent in Co. Leitrim. Five minutes after she had arrived there it had occurred to her that there were two ways out of it – one was to be carried out in a coffin and the other was to be booted out. She did not bother to consider running away because she had done that before from a previous convent (in County Mayo) and that was why she had ended up in the back of beyond. Twenty odd years later when many of her friends were purchasing country homes and both Leitrim and Mayo were among *the* places, Kitty O'Dowd briefly wondered whether she would be capable of visiting any of these cottages. Brief consideration it was. She knew immediately that she could not, that she would not ever cross the borders into either of those counties again.

Leitrim, to her, was for ever that ghastly cold convent and the echo of footsteps on empty corridors peppered with statues portraying various degrees of misery, both human and celestial, and fields and fields of cattle and cow dung, and her legs blue and purple with the cold, and chilblains on her fingers, and long, long lonely nights. And she had had to push very hard to actually get expelled. The nuns had other ways of dealing with recalcitrant pupils.

She sighed. Eff the lot of them, she thought as she pattered barefoot along the corridor back to bed.

Chapter Two

Turn back the pages in their lives and here is Mary Olivier, two years old, toddling down the garden of her home outside Paris. The sun shines on her dark hair and her olive skin, which looks sallow in winter and goes a lovely golden brown in summer. 'Papa, Papa,' she calls. She is the light of his life but this is not what Maman tells her when she is old enough to understand.

'*Viens ici*, Marie,' he calls to her. He is just home from work and he scoops his little bundle of joy up into his arms. This is the last time he will ever do this because after he leaves for work tomorrow morning he will not see this little bundle for fourteen years and by then she will be too old to scoop up into his arms. He tosses her in the air and she squeals with delight, and he carries her into the house where they are going to have supper – baguette, salami, thinly sliced smoked ham, tiny cucumbers pickled by the neighbour, tomatoes off the vine. (It is the neighbour who has the vegetable garden, not the Oliviers.) She sits beside him and holds his hand every time it is free.

It is late summer, not just seasonally but also figuratively – the late summer of her childhood.

Au revoir, Papa.

In the morning he comes into her room and plants a kiss on her little fat cheek as she lies like a sleeping cherub in her cot.

'*Au revoir*,' he whispers and he is gone.

Fast forward nearly three years and Mary Olivier lives with her mother, an Irish woman whose name is Deirdre Olivier (née O'Brien), in a basement flat in Bayswater in London. They speak no more French. Mary Olivier remembers the word *Papa* but she knows not to use it. Her mother is hard put to keep them going, and Mary is minded by a woman in the other basement flat and is taken out daily for a walk in Hyde Park. When they go out she brings her teddy Boubou with her. He is her constant companion. Her name is on a register of missing children in France but it is only the early sixties and there is no serious co-operation between the European countries. Monsieur Olivier has been to Dublin to the Department of Foreign Affairs, looking for assistance in tracking his missing daughter. They are unable to help.

On Sundays Deirdre Olivier brings Mary to Mass. She tells Mary to pray for the wicked people in the world, including Mary's father. Mary's memories of her father laughing and cuddling her and tossing her in the air are very blurry now. It is difficult to hold on to such images when you are constantly being told how dreadful the perpetrator actually was. Mary wonders sometimes if the man she remembers might in fact be someone else, like a neighbour or someone. She is a bit vague as to whom that someone might be.

Deirdre Olivier is a secretary. She works from nine until six five days a week, and sometimes on a Saturday. She has a strange quirk in her personality, which leaves her fed up with people after a while. This has led to her marital breakdown, if such can be the word to describe what happened that late summer evening a few years earlier in the Parisian suburbs when she looked at her husband, a successful and hard-working young man rising at a smooth pace in the French diplomatic service. She had looked at him at the supper table as he held Mary's little plump hand in his and she suddenly thought to herself, Mother of God, I can't stand this.

The following morning, after he left for his regular day at the office, Deirdre Olivier took her daughter and one suitcase, popped into the bank and emptied both accounts and went to the railway station.

It was an arduous enough journey, with a suitcase and a two-year-old, by train and boat and train again. It was several days before she found the flat in Bayswater and she and the exhausted Mary finally lay down to sleep in a bed.

Prior to that a pattern was already apparent in Deirdre Olivier's behaviour but her young husband was not privy to it. On leaving school,

Deirdre had cut all contact with her classmates and simply moved on into the life of a secretary, which actually quite suited her as she rarely needed to see anyone for longer than six months because she kept changing jobs. On marrying her young and upwardly mobile French diplomat (whom she had met while sheltering from the rain at a tram stop in Dublin) she had cut all contact with her family, and the four years she put in with Monsieur Olivier were four years longer than she had ever given anyone else in her life.

Mary Olivier, beware. Watch your back. The space you're taking up may be needed for someone else.

Three years in the basement in Bayswater have left the cherubic Mary Olivier with her sallow skin and dark brown hair looking pale and jaundiced. She is now a skinny little five-year-old with huge dark eyes and very pink lips. She says 'Mummy' with an English accent, and she goes to school. She's bright. She has an aptitude for languages, though this is not yet apparent because under the English system she just learns English. Quickly she learns how to read, and in the afternoons after the basement neighbour has brought her back home and let her into the one-bedroom flat where she waits alone for Mummy to return from work, Mary Olivier reads to Boubou, or listens to the wireless.

She has recently heard about a chimpanzee called Ham whom the Americans have sent into outer space, and on his return they have debriefed him. This fascinates her. Can chimps talk? If so, what do they say? If not, why would you send one hurtling into outer space and then bring it into a lab for debriefing? She looks at Boubou. She would never hurl him into outer space and he is only a furry teddy bear. If she had a chimpanzee, a real one, whether it could talk or not, the last thing she would do would be to arrange for it to orbit the earth.

Mary Olivier has a lot of time for thought. She decides to pray for Ham, because really only God can help him. She prays when she gets into bed that night.

> As I lay me down to sleep
> I pray the Lord, Ham's soul to keep
> And if I die before I wake
> I pray the Lord, Ham's soul to take.

Then it transpires that Ham doesn't have a soul. 'Are you sure, Mummy?' she asks when Deirdre Olivier breaks this piece of news to her.

Deirdre Olivier is absolutely sure. Apparently chimpanzees, dogs and most men don't have souls.

'So what happens to them when they die?'

It appears they go to sleep and that is that.

Mary Olivier is afraid to go to sleep that night, even though she is not a chimp, a dog or in any way male.

'Mummy?' It is breakfast time and they are in a bit of a rush. 'Mummy, do they dream?'

'Who? Does who dream?' Deirdre Olivier is putting on her face, moueing into the mirror as she deftly puts lipstick on.

'The dead ones.'

'What dead ones?'

'You know, the dead chimps and dogs.' Mary Olivier is nearly in tears with tiredness and distress.

'They're completely peaceful,' says Deirdre Olivier authoritatively, with no idea or care how these observations may affect her only daughter.

Mary Olivier decides that completely peaceful is acceptable and she goes to school and falls asleep at her desk, black smudges under her eyes. The teacher lets her sleep right through two classes and wakens her gently at break time to make sure she gets her milk.

Mary goes home from school with the neighbour and is let into her flat where she turns on the wireless, hoping for an update on Ham. She hears no more about him, and in due course feels that he has probably gone back to the zoo, which is the right place for him. She listens to a report on Adolf Eichmann and she hopes, indeed she is almost sure, that he doesn't have a soul. *If any evil comes to me, Mother of Jesus waken me.*

No guarantees.

Sometimes, when she's asleep, terrible things happen. She once dreamt that she was in a little cot in a pink room and the light was coming in the window and Papa was standing there ready to kiss her goodnight and suddenly Mummy came into the room and said, 'You're Adolf Eichmann,' and Papa turned and walked out. She woke up and she was shivering and

28

she had wet the bed. She stayed where she was, though, because Deirdre Olivier wasn't keen on being disturbed during the night (and she wasn't around to be disturbed during the day).

One day, Deirdre says to Mary, 'I'm getting married tomorrow,' and she does.

She marries William Whittaker. He tells Mary he would like to adopt her and then she could be Mary Whittaker, but Deirdre says it wouldn't be a good idea. He gives Mary the impression that he thinks her real papa is dead, and Mary isn't sure anyway if he is or not, so she doesn't say anything.

Life becomes more comfortable. They move from their basement flat to a four-bedroom terraced house and Deirdre stops working from nine until six (and sometimes on Saturdays) and shortly afterwards this tiny baby is found under the bushes in the back garden and she comes to live with them.

'It was a good thing you found her, Mummy,' says Mary Olivier, counting Lucia Whittaker's tiny toes. 'She could have died out there in the garden if you hadn't. And then she couldn't have gone to heaven because she hadn't been baptised and she would have gone to limbo for ever and ever.'

William Whittaker suggests to Deirdre Whittaker (formerly Olivier) that perhaps it would be better for Mary to attend a 'normal' school. Deirdre Whittaker, holding baby Lucia in her arms and pushing the teat of a feeding bottle into her tiny mouth, shakes her head and says no, definitely not. Mary is going to stay at Catholic school, and not only that, in due course she wants to send Mary to a Catholic boarding school in Ireland; that she, Deirdre, was educated like that and she would like Mary to turn out as well as she has. William Whittaker sits Mary on his knee and cuddles her. He wonders what terrible things are going on in her head.

'What's limbo like?' he asks her that evening as he tucks her into bed.

'It's full of devils with prongs,' she says. 'They keep the babies there and don't let them out. They're not allowed to touch the babies with the prongs, but they keep them there.'

William Whittaker nods slowly. 'Is there anyone else there?' he asks.

'Yes.' She nods. Mary Olivier knows her stuff. 'All the people who are good but who were never baptised. There aren't very many of them because really only Catholics are good, and they get to heaven, but mostly they have to go through purgatory first.'

William Whittaker swallows. 'If I die,' he says slowly, 'where will I go?'

Mary looks sadly at him. 'At the moment,' she says, 'you don't stand a chance. But I'm praying for you. And remember last Sunday when you were in the garden lying in the deckchair and I spilt some water on your forehead?'

He nods.

'Well, that wasn't an accident. I was baptising you.'

He kisses her on the top of her head and tucks her in. 'Say a little prayer for me.'

'Oh I will. I do all the time,' she says.

> *There are four corners on my bed*
> *There are four angels overhead*
> *Matthew, Mark, Luke and John*
> *God bless this bed that I lie on*
> *And God bless Daddy, Mummy and baby Lucia,*
> *but especially Daddy because he's English and a pagan.*

Lucia Whittaker is adored by Daddy and Mary. During the day Daddy goes out to work, and Mary goes to school, and when she comes home Deirdre Whittaker (née O'Brien, once Olivier) is usually busy, so Mary takes Lucia and she cuddles the baby and they listen to the wireless. Both Adolf Eichmann and Marilyn Monroe are dead. Because of some distraction, which took place during the period when these two characters bought their final tram tickets, Mary Olivier is under the impression that they were, in some way, partnered.

Mary's wireless world is very important to her but the crying of the baby at inappropriate moments over weeks, indeed over months, has blurred and changed the edge of time. The big question for Mary is this: did Marilyn Monroe have a soul? Clearly Adolf Eichmann did not, as he is male and must fall into that category outlined by her mother. Marilyn

Monroe was curvy. Her mother, Deirdre, is curvy too. So is the Queen. *God save our gracious Queen.* That is what is sung when she goes to the cinema with William Whittaker.

In fact, that is what is being sung when William Whittaker keels over dead at the end of *The Sound of Music.* The year is 1965. William Whittaker holds his chest, and Mary thinks it is for love of the Queen, but then he makes a funny gasping sound and he slips down on the floor between the rows of seats.

Mary stands and looks at him, wondering if there is something happening that she doesn't know about.

And indeed there is. This is death.

She gets shifted out of the row during the next few minutes as people come to help and an ambulance is called and William Whittaker is carted away and Mary Olivier can't get through the gawking crowds to be with him. She is swamped by people and carried with the crowd as it surges one way and then the next. When she is finally deposited outside the cinema, she makes her way back to the foyer and hopes that William will yet appear as she doesn't know that he is gone.

The time has come for me to say goodbye, adieu, adieu, to you and you and you.

She stands there for a very long time, waiting patiently like she has been told to do if she gets separated from him. She is spotted by an usher, who keeps an eye on her, thinking she must be waiting for a parent who has gone to use the conveniences.

In due course the manager approaches her. 'Are you lost?' he asks kindly.

She shakes her head. No, she is not lost. She knows exactly where she is.

'Are you waiting for someone?'

A nod of the head. 'My daddy.'

'What's your name?'

'Mary Olivier.'

A momentary suspicion that she might be connected to the dead man is dismissed as the dead man had a totally different name.

Meanwhile, the police have been in touch with Deirdre Whittaker and Deirdre (now quite a well-off widow) heads for the hospital for the purpose of identification. She has forgotten completely about Mary's existence and it isn't until later in the evening, with William Whittaker's family around comforting her and William's sister putting the three-year-old Lucia to bed, that it is observed that Mary is nowhere to be seen.

'Very distressed, is she?' asks William's brother of Deirdre, and Deirdre, startled, puts her hand to her mouth and says, 'Where on earth is she?'

William's brother (Anthony Whittaker) starts to reassemble the jigsaw of the afternoon and he heads for the cinema, which is now closed. He calls into the police station where Mary is sitting drinking milk and looking scared.

Mary, whom Uncle Anthony thinks of as being a bright little poppet, gives the impression of not knowing what is going on. Even when he explains to her about William's demise in the cinema, there is something bewildered about her. It reminds him of the day William and Deirdre got married. There was a lot of bewilderment that day too because that was the day both William and his siblings discovered that Deirdre (whom they all believed was a widow) actually had a daughter. (Yes, Deirdre never got a divorce. This is bigamy.)

Uncle Anthony thinks back to the bewilderment that day when Mary's existence became apparent as she walked with her mother into the civil ceremony. Mary had looked bewildered that day too, much like now, but back then she was five and she sat on his knee and told him about Ham, whereas now she was almost nine and she appeared to be catatonic.

He brings her home and William's sister gets her into bed, and when he checks on her the following morning she seems more lucid and she understands that Daddy is gone. He holds her hand at the funeral and he watches out for her over the next few years, which is just as well because no one else does.

Uncle Anthony takes Mary Olivier to Regent's Park to see Goldie. Mary has heard about Goldie on the wireless. He is a golden eagle and he is free after ten years in captivity. Provided no one takes a pot shot at him, he could live for forty-three years, which is way longer than either of Mary's fathers lived, or so she thinks. The man on the wireless said that Goldie could live quite well on one duck a day from the pond. Mary has considered this and is unsure if this means that Goldie would need to kill a duck and eat it or that he could live on top of a duck. She would prefer that he could live on top of a duck but it doesn't really make any sense.

When things don't make sense, Mary prays. *God bless Mummy, and Lucia, and Uncle Anthony and Goldie. And please, please let Daddy into heaven even though he is a pagan because I did baptise him and he was a very, very good man, and I miss him.*

The years pass.

'I'm sending her to boarding school in Dublin,' Deirdre Whittaker says of Mary to the Whittaker siblings.

The siblings look at each other. They have seen this coming.

'Obviously it will be your choice,' is tentatively said, as if a decision has not yet been reached. 'But it's early days yet, isn't it? She's only thirteen, and what's the rush?'

'She'll be fourteen when she goes, next September. And it's only for three years.'

'She'll be finished with school very young, won't she?' says William's sister, Joan.

'And she's doing so well here,' interjects Anthony. 'Why change a winning team?'

They are on a losing wicket. Deirdre has had thirteen years of Mary and that's more than she's ever had of anyone, and there will be no shifting her.

'Her poor dead father would have liked her to have had more religion,' says Deirdre, taking out her secret weapons.

'Oh, I don't think William ever thought like that,' says Joan Whittaker.

'I'm not talking about William,' says Deirdre. 'Mary is not a Whittaker,' she reminds her dead husband's brother and sister. 'She's an Olivier and as her only real living relative I have to do what is right for her.'

The Whittaker siblings try again on Mary's behalf, but Deirdre Whittaker needs air and space and Mary's number is up.

Uncle Anthony tries to coax Mary into going to the cinema with him. '*Chitty Chitty Bang Bang,*' he says. 'It's light and funny and we'll love it.'

Mary shakes her head. She has not been to the cinema since *The Sound of Music.*

Uncle Anthony is keen to get her to go to it because he wants her to slay a few dragons before she gets sent off to the Emerald Isle. He knows that in Ireland she is going to be even more isolated, with her English accent and her French surname and war looking as if it's breaking out north of the border.

'Tell you what, Mary,' he says. 'I'd love to take Lucia to see it but not without you.'

'But you could take her without me,' says Mary. 'I don't need to be there.'

He shakes his head. 'No, there is no way I'll take her without you. She'll just have to do without.'

Mary has never been able to identify manipulation and she adores Lucia, she can't bear the idea of Lucia being deprived of a treat. She agrees. They go to the cinema and all three emerge alive, which is a great relief for Mary who still has not identified what it is that she feared. Nonetheless, an afternoon well spent.

Deirdre Whittaker flies with Mary to Dublin in June for an interview with Mother Immaculata. It is agreed that Mary should go into Fourth Year in St Martin's in the Fields (fields yet to be seen) in September and that Mary should do an Irish course during the summer as she knows none even though she is exempt from doing it in her Intermediate Certificate. (Mother Immaculata forgets to check on Mary's French, which is non-existent, but that will come out in September and Mary will find herself doing extra French every afternoon as Sister Rodriguez crams three years of French into her within three months.)

Mary Olivier is sent to Irish College in a seaside village north of Dublin where, having none of the language, Mary has this strange feeling of living someone else's life, someone she has not yet managed to identify, or, at the very best, it is as if she is living on the periphery of her own life and has not yet found out how that life is supposed to be lived. There are no fixed givens where she comes from. The men who once offered stability in her background have disappeared. Her mother is a vague and blurry non-maternal figure who has never worked anything out properly, and Mary finds herself in a large school on the seafront for a month during that summer, where no one is supposed to speak English.

However, there is a church attached to the school, and Mass and lots of

34

statues, and these are what Mary can identify with. *Our Father, who art in Heaven* ... both fathers, in fact, Papa Olivier who might be in heaven if Mummy got it wrong, and Daddy Whittaker who just might have slipped through the net thanks to the timely baptism and, with a bit of luck, a clear conscience and an act of contrition.

Dear Mummy,

Two and a half weeks here now and missing you and Lucia. The day is well structured between classes in the morning and sport in the afternoon which as you know I am not very interested in, but Maistir O'Fluthúlach (my teacher) says that I have a definite aptitude for the language and I am making great progress. It's more interesting than Latin because once you get the hang of it you can actually use it. (Not that I am decrying Latin in any way because I see it as the foundation of modern European languages as well as being the central language of the one true Church.)

I was thinking, Mummy, that instead of my going home for the month of August and then back to Dublin for school in September, is there any way I could stay here for a further month to improve my Irish? Maistir O'Fluthúlach says that at the rate I'm going I will be able to do at least Pass Irish in the Intermediate Certificate exam next summer, and there is even the chance that I may be good enough to sit the Honours papers.

I do realise the expense that this will incur, my staying on here I mean, but it would save the fares back to London and then back here and I could go straight from here to school. Maistir O'Fluthúlach says any number of people will be driving up to Dublin at the end of August and he will arrange a lift if it suits you. He also says that he will write to you as well and see what you think.

I'm very well. Please give Lucia a kiss from me.

Love,
Mary

This arrangement suits Deirdre Whittaker down to the ground and so

35

it is that Mary Olivier finds herself ensconced for a second month in this large grey edifice perched on the coast. There is something reassuring about it. She likes the sea and they go there most afternoons to clamber on the rocks or to wade into the water in their swimsuits, shrieking at the chilliness of the water.

She has not integrated very well by the end of the first month, but come the start of the second month and she is the only girl to have stayed on, she finds herself in a more secure position as the new girls arrive. She chooses a different bed for the second month, a top bunk beside the window in the airiest dormitory. There is a twenty-four-hour lull between the July girls departing and the August girls arriving. During that period Mary wanders through the empty rooms and spends time in the little church in the school grounds. She likes the church with its stained-glass windows depicting various saints, some of whom she can recognise. Saint Francis holding his hands aloft to the birds, Saint Patrick pointing down to the ground where there are wriggling snakes going in the opposite direction. She ponders on these matters, why birds are acceptable and snakes are not. She wonders what would have happened had it transpired that birds were unacceptable in Ireland. Would Saint Patrick have rid Ireland of the birds? Don't all animals have a place in the order of things? Why did Saint Patrick go for the snakes? Mary Olivier has seen snakes in the zoo, both with William Whittaker (Daddy) and with Uncle Anthony. Neither had said to her that snakes were unacceptable in London Zoo, or indeed in England. She quite liked the snakes with their sleepy eyes, but clearly Saint Patrick did not. Did Noah take two snakes into the Ark? And if not, why not? *All things bright and beautiful, the Lord God loves them all.* But not snakes.

The new girls arrive. Mary Olivier, sitting on her top bunk, watches them come and choose their beds. She exchanges information with Aisling who takes the lower half of her bunk. Aisling has been here the previous year and goes to a school in County Westmeath. Aisling says there are two girls who were here last year and are back this year and they, too, go to St Martin's in the Fields where Mary says she is going in September. Aisling saw them out front saying goodbye to their parents. 'I'll point them out to you over tea,' says the friendly Aisling.

And so Mary Olivier meets Bernadette O'Higgins and Treasa O'Donoghue who have a bunk in another dormitory but who, quite dextrously, persuade two girls in Aisling and Mary Olivier's dormitory into swapping beds with them. Treasa's smiling open face spells good humour and friendliness, and Bernadette, somewhat more reserved and very self-contained, follows Treasa's example in displaying goodwill towards Mary.

They have tea, which consists of bread and butter and jam, and an odd fluffy kind of cake which is filled with cream and covered in coconut, and enormous teapots full of tea, and there is a lot of friendly giggling at the table. Treasa is open, and the questions flow. Where are you from? Why are you here? Oh, your mother is Irish? And what about your father? Will your sister come to St Martin's too? When? What year have you completed? Do you have to learn Irish? And then, in a lower voice, with their heads bowed and their eyes raised towards her, Bernadette and Treasa ask: do you smoke? Would you like to? Have you ever been in trouble in school? Why St Martin's? You know how strict it is? Do you know any boys?

And Mary Olivier smiles. She is smitten. She will always be a loner, will always be easily damaged, will always have a problem identifying what is right and what is wrong and how to tell someone to leave her alone. But in this moment, looking at these two girls, she is hooked by their genuine smiling faces, by their ease and self-confidence, by their self-knowledge and their ability to include her.

I want to belong, she thinks.

And in many ways she is safer here, outside her mother's ill-guided and controlling hand, and the following morning she ties her dark hair into a ponytail like Treasa's and Bernadette's, and she looks forward to being one of the group.

He the magpie, she the raven, tapping tapping on the door
Dreaming, scheming, dreaming dreams, no mortal dare to dream before
But the silence was unbroken and the stillness gave no token
Not a word was spoken, not a word and nothing more
But we whispered ever hopeful, whispers echo cross the floor
                    Quoth the Raven, 'Nevermore.'

Chapter Three

Mary Oliver stirred on day two of the Retreat in her bed at the window in the sickbay. She wondered what she was doing there. In fact she wondered where she was at all, as she had no recollection of the events of the previous afternoon and evening and had never been in sickbay before, so had no way of identifying her surroundings. She lay very still. She appeared to have no energy; even lifting her hand from the counterpane took every bit of concentration and effort, so she just let it drop back.

Sickbay Sister entered and came over to take her pulse. Mary Oliver looked at her and slowly identified where she was and realised that she must be ill. Sickbay Sister tut-tutted a bit.

'You're on Retreat still, Mary,' she said. 'Try not to break your silence unless you feel you really have to.'

Mary felt that she did not have anything to say, so she said nothing.

'You fainted,' Sister Sick continued. 'You really have very low blood pressure.' She said this severely as if it were something Mary had concocted just to cause trouble.

Mary Oliver looked at her and suddenly wondered (the first critical question she had come up with in her entire life) why her mother would have sent her to a place where even your blood pressure was a fault. She wondered where her nails were as she would quite like to have them in the palms of her hands for safety and comfort.

'Your pulse is fine. I think we'll get you up and you can have some tea and bread,' Sister Sick told her.

Mary Oliver wondered did her mother know she was ill, but she did not like to ask.

'Tea and bread,' repeated Sister Sick. 'And then we'll get you down

41

to chapel to join the others. That will make you feel better, won't it, my girl?'

Mary Oliver nodded.

Washing in the bathroom after her tea and bread, Mary Oliver took herself into the toilet cubicle and put her fingers down her throat, for the first but not for the last time. Afterwards she was not sure why she had done it, but she knew that she felt the better for it, and that was good enough at that particular moment.

Treasa O'Donoghue, whose bottom was such that the pleats of her uniform did not hang smoothly over it, strode along to sickbay as soon as breakfast was over.

''Scuse me, Sister,' she addressed Sister Sick. 'May I visit Mary Oliver?'

'You may not,' Sister Sick replied. 'You're on Retreat and there is silence, and anyway Mary Oliver will be joining you as soon as she is dressed. I brought her breakfast in her room,' she added piously.

Looking for a few indulgences, are we? thought Treasa O'Donoghue to herself. 'If Mary is going to join us for chapel, may I wait and accompany her down there? I mean, seeing as she fainted, it will save you bringing her down there as I'm sure you wouldn't be sending her by herself,' Treasa suggested pleasantly.

Sister Sick was snookered and she nodded in agreement, reminding herself to report Treasa for breaking silence.

Mary Oliver wrote to her mother that night in bed.

Dear Mummy,

I wasn't well yesterday but I've managed to stick with the Retreat, total silence now for two days. I miss you and Lucia and hope you are both well. I know you sent me here because it was your old school, and I did settle in well, but I keep thinking about you saying you're thinking of sending Lucia next year so that she will have six years here, instead of the three I'm having. I'm not sure if that's such a good idea. She's happy in school in England, and I don't know if she'll adapt as easily as I did.

She sucked the top of her pen and thought about the things she couldn't say, like, 'It's difficult hiding the fact that your mother lives in England, which might appear to be criminal here.' Or 'I'm terrified people will find out my father was French and wonder why I don't speak the language.' Or that not only have I lost one dad, but I've managed to lose two. Of late she had wondered if the man she used to call 'Papa' might indeed be still alive, but the feeling was vague, intangible, blurry, not one she could focus on properly. She would have liked to have asked her mother, but she was afraid to.

She thought about all the things you couldn't say to parents. Later, when she was a mother, she made sure there was nothing her daughter couldn't say to her, to such an extent, in fact, that sometimes she wondered why her daughter told her so much. As the years went by her daughter's mouth seemed to get bigger and bigger and there was nothing she would not and did not come out with.

'Jayzus,' Kitty O'Dowd said to Treasa some twenty-two years later. 'I wouldn't take that from my child. What a mouth. What lip.'

And Treasa said, 'That's Mary for you. She never managed to find the balance.'

'Three more days of Retreat,' continued Mary Oliver in her letter to her mother, 'then six weeks until my Leaving!' The thought of that did not bring her much comfort. What to do when she was finished school?

During the course of day two of the Retreat, various events had contrived to assist her to recall a lot of the previous day, right up to being in the confessional, but no further, which, under the circumstances, was probably just as well. There is a limit to how much the human mind can cope with at any given time, and Mary's mind was in such a state of turmoil that she found no peace at all on day two. She varied her time between kneeling in the chapel praying, walking in the cloistered garden praying, sitting on a bench in the garden praying, and finding herself in one of these places staring into space having no idea whatsoever as to how she had got there.

Sister Rodriguez, noticing how pale she was, had insisted that she had an extra portion of potato at lunch, which meant that she had almost twice as much to throw up afterwards, which left her with her ribs and throat hurting, and the burn of tears behind her eyes, and feeling very tired.

Her letter continued:

Maybe your suggestion that I take a year out was a good one after all. I shouldn't have shot it down like that at Easter. I am a year younger than most of the others, as you pointed out, and it would give me time to get my thoughts together. I could do a secretarial course and some voluntary work at the same time and both would stand to me. That doesn't mean that I don't want to be a nun, it's just that I realise that you are right and another year won't do me any harm. Please give my love to Lucia and please write back. I'm sorry for the stance I took over Easter. Love from your elder d. Mary.

Mary thought about that argument at Easter and how she had confessed it immediately afterwards, and although the sin was gone because the priest had absolved it on God's behalf, and she had said the three Hail Marys which he had instructed her to say, she now felt better for apologising to her mother.

Kitty O'Dowd, in the cloistered garden at the Sister Chapel, looked at Treasa O'Donoghue and grimaced. 'Lunch made me puke,' she muttered.

Treasa took her literally and nodded, 'You're not the only one,' thinking about Mary Oliver who was now back in the chapel with her white and sweating face glowing in the hushed semi-darkness. At two in the afternoon, the sun was blocked by one of the taller buildings behind the church and so did not shine through the stained-glass window. Mary Oliver therefore could not see the bleeding heart of Jesus in the stained glass. Its crimson colour on his white clothing was dull without the light. So Mary Oliver, with eyes closed, was trying to work out what to do. She wanted to go to confession, but could not. The thought of being in that small box was more than she could bear, and she missed her nails. Looking up at the crucifix hanging on the pillar to the right of the altar, her eye was caught by the nails in the palms of Christ.

She wanted those nails.

'I'm going out for an hour,' Kitty murmured to Treasa. 'Cover for me.'

Treasa smiled. 'No problem. Are you by any chance skipping the trip to the workshop?'

Kitty stuck up two fingers in the general direction of the Chapel Sisters' 'Sweatshop', as she called it. Taking that as an affirmative, Treasa continued, 'Where are you off to?'

'Meeting a fella in Sutherland Square.'

'What's he like?'

'Interesting. A year older. Funny.' Kitty shrugged. She couldn't think of anything else to say about him.

'What does he look like?' Treasa asked in an effort to keep the conversation going and to postpone the inevitable boredom which would shortly creep back in anyway.

'Very tall. Dark. Talks with a Scottish accent,' Kitty obliged.

'Wears a kilt?'

'Dunno. Haven't seen him in one yet.'

'Why is he Scottish?'

'Dunno. I suppose someone has to be,' Kitty replied.

Treasa laughed. 'I meant, why is he in Ireland?'

'His father is in the British Embassy,' Kitty said.

'The late British Embassy!' Treasa laughed again. 'I'm surprised they didn't try and hang you with that particular piece of arson.' She was referring to the burning down of the embassy some weeks earlier.

Kitty laughed too. 'I'm off,' she said. 'Have fun in the Sweatshop, and tell me about it afterwards in case I need an alibi.'

'Think of me,' said Treasa miserably. 'First stop is the Bakery.'

Kitty headed in the direction of the loos, from where she successfully made her exit to the basement and so out onto the street.

Anna McBride, known as Bridie to her friends, was sitting at the other side of the garden, complete with a handful of pamphlets which the nuns kindly made available to the girls. These included such gems as 'Growing up as Jesus wants us to' and 'Walking with the Cross while we mature'. Bridie had just come across the word 'scrotum', the pronunciation and meaning of which she was a little unsure. She read the sentence through again and concluded that it was a euphemism for penis.

What a nice word, she thought, seeing the potential for a whole new line of conversation and experimentation with Jean Jacques Versailles, as she was uncomfortable with the word penis.

'May I handle your scrotum?' She tried the words in her mind. 'Is this your scrotum that I see before me?'

She wondered if it was declinable as in '*Et tu scrote?*' or maybe even '*scrotibus*'. Jean Jacques might, in a moment of extreme stress, call, 'By my scrotibus.' Or maybe just '*Scrotibus meus*' seeing as that would include the word 'by' or 'from'.

She contemplated the possibilities.

Kitty O'Dowd entered Sutherland Square from the Northumberland Road end to find Andrew MacDonald already ensconced on her park bench. He stood up as she approached and apologised for missing their assignation the previous day.

'No problem,' she said. 'I was glad to get out of the place anyway. What happened to you?'

'I got nabbed by one of the masters as I was about to leave the building, and ended up doing extra chemistry in the lab.'

'What if they miss you today?' she asked.

'I didn't go in today, studied at home and have come out now for a breather. How about you, if they miss you, I mean?'

'Don't ask. I don't give a fuck anyway.'

'How's the praying going?' he asked with a grin. He couldn't think of a person less likely to pray than Kitty O'Dowd, and the idea of her trapped in a Retreat was quite amusing.

She did not bother to answer.

'Go on,' he persisted. 'What are you missing right now?'

'You wouldn't believe me if I told you,' she said.

'Try me,' he said.

She snorted. 'This afternoon we're having a whole hour in a place we've christened the Bakery, seeing how the wafers for Communion are made.'

'That sounds like it might be a handy thing for you to have on your CV later,' he said drily.

She laughed. 'It's probably better than praying.'

'What do you all pray for?'

'I pray for the Retreat to end. But what we're supposed to be praying for is a vocation, and indulgences.'

'A vocation?'

'Yes, to be called to become a nun.' She grinned at the look on his face.

'Sister Kitty,' he said with a chuckle.

'Sister Kitty, my arse!' she replied.

'Well, Sister Kitty, what, may I ask, are indulgences?'

'Don't call me that. I don't know how you'd describe them. They're sort of like . . . oh, I don't know. The more you pray, the more of them you get and you can use them for things – like getting your grandmother out of purgatory!'

'Like bonus points?' he asked.

'I don't know,' she said. Kitty got bored by things so vague.

'No, go on. I really want to know.'

'Well, sort of. You get extra ones on certain days.'

'Like when?'

'Well, if you go to Mass on the first Friday of each month, I think you get a bundle. And if you go every day during Lent.'

'And how many do you need to get a grandmother out of purgatory?'

'God, I don't know,' said Kitty irritably. 'I suppose it depends on what the auld grandmother did that got her into purgatory in the first place.'

Bernadette O'Higgins's navy blue eyes skimmed the lines in her illustrated version of *Scrumptious Sex*. She wondered if the book was correct in saying there were seven hundred and twenty photographs and illustrations. One way to find out, she thought, and decided that if by Friday she had run out of reading material, she would begin to count. If there were less than seven hundred and twenty and she wrote to complain to the publisher, she wondered what recompense she might receive. She smiled to herself. Perhaps the publisher would turn up on the doorstep of the school to demonstrate in person the missing illustrations.

A shadow fell across her book. Her breath caught in her throat. She closed the book and looked up in one movement. The Maple stood in front of her. Their eyes met. Bernadette forced herself to breathe again and prayed her cheeks wouldn't redden.

The Maple smiled at her. 'Nice to see you reading *The Lives of the Saints*, Bernadette. You're quite exposed here . . . to the sun I mean.'

Bernadette swallowed, and nodded.

The Maple moved on. Perhaps there was a small smile at the corner of her lips.

In the workshop Mary Oliver looked in amazement at the Hosts being prepared. She noticed that no one else seemed to be surprised, and that surprised her too. She wondered vaguely why it had never occurred to her that someone must actually make the wafers of bread. But she had never thought about it. She had always assumed that it was just part of the miracle of Transubstantiation. First there was bread and then there were Hosts. She realised that she had always thought of the bread in terms of a batch loaf or a sliced pan, and had never pursued the matter any further than that. Trays of them, she noticed. She felt uncomfortable looking at them lying there like that. Trays and trays, and she felt terribly hungry suddenly. She wished she knew where her missing nails were. There was very little comfort to be had from holding a rosary, even with the crucifix pressed hard into the palm of your hand, after you had held nails.

The Chapel Sisters were now showing the girls out from what Kitty referred to as the Bakery and they were ushered into another long room, which Kitty called the Sweatshop. Mary Oliver had the distinct impression that she must have missed something somewhere, because here the nuns appeared to be sewing sheets.

She wondered if they were for the convent beds in the Mother House. There was something very odd about them. She looked over at Bernadette O'Higgins who was looking out of the window. She glanced around for Bridie, but Bridie looked as if she was in a trance. Treasa O'Donoghue caught her eye and smiled at her. Mary Oliver wondered what on earth was going on. Treasa coughed and caught her eye again and winked. There was something quite comforting in the wink. She felt distinctly light-headed. Perhaps she would skip confession that evening after all, she thought, although it meant she could not receive Communion until she had made confession because yesterday's confession had been a bad one and needed to be confessed.

'Jayzus, Andrew, will you take your hand out of my blouse,' Kitty said as she sat back sprawled on the bench in Sutherland Square. Reluctantly Andrew obliged, and she buttoned up the top of her gymslip.

'You OK for tomorrow?' he asked.

'Not if you're going to do that. Can you imagine if Mother Immaculata strolled along.'

'Thought you didn't care,' he said.

'Well, I don't, but on the other hand . . .' Her voice trailed away.

'On the other hand what?' he asked.

'I can't really afford to be expelled,' she said. 'Not again.'

'Were you expelled before?'

She shrugged. 'Twice.'

He laughed and leaned forward to rest one elbow on his knee as he looked at her. 'Really? Go on, what did you do?'

'Which time?' she asked.

'Either, both. Go on. Tell me.'

'First time, I ran away,' she said. 'Jayzus, is that the time?' Her eye had caught his watch. 'I have to go. I'm now a choir girl and I have to be in at four.'

And she was up and gone.

'See you tomorrow,' he called after her.

A few minutes later he observed a thin woman in a very tight checked suit and high heels heading in his direction across the square. He had the immediate feeling, based on nothing really, that Kitty O'Dowd had just had a near miss.

Miss Ní Ghrian (Grinny to the girls) was scouring Sutherland Square for any girls out of bounds. She felt there was not sufficient discipline while they were on Retreat, and there was far too much trust put on them, and having been sure she had seen Kitty O'Dowd the previous afternoon, she was leaving nothing to chance and was continually checking up on the likely suspects. The problem was they were all terribly elusive. Because they had a certain amount of freedom within the confines of the Sister Chapel during the Retreat and were only obliged to be in particular places at particular times, it was fairly impossible to check up on each girl all the time.

Grinny felt that for all her strictness, Mother Immaculata was way too lax when it came to the Retreat schedule. No roll calls were taken to see who had visited the Host workshop on which day, or who was in chapel and who not. Mother Immaculata seemed to assume that the girls would give it their all.

Grinny knew better.

That evening, in the dormitory, Treasa O'Donoghue stretched out on her bed and filled in Kitty O'Dowd on what she had missed that afternoon. 'After we left the Bakery,' she said, 'you'll never guess what we did next.'

Mary Oliver, lying on the bed to the right of Treasa, writing a letter to her mother, listened with a certain amount of interest, mainly because she had no idea what they had done next.

'What?' Kitty asked as she painted her toenails.

'No, I'm not telling you. You're to guess. I really want you to guess,' Treasa said.

'I don't know. They let you eat the Hosts,' Kitty suggested.

'Nope. Try again.'

'They gave you all a cigarette and sent you home.'

Mary Oliver, pen in hand, lying on her stomach, paused with the pen poised and waited for Treasa to get on with it.

'They took us to the dressmakers,' Treasa said with a giggle.

'What do you mean?' Kitty asked, sufficiently curious to look up at the giggling Treasa.

'Really, they took us into this other room, where the Chapel Sisters were sewing shrouds.'

'Shrouds?' Kitty looked incredulous.

Mary Oliver had this strange feeling that she was hallucinating, partly because she had managed to get through the day on no food (or rather on purging it as soon as was possible after it had been consumed) and partly because she couldn't see how she could have been present in that sewing room and it had never dawned on her what was going on.

In the next dormitory Anna McBride (Bridie to her friends) was already tucked in under her covers and was discussing escape with Jean Jacques by means of a tumbril and a shroud.

'*Ma chérie*,' Jean Jacques whispered to his one true love. 'I will have you out of here before the week is up. You trust me, don't you?'

The red-haired Bridie, languishing in her prison cell, dressed in rags, lifted her brave face and her hopeful green eyes to his and said, 'Promise me, Jean Jacques.' (She had wondered briefly about calling him J.J. but decided against.) 'Promise me, Jean Jacques that we will flee this place together, that you will never leave me, and one day your scrotum will be mine for ever.'

'*Ma petite*,' he whispered. '*Et in secula seculorum scrotumorum maximum.*'

Downeyone and Downeytwo headed for the bathroom to share a bath. As senior freshmen in Trinity College two years later, they would become legendary for wearing long black pvc coats in winter, completely starkers underneath. For the time being the most extreme action either took was to bathe together and to admire each other's face and body. As identical twins this brought them a lot of mutual comfort and built their confidence.

They did not waste words on normal conversation with each other, mainly because they each knew what the other was thinking, and it was only when it came to mutual admiration that they bothered to break their silence when alone. However, on the evening in question, their thoughts were elsewhere. Having run their bath and undressed, they climbed in and sat facing each other, knees pulled up in front of them. Downeyone shivered.

'I didn't like the shrouds either,' Downeytwo reassured her.

Downeytwo looked out of the window and pulled a face.

'I don't like the priest either,' Downeyone said.

'Why do you suppose they make so many shrouds?' Treasa asked.

Kitty said, 'Hopefully they're planning a mass suicide.'

Mary Oliver shivered. There had been hundreds of shrouds in the room. Dozens and dozens at least, she thought. Maybe they're for lepers in Africa.

She continued her letter.

Silently, as on roller skates, The Raven glided into the room. Bugger, Kitty O'Dowd thought, as yet again she smudged her nail polish. She slipped off her bed and stood beside it.

One by one the girls became aware of Mother Superior's presence.

All but Mary Oliver.

Treasa coughed in an effort to warn Mary as well as to attract Mother Superior's attention away from her.

'Hand me that at once, Mary Oliver,' The Raven addressed the unfortunate Mary Oliver who, lying on her stomach, had been totally oblivious of her arrival.

Mother Superior took the writing pad and the pen from the hapless Mary, who that moment had just signed her name, and said, 'Right. Next Monday morning, first break you will report to my office. Letter-writing is banned for the duration of the Retreat, as you well know. It is the equivalent of talking, and the Retreat is a silent time. I will deal with you on Monday. It's five minutes until lights out. Hurry up, girls.'

> *See the nuns in flowing robes*
> *White on black, and black on white*
> *Immaculata rules the roost*
> *Controlling all by day and night*

Mary Oliver sank back onto her bed, white-faced and shivering.

'It's OK, Mary,' Treasa said. 'You're never in trouble. It'll blow over.'

'What were you writing anyway?' Kitty O'Dowd asked.

'She was writing to her mother,' Treasa replied.

Mary wondered vaguely how Treasa knew, forgetting that there was little that passed Treasa by.

'Sure that's nothing,' Kitty said. 'It's not as if you were doing something illicit.'

'Someone's learnt a new word,' Treasa teased.

'Does it mean *really* bad?' asked Kitty hopefully.

Mary Oliver wondered if Mother Immaculata would read the letter, and if so how she would feel when she read that she was recommending that her sister did not come to the school in September.

*   *   *

Mother Immaculata (known as The Raven to the girls) handed the confiscated letter to Sister Rodriguez.

'Did you know Mary Oliver is harbouring ambitions to become a nun?' she asked.

Sister Rodriguez perused the letter and then sniffed. 'So why doesn't she want her sister to join us next year?'

Mother Superior looked at the statue of the Infant of Prague sitting on a shelf to the right of her desk.

'That's unclear,' she replied. 'Though it may be connected.'

'She is a very pious and religious girl,' Sister Rodriguez said thoughtfully. 'And intelligent.'

'But immature,' Mother Immaculata said.

'No more than most of them,' Sister Rodriguez pointed out.

'True.' Mother Immaculata took the letter back and read it again.

'There are certainly less obvious candidates for a vocation,' Sister Rodriguez continued.

'There are very few, if any, this year,' said her Superior. 'But she would need to go for a degree so that she can teach. I mean, what use is a secretarial course for a nun in here?'

'So we should encourage her to go on to university?' asked Sister Rodriguez.

Mother Superior nodded. 'Yes, a nice solid degree in English and French, that would suit us well. She's not mathematically orientated, going by her marks in maths.'

'But maybe we could encourage her in that direction. We only have lay staff teaching maths at the moment. A sister in that department would be most helpful. If, and when, we are forced to teach science, we will have to have lay staff for that, and it would be helpful to have a sister in charge.'

'Yes, so from next week, when Retreat is over, we will increase her time in maths, and if necessary organise extra tuition for her.'

'The Work of Our Lord will be done.'

'Amen.'

The hapless Mary Oliver lay on her side in her bed and pulled her knees up into a foetal position, with no idea that her future was being planned even as she lay there. She missed her nails so much and wondered yet again where they could be. She started to realise that they were really gone. How could she replace them?

With that thought on her mind, she began to slip into sleep but was distracted by the return of the Downey twins (each of whom had picked up one of the nails in question when Mary Oliver fell out of the confessional, and now each had one in her zipped gymslip pocket). Downeyone and Downeytwo, dressed in baby-doll pyjamas, and smelling of deodorant and talc, drew the curtains partially round their beds and then slipped in under the covers and lay facing each other.

Bernadette O'Higgins lay flat on her back and wondered, not for the first time, what on earth this Retreat was all about. It had no relevance to her at all. She folded her hands under her head and wondered why her brothers had not been expected to undergo such a trial. The previous year she had worked out that the only way of handling it was to keep oneself as occupied as possible, but with three more days to go, she was beginning to realise that it was fairly impossible to keep oneself occupied.

It's the boredom, she thought. From the moment we get up until we can finally escape to our beds at night, the sheer unadulterated boredom of it all. What is the point in pushing a group of reasonably bright girls to such extremes?

They were not allowed to enter their Common Room to pass time listening to music, or even to the news. The worst point of the day for her was when the Gospels and the lives of the saints were read out during mealtimes – probably to distract them from the awfulness of the food, she thought. The sheer unending boredom, and for what? She wondered how the others were coping. For her part, she had decided to keep to the silence to see if it had any effect on her. Yes, she knew she would have to do confession at some point during the week, and then she would whisper the same sins as ever through the grid in the confession box. She had long since decided she would only go when the more ascetic priest was hearing confession. She wondered if the other priest had said something to Mary Oliver or whether it was just that Mary had not been well. No one seemed to care. She couldn't believe it when Mary had turned up in chapel that morning escorted by Treasa who was mouthing about Sister Sick being sick. Mary, of course, had said nothing, just looked pale and miserable.

Sisters of Care, thought Bernadette, wondering what it was that they did care for. Themselves? she wondered. Or is it order and discipline? It certainly was not the individual. There was no place for the individual. She grimaced. Six weeks to go, she thought. That is surely feasible. As long as I manage to get through this week, through this Retreat.

Maeve Maple had a drink with a friend on her way home that evening. 'How's it going?' asked the friend as he put her drink on the table and took out his cigarettes.

'This is always the worst time,' the Maple replied. 'The girls are pent up for the week, total silence bar the singing, hormones going wild, the food is dreadful – part of the penance attached to the whole caboodle. I don't know. One of the girls fainted yesterday evening, and there she was today putting in the whole day on Retreat in silence, looking like death, and when I asked her was she all right, she just shook her head, wouldn't speak because she won't break the silence.'

'Does it serve any purpose, the Retreat, I mean?' asked her friend.

'On one level, yes, it probably does, but it's so protracted and if you silence girls like that and give them nothing to do to stimulate them or to occupy them productively, you are just breeding trouble. You can see it on day one. Some of them will get through it, it may even strengthen them in certain ways, but don't, whatever you do, ask me what those ways are, because I cannot for the life of me imagine.'

'You sound like it's getting to you too,' he interjected.

'I know,' she said, 'and I'm not committed to the silence. Can you imagine what that's like – five full days and nights at their age? For every one of them it may give something to, I can't help feeling it's pushing others closer and closer to the edge.'

She was right about that.

That very night Mary Oliver sleepwalked for the first time.

No one knew. No one even suspected. But Mary Oliver was puzzled when, the following morning, getting out of bed she saw how dirty her feet were. She looked at them in horror. There was dust and dirt on her legs and on her nightdress, and the soles of her feet were completely black. Needless to say, she kept it to herself, just hastened to the bathroom where she washed her feet and legs thoroughly and tried to wash away the bewildered feeling that seemed to swamp her. When she was clean, she wondered if perhaps she had imagined the state they had been in, but the dusty marks on her nightie belied that thought and she washed it too and hung it on a rail in the bathroom.

Treasa O'Donoghue was bored out of her tree. There was no other way she could describe it. She was puzzled as to how the others were getting through it. Bernadette seemed absorbed in an old leatherbound copy of *Lives of the Saints*, which was extremely unlikely and probably meant that Bernadette was up to something else but at least she didn't look bored. Anna McBride was behaving as if she weren't there at all, which probably meant that Bridie had something better to think about. Mary Oliver appeared to have gone over the edge, and Treasa increasingly felt there was little she could do to assist her other than to smile at her and to wink, but as she got no reaction whatsoever, she was unsure how long she could keep this up. And Kitty, well, Kitty had found an 'out', and even if it was only for an hour in the afternoon, it meant escape for her. The lucky wagon. Treasa envied her that hour. In fact, now that she thought about it, Kitty was the only person in the group who was behaving normally.

Treasa, who was quite lackadaisical in her approach to life, was actually afraid to break out like Kitty. She couldn't afford to have the wrath of her father brought down upon her. She wondered how Kitty got away with it. She knew Kitty had been expelled twice before but for some reason it had not really changed the essence of Kitty.

The essence of Kitty was the 'fuck you' attitude that steered her slowly through school, skirmishing with the nuns and toying with her schoolwork. And that same attitude would ultimately propel her out through the front door of the school and she would not look back other than mentally to stick two fingers up at Mother Immaculata.

But of course Treasa did not know that at this point. Treasa, lying in bed, was trying to think of one thing to look forward to during the remaining three days of the Retreat. She came up with a blank.

Chapter Four

Turn back the clock and meet Anna McBride as a little girl, pale-faced with dark red hair, large green eyes, little thin legs and arms and a hopeful look on her tiny oval face.

She is born with a silver spoon in her mouth. An only child. Her parents own a large house about eight miles out from Dublin city centre. A large detached house with two and a half acres of exciting garden, complete with a swimming pool and lots of bushes for hiding in.

Anna McBride is taught at home because it is more convenient. Every day her tutor arrives and she, clothed in a dress and cardigan with a matching ribbon tying back her long red hair, waits in the study to begin her tuition. She was reading fluently by the age of four, and had taught herself multiplication by the age of six (but only up to the 16 times table at that stage). It is amazing what emotional deprivation does for a child.

Anna McBride (later Bridie to her friends) lives in this large six-bedroom house in the outer extremes of Dublin suburbia and, apart from conversing with her tutor, has very little human contact during the day. Her father is a busy lawyer and her mother is just busy busy. There is not a charity in South County Dublin where her mother does not put in her twopence worth, with golf and bridge for relaxation.

Anna McBride is not allowed outside the gates of their secluded home for fear that she might meet unsuitable friends. (Would unsuitable friends be better than none? she would later ask her husband.)

'Children will be attracted to you because of our swimming pool. But only during the summer,' her mother says. 'Come winter they will abandon you, and you will have no one to play with.'

But I have no one to play with anyway, thinks Anna as she looks up at her mother. 'Yes, Mummy,' she says sadly.

'Don't feel sorry for yourself,' her mother says reassuringly. 'This way you won't be abandoned by friends.'

And so Anne McBride is prepared for life.

'Now go out and play, Anna, and get out from under my feet. We've acres of garden for you to have fun in,' says Mrs McBride.

When Anna is three she meets Tom and Mary. They are in her first reader. *Run, Tom, run, Mary, run run run.*

She takes them in her mind into the garden and they play in the bushes. There are no pictures in the book and she knows no children other than the one she sees in the mirror.

Tom and Mary have dark red hair.

Later she reads *The Bobbsey Twins*, and Tom and Mary are given a surname. *Come, Tom Bobbsey, come, Mary Bobbsey, come come come.* They follow her through the trees, under the lavender bush, down by the laburnum. *Smile, Tom, smile, Mary, smile smile smile.*

When she is four she gets a present from Canada. Her mother says, 'This is from a distant cousin who lives in Canada where there are grizzly bears.'

Anna opens her parcel, and inside is a teddy bear. She names him Grizzle.

A week later Grizzle looks at her and says, quite clearly, 'Take me with you.'

She looks in surprise at Grizzle because she didn't know he could talk. He wears red dungarees and has a very pointed black-brown nose and he usually sits on her bed. She stops at the door and waits to see if he will say anything else.

He doesn't.

She thinks that she ought to bring him with her just in case he says something after she has left him. She takes her doll (Melissa with long blonde hair and blue eyes) out of her doll's pram, and pops Grizzle in instead.

'Thanks,' says Grizzle as he settles down for his first journey in a perambulator. He looks with interest at the trees and the bushes as she wheels him around the two and a half acres of well-kept rolling gardens.

Isn't this fun, Tom? Isn't this fun, Mary? Isn't this fun, Grizzle? Fun fun fun.

When she is nine she is brought by her mother to a convent school in a row of Georgian houses situated in the city, in that area of town known as Dublin 2.

Mother Immaculata, in head regalia which makes Anna think of seagulls flying on the seafront, interviews her in an office which smells of polish with the faintest waft of cabbage thrown in for good measure.

'We were thinking next September would be a good time for Anna to commence school,' says her mother in that funny voice she puts on when she is trying to impress.

Anna's eye is caught by the statue on the mantelpiece.

'Do you know who that is?' Mother Immaculata asks the large-eyed, pale-faced child.

'Is it Jesus?' Anna asks.

'It is the Infant of Prague,' retorts Mother Immaculata.

Anna blushes. She thought it looked a bit like Jesus and she has never heard of the Infant of Prague.

'She has had religious instruction,' her mother hurriedly puts in. 'Our priest, Father McMorrow, from the parish, you know. He comes regularly and teaches her.'

'Has she made her First Communion?' asks Mother Immaculata, eyeing the blushing Anna.

'Oh, yes, indeed. There have been no short cuts in her education,' reassures Mrs McBride. 'Confession and First Communion at the age of eight. In our local church. The priests arranged it that she could make it with the . . .' (pause as Mrs McBride has a problem with certain 'types' of people), 'local children . . . from the, er, err . . . local school.'

'I see,' says Mother Immaculata, and she prepares a barrage of tests for Anna to undergo.

Anna sits at a desk in a classroom by herself. The June sunlight shining through the window makes her hair look as if it is on fire. Her small hand works its way quickly across page after page. Level after level of sums completed. Page after page of writing. All her reading coming to good use as she answers questions on comprehension and writes an essay about the best day of her life (which is based on nothing in reality). Her Irish and French are excellent, as is her Latin.

'We have a problem, Mrs McBride,' says Mother Immaculata behind her desk in her school office in the Georgian house in Dublin 2.

'Oh dear,' says Mrs McBride. 'What's happened? What's gone wrong?' Anna, pale-faced and large-eyed, swings her white-socked legs and sucks her bottom lip.

The problem appears to be that Anna is ahead of her peers.

'If we put her in with girls of her own age she will be bored,' says the wise Mother Immaculata, who doesn't worry about boredom with regard to any other part of her charges' lives. 'Really, her level is that of First Year, the thirteen-year-olds, but she has done no geometry.'

'No problem,' says Mrs McBride with a sigh of relief. 'Come September her geometry will be at the right level.'

Anna looks out of the window, knowing deep in her heart that come September, her geometry will be of the level of at least fifteen-year-olds, if her mother has anything to do with it.

Mother Immaculata nods, satisfied. Another pupil. More money in the coffers.

The fees are not inexpensive – in fact this is one of the most expensive private girls' schools in Ireland.

Mother Immaculata is very pleased. A good family. Father a lawyer. Nice accent. Refined. The right type of girl.

'Were you thinking of having her board?' asks Mother Immaculata.

'It's certainly open to discussion,' says Anna's mother, willing to be convinced that boarding is the right option for her only child.

'See you in September, Anna,' says Mother Immaculata.

Anna nods her head up and down in excitement. A real school. Long corridors, a smell of wax and polish. A dormitory. And lots and lots of girls.

Goodbye, Tom, goodbye, Mary, goodbye goodbye goodbye.

It is 'Goodbye, Tom and goodbye, Mary', but not quite yet. Nor is it 'Hello, school'. Not yet.

Before Anna gets to school she is going to have an accident, and come September she will be in hospital not in St Martin's in the Fields.

On the way home from the school interview she says to her mother, 'Why is it called *in the fields* when there aren't any?'

'Aren't any what?' asks her distracted mother whose mind is thrilling with the fact that her nine-year-old is going into a class with thirteen-year-olds. She'll be ten by then, but so what. What a feat! What a coup! Wait until she tells them at bridge and at golf.

'Fields, Mummy,' says Anna, puzzled.

'That's just an anomaly,' says her mother vaguely. 'And there are gardens. Behind the houses. Mother Immaculata showed me around while you were doing your tests. Quite lovely, in fact. There are four houses, all with interconnecting doors. And behind the houses there are these gardens – idyllic, in fact. There is a vegetable garden, and then three other ones. They are walled in but there are arched entrances between each.'

'But what about sport, Mummy?' asks the enthusiastic Anna who had read all the Enid Blytons by the age of eight and knew to expect hockey and lacrosse, tennis and netball, and possibly horse-riding, with a bit of luck. The Chalet School novels had offered skiing, but Anna knows instinctively that skiing is out.

'I forgot to ask,' says her mother. 'Don't worry about it. There is a tennis court. It'll be wonderful, dear.'

It will be, won't it? thinks Anna hopefully. She pushes aside the thought of a school with no playing fields. No sports mistress. No gym.

In some instinctive way (and Anna McBride is instinctive) she knows that girls without fields will use their imagination. That a tennis court will get used, not just as a tennis court but also as a makeshift basketball court where enthusiastic girls bend wire coat hangers into the appropriate shape and wedge them into the wall. So what that both goals are at the same end? The girls just twist the rules to fit the cloth that's given to them.

And those who don't play tennis or basketball use the next garden for reading, or the end garden for climbing over the back wall into the lane to escape. And those who do some of the above also climb out through the skylight on the roof of the dormitory house and scamper across the lethally dangerous roofs among the chimney pots to smoke and sunbathe.

But there's a while to go before Anna McBride gets that far, before she, as a flat-chested child, slips into the dormitory where her thirteen- and fourteen-year-old classmates turn and stare in horror at their new companion.

She doesn't know not to be in a rush. Where she is is not much fun, but she is optimistic. She is sure that St Martin's in the Fields will offer her more.

Anna McBride goes home to learn geometry. Unfortunately her tutor doesn't teach geometry.

'You employed me to teach her maths, Irish, English, French, Latin, history and geography. I've brought her to an acceptable level, Mrs McBride, and I don't teach geometry.'

It's summer time. The lawyer father sighs and says that he will teach her geometry. 'I'll teach you one theorem each Sunday until the end of July, and then we can do an hour a day during August.'

This turns out to be one hour every Sunday morning. Initially Anna is delighted. A whole hour of uninterrupted work with her father whom she adores from a distance. But distance is the best place to be with a father who is not known for patience.

The classes start well. She is enthusiastic, excited, attentive. He is irritable at losing an hour with his papers on a Sunday morning.

'I don't see it,' she says, looking at the triangles in her copybook.

'Well, why don't you see it?' he asks. 'It's right there in front of you.'

It is tough going. She starts to dread Sunday morning, and he has a habit of slapping her with a ruler when she doesn't catch on.

She takes a flying leap off the garden wall with Grizzle in her arms. She had jumped it before, many times in fact, but only in her mind.

Jump, Tom, jump, Mary, jump jump jump.

'That wall is seven feet high,' her father says to the doctor in casualty. 'She jumped seven feet, I can't believe it.'

'Not seven feet, Daddy,' she interjects. 'The wall is seven feet high. The flowerbed is four feet across. I jumped just over eight feet.'

'What? What do you mean?'

'The square on the hypotenuse is equal to the sum of the squares on the other two sides. Seven by seven is forty-nine plus four by four, which is sixteen, equals sixty-five feet. And the square of that is eight point . . .' Her voice trails away as the anaesthetic takes hold.

A lesson well learnt, Anna.

Broken legs are operated on and then they need traction. Anna is in hospital for the long haul.

'Are you lonely, Anna?' asks her mother during visiting hours.

'No, Mummy. I'm fine, thank you.' Anna has been disappointed to have the start of school postponed but quickly realises that few places would offer her the companionship of hospital. In a ward with thirteen other children, all in various stages of distress, she lies on her bed (she has no choice) with her legs hoisted at different angles, and Grizzle tucked in beside her, and she chats and chats all day long.

Then it is time to go home and recuperate.

Welcome back, Tom, welcome back, Mary, don't go away away away. Her big bedroom with its flouncy pink curtains and candy-striped bedclothes is very empty and quiet. She lies on her bed clutching Grizzle and thinking about all the children she's met in hospital. Really, she thinks, this room is big enough for more than just me (and Tom, and Mary, and Grizzle).

And just like that, in walks Tess and Sue. They have red hair and freckles and very laughy faces. They sit on the chairs while she sleeps and they are there when she wakes in the morning. They encourage her on her crutches, and because she can't carry Grizzle now, he stays on her bed and Tess and Sue walk around the garden with her.

It is coming up to Easter. She is sitting by the pool and the window into the dining room is open. Her parents' voices filter through, lifted on the thin white curtain which floats outwards.

'She's missed six months of school. She'll have to start after Easter,' her mother says.

'I don't think we can let her board for this coming term,' her father says. 'The doctor said more home care and he didn't seem to think she should start until next September.'

'I can't have her lying around. It's inconvenient and it's bad for her.'

'Do you want to get the tutor back for the coming term?'

'It'd just be easier if she went into school even if it's only on a daily basis for the coming term.'

'Isn't she still a bit frail?'

'She'll be grand. It'll toughen her up.'

And so it is that, aged ten, Anna finally goes to school.

Tess goes too. Sue stays at home.

Anna's lawyer father drives her (and Tess) in the mornings. They sit in the back of the car because he likes to travel with his briefcase on the seat beside him. It is all very inconvenient for him, because when he gets to the school each morning, he has to carry Anna's bag in for her because she is lumbered with her crutches.

She loves her uniform. It consists of a bright green gymslip that buttons on her shoulders, and a belt that buttons round her waist. A matching green tie, a crisp white button-through blouse (five of them, in fact), white knickers (they are supposed to be green but as her mother says, 'Who would know?' as there is no sport, and white knickers are more attractive anyway), white socks and smart black shoes. (Good thing they aren't patent leather shoes or the nuns might find out about those white knickers!) A bright green blazer with a crest which says *Humanitas et Virtus* (she won't encounter much of the first and she'll need all she can of the latter) and a gaberdine for the cooler weather.

There is no school scarf as such, but there is a knitting class for the boarders on Saturdays and there they knit a green and white striped scarf of any length they like, which they wear wrapped like muffs round their necks in the damp and badly heated Common Room in winter.

Anna McBride arrives on her first day, as a day pupil, on her crutches with her impatient father in tow, carrying her bag. They enter the building and she is suddenly swamped by the size of the place and the number of girls (though it is not a large school), and she tries to take a step closer to her father as she is now nervous of being knocked off her crutches.

'Ah,' says an approaching nun complete with seagull wings on her head, 'this must be our little brain.'

Mr McBride is now smiling proudly, but somehow Anna feels that didn't sound very nice. Her father leaves her with this nun whose name for some unknown reason seems to be Sister Rodriguez. Anna wonders if she's Spanish, but doesn't like to ask. Sister Rodriguez gets Anna off to a great start by bringing her to her classroom, handing

Anna's schoolbag to a girl in the room, and introducing Anna as 'Anna McBrain'.

Anna McBride blushes and says hello to the girl who has taken her bag. 'Are you sure this is the class you meant to bring her to?' asks the girl of Sister Rodriguez.

'Oh, yes,' says the nun with her sugar-sweet voice that makes Anna think of burnt toffee. 'Our prodigy is nine years old.'

'I'm ten,' Anna says. 'Nearly eleven,' she adds hurriedly.

'Don't you dare contradict me,' says Sister Rodriguez.

And Anna, ten going on eleven, is relegated to being a nine-year-old in a class of girls aged fourteen who look at her with a mixture of curiosity and disgust. In three years' time, these girls will be doing their Leaving Certificate. So will Anna. She has an awful lot to learn.

She puts her head down and works for that term, getting rid of her crutches three weeks on, which makes things easier for her father because now he can just drop her off outside the school and pull back into the traffic almost in one movement. And she, now carrying her own schoolbag, accompanied by Tess, heads in through the door into the building that smells of wax and polish, with a whiff of cabbage which is much stronger in the house to the left where they have lunch and where the boarders eat breakfast and their evening meal. Strangely, cabbage is not served that often, but it is definitely cabbage which one can smell. (Except on Fridays when the smell is decidedly fishy.)

Anna McBride has no friends. She will have later, but not yet. Friends take time to make and she has no idea how to go about it with girls of any age, let alone girls three years her senior who have been led by a nun to believe that they are four years her senior. So Anna studies and, horror of horrors, Anna comes top of the year even though she has only been there one term.

They break for the summer holidays and Anna's heart is broken. She is unable to balance what has happened. Surely to come first is a reason for joy. It is an achievement. Her parents are pleased, although she only got 92 per cent in her Latin. 'Room for improvement,' her father says. But she knows he's pleased. He has to be. But on the last day of term there is prize-giving, and the applause is hesitant and broken when she is called up as pupil of her year. The teachers applaud, and girls from other classes clap away, but she knows that her classmates are displeased. And afterwards, back in the classroom, as they clean out their desks they are all swapping addresses and sharing information about where they are going and who will phone whom but no one says anything to Anna McBride. She bites back the tears and puts her books in her bag.

Home she goes with Tess. *Hello, Tom, hello, Mary, hello, Sue, hello, Grizzle, hello hello hello.*

'Daddy and I were thinking a month in Irish College would do you good,' her mother says; her golf card appointments are filled up and she is busy busy busy. 'I booked you in today. You leave on Monday.'

Anna McBride digests this. Could it be worse than school? Is there any information she has learnt in school with which she can arm herself? Don't be a goody-goody, suggests itself.

So Anna McBride, just turned eleven, goes to Irish College with Grizzle in her bag and Tess and Sue in her mind, and a suitcase full of summer clothes and several books, alone by train.

It takes for ever to get to Cork, and she reads a book, and tries to fight the hunger pangs because her mother has forgotten to give her a packed lunch and she has never been on a train before and doesn't know there is a dining carriage.

She is found on the platform at the other end, by a teacher from the Irish College who is calling out names and ticking them off on sheets of paper. The next thing she knows she is on a bus with dozens of screaming and yelling girls who give the impression of knowing each other for ever even though it later transpires that most of them only know two or three others.

The dormitories are individual chalets housing four or six girls each, and as the girls who know each other pair off, Anna McBride finds herself in a chalet with three other loners. Two of these girls are twins who appear to have no interest in or need for anyone's company other than their own. The other is an older girl called Kitty. She is fourteen.

Coincidence?

Yes. Life is full of coincidences. (The Mother Church would probably call them miracles.) These are the Downey twins, due to start at St Martin's in September, and Kitty O'Dowd, not yet expelled from her second school. A chance for Anna McBride to make friends, although at this point she has no idea that these three girls will be in the next dorm to her for the next three years.

It seems unfortunate to Anna that she has ended up in a chalet with girls so much older than she is, but being an optimist at heart she gives it her all. She hides her books and pretends not to care, this being what she has picked up during her first term at St Martin's as being the safest way to survive without attracting attention.

'Jayzus,' says Kitty to the twins. 'We can't smoke in here because of the child.'

'I don't mind at all,' says Anna. 'I used to smoke myself but I got a chest infection and now I can't, but I won't tell.'

And Kitty O'Dowd takes another look at her and knows that Anna is lying about being an ex-smoker. But she sees something that she identifies with, even though it will be years before she can put her finger on it, and she grins at Anna and says, 'Would you like one?' And with that one question, Anna is accepted.

Anna McBride makes her first three friends that summer (other than her imaginary ones). Tess and Sue go home at the end of the first week, and Anna runs errands for Kitty and the twins. She trails along behind them to class. She goes to sports in the afternoon and swims and plays every game you can imagine, which strengthens her legs, and her skin gets tanned under the sun which seems to shine all day every day during that month. Her face becomes freckled, and her thick dark red hair becomes lustrous, and Kitty snips the ends of it to even it off. Kitty christens her Bridie, which she loves, both because it is the first time she has ever had a nickname, and because it is Kitty who has thought it up and Anna adores Kitty.

Adores Kitty? No, she worships Kitty. In her eyes Kitty can do no wrong, which of course is interesting because in the eyes of everyone else Kitty comes in contact with, Kitty can do no right. At the end of the first week in the Irish College, Kitty is called in and admonished for smoking, for skipping class, for not turning up to any sporting events and for talking only English.

'What do you hope to get from Irish College?' the principal asks Kitty, who shrugs.

A nice even tan, she thinks. A bit of a break from the usual. To be left alone.

None of these sentiments are uttered aloud.

'If you get sent home,' the principal persists, 'and the way you are going you will get sent home, your parents won't be pleased and we will inform your school.'

Kitty curtails her activities and turns up to class and makes a bit of an effort, which brings Bridie no small joy.

'Will you do my nails for me, Kitty?' she asks. And Kitty surprises herself by polishing them for her, and is quite pleased at Bridie's evident delight.

'I wish I had a sister like you,' Bridie says.

'Do you have a sister?' Kitty asks.

Bridie shakes her head. 'I'm an only child. How about you?'

'I've two older brothers,' Kitty replies. 'A sister mightn't have been bad, actually,' she adds. 'I think my parents really wanted three boys.' (In fact they had only wanted two boys, but it hasn't occurred to Kitty that she might not have been wanted – she just thinks she's the wrong sex.)

And the following day when Bridie slips on the rocks down at the beach and cuts her leg, Kitty puts an arm round her as they walk back to the college and Bridie thinks, she's as good as a sister.

But then the month is up, and the train journey up to Dublin is horrible, as Kitty retreats into herself, and the twins have been collected by their parents in Cork. And Anna McBride, with Grizzle in her bag, contemplates the rest of the summer alone in her back garden.

When she says goodbye to Kitty O'Dowd on the platform in Dublin, Kitty just nods and takes her bag and walks off. Anna suddenly finds a new friend called Odette who looks very like Kitty, with the same high cheekbones, porcelain skin and the same cheeky grin and lackadaisical walk. Odette sits in the back of her father's car with her and holds her hand and calls her Bridie, and the rest of the summer no longer seems to stretch out so frighteningly empty.

And in September, when she goes back to St Martin's, this time as a full term-boarder, there are the Downey twins, and while they are not particularly nice to her, they are certainly more pleasant to her than they are to anyone else.

'Do you ever hear from Kitty O'Dowd?' she asks hopefully.

'We don't write letters,' say the Downey twins as one.

But seeing Bridie's crestfallen face, they return her question, and she is delighted that they might think that Kitty O'Dowd just might have kept in touch with her.

'Why are you in the same year as we are when you are three years younger?' asks Downeyone, echoing aloud the thought of Downeytwo.

'Some clerical error,' Bridie says vaguely, trying to obliterate the memory of Sister Rodriguez and her Anna McBrain comment of a year before.

'Someone said you're a bit of a whizz in the maths department,' Downeyone continues.

'No, not me,' Bridie says. 'I prefer subjects to do with people – English and history – subjects where people interrelate.'

Downeyone and two look at each other. Interrelate, they think. They say nothing.

Bridie starts to retreat. She knows that look. She's seen it before in her classmates' eyes.

'Give us a hand with maths, Bridie,' the Downey twins say as one.

And Bridie, thrilled to be called Bridie and asked to help, agrees.

'But we thought you weren't any good at maths,' says Downeyone.

Bridie is caught by their duplicated logic, and she stands there with her face blushing until it clashes with her hair, words of consternation falling over each other inside her head.

In due course Kitty O'Dowd is expelled from her second school and turns up at St Martin's. Things get better as Bridie learns how to balance being a brain with being one of the class. She never gets it quite right because of the age difference, but after Kitty arrives on the scene, those who had mocked pull back, and the more decent girls learn to accept her.

Around this time, Odette disappears, puberty sets in and Anna McBride meets Jean Jacques Versailles.

Forward to the chamber turning, all her soul within her burning
Soon again she heard a tapping, tapping louder than before.
'Surely,' said she, 'surely that is something at my window lattice;
Let me listen to what that is, and this mystery explore –
Let my heart be still a moment, and this mystery explore; –
                                        'Tis the wind and nothing more.'

Chapter Five

M ary Oliver's feet were black again when she got out of bed on the Wednesday morning. There were matching black shadows under her eyes. During breakfast Sister Rodriguez read from the Gospels in a well-practised monotone which seemed to Bernadette O'Higgins with her navy blue eyes to be designed to put them all to sleep. Bernadette kept herself concentrated and awake by counting in her mind as many of the illustrations and photographs in *Scrumptious Sex* as she could recall.

It was raining and much cooler that morning as the girls left the convent for the Sister Chapel. They had their gaberdines on.

'Hoods up, girls,' Sister Rodriguez said as they trooped out into the wet. Kitty O'Dowd checked her tunic pocket for her packet of cigarettes, but she could already see a problem about where she was going to smoke if it kept on raining.

Mass took place nearly two hours later in the Sister Chapel, by which point Kitty O'Dowd was desperate for a smoke. She was about to slip out the back of the church when Miss Ní Ghrian grabbed her by the arm and instructed her to go and sit at the front of the church.

Treasa joined her and they knelt side by side in the front pew. The priest walked out onto the altar with his altar boys trailing behind him. Kitty looked at Treasa and raised her eyes to heaven. It was the younger, chubbier priest with the well-fed cheeks and the blond curls, Father Michael McMorrow to those in the know. Mary Oliver shivered in her pew but didn't know why. The Downey twins glanced at each other, and they let their knuckles touch each other's hands as they knelt to pray.

It was midway through Mass when Kitty whispered to Treasa O'Donoghue, 'Which part of him would you least like to have touch you?'

Unfortunately this came at a moment when Treasa was least expecting such a query and she gave a guffaw of laughter, which she tried to turn into a cough. She sounded remarkably like a chicken being strangled. The priest, who had been about to pour the wine into the chalice, turned to see what had happened and caught Kitty O'Dowd's eye.

Kitty (who later pointed out to The Raven that it wasn't her fault that her face was the way it was) gave the priest one of those looks that her friends' parents weren't keen on, and the priest, on seeing Kitty with her wide eyes and her raised eyebrows and who had never been looked at like that before, accidentally poured the wine on the Hosts, giving rise, as Treasa later commented, to a whole new type of miracle.

The altar boys rang the bells and the whole congregation bowed their heads and while the wine and bread were changed into the blood and body of Jesus Christ, Kitty and Treasa looked at each other.

There wasn't much the priest could do. When he came to give out Communion some ten minutes later, he was forced to press a sodden piece of wine-drenched Host onto each of the girl's tongues.

'How dare you distract Father McMorrow like that, Kitty O'Dowd.' Mother Immaculata and Sister Rodriguez had cornered Kitty in the chapel porch.

'It wasn't Kitty,' Treasa interjected. 'I was the one who coughed, not Kitty.'

'How dare you interrupt, Treasa O'Donoghue, AND you are on silence.' The Raven turned back to Kitty O'Dowd. 'Take that look off your face.'

This was when Kitty said, 'I can't help my face.'

Where or how Father McMorrow managed to appear at this moment is unclear, but something flashed across the face of the young priest, and he said smoothly to Mother Immaculata, 'Perhaps I may have a word with her.'

Kitty O'Dowd turned and looked at him. Her full pink lips above her slightly pointed chin quivered. The wrath of a priest was more than even she could handle.

'I'm sorry, Mother,' she said suddenly to the head nun.

'You may go with Father,' said The Raven, irritated that the priest was stepping into her patch.

Kitty hesitated.

'Now,' said The Raven, her voice cutting the silence with devastating precision.

Slowly Kitty followed the priest to the furthest corner of the porch.

'Would you like to say confession?' he asked her, although his tone implied that it was not a question, more a statement of fact.

She shook her head. Out of the corner of her eye, through the open door into the church, she could see dozens and dozens of candles lit before one of the statues of St Martin. They flickered and she turned her head to look at them.

'You cannot behave like that in church,' he said to her.

'I didn't do anything,' Kitty replied, as Miss Maple appeared beside her.

'I don't want to make confession now,' Kitty O'Dowd said to Miss Maple, moving closer to her.

Some kind of power struggle going on here, Maeve Maple thought to herself, looking at Kitty's pale face and her trembling lips. 'Perhaps tomorrow, Kitty,' she said aloud.

'I'm not making confession,' Kitty said. 'I didn't do anything.' With that she turned on her heel, and pushing past Mother Immaculata and Sister Rodriguez she ran out of the front door of the chapel and down the street.

There was a stunned silence, reminiscent of when Mary Oliver fell out of the confessional. Miss Maple turned and looked after her in surprise.

Treasa, disbelieving, and expecting something to happen, hovered, unsure whether to follow Kitty or to stay and do something. Miss Maple, who felt she must have missed some part of what had happened, said to Mother Immaculata, 'I'll go after her,' and hurried out onto the street.

Father McMorrow, turning to Mother Immaculata, said, 'You really ought to control these girls better. They lack discipline.'

Miss Ní Ghrian, torn between loyalty to the sisters and satisfaction at what she always felt was the case, pursed her lips and looked from one to the other like an inquisitive hen.

The rain had eased off for the time being and Maeve Maple hastened in the direction of Sutherland Square where she correctly guessed that Kitty

O'Dowd was heading. She caught up with her just inside the gate. 'Come and sit, Kitty,' she said, putting her hand on Kitty's arm.

Kitty shook her hand off.

'Come and sit,' Miss Maple repeated, and taking a packet of cigarettes from her pocket, she offered Kitty one. Kitty looked at the cigarette and up at the Maple, then she took one from the proffered packet and slipped it between her lips. Miss Maple lit it, and lit one for herself. There was silence between them for several minutes, then the Maple said, 'What happened?'

'I didn't do anything,' Kitty said. 'And that bastard wanted me to go to confession.'

Another silence, and Miss Maple said, 'Why did he want you to go to confession?'

'I don't know,' Kitty said. 'He poured the wine in on top of the bread during Mass, and for some reason he appeared to be blaming that on me.'

A further silence while the Maple digested this.

'Have you any idea why he blamed you?' she asked.

Kitty shook her head. 'I didn't do anything,' she repeated.

They finished their cigarettes, and stubbed them out on the path.

'We're going to have to go back,' the Maple said.

'I'm not going back,' Kitty said. 'He's a fecking pervert, and The Raven has it in for me . . . always has had it in for me . . . and no one will listen to me or believe me.'

'Gently, now,' Miss Maple said carefully. 'Just take it gently. I believe you. That's why I'm sitting here with you. But you need to be very careful. It's a very strong institution and you have to protect yourself because, believe me, they will protect themselves.'

Kitty scowled. 'I don't stand a chance against them. I don't want to go back.'

'You listen to me now,' Miss Maple said. 'Don't let them win. If you don't go back, that's just what happens. They win. They'll love that. I believe you that you didn't do anything. So stand up and say it. Don't let them win. You're so close to the end, six more weeks then final exams. Stick with it. Don't give them the satisfaction.'

Kitty sighed. They stood up together and started the walk back to the Sister Chapel.

Lunch was under way when they returned. Miss Maple directed Kitty to go to her table and sit down.

In the corridor outside the refectory, Maeve Maple addressed Mother Superior.

'Mother Immaculata,' she said. 'I don't know the whole story, but I am absolutely confident that Kitty O'Dowd did nothing. Confession is supposed to be voluntary, and she felt that she was being coerced into going. And I, on her behalf, would like an explanation. This is truly unacceptable.'

Mother Immaculata was surprised to find Miss Maple taking this stance, surprised and not pleased.

'I'm busy now, Miss Maple,' she said. 'We can pursue this tomorrow if I have sufficient time.'

'That will suit me fine,' the Maple said, and she turned and went into the refectory.

In the refectory the girls sat at long tables, and Kitty O'Dowd slipped into the place beside Treasa.

Treasa O'Donoghue looked at her and mouthed, 'I'm sorry.'

Kitty shrugged and poked her food around her plate.

Sister Rodriguez was reading about the creator of mankind possessing power and intelligence without limit. 'Make the following supposition,' she intoned. 'Suppose that all the parts of mankind lay scattered about on a table . . .'

The few girls who were listening dropped their heads to hide their smiles.

'. . . and suppose you saw them rise up and move towards one another and fit themselves together – would you say that this happened by chance?'

Treasa O'Donoghue nudged Kitty O'Dowd in an effort to get a grin.

'She's a mad pervert,' Kitty whispered without moving her lips.

'No,' read Sister Rodriguez from *The Creation of Man*. 'You would say that this indeed was a miracle. That this indeed could only have been brought about by intelligence, invisibility, the ultimate Creator, and you

77

would know that he possessed faculties beyond our comprehension. And that is what our Creator did. He made the pieces of mankind and put them together in the ultimate act of creation . . .'

Where does that leave evolution? wondered Bernadette O'Higgins to herself.

Mary Oliver gagged and covered her mouth with her hand. Bridie asked Jean Jacques Versailles if he would bring her something to eat the next time he was visiting her in her cell.

'Jean Jacques,' she whispered. '*Je suis seule.*'

'*Jamais,*' he replied. '*Jamais, ma petite. Tu n'es pas seule.*' (He had recently progressed to the second person singular.) '*Nous sommes ensemble.*'

Bridie, totally tuned out from Sister Rodriguez's monotonous tones, held Jean Jacques' hand over her small right breast. She looked into his eyes and her heart melted as he brought his lips down to hers.

The hour passed.

Mary Oliver returned to the chapel after lunch when the others headed for the dayroom to read or to walk in the sheltered part of the cloistered garden – it had started to rain again. In the chapel she knelt before the small wooden crucifix on the wall and watched the hands of Christ. She prayed for guidance on a pathway she no longer understood. Things which had seemed clear to her before were now blurry and out of focus. She felt afraid. The stained glass of the windows around and behind the altar was dulled by the darkness of the day, and in some way this reflected where she was or, indeed, where she was not. She noticed one of the pieces of glass was missing. She felt light-headed almost to the point of being faint. She dropped her head onto her hands and closed her eyes.

'Please, please help me,' she prayed.

She stayed like that for the best part of ten minutes, until suddenly she felt something change, a coldness, a shadow, something cast over her, and she lifted her head. Father McMorrow was standing facing her in the pew in front. She felt her skin prickle, an iciness slipped down over and around her. She felt the stirring of panic, her heart beginning to pound, and yet she did not know why or what was happening. She cast her eyes back down and tried to go on praying, but she felt real fear.

* * *

That evening at the dinner table, Maeve Maple's parents asked how day three had gone.

'Sinking fast,' she replied. 'Something happened today . . .'

It took her a while to continue, and they did not push it, just waited until she was ready to unload.

'Kitty,' she said. 'Kitty O'Dowd . . .'

'New to the choir,' her mother encouraged her. Another silence ensued.

'She had some kind of run in with one of the priests,' Maeve Maple continued eventually. 'At least I think that is what happened. I couldn't follow. She's so . . . I don't know . . . poised? Is that the word? You know what she's like. You know the way she has such an impassive face.'

'Such a pretty girl,' her mother said. 'And you're right, she is impassive. I remember once watching her, down in the hotel, and I thought to myself, that girl doesn't know joy – and then suddenly she smiled. It was mischievous, lively . . . such a pretty girl, I thought.'

'Well, she's always like that,' Maeve Maple said slowly as she pieced together the Kitty she knew. 'She's very self-contained. The impassivity is usually impregnable. She deals with the frustrations of school by simply ignoring them. They seem to pass over her – you know, the pettiness of some of the rules, the unfairness I've sometimes told you about. It washes straight over her . . .'

There was a long pause while Miss Maple tried to piece Kitty O'Dowd together.

'She seemed to lose her aplomb this afternoon – that's the best way I can put it. Something happened in church. I missed it, I don't know what. The priest claims, I think, that she distracted him during Mass, and he wanted her to make confession. And she refused . . . point blank. It was terribly odd.'

Both her parents raised their eyebrows in a gesture of surprise and both waited.

'Needless to say,' Maeve continued, 'Kitty ran off and I went after her.'

'Was she all right?' they asked.

Maeve was silent for a while. 'Yes, yes, I think so. I talked her into going back. She didn't want to return. It was as if she had had enough.'

'That's probably understandable,' her mother said.

'There's something else,' Maeve said. 'Something . . . I'm not sure. I'll leave it for now. I need to think.'

Later that evening she returned to her parents in the drawing room where they were drinking coffee.

'I'd like to tell you what she said,' Maeve said. 'Kitty O'Dowd, I mean. She was talking about Father McMorrow, and she said, "He's a fecking pervert."' She looked from one parent to the other. 'Would you say that about someone who wanted you to go and make confession? Does that tie in? Does that make sense?'

'You might say it,' her father replied. 'One might. She might. What's the problem?'

'Nothing,' she said. 'No problem. You're probably right.'

Mother Superior (The Raven to the girls in her care) and Sister Rodriguez were back in the Mother House having afternoon tea in the office.

'She's disruptive,' Sister Rodriguez said of Kitty O'Dowd.

Mother Immaculata nodded. She was torn between different feelings on how to handle what was going on. Father McMorrow's observation about discipline within the school was a direct attack on her, an observation which she felt to be both unfair and unbalanced. She ran a tight ship and she knew it, but every so often up turned a bad egg, and one did one's best to handle the bad egg and to make it conform. Against that, of course, was the problem of Miss Maple who seemed to feel that an injustice was being done to Kitty O'Dowd, and Miss Maple was known for her tenacity and sense of fair play.

Mother Immaculata felt quite weary as she looked at the different players who were involved – the self-righteousness of Father McMorrow, the unruliness of Kitty O'Dowd, and the persistence of Miss Maple. She wished Sister Rodriguez would look a little less pleased. She was loath to let the side down by speaking about Father McMorrow, but she could not help but feel that he had been unfair in what he had said. After all, he was new to the Retreat, and going by what she had read about him he would move on from this to something else. He would only be giving St Martin's this one week and then he would be gone. He was really in no position to make any judgement. The school was very strict and discipline was not a problem, she was confident of that, so how dare he make such a comment and in front of so many people.

Treasa O'Donoghue, sitting in the dayroom, thought she was going to go out of her mind with boredom. The rain was pelting down outside now, and there wasn't a pamphlet left in the room which she had not read. She looked around for Kitty O'Dowd. Kitty was sitting by the window scowling, legs crossed, stocking tops exposed. Treasa could feel her frustration across the room. They made eye contact and Treasa jerked her head towards the door. She got up and left, and a few minutes later Kitty followed her. They headed for the chapel, which they thought might be a quiet place for a chat. There really was nowhere to smoke when it was raining. Arriving first, Treasa ran up the steps to the gallery where she would have a clear view of the whole of the nave. Down below, Father McMorrow, hearing her footsteps on the stairs, stood up from his place beside Mary Oliver who was sitting rigidly on the second front seat, motionless as if frozen.

Treasa got the impression she had interrupted something serious and she was about to step back from her viewpoint when she suddenly changed her mind. She moved forward so that she was clearly visible to Father McMorrow. Kitty came and joined her.

Father McMorrow, standing beside the frozen Mary Oliver, looked up at the two girls, then he left the pew, turned and walked up the aisle and disappeared through the doorway to the left of the altar.

Treasa stood and watched Mary Oliver's bowed head and wondered if by any remote chance McMorrow had been offering her comfort.

'What's up?' Kitty O'Dowd whispered.

Treasa shook her head. 'Nothing.'

They both contemplated the back of the disappearing priest.

'Did I mention . . .' said Treasa slowly, 'that Father McMorrow is my uncle?'

'Your what?' whispered Kitty in surprise.

'Me muvver's bruvver,' Treasa said in a joking way.

'Well, aren't you the right holy Joe,' said Kitty, taking in this bit of information. 'Are you sure?' she added after a moment.

'Don't you see the resemblance?' Treasa asked. 'We both have large bottoms.'

Kitty giggled. 'Yours is sexy, Treasa. Trust me,' she responded.

'Oh, fancy me, do you?' Treasa asked with a laugh, looking down again at the immobile Mary Oliver.

'Oh, dahling, I adaw you,' Kitty said. 'But I have other plans for my virginity.'

'Do you?' asked Treasa with interest. 'Personally, I think there are too many virgins around us. It's unhealthy.'

'And they're not a happy bunch, are they?' Kitty said, looking down at Mary's bowed head in the nave below.

When the girls filed out of the chapel that evening to walk back to the Mother House, two men were placing their ladders in the chapel porch. One of them winked at Kitty O'Dowd, and she winked back. The other man said to the Chapel Sister, 'We'll repair the stained-glass window now, and we'll leave the ladders and our tools here for the night and start cleaning the windows outside this time tomorrow, when the girls leave. It was too bad about the weather today.'

'Could we escape by ladder?' Bridie asked the ever-willing Jean Jacques Versailles.

'*Oui, c'est une possibilité,*' he replied as he pulled up the hood of her gaberdine and linked his arm through hers to escort her from one prison cell to the next.

Treasa walked beside Mary Oliver who looked even paler than she had earlier in the day.

'You OK?' Treasa whispered.

Mary Oliver looked at her. She wasn't sure at all if she was OK. She couldn't really feel anything. She nodded at Treasa, and stumbled slightly on the pavement; she would have fallen had not Treasa grabbed her arm.

'Let's link,' Treasa said to her, and she slipped her arm through Mary's. There was something very reassuring about Treasa's open face and brown eyes, and her laughing mouth. Mary knew that Treasa was bored a lot of the time, but still, or maybe in spite of that boredom, she always seemed to have time for other people.

'Did Father McMorrow ... was he ... did he talk to you about you fainting the other night in confession?' Treasa asked. She felt uncomfortably prurient in asking the question, but she did not know any other way of asking it, and she instinctively felt something was wrong.

Mary Oliver looked at her as if she had no idea what Treasa was talking about. A puzzled expression passed over her face, and then she nodded again at Treasa, really because it was the easiest thing to do.

'Will you take Communion tomorrow?' Treasa asked, knowing that Mary hadn't received Communion since Monday morning.

Mary dropped her head and shook it. She still had not been to confess, and she could not receive Communion until she had done a proper confession, and there was no way she could confess because she was afraid to go into the box. She felt like crying, and yet she had no idea what was wrong.

In the dorm that night, Kitty O'Dowd announced that Treasa O'Donoghue had holy blood running through her veins.

'What do you mean?' asked the Downey twins as one. Mary Oliver looked up at Kitty.

'Father McMorrow is my Uncle Mick,' Treasa said, shoving her washbag back into her locker. 'I am of the Lord,' she continued with a grin. '*Not of works, lest any man should boast.*'

'You're made out of a rib,' Kitty said with a snort.

'That's right,' Treasa replied. 'But wouldn't you wonder how a male rib would turn me out the way it has?'

''Tis a miracle,' said Kitty. 'Isn't it wonderful how, out of all the bits of a man which God laid out on a table and then pieced together, he chose to make women out of a rib?'

'I think it's a euphemism for a penis,' said Bernadette from the doorway, where she appeared to be standing plaiting her hair. 'I mean a rib – for goodness' sake. They just couldn't bring themselves to use the word "prick". It's what the snake in the Garden of Eden was all about. That's what that myth means but they had to tart it up and have a devil disguised as a talking snake.'

'Gawd,' said Kitty. 'It's no wonder we have no snakes in holy Catholic Ireland if that's what a snake stands for.'

'Hush,' whispered Bernadette, glancing down the corridor. 'Nun on skates approaching.'

That night Mary Oliver had a dream.

It was, without any doubt, the worst dream she had ever had in her life. She was walking down a corridor in her white nightdress, and across into the main part of the convent. She walked on bare cold feet down the wooden stairs, down into the basement. There she unlocked the heavy wooden door that led to the stores and was out of bounds to the girls. Past the shelving to the grid at the end. She lifted the key from the hook on the wall, and she unlocked the grid and pulled it open. Down old brick steps she went, into the bowels of the earth. In her dream she could feel the cold stone under her feet and the dampness of the air underground. The passageway was lit. Far above her there was the sound of the occasional car on the street, and on she walked, her eyes focused ahead of her until she came to another set of steps. She climbed up them slowly but surely, like someone who had climbed them before.

The grid at the other end opened easily and smoothly, as if recently oiled. Mary Oliver left it open and passed down the passageway beyond. And then she felt nothing. It was all just happening, just as if she were gliding on Mother Immaculata's roller skates. Up the stairs to the porch, and she slipped into the chapel, letting the door swing silently closed behind her. There was a light above the altar, and the moonlight coming through the stained glass lit the apse in an eerie way. She walked up the aisle and over to the pillar on the right where the crucifix was hanging. On silent feet she returned to the porch where she got the ladder the window cleaners had left the previous evening. In her dream the ladder was both long and heavy and she had to drag it up the aisle. It propped easily enough on the pillar where the crucifix hung. She climbed up it and looked at how the crucifix was attached to the pillar. It appeared to be on wire attached to a hook. She tried to shift it, but it was too heavy. She ran her hands over the wood which was surprisingly rough and uneven.

Back in the porch she searched through the toolboxes left by the workmen. There she found wire-cutters.

When she cut the wire that attached the crucifix to the wall, there was a loud sound as it snapped, and then a momentary pause as if time stood still before the crucifix fell to the floor, just missing taking Mary Oliver with it. The crash it made as it landed and broke resonated through the chapel, and it seemed to Mary in her dream that it echoed on and on.

In their beds the Chapel Sisters stirred as one, and then returned to their pure and untroubled sleep.

Mary tried to remove the Christ from his broken cross lying on the ground. His face was full of pain and anguish. His eyes, which while he was hanging on the pillar looked down on her, now seemed to avoid her eyes. She ran her hand over the wound on his side, over his forehead mutilated by the crown of thorns, over his torn and bleeding hands and feet.

In her dream Mary Oliver wept. She wept for Christ, and for herself.

In her dream she heard a voice saying, 'Flesh of my flesh, blood of my blood,' and so she approached the altar and there she committed the ultimate sacrilege by taking the chalice from the tabernacle. She laid the Hosts on the wound in Christ's side. She tried to remove the nails from his hands but could not, so she placed Hosts on the nails, hoping they would heal him. 'Flesh of his flesh,' she whispered.

She took a lighting candle from the altar and made her way to the room which the girls called the Sweatshop and there she took a shroud. On the way back to the crucifix she took two nails from the toolbox in the porch. Back at the shattered cross, she wrapped the Christ as best as she could in the shroud, before kneeling beside him and praying.

It seemed as if a storm had broken out. There was thunder and lightning, and the chapel seemed to light up. The sudden sound of rain belting down hit the windows and they shuddered in their frames.

The Chapel Sisters stirred again.

Mary Oliver seemed to be removed from herself; it was as if she could see herself, a slim, dark girl in a long white nightdress kneeling beside the broken cross with its shrouded Christ, her head bowed, her hands joined in prayer.

'*Absolvo meo*,' she intoned. '*Mea culpa, mea culpa, mea maxima culpa.*'

She looked up and around her and in the shadows of the church she thought she saw the Chapel Sisters, dressed in black, encircle her and the shrouded Christ, and they joined in her intonation.

'I am Mary and I am Martha,' she said to the broken body shrouded on the floor. 'I am the Lamb of God.' And she rolled the nails in the palms of her hands.

And when she looked again, there were no sisters there, just the stations of the Cross on the walls around her, and the statues of the saints with their blind eyes gazing into the darkness of the church.

Horse and rabbit quite beguiling, her happy soul into smiling,
Straight she left the farm and field, heading for the Grennit's door.
There within the nursery sinking, she betook herself to linking
Fancy unto fancy thinking; childhood friends and days of yore
Enjoy them now, these passing childhood days of yore
Quoth the Raven, 'Nevermore.'

Chapter Six

Treasa O'Donoghue seemed born to giggle. By the age of four months her two older siblings (there were just the three of them) had taken to tickling her, and baby Treasa, with black curly hair, rolled on the floor laughing.

'But she's a joy to tickle,' said her eight-year-old sister and six-year-old brother when their father suggested they desist. And a joy to tickle she was. What could be nicer for the perpetrators than to have the tickle-ee beetroot in the face and rolling on her nappy-covered bottom, positively squeaking with happiness.

Treasa's first word was 'More', and while it referred to many things, it mostly was to do with being tickled. Her face was in a permanent grin, and she liked nothing more than to have Maria and Michael come home from school and head in her direction.

Her dark curly hair grew long and knotted easily, but either Maria or Michael would take a comb to it, and with the most infinite patience and without causing her one gasp of anxiety they would remove the knots and then settle in for a tickling session.

No wonder Treasa had an open face and a laugh on her lips as she scooted around the floor, first on her back wiggling along, then on her knees as she learned forward propulsion, and finally pulling herself up onto her legs. She learned quickly how to clamber up and over the bars of her cot, and it wasn't to her parents' room she went at three or four in the morning but in search of Maria or Michael who always just lifted their bedclothes and let her slip in beside them.

'Such an easy child,' her parents said. 'She's never woken us at night, she's so easygoing, all she wants to do is be with people and to laugh.'

Her uncle Mick, a priest, and her aunt Concepta, a nun, on a visit to Wexford to the O'Donoghues' farm, nodded sagely, and noted Treasa's open, laughing face.

'God bless her,' said Sister Concepta, home from Malaya after a four-year stint, and due back in two weeks' time to spread the Word and enlighten the Orient.

'Indeed, indeed, blessed she is,' said Uncle Mick as he watched the toddling Treasa work her away around the room holding onto the edge of the furniture. 'If they were all that agreeable,' he said, thinking about his parishioners in a wealthy urban suburb, 'sure the world would be an easier place.'

Treasa, heading for the coal scuttle, is waylaid by Michael and taken out to see the farm animals. She loves that. After the word 'More', her next word is 'Moo', and the next one is a strange whinnying sound and means, 'Time to bring me to the stables'.

The O'Donoghues' land backs onto the local squire's, whose heart is closer to Belgravia than it is to the rolling fields of County Wexford. The same month that Treasa is born, so is the squire's daughter, Vita, blonde-haired, blue-eyed, with a whole canteen of silver spoons in or around her mouth. Neither child knows of the other's existence until Treasa, aged four, slips under the barbed wire and heads off on an adventure.

Across the fields on straight little legs with a friendly but determined expression on her face, Treasa goes to look for 'other animals', as she later tells her parents. (Maria and Michael had read her *The Wind in the Willows*, and one of them had said that Ratty and Mole lived out there beyond the wire.)

Across the fields, armed with her copy of the aforementioned book so that she can show Ratty and Mole what they look like in the illustrations, goes Treasa. She is not missed for two hours because her mother is busy in the kitchen and thinks Treasa is with her father, and he is busy in the stables and assumes Treasa is with her mother. A misunderstanding which will not be repeated.

Treasa heads off into the wide blue yonder, into uncharted territory because, although their land adjoins, the squire and her parents are only passingly acquainted. It is a lonely part of Wexford, with little contact between the large farms, except at church on Sunday, or between the men at the creamery where they daily bring the milk churns.

Treasa covers quite a distance, her determination to find the animals propels her ever onwards, and she finds herself approaching a house a lot larger and grander than her own. As the crow flies, it is not that far from one house to the other, and Treasa takes the territorial route but follows the crow's flight path with a singular sense of direction. She comes in across the fields and onto the pebbled driveway and she looks up at what she thinks is the castle from *The Sleeping Beauty*. With a handful of tiny stones in her hand, and her book under her arm, she heads for the house where she is spotted through the window by both Vita and Nanny.

Nanny, stiffly starched in white, and holding Vita by her hand, comes to the hall door and opens it to admit the tousle-haired child who grins happily at the perfectly and primly dressed Vita.

Nanny, at first nonplussed, quickly realises from Treasa's speech that she is not a Gypsy child but that she has clearly travelled from somewhere. Treasa is brought into the nursery where Mrs Moore the cook and Brigid the maid both come to take a look. They bring her milk and biscuits.

'Sure, she has to be an O'Donoghue,' says Mrs Moore, 'with that dark curly hair and those big brown eyes. Sure, isn't she the image of her father, God bless him indeed.'

And so Treasa is identified. Vita's parents are away and Billy, the stable hand, is despatched to the O'Donoghue farm by horse, a good five miles away, the long way around, by road and boreen.

Treasa, sitting in the nursery opposite Vita, entertains both Nanny and child with stories about Ratty and Mole, and how to bake bread, and that she hopes to get a rabbit for her birthday, which observation is later repeated by the excited Vita to her parents on their return from wherever. ('Oh, Mummy, Papa – pronounced paw-paw – please, oh please may I have a rabbit for my birthday, and if not a rabbit, then a rat or a mole?')

In the meantime, Mr and Mrs O'Donoghue set out in the Land Rover to collect the missing Treasa, whose absence was unknown until the arrival of Billy, the Grennits' stable boy.

The excitement is palpable in the Grennits' nursery as the two little girls, both of whom had hitherto known no other child their own age, eye each other and smile, and both are already planning how to repeat the afternoon.

In the Grennits' drawing room Nanny explains to the O'Donoghue parents about Treasa's arrival, and what a delight she has been, and how unfortunate that Vita's parents are away. Then both little girls are brought in and Vita shakes hands in the most agreeable of ways and Treasa is hugged by both parents who are only too aware that this escapade has turned out lucky.

'Please may Vita come to tea?' says the excited Treasa, and somehow she and Vita are suddenly holding hands and staring hopefully up into Mrs O'Donoghue's smiling face, and all is agreed. Vita will come to tea. The Grennit family chauffeur will drive her and Nanny over the following afternoon, and tea will be taken in the garden.

Mrs O'Donoghue and Treasa bake in the morning so that afternoon tea will be fun, and Treasa is shown how to make tiny cucumber sandwiches (crusts off). Later, when the chauffeur-driven car arrives, Mrs O'Donoghue is glad she has gone to so much trouble because there in the back seat beside the demure Vita with the sparkling blue eyes is Lady Vanessa Grennit, just in from London.

Lady Vanessa is charm itself, clad in a summer dress and silk stockings, with an elegance and a poise that the O'Donoghue farmhouse has not yet encountered. The girls disappear up to the bedroom, down to the breakfast room, out to the yard, over to the swings, up into the oak tree using the little wooden ladder which the O'Donoghue children always use.

Lady Vanessa and Jennifer O'Donoghue sit outside and sip tea and talk with care about their two little girls. Their plans unfold, and both are pleased with the other and hope that their children's friendship will develop.

Mr O'Donoghue comes into the garden to meet Nanny, as he thinks, and is more than startled to find Lady Vanessa, who raises her gloved hand to his, and he is unsure whether to shake it or to kiss it. He is speechless to find her sitting at the garden table, chatting with his wife and breaking into melodic peels of laughter.

'Sure, I thought it was the nanny,' he says that evening to Jennifer

O'Donoghue who is exceptionally pleased at the way the afternoon went. 'I haven't seen Lady Vanessa in eight years or more, and then it was only once, you remember, when they got a puncture down outside the creamery.'

And Treasa, in bed that night, rolls around thinking about Vita and planning their next encounter. Michael and Maria are happy for Treasa, but they both miss her midnight ramblings into their room looking for their companionship, because Treasa now sleeps through, and when she wakens in the morning, she climbs on a chair and looks out of her window across the fields and thinks of Vita in her grand house across the valley.

The girls get to visit each other at least twice a week for the rest of the summer, and then, come September, Treasa starts in the local national school where both her siblings have been before they moved on to secondary.

'I wish you were coming too,' Treasa says to Vita, high up in the oak tree where they are not allowed to climb.

'Me too,' replies Vita. 'I asked Mummy and Papa, but they said no, I have to have a governess. Papa said, "That is that," so I can't argue.'

In fact Lady Vanessa had suggested briefly to her husband that perhaps Treasa could share the governess, it would be company for Vita. But he had said, 'No. Each to their own. Nice and all as Treasa is, she is a local child, and the local school is for her. Vita is different, and must be educated differently.'

As a pre-school treat Lady Vanessa has the chauffeur drive herself and Jennifer O'Donoghue and both little girls to a pet shop in Dublin and there the girls choose two rabbits – one each from the same litter. White, fluffy, floppy-eared, just what little girls like.

'Mine is George,' says Treasa firmly in the car going back.

'But how do you know he is a he?' asks Vita, examining her rabbit's face for signs of gender.

'Because he looks like a George. What are you going to call yours?' asks Treasa with a certain authority.

'Well, mine is a girl rabbit,' says Vita, guessing wildly. 'Her name is Georgina.'

'Perfect,' says Treasa, who sees a certain symmetry, and both Jennifer

O'Donoghue and Lady Vanessa put a hand over their mouths, catch each other's eye, and look out of the window to hide their smiles.

Hutches have been purchased too and these are carefully positioned in sheltered places in each child's outhouse. But George gets to live indoors most of the time. He hops happily around the breakfast room and Michael makes tiny rabbit jumps for him out of lollypop sticks, and George obliges when he feels like it and hops over them, only to find that they have been raised by a quarter of an inch the next time he tries.

Treasa starts school and settles in comfortably. Sometimes she pronounces words the way Vita does and she gets teased and pointed at, so she quickly reverts to saying 'bath' with an open vowel and not to pronounce it 'bawth'. And hot press is acceptable, but airing cupboard is not, and the same with face cloth, but not flannel.

You live and learn.

She only gets to see Vita at the weekend now, and although she misses Vita, it is nothing to the way Vita misses her. Vita's life is made up of the governess, the nanny and the rabbit, whereas Treasa has loads going on around her, both in school and at home.

Treasa smuggles George over into the Grennits' house; she and Vita have great hopes of Georgina having babies. But for some reason it doesn't work. (Both rabbits are female.) There is great high jinx as the two rabbits lollop around the nursery and they have to be hidden when Nanny comes in with tea. There are lots of giggles from the two girls as the rabbits hide out in Vita's toy trunk and one or other of the rabbits must have pressed on something in the trunk because suddenly out of the blue comes the sound of Vita's little clockwork drummer.

Nanny says nothing until Treasa is leaving, and then she asks, 'Do you have *everything* with you, I mean *everything* that you brought here with you?'

And Treasa blushes, and Nanny smiles and pats her head.

A joyous childhood. Truly. Innocent, peaceful. Indeed it is idyllic.

And suddenly the year is 1965 and the girls are ten plus, and Vita knows that in a year's time she will go to boarding school in England.

'It's not fair, Treasa,' she moans. 'I want to stay here. I'll miss you.'

'But we'll write,' Treasa says. 'We should start practising now so that we can write each other great letters when you go.'

And so they write to each other and they wait for the other's letter to drop through the letterbox once a week so they are quite up to date.

Tom Jones is singing 'It's Not Unusual', and Sonny and Cher sing 'I've Got You, Babe', and Maria has finished school and is going to do a secretarial course, and Michael is about to do his Leaving Certificate and head for University College Dublin to study agriculture.

Aunty Oonagh, Mr O'Donoghue's sister who has a large house in Rathmines, offers to take Michael in for the three years that he is in Earlsfort Terrace. But Michael has other plans, which do not include residing with a maiden aunt.

Maria moans to her mother, 'It's not fair. I have to stay here and travel into town to do my course, and he gets to go into digs in Dublin, just because he's a boy. If I were going to Dublin, you'd make me stay with Aunty Oonagh, wouldn't you?'

Jennifer O'Donoghue says, 'Don't start that nonsense, Maria. You chose to do a course locally, so it doesn't arise where you'd stay in Dublin.'

'They'd make you stay with the Archbishop,' teases the exultant Michael, 'or with Uncle Mick,' after whom he has been named.

'How come both your brother and sister are terribly religious?' Treasa asks her mother in an effort to change the subject and the argument, which she can see is going nowhere.

'They both had a vocation,' says Jennifer O'Donoghue, smiling at Treasa as she recognises her youngest, typically, trying to deflect the argument. 'Uncle Mick always wanted to be a priest, and Concepta, well, it was the same for her and so she became a nun.'

'And you never wanted to?' persists Treasa. 'Become a nun, I mean?'

Jennifer O'Donoghue shakes her head. 'No, I wanted everything. I wanted the whole world, and I wanted you three.'

'And did you get that?' asks Treasa.

'In some senses I did,' says Jennifer, looking at her three offspring. And in some senses I most certainly did not, she thinks but does not say aloud, as her mind wanders around the confines of the farm and the limitations of country life.

Treasa gets her optimism from her mother, because Jennifer made the best of things. From the day she got her car, which in fact will be the death of her, Jennifer has travelled up to Dublin, and into the local town, she's big in the Irish Countrywomen's Association, she takes tea with Lady Vanessa (and they are on first-name terms). She is a busy person who has done all she can with her life. And she wants her children to spread their wings and to live a full life. This is why she has raised no objections to Michael not staying with Aunty Oonagh in Rathmines. She knows that in due course he will probably come back to live on and run the farm, and she wants him to be able to do that by making the choice, and by understanding the choice he is making.

She has told her three children this over and over. She has told them about life out there, and life in County Wexford. 'Spread your wings,' she says. 'Taste it all, and then you can choose.'

Her time is almost up.

She drives a Morris Traveller with wooden panels and nice upholstery. She knows her way around the unlit lanes in every direction from the farmhouse. She is a careful driver and she is coming home late one Wednesday evening from a meeting. A normal evening after a normal day, or so she thought. At the S bend just outside the Grennits' estate, she slows to twenty miles an hour – any faster would be lethal there – but unfortunately Father Corry, with two pints of bitter and three shorts under his belt, coming in the other direction, does not show such caution.

He's driving a chocolate-coloured Rover with leather seats, and in the pocket in the dashboard is a quarter bottle of Paddy, which the local garda will remove and slip into his own car for another day.

Father Corry survives the crash, Jennifer O'Donoghue does not. There is no justice here, nor will there be, even though it is well known that Father Corry is a bit too fond of the drink.

Mr O'Donoghue asks how the accident happened, why Father Corry's car is on the wrong side of the road, would someone please explain.

There is no explanation forthcoming. The cover-up is absolute, and there are no answers to his shocked questions, only the reassurance from the doctor that Mrs O'Donoghue died immediately.

At Jennifer's funeral, her three children stand white-faced, the older two holding Treasa's hands tight in theirs. Their father, stoic but numb, stands beside them.

And just like that, the idyllic childhood is over.

The Grennits come over to see if they can help. It is a few weeks later. Michael has done his Leaving Certificate and will make UCD in autumn, and Maria is finishing her course and has a job lined up.

'I don't know what to do with Treasa,' the farmer says, occasionally shaking his head or wiping his hand across his forehead.

'Can we help?' asks Vanessa Grennit. 'You know Vita starts in Benenden in September. Would you consider Treasa going there too?'

But Treasa is a Catholic, and so Benenden cannot be considered.

'Sure it's in a different country,' he says. 'It's far away. I can't do that to her. It's bad enough that I'm going to have to consider a boarding school at all. Sending her away from here is going to be dreadful.' He can't go on. He is truly devastated but knows he can't handle Treasa as well as the farm.

'I've a sister in Rathmines,' he says eventually to the Grennits, who are sitting politely but are aware they have intruded with their suggestion of taking Treasa out of her own culture and spiriting her abroad.

But Maria puts down the suggestion of Aunty Oonagh in Rathmines. 'Don't do that to Treasa, Dad,' she says. 'Let her board, and be with children her own age, not with potty old Aunty Oonagh.'

And so it is that in September Treasa O'Donoghue heads for St Martin's in the Fields, and Vita heads across the Irish Sea.

In St Martin's, the girls whisper to each other, 'She's the one whose mother died in the car accident,' and they watch Treasa to see how she will cope.

Initially Treasa has a problem, but it's not to do with her mother's loss, which loss she has somehow dealt with in the calmest of ways, by storing up the memories and taking them out slowly, one by one.

Treasa has other problems. Some of them are to do with the noise of the city, the traffic at night, the shaking of the window panes in their rather tired frames, the bustle of a busy school, the banging of locker doors, the jostling in the corridors, the racing to get to the bathroom first – these are things that she and Vita had skirted around, not knowing what they would be really like. Their information was picked up from books, and they were unsure what was fact and what was fiction.

Dear Vita,

It's funny, isn't it, that this is the one thing we never thought of, I mean that I would be in boarding school too. How was your journey? How did you feel when they left you? We came up by car, Daddy and me, and Michael too, because he is looking for digs. I wanted to cry when Daddy left but I didn't. Mummy would have said, keep your tears, and protect yourself by not letting other people see when you're upset, unless you know the people well enough to trust them. So I didn't cry until I got into bed that night. And then I didn't cry much about Daddy going, but funnily enough I cried about George and Georgina – isn't that odd? It's two years since they died. I'm glad we buried them together.

I'm in a dormitory with fourteen beds. There is a curtain between each bed, and we each have a locker and a small cupboard and a chair beside the bed. We have to hang our uniform on the chair and our clothes for the next day folded neatly on it. Most of the girls are boarders, even though a lot of them seem to come from Dublin. They all seem nice enough and I'm sitting beside Bernadette O'Higgins who I met before when Daddy brought me up for my interview. And then again in Irish College. Remember? I told you about her. She is really nice, and if we're allowed out for a walk at the weekend, we're going to partner each other.

Please write and tell me about you. Everything. Uniform, teachers, girls, sport (there doesn't seem to be any sport here – well, not much anyway).

Can't wait to hear from you.

Love,

Treasa

Dear Treasa,

I got your letter this morning. I'd meant to write earlier. It's ghastly and I miss you like anything. Mummy said it's good for me, that it's part of growing up. But I'm sure it isn't. The food is horrible. I keep thinking of toast in the nursery with Nanny and you, and lots of butter and strawberry jam. Do you remember when we hid Georgina and George in the toy trunk? Wasn't that funny? It seems so long ago now. I missed them too when I got here, and like you I thought that was odd, seeing as it was years ago.

I miss the oak tree with the little ladder down by your farm. Oh, and we have to wear the silliest of hats. Do you have to wear a hat? I hope you do, as I'd hate to be the only one of us having to.

It's not a bit like being in Mallory Towers or the Chalet School, is it? And I haven't seen a sign of a horse, but Mummy promises that Christabel is fine and is being exercised daily. She wouldn't say that if she didn't mean it, sure she wouldn't?

And everyone sounds like my relatives, and no one sounds like you.

Write soon.

Love,

    Vita

Dear Vita,

We have to wear a beret and it looks ridiculous. It has a badge with the school motto on the front, and we're supposed to wear it sort of plonked on top of our heads. What about your hat? I keep imagining something with a feather.

I got a letter from Daddy and he said both Christabel and Yammy looked fine when he saw them out on the hill last weekend.

I meant to tell you something about Uncle Mick. Do you remember he came to stay after the accident? I wanted to tell you something about that. But it can wait.

Do you have any nuns at all in your school? There are mostly nuns here. One of the girls says that they wear seagulls on top of their heads. I don't know if you've ever seen that – it's a big white headdress and it looks awfully like a seagull. I laughed when Anna McBride came out with that. Isn't it funny how nuns have to wear things like that and yet you never see a priest with something on his head? Our top nun is called Mother Immaculata, but everyone calls her The Raven. She's an awful cow.

I know, I can just hear you saying cows are nice, but it's a term all the girls use. It means she's just awful. And she has this second-in-command called Sister Rodriguez – do you remember when Georgina was doing a poo she used always make this funny little rabbit face and her nose twitched. Well, think of that and you've got Sister Rodriguez.

Do your teachers have strange names like ours do? All the nuns, except The Raven, have a man's name.

Vita, will you be home for Christmas? I do hope so, and yet Daddy seemed to think you mightn't be.

Bernadette is really nice, I just know you'd like her, but I miss you anyway.

Write soon.

Love,

Treasa

Dear Treasa,

What are you talking about when you say your Uncle Mick came to stay? I don't really like him, but I suppose I shouldn't tell you that seeing as you are his niece.

I've made a friend called Jessica. She's OK, but not like you.

I have a horrible feeling I won't be home for Christmas. I really wanted to see you and ride Christabel. I know it'll be nice here. We're going to stay in the house up in London, but I'd much prefer to be at home. Remember last year you came over and we put up our tree together. That was the best fun ever, wasn't it?

My school hat is the most ridiculous thing you ever did see. In fact we have two. Don't laugh. In summer we wear a boater, and, wait for it, in winter, which is now, we have a thing called a jelly. No, you can't eat it. It's a bit like Wee Willie Winkie's night hat with a pompom on the end in the colour of one's house. Isn't a beret a very French thing? Why do you have one? When we finish school, let's burn my jelly and my boater and your beret down at the stream. We'll do it at Hallowe'en. Here they celebrate Guy Fawkes. Ever so odd.

Please write soon. Jessica says hello.

Love,

Vita

Dear Vita,

Do you think I can go and ride Yammy over Christmas? Would you ask your mother? Please. I know she said before we all left that I could, but I'd just like to hear it again.

I'm not really looking forward to going home for Christmas, although Michael is going to collect me and we'll travel down by train together, but there will be relatives staying there. How I wish you were at home, and maybe I could go over and stay with you for a bit.

What are you getting for Christmas? I'd love to get a pet, but there isn't any point as we're not allowed pets here in St Martin's.

I'm hoping Bernadette will ask me to come and stay for a few days.

Please write. It's nearly three weeks since I've heard from you.

Love,

Treasa

Dear Treasa,

When I get home, I'm going to be the fastest eater in the world. We eat by bells, can you believe that? Or is it the same at St Martin's? A bell to start eating, and no talking while eating, and if you want seconds you have to have them before the next bell rings.

Mummy says you're to please go and ride Yammy, and if you have a friend down staying with you, you're to take Christabel too.

Please write.

Love,

Vita

Dear Vita,

At least you get seconds. I'm hungry all the time. I'm planning on bringing loads of food back after Christmas, but I'm not sure where to hide it as we're not allowed to keep food in the dorm and there isn't anywhere else. So much for tuck and midnight feasts. Remember we talked about cherry cake and bottles of gingerbeer. I don't think Enid Blyton knew much about Irish convents. Sometimes the day girls smuggle something in to us, but as Sister Rodriguez (she who looks like a rabbit doing a poo) says, 'Woe betide any girl caught with food.'

I keep thinking about Christmas dinner. Aunt Oonagh (the mad one who lives in Rathmines) is coming down to help Maria cook the dinner. It'll be a first for both of them. Aunt Oonagh asked Daddy would we like the turkey stuffed with brussels sprouts for a change. Can you imagine?

Love,
Treasa

Chapter Seven

Shafts of light through stained glass windows
Beating on a prostrate form
Shadow waiting in the shadows
Will the girl survive till dawn?

'Two days to go,' Kitty O'Dowd mouthed to Treasa in the bathroom.

'What have you lined up for today?' Treasa asked.

Mary Oliver came out of one of the bath cubicles. Her body was wrapped in a towel, she had slippers on her feet, her hair was wet, and she came and stood in front of one of the mirrors and started to brush it out.

'What happened to your hands?' Treasa asked, aghast.

Mary looked at her hands as if she had never seen them before. She seemed truly amazed at the state of her cut fingertips, and her bruised fingers.

'I just slipped getting into the bath,' she whispered, briefly breaking her silence.

'They look sore,' Treasa said.

Mary shook her head, as if dismissing the notion of pain. But she looked upset, and she was very pale with dark shadows under her eyes.

'You better hurry up, Mary,' Treasa continued.

'Anyway,' Kitty O'Dowd continued, eyeing Mary's hands with mild curiosity, 'I've a three o'clock rendezvous with Andrew, usual place.'

'You getting keen on him?' Treasa asked. 'I thought he wasn't your cup of tea.'

Kitty smirked into the mirror. 'A woman's prerogative, if that's the right word, is to change her mind. By the way, he's having a party on Saturday, and you're invited.' She glanced at Mary's pale face in the mirror. 'You too, Mary,' she said.

Mary was combing out her hair. She didn't appear to hear. Her eyes had a glazed look about them, and she turned suddenly and rushed into one of the stalls.

Kitty and Treasa looked at each other as they heard Mary retching repeatedly.

'You OK, Mary?' Treasa called, although it was clear she was not.

'Something I said?' Kitty asked, puzzled.

'No,' Treasa replied. 'Nothing to do with you, Kitty. Just look at her. I think she's ill.'

They waited until Mary came out, and then Treasa walked her back to the dorm and made her sit on her bed while she dried her hair with the drier.

'I think you should go back to bed, Mary,' she said. 'I'll tell The Raven that you're not well.'

Mary shook her head vehemently.

'Well, lie on my bed then while I do your cubicle for you, and then you can get dressed.'

Mary nodded gratefully and lay down on Treasa's bed on her side. The towel slipped down her back and displayed the outline of her ribs but she was too tired to pull it back up.

Treasa didn't notice because she was making Mary's bed, and straightening her curtains. Kitty took Mary's school clothes from her chair and put them on Treasa's bed.

'You sure you don't want to go to sickbay, Mary?' she asked.

Mary sat up and started to pull on her clothes as quickly as she could, and Kitty left her to do her own hair.

Treasa was straightening Mary's pillow, she lifted it to fluff it up, and underneath she saw two nails.

'Hey, Mary,' she said. 'What are these?'

Mary turned and looked at her bed. 'I . . . I don't know,' she said. She came over and picked them up. She stared at them lying in her hand, and then slipped them into her pocket.

Treasa pulled up the bedclothes, and the moment was gone.

Mary Oliver felt a warm feeling of comfort and security flooding through her, and she patted her pocket as they left the dormitory.

They got down to breakfast on time and as they ate Sister Rodriguez read out the Corporal Acts of Mercy over and over. Several times Mary glanced puzzled at her cut fingers, but then she patted her pocket and the feeling of unease passed. How silly of me, she thought. All the time my nails were under my pillow. After eating a slice of bread and drinking two cups of tea she felt a little better. She had a feeling of impending doom but had no idea to what it was related.

'Feed the hungry,' intoned Sister Rodriguez. 'Visit the sick.'

Treasa glanced across the table at Mary and thought she looked a bit better. Less likely to keel over, she thought.

'Bury the dead,' said Sister Rodriguez.

Mary's feelings of unease suddenly increased. I had a dream, she thought. It was a dream, she repeated to herself.

The girls walked down to the Sister Chapel. As they approached it, Treasa and Bernadette, at the front of the group, became aware of a commotion outside the chapel. There were two squad cars and lights flashing.

'Let's just go in,' Treasa whispered to Bernadette. 'At least that way we'll fnd out what's happened.'

Kitty joined them and they walked purposefully into the chapel porch where they were immediately stopped by two policemen.

'Sorry, girls. No entry,' one of them said.

'What's up?' Treasa asked pleasantly.

'Been a bit of desecration,' the younger one said.

'We have to go in to pray,' Treasa tried.

'Not today, miss,' he said. 'I'm sorry. No one is allowed in.'

One of the Chapel Sisters appeared. She looked pale and shocked. 'Girls,' she said. 'Straight back to the convent with the lot of you. Who's accompanying you?' She pushed past the first group of girls and out onto the street. 'Miss Ní Ghrian,' she called to the Irish teacher who approached with her customary tight-lipped face. 'The girls have to go immediately back to the convent. There has been ... a ... a ... an incident ...' She hesitated and then she and Miss Ní Ghrian stepped away from the chapel and she whispered to her.

Bridie, watching with interest, reported afterwards that Grinny's eyes had widened and then she put her hand to her mouth and said, 'Oh, no. No. No. Oh, my goodness, no. No.'

'Did she say anything else?' Treasa asked.

Bridie shook her head.

'Well how shocked would you have described her?' Treasa was nothing if not persistent.

'Well,' Anna McBride said, 'she was more shocked than the day Kitty said "shite" in class.' (Kitty had said 'shite' when asked in Irish during Irish class what dogs do in parks. The correct answer had been, 'They run and play.')

Back in school the girls were told to go to the Common Room and to read either from their missals or from the religious books which were available on one of the shelves. There was a buzz among them; clearly the unexpected had happened, whatever that might be.

Kitty sat at the window and got her nail file out of her gymslip pocket and commenced filing. Treasa pulled a chair over and sat beside her, putting her feet up on the windowsill. Bernadette, complete with her *Scrumptious Sex*, pulled up another chair. (She was about to commence counting the illustrations.)

'Now what?' Treasa asked.

'Party at Andrew's on Saturday, Bernadette,' Kitty said by way of invitation.

'Oh good,' replied Bernadette. 'Oh no, there is no way I'll be allowed home for the weekend, not so soon after Easter. Daddy will be going on about the Leaving and studying and stuff.'

Treasa grinned. 'I can't go home either, because if I did I wouldn't be able to get up to Dublin to the party. We'll get the Downey twins to cover for us and we'll go late. Sure, it'll be grand.'

Anna McBride came in the door and went over to the window to join the others. For the first time during the week, she ignored Jean Jacques.

Kitty, looking at her, knew immediately that Bridie knew something.

'What's up, Bridie?' she asked.

The younger girl looked at the other three and put a finger to her lips.

'Mum's the word,' Kitty said. 'Now, what's up?'

106

'From what I can make out,' Bridie began.

'Hurry up, Bridie,' Treasa said. 'We're all agog.'

'The crucifix in the church was removed.'

'Removed?' All three looked surprised. Even Kitty stopped filing her nails.

'Taken off the wall ... and something was done to it, but I don't know what.'

'How did you hear this?' Treasa asked.

'I was just, well, just sort of on the upper landing, sort of,' Bridie said hesitantly, 'and I sort of heard Grinny telling the Maple.'

'Aha,' said Treasa. 'The plot thickens.'

'What do you suppose was done to it?' Bernadette asked.

'Can't imagine,' Kitty said. 'It was an ugly piece of work anyway – they're better off without it.'

Treasa looked out of the window at the street, and suddenly thought of Mary Oliver's fingers. Her eyes narrowed and she tried to shrug off the thought. Glancing around, she saw Mary skulking at the bookshelves. Treasa got up off her chair and went and brought Mary over to the others and told her what had happened. Mary said nothing. She just sat on the floor with her back to the bit of wall under the window and her arms round her knees.

'So will the five of us go to the party on Saturday?' Treasa asked.

Kitty looked at Bridie and felt she would be out of place, but then she looked at Mary and thought how she wouldn't fit in either, so she shrugged and said, 'Yes.'

'What party?' Bridie asked.

Treasa explained.

'I'm going home this weekend,' Bridie said. 'I wonder will the parents let me.'

'Why don't you invite Mary for the weekend,' said Treasa, thinking it might do Mary good to be out of the place as she was always stuck there for the whole term, and also because she couldn't imagine Mary breaking out with herself and Bernadette. 'Your parents won't mind, and if they see it as an end of Retreat party or something, it'll be grand.'

Anna McBride grinned. She loved it when she got included even though that often brought its own problems because she looked younger than the others.

'Brilliant,' she said. 'Andrew won't mind me coming?' she asked Kitty.
Kitty shook her head. 'Nope. He said I could bring some friends.'
Bridie smiled again.

Miss Maple and Mother Immaculata entered the Common Room. The girls all got to their feet.

'Girls,' said Mother Immaculata. 'You may sit. In order to dispel rumours, I have decided to inform you that sacrilege took place in the Sister Chapel during the night. The police are confident that they will catch the perpetrator so you have no need to worry. They are taking fingerprints from the scene of the ... crime. He will be caught, and severely dealt with,' she said with assurance. 'In the meantime, you will have a quiet day here in school. Father McMorrow will be over later to continue with confession and there will be prayers in our oratory later. Miss Maple and Miss Ní Ghrian will supervise you for the rest of the day. You will pray for the criminal to be caught, and God willing the Retreat will continue tomorrow in the Sister Chapel.'

And as on roller skates, she was gone.

There was a certain amount of shuffling as the girls settled down again. Bernadette O'Higgins whispered to Treasa, 'What was the Act of Mercy Sister Rodriguez read out this morning – be merciful to those who have sinned?'

Treasa snorted with laughter and turned it into a cough. Kitty dropped her head to hide her smile. Mary Oliver slipped her hands under her bottom so they were hidden from view.

'Do you think they will take our fingerprints?' Bridie whispered.

'That'd be a laugh,' said Kitty.

'No, they won't,' Treasa said as she saw the startled and worried look on Mary Oliver's face. 'Of course they won't. They're looking for a hardened criminal or a thug or someone. They'll take the fingerprints from the chapel and then compare them, down in the station or somewhere, with all the fingerprints they have on file.'

'Pity,' said Kitty, as she saw the only bit of excitement on the immediate horizon slipping beyond her grasp.

Treasa noticed that Mary Oliver looked relieved.

Mary Oliver patted her gymslip pocket and Treasa wondered why.

Miss Maple addressed the room. 'Sixth Year girls, I have prevailed upon

Mother Immaculata to kindly let you go to your classroom and put in some study for your forthcoming Leaving Cert. The rest of you can remain here and Miss Ní Ghrian will look after you. Sixth Year girls, in silence, head for St Anthony's and don't get lost on the way.' The irony in her voice was clear. The statue of St Anthony, patron saint of lost objects, always had a candle lit in front of it in the recess outside the classroom which was named after him.

It was flickering in its little glass casing as the girls passed it.

'Have you ever wondered who replaces that light?' Treasa asked Kitty in a whisper.

'It's one of the perpetual miracles,' Kitty replied. 'It burns in perpetuity.'

'Someone's learnt a big word,' Treasa whispered. 'I'm impressed.' Kitty was not known as a user of words which had more than four letters in them.

'Never thought I'd be so glad to get back to work,' whispered Treasa to Kitty as they sat down.

And even Kitty was forced to agree.

'Do you think that's the purpose of the Retreat?' Treasa asked Bernadette later.

'Well, if it is,' Bernadette replied, 'it certainly worked.'

'Are we going to be locked up in St Anthony's all day?' Bridie whispered to them.

'Unclear,' replied Treasa.

'Better than St Christopher's.' This was from Bernadette and brought a chuckle from the others but a glare from Kitty O'Dowd.

The classrooms were referred to by the names of saints, and each name carried its own meaning. The reference to St Christopher was to do both with the fact that he was the patron saint of travellers and that his classroom was on the top floor and therefore the furthest away.

It also brought memories of an incident when Kitty O'Dowd had, in a moment of recklessness, placed a bag of flour on the top of the door the previous term. It had been meant to land on Treasa as a joke. But Mother Immaculata had overtaken Treasa on the stairs and with her head held high she had glided into St Christopher's seconds before Treasa, and the open bag of flour had toppled over and neatly landed on her headdress. The flour had covered the nun completely so that she resembled a dusty ghost.

Treasa giggled as she recalled the sight.

'It wasn't funny,' said Kitty. 'The fecking Raven turned and went down the corridor spreading clouds of the bloody stuff everywhere. It took me all day to clean it up, and she beat me black and blue.'

'Oh, you'll look back when you're older,' Treasa mouthed, 'and I bet you won't be able to stop laughing about it. You'll share that wonderful moment with your children, and they'll look at you in amazement and say, "Mom, you didn't!" And you'll be glad you did it.'

Kitty looked at her in amazement. 'Have you any reason to think I'll ever have kids?'

'Well, you might. Just to share those wonderful moments with them.'

'I'll never have kids,' Kitty said fiercely. 'Never. And if I did I'd never send them to a convent.'

'Well, there isn't a lot of choice on the school front,' Treasa said.

'Yeah, well ...' Kitty said. 'I'm not planning on bringing any into this world.'

'But it's your duty, Kitty,' Treasa teased. 'Four children minimum. Isn't that right? One to be a priest. One a nun. And any left over to marry and do the same.'

'Watch me,' said Kitty fiercely. 'There won't be any little Kitty O'Dowds arriving on planet earth!'

'That's what they all say,' Treasa giggled.

'Silence, girls,' Miss Maple said. 'Just because you've been given a reprieve from the Retreat, however short-lived, does not mean you can talk.'

The girls settled down with their books.

In due course, Miss Maple left them, 'on their honour', to study in silence when she was called out by a Fifth Year girl because the police wanted to address all the staff.

'What do you think will happen next?' Treasa asked, keeping an eye on the door.

'Jayz, I hope we'll be interviewed,' said Kitty. 'It'd be such fun. *Yes, Sergeant,*' she mimicked, '*I saw Miss Ní Ghrian with a hatchet in the Sister Chapel.*'

'Brilliant.' Bernadette laughed. 'A whole new game of Cluedo. *I accuse Mother Immaculata of commiting arson with a candle in the Sister Chapel.* Your turn, Mary.'

Mary shrugged sullenly and looked back at her books.

'Oh, OK, Mary. How about you, Treasa?'

'*I accuse Sister Rodriguez of being a two-faced bat whose aim in life is to make our lives miserable.*'

'That won't do,' Kitty said. 'You've got to abide by the rules. A crime in the Sister Chapel is what this is about.'

'Oh, OK,' Treasa said. 'I was going to say that that was why I murdered her in the Sister Chapel with the lead piping. Your turn, Bridie.'

Bridie looked to Jean Jacques for support. Jean Jacques nodded to her to continue.

'*I accuse Mother Immaculata of doing something unspeakable with a candlestick in the Sister Chapel,*' she said. She wasn't quite sure what that meant but it certainly got a reaction from the rest of the class, both because of what she'd said, and the fact that *she*, innocent Bridie, had said it. She tried not to look bewildered, but she did wonder what on earth it could have meant. 'Your turn, Downeyone,' she said quickly to get the attention away from her.

'*I accuse,*' Downeyone looked slyly at her twin, whose mouth twitched as she knew what was coming. '*I accuse Mary Oliver of the crucifixion of Father McMorrow in the Sister Chapel.*'

Mary Oliver looked up, startled and pale-faced. She began to shake.

'I was just joking,' Downeyone said as Mary jumped to her feet.

'It was only a joke,' Downeytwo reiterated, as Mary headed for the door.

'What's got into her anyway?' Downeyone asked.

'That time of the month?' asked Downeytwo.

'She's just not in the mood to be teased,' Treasa replied and followed Mary out of the door.

'You OK?' she asked Mary when she caught up with her in the loos.

Mary was standing in front of the mirror looking as if she had seen a ghost.

'I didn't do anything,' she said. 'I didn't.'

'They were kidding,' Treasa said. 'You know what they're like.'

Mary looked down at her hands and so did Treasa.

'What happened to them?' Treasa asked, nodding at her raw and bruised fingers.

111

Mary looked up with frightened eyes and shook her head. 'I don't know,' she said. 'I have no idea.'

'Just keep them out of sight,' Treasa said. 'Hey, it's all right.'

Mary had started to cry.

'Look, it's all right. Whatever happened happened,' Treasa said gently. 'Wash your face and just keep your hands out of sight. They'll heal.'

Mary looked at her fingers. If one's hands would heal, would one's soul heal too? she wondered. What is there without prayer? she asked herself in the depths of her mind, as one hand sought the nails in her pocket. What is left when God leaves you?

'There's the bell for lunch,' Treasa said. 'We need to hurry or we'll be missed.'

By the time they got to the refectory and took their plates of stew to their places, Grace Before Meals had been delayed until they were standing at their table.

'*Bless us, Oh Lord, and these thy gifts,*' said Bernadette O'Higgins, leading the girls in prayer as there were no nuns or teachers present because the meeting with the police was taking longer than expected.

'In The Raven's absence,' Kitty O'Dowd announced, picking up Bernadette's *Lives of the Saints* from the table (unnoticed by Bernadette), 'I will read to you to keep your minds clean and your thoughts on a higher plain.' There were a number of giggles as Kitty had got The Raven's voice to perfection. She approached the rostrum, imitating Mother Immaculata's skate-like gliding. 'Gerls of St Martin's,' she continued, 'you may begin to eat. *Credo in una Immaculata,*' she intoned. '*Mater omnibus.*'

Kitty O'Dowd was not known as a Latin scholar. Bernadette, who was, snorted with laughter and kept an eye on the doors.

'*Agnus Dei,*' tried Kitty again. 'Well, agnus something . . . that is lamb you're eating, isn't it? *Mater vobiscum,*' she continued, '*et Satan vostrum . . .*'

A hissing sound from a dozen or more girls and loud coughing from Bernadette pulled Kitty up short.

There in the doorway on silent roller skates stood Mother Immaculata. 'What are you doing, Kitty O'Dowd?' she snapped.

'In your absence, Mother, I thought one of us should read from this,' Kitty said glibly, gesturing towards the book in front of her.

112

The Raven eyed her with suspicion and general disbelief.

'Then pray continue,' said The Raven.

'I've lost my page, Mother,' said Kitty, fumbling with the book.

'I'm sure you can find it, my girl,' said Mother Immaculata, looking down her aquiline nose at the now less confident Kitty.

Kitty, trying to stay calm, frantically turned the pages, looking for something she could identify and realising with slowly mounting horror that the book she was holding was most definitely nothing to do with the lives of the saints.

'I'm waiting,' said The Raven in the doorway.

Bernadette, reading Kitty's consternation correctly, glanced at the book in her hands and then back at the table in front of her and realised with the most horrible shock that *Scrumptious Sex* (the illustrated version) was in Kitty's hands at the rostrum.

'I'm waiting,' The Raven repeated.

There was silence in the room as the girls watched, wondering what on earth was the problem. The silence extended and the tension in the room grew. Bernadette tried to think what to do. Jump up? Fall over in a dead faint? Oh, my God, she thought. Oh no, Kitty, do something.

'Because it is the Retreat,' Kitty said, trying to keep her voice as calm as possible as it dawned on her what had kept Bernadette O'Higgins so busy for the past three days, 'I am going to lead you all in prayer. Sister Rodriquez has read to you all week during mealtimes, but we are sadly going to miss out on prayer time today because of what has happened in the Sister Chapel.' Out of the corner of her eye she could see The Raven still looking suspiciously at her. She closed the book and held it close to her chest.

'*Our Father,*' she prayed. '*Who art in Heaven . . .*'

The Raven stayed for the whole prayer. When Kitty finished, she was obliged to start another one.

'*Hail Mary, full of Grace . . .*' she intoned.

Towards the end of the fourth Hail Mary, The Raven turned and skated out of the room. Kitty raced over to Bernadette and returned the book, and then went back to the rostrum, still reciting prayers – any prayer she could think of. '*Hail Holy Queen, Mother of God, hail our life, our sweetness and our hope . . .*'

Kitty O'Dowd kept up the praying until lunch was over just in case The Raven returned.

'Jayzus,' she said to Bernadette afterwards. 'You mean old cow!'

'Hey, what do you mean?' asked the indignant Bernadette. 'It's not my fault you decided to take my book off the table.'

'No, I meant you're mean because that's what you were reading all week while the rest of us were going out of our minds with boredom.'

'That was awful,' Bernadette said. 'I'm still in shock. I thought I was going to faint when I realised what book you had. Thank God The Raven didn't take it from you.'

'Wasn't I wonderful?' Kitty said. 'I could be a politician – smooth-talking my way out of any tight corner.'

'You were jolly lucky,' Bernadette said.

'Well, so were you,' Kitty responded quickly. 'Can you imagine The Raven's face if she'd seen those pictures?'

'It's not her face that would have bothered me. It's what she would have done to us.'

The afternoon passed in study in St Anthony's, with the odd scribbled suggestion of further accusations from the morning's game of Cluedo.

'*I accuse Kitty O'Dowd of imitating The Raven in the refectory with a pornographic book,*' wrote Bernadette O'Higgins on a torn-out scrap of paper.

'*I accuse Bernadette O'Higgins of being the purveyor of porn,*' came back the response.

Nonetheless, a fair amount of study was done, and at teatime they were released.

'I understand from Mother Immaculata,' Miss Maple addressed the class as they cleared away their books, 'that Kitty O'Dowd led you all in prayer over dinner.'

Twenty-five girls looked at her in anticipation of what might follow.

'It appears that Mother Immaculata was so impressed, Kitty, that she would like you to repeat the performance over tea.'

Kitty knew from the way Miss Maple was looking at her that she, her form mistress, had not been fooled, not for one moment. She had the good grace to blush.

114

'Kitty,' Miss Maple continued, 'when Mother Immaculata asked me what I thought of you saying prayers over dinner, I did point out to her that I have found you a changed girl, that joining my choir was a sign of your new maturity. I am very pleased with you.'

The edge in Miss Maple's voice spoke volumes and Kitty nodded, realising she was being warned by Miss Maple that those on high remained sceptical.

'I'd make a very good job of reading at tea, if I were you,' Miss Maple said, noting the grins on the faces of the rest of the girls.

As soon as they had poured out of the classroom, Kitty shot over to the Common Room and carefully perused the bookshelves, looking for something to entertain her captive audience for the three-quarters of an hour which tea would take.

'Jayz,' she said to Bernadette. 'The most exciting thing I could come up with was *The Apologetics and the Ultimate Doctrine* by one Timothy Bigott, DD, God love us all.'

'She's awfully decent,' Bernadette whispered to her as they headed for the refectory, from which the smell of cabbage seemed permanently to emanate. 'The Maple, I mean.'

'Well, I'd find her an awful lot decenter if she'd come along and do the reading.' Kitty mumbled. 'It's one thing entertaining you all by imitating The Raven, it'll be another thing having to read out of this for the best part of an hour.'

'Offer it up,' Treasa said. 'For the black babies, and the sinners in the world, time off in purgatory, and . . .'

'Oh, shut up,' Kitty said. 'This *is* my purgatory.'

Maeve Maple closed the staff-room door at six that evening and headed down the hall to the main steps. She contained her sigh of relief until she was outside on the street.

Downtown she walked briskly, hoping the events of the day would blow free in the evening breeze. But those same thoughts still had not been evicted from her mind by the time she had reached the Grafton Street end of Nassau Street where the Berni Inn and her old college chum awaited her.

She pushed the door open and went into the friendly darkness.

'Gemma,' she said, greeting her friend with a smile. 'What'll you have?'

'I've already ordered. For us both, I might add. Same as last time, I presume,' Gemma said. 'Goodness, you look exhausted. How are things?'

'Just another day,' Maeve Maple replied. 'Another day in Ireland's most exclusive establishment for young ladies! Don't get me started.'

'Talk away,' Gemma encouraged her. 'Let it all out. And then I can update you on the halls of academia where the same young ladies will no doubt be this time next year.'

'I don't think you'd believe what happened today,' Maeve said. 'Honestly, Gemma, school is difficult enough without added drama from outside!'

'Let me guess,' said Gemma. 'Are we by any chance referring to the desecration of one Sister Chapel in Dublin Two?'

'What? How do you know?'

'Evening papers, Maeve. They're full of it.'

'Oh, my goodness. For some reason I didn't think of that. The whole day has been spent yo-yoing between hysterical nuns, pent-up girls whose hormones are fit to explode, policemen lurking in some underground passageway in the school, which I didn't even know was there, and the all-seeing eyes of Mother Immaculata. The Raven to the girls!'

'Are they on Retreat?' Gemma asked. 'That's what it implied in the papers.'

'Yes, they are. Ridiculous, isn't it? Leaving Cert. in a few weeks' time. However, at least the dreaded silence got somewhat suspended today.'

'What's the story on the desecration?'

'Some thug, lout or lunatic, the police seemed to think.'

'That's the implication in the papers too.'

'Though it's funny, you know,' Maeve said thoughtfully. 'It was the oddest sort of desecration. As far as I could make out, someone tried to dismantle the crucifix in the church, and then wrapped the body in a shroud!'

'Odd,' Gemma agreed. 'Not your everyday run-of-the-mill vandalism.'

'No. And then on top of that something was done to the chalice but they're not saying what.'

'And how are the girls coping? Especially that girl – you know, the one whose parents own the hotel out near you in Bray?'

'Oh, Kitty. Kitty O'Dowd. Well, she's hanging in there. You know, she's always up to something, "don't-care-mischief" is how I'd describe it. I'll be glad to see her finishing in June. I'm fond of her and she's never given me any trouble, but in the staff room you'd think she was a daughter of Satan, the way they go on! There's one of my colleagues, Áine Ní Ghrian, who—'

'What, Áine Ní Ghrian? Not Áine Ní Ghrian with the frizzy hair?' interjected Gemma.

'Hatchet face? Hygiene questionable?'

'Oh, goodness.' Gemma laughed. 'I don't believe it. She teaches in St Martin's? Oh good, drinkies!' she added as the waitress placed their glasses on the table with a smile. 'We won't order yet, we'll wait until we've had these, thank you.'

'How do you know her?' Maeve asked. 'Áine Ní Ghrian, I mean.'

'We were at school together. We're from the same neck of the woods. Didn't you know? The same Áine who, like the rest of us, used to blacken her legs with shoe polish when she tore a hole in her stockings, only in Áine's case she never washed her legs. Come summer when we had to wear ankle socks, her legs were covered in black marks of varying sizes and density, depending on how long they had been there!' Gemma laughed. 'Imagine, she's in St Martin's.'

'She's vicious towards the girls,' Maeve said, smiling at Gemma's tale.

'She was always a nasty piece of work,' Gemma said.

'I think she's the person I least like working with. You always know she's out to get one or other of the girls. She has favourites and she shows it at the expense of the others, which needless to say doesn't do any favours for anyone. And she's gleeful when she has her victim in hand.'

'That's Áine all right. How did she cope with the drama today?'

'Well, on the one hand I think she was sorry that she couldn't pounce on unsuspecting, whispering girls and report them. But on the other I heard her ask some of the sisters if they were concerned that the person who had vandalised the church might find the passageway to the school and come in and get them.'

Gemma chuckled. 'I bet that went down a treat!'

'Don't talk! Interesting, though, that there is a passage connecting the two buildings.'

'It's not that unusual,' Gemma said. 'If you think about it, a lot of older buildings have passageways, like the one down at St Michan's. That stretched right under the Liffey – still does, for all I know. So whoever built those Georgian houses probably just utilised whatever was already there. Anyway, how did the good sisters react to Áine's concerns for them?'

'Oh, as you'd expect. Some of them were twittering about "the poor girls" but were probably thinking about themselves. No, I'm not being fair. Some of them were genuinely concerned about the girls, but it wasn't all altruism. Mother Immaculata fixed Áine with a gimlet eye as if to say, "Just let some vandal, rapist or thug come in here, and I'll show him what's what!" And she would too. I'd pity him by the time she had finished with him.'

'Just remind me, Maeve, why you stay there.' The irony in Gemma's voice was clear.

'Nothing has changed, Gemma. It's so difficult to get a teaching post. And it is a good school, with high standards, and while I have a big problem with the way it is run, I have to admit it is efficient ... Oh, you know, the usual. And if I did manage to get a position somewhere else, I'd have to go right back to the bottom of the teaching scale and start over!'

'So you're stuck unless you get out of teaching.'

'Now there's a thought!' she said with a sigh. She ordered another round, and opened her menu. 'Mmmm, prawn cocktail. Followed by a gammon steak with pineapple ...'

Ah, distinctly I remember, it was in the bleak December,
And each separate dying ember wrought its ghost upon the floor.
Eagerly I wished the morrow: — vainly had I sought to borrow
From my books surcease of sorrow — sorrow for the days of yore
For the rare and radiant days, the endless angel days of yore
                                        Nameless here for ever more.

Chapter Eight

Bernadette O'Higgins, as a toddler, could be seen through the hedge from the road, playing safely in her garden. Even pottering around among the vegetables she was neat and well cared for. The corners of her mouth turned up whether she was sad or happy. Her fair hair was shiny and was brushed and carefully combed by her mother every morning. She had two older brothers and once upon a time she had a baby sister too, but only for six hours.

Bernadette remembers that night clearly. Her brothers (Seamus and Cian) and she were taken from their beds by their father (Dr O'Higgins) at one in the morning. Bernadette was three. He got them into the back of the car and tucked them in with blankets and then he helped their mother into the front seat. No seat belts then, but in those days it didn't seem to matter, and Mrs O'Higgins was so large anyway at the end of her pregnancy that no normal seat belt would have fitted round her. They sped through the night. Bernadette remembers seeing the moon filtering through the trees as they wound their way up the long driveway to the nursing home where Helen O'Higgins was about to be born. Had Helen been a boy he was going to have five different names because no one had been able to agree with anyone else as to what would suit the unborn baby. Bernadette had opted for Rudolph because it was just three weeks after Christmas and she could sing 'Rudolph the Red-nosed Reindeer'. No amount of teasing by her brothers would distract her from her choice.

Their father tells them to sleep and he will be back as soon as possible. Seamus and Cian fall asleep immediately, but Bernadette lies there curled in her blanket and watches the bright lights of the nursing home and wonders about what is happening inside.

She dozes fitfully and wakens to discover that her father is back in the car and they are driving home. There he carries each of them into the house and puts them in their beds.

'No, the baby has not yet been born.'

Mrs O'Dea from next door will come in and mind them because he is going back to the nursing home to be there. Bernadette feels there is something wrong. His face is not smiley-laughy like it usually is. His mouth seems firmly closed between sentences. There are lines on his face that she has never seen before.

Later, much later, she wonders if he knew before baby Helen was born that she was not going to live, or did she, Bernadette, twist all of these facts around. She cannot ask him because it is too painful, and so she never finds out. But she seems to remember being back in her own bed and her body heat gradually warming the bed, and feeling uneasy, unsafe and concerned. Yet those feelings may only have arisen from the fact that for the first time in her life neither of her parents was in the house in the early hours of the morning.

It is the following evening before Dr O'Higgins returns. There are shadows under his eyes, and the three children fight to climb into his arms. He tucks Bernadette safely in against his chest, and the boys sit on either side of him while he tells them of Helen's tiny little body and her little lungs, and Helen's baby struggle to hold on to life.

They bury Helen three days later in a little white coffin in a plot inside the churchyard in the country, where her grandparents are buried.

Bernadette watches her father's face. There are lines from his eyes to his mouth. His skin seems grey.

'It's a special place for her,' he says. 'It's . . .' His voice breaks. He pauses for a very long time, and Bernadette wonders if he's breathing. Then he says, 'Tiny babies, little tiny babies like Helen, don't always get buried in the big cemeteries. We are very lucky, all of us, especially Helen, that she is beside her grandparents.'

Bernadette watches his face carefully. (Dr O'Higgins has fought for Helen to be buried inside the walls of the cemetery. He has struggled with the church to have his daughter in consecrated ground. 'I baptised her,' he says to the parish priest who arrived too late in the nursing home. 'I'm a doctor – I saw there was the likelihood she wouldn't survive . . . I took it on myself . . . I baptised my daughter. You can't . . . you cannot . . .' He regains his composure. 'I baptised my daughter. You were not here. You had been called. My daughter will lie with my family.' And the parish priest yields.)

Five months later they get a stone with an angel carved on it and Helen's name and six-hour life is recorded for posterity (or maybe just for as long as the cemetery survives because by the turn of the century it will probably transpire that the land has long been zoned for housing or a shopping centre). Bernadette would have liked a duck on the headstone beside the angel, but Dr O'Higgins thinks not. He tries to keep the children involved but he has quite a difficult situation on his hands because for two years after Helen's death, Mrs O'Higgins grieves.

She weeps. She lies in bed. When she gets up she sits at the window staring out at nothing. When she speaks she says things like, 'My baby is gone. I have no baby. How long is for ever?'

And Bernadette, who had assumed that she was the baby until Helen's birth and that she would return to being the baby after Helen's demise, finds that there is no real place for her at that time in her mother's affections.

Dr O'Higgins sees them all through this rough time as well as continuing to build his practice.

Mrs O'Dea, next door, kindly takes Bernadette during the day so Mrs O'Higgins can rest, while Seamus and Cian are at school. Sometimes Bernadette sleeps over at the O'Deas', which she really likes, as the O'Dea girls, aged seven and eight, are good fun. It is a house full of mischief, while the O'Higgins house is serious.

The O'Deas have a television set which often has truly dreadful reception but this does not bother Bernadette at all. (There is no television in the O'Higgins household, and in fact there will not be one until Bernadette is sent to boarding school aged eleven. It will be purchased after the World Cup in 1966 because Dr O'Higgins suddenly feels that the boys may have lost out by not being able to watch the World Cup at home.)

Bernadette likes *Uncle Ed the Talking Horse* and *The School Around the Corner*. And Mrs O'Dea always makes scones in the afternoon because her girls love them when they come in from school. The kitchen smells of fresh baking, and the strawberry and raspberry jams are homemade.

In due course Bernadette starts school too and the O'Dea sisters take her with them in the mornings and they pretend she is their little sister and they check on her at break and fuss over her and show her off.

Bernadette is reserved and cautious.

She knows you can be two different people. At home she is serious little Bernadette who reads endlessly and plays with her brothers' Meccano (when they let her) and lays out her toy farm in the playroom, each tiny chicken carefully tucked in behind the mother hen, and each calf beside its bovine parent. At the O'Deas' she is like a little O'Dea bouncing from one room to the next, sprawled on the floor with the O'Dea girls, legs over the arm of the sofa, knickers showing and who cares. At home she has to sit with her legs together because she will be a lady when she grows up, and that's how ladies sit, her skirt pulled down to her knees.

'Mrs O'Dea,' she once said to the aproned, happy, next-door neighbour. 'Please, Mrs O'Dea, may I call you Mummy?'

'Oh, my dear,' said Mrs O'Dea. 'I don't think that's a good idea. I don't think your mummy would like it.'

'Well, could I call you Mummy O'Dea,' persisted the child Bernadette.

'How about you call me Aunty Moll?' said Mrs O'Dea, giving Bernadette a cuddle and a scone.

So Aunty Moll she was, and Bernadette lives these two personalities as she moves from one house to the other. She plays the introvert at home, neat and tidy, seen but not heard. She feeds the birds in the garden and chases away any cats who come over the wall, in order to protect the birds, even though she would quite like to have a pet, and a cat would be nice, but her mother doesn't want any pets in the house. She knows one of her strengths is that she can be invisible when she wants to be. Often she is not noticed as she sits quietly by the window reading. Her brothers come in to get something and then they amble out again. Her mother comes in and dusts. No one says anything. She turns the pages of her book. She is going through her childhood fiction phase, which she will soon grow out of. *Billy Bunter, Biggles, William*, she reads her brothers' books and browses through their comics, *Hotspur, Eagle, Valiant*. She tires of them soon. She will be a serious reader later when she finds her métier. For now, having dealt with what the boys have on offer, she moves to the bookshelves and starts there.

In the O'Deas' house, Bernadette lets her extrovert side out. She will never be as forthcoming as the O'Dea girls nor as wild, but she does her best. Her hidden strength is assessing a situation and making quick decisions, but she doesn't know this yet. She likes both households but for different reasons. Often she hates leaving the O'Deas, hates climbing through the hedge and going into her own quiet home, but other times she is glad. When she is tired and it's time to go, there is something reassuring about going in the door of home, and feeling the quiet calm that is re-establishing itself in the O'Higgins' house as Mrs O'Higgins returns to normal.

By the time Bernadette is six, Mrs O'Higgins has regained her equilibrium, but it is too late for Bernadette to be 'the baby' again, and so instead she and her mother forge a new relationship and she allows her mother to take pleasure in dressing her nicely and having her always look neat and tidy, but she never clambers onto her mother's lap again. Instead she takes solace from Aunty Moll, and sometimes sits on her knee and sucks her thumb and plays at being the baby, and then up she gets and tumbles on the floor with the O'Dea girls.

In the summer holidays Aunty Moll takes her own two and the three O'Higgins children across the road and down the lane to the sea every day. The five children collect crabs in buckets, having carefully fished them from their rocky dens, and they add to them as the day goes on, feeding them bait to keep them happy, keeping the little ones in a separate bucket so that they won't be bullied. In between this crab activity they swim, play ball, clamber over the rocks and go to the sweet shop for shiny satiny sweets that can only be bought there. Come evening, they return the crabs to the sea and trail, with salt on their skin and in their hair, after Aunty Moll back up the lane, carrying their empty buckets and their spades, and so back home.

In the O'Higgins household they are sent for baths and then they have dinner. In the O'Dea house the girls peg their swimsuits on the line and then sprawl on the grass in the back garden with their mother who says,

'Sure the housework will wait until tomorrow, let's pick raspberries and we'll have them with cream.'

Both homes offer different comforts.

There is nothing as nice as lying on the O'Deas' grass spooning apple tart or raspberries and cream into one's mouth, or rolling onto your back licking a choc ice, and then getting out the container in which the girls collect the wooden spatula-like ice pop sticks, and making intricate wooden latticework. But there is also nothing as awful as going to bed with sand between your toes and in other unmentionable crevices in your body, and your hair sticky and knotty with salt and wind, as Bernadette well knows, as she has stayed overnight on numerous occasions in the O'Deas' house. Bernadette loves that feeling of slipping, smooth-skinned and washed, down between the clean cool sheets and resting her cheek on a smooth fresh pillow.

Long heady days of summer and Bernadette is now seven and the O'Dea girls are eleven and twelve, and their cousin Simon, aged seventeen, comes to stay.

Simon, from the North of Ireland, has a penchant for little girls. He is tall and tanned, and has an interesting and interested face. He is handsome. He looks at his prepubescent cousins and smiles his greetings, and then later that day in comes Bernadette who promptly slips into her 'O'Dea household persona' and she rolls on the floor so that her little white knickers are showing, and Simon smiles all over again.

'*I can't stop loving you,*' he sings to Bernadette as he lures her into his room with a little set of pigs for her farm, about which she has told him in detail. She giggles. She's heard the song on the wireless. He sings it very well, and she tells him so. She asks him about his northern accent and why he uses the word 'wee' all the time. '*The answer, wee Bernadette, is blowing in the wind, the answer is blowing in the wind.*'

She sits on his bed and he rubs her knee and a little bit further up her leg while he chats and sings to her.

Bernadette sits on his knee while they watch television (*The Crisscross Quiz*), and when she has to go home in the evening he walks her over to the hedge and as she slips through it into her own garden he lifts her skirt and gives her a little slap on the bottom. And Bernadette turns and peeps back through the hedge at him and she giggles before she changes her personality and goes up her driveway for her bath and supper before bedtime.

And of course it doesn't stop there.

Simon gets to take the girls to the beach and Mrs O'Dea follows along later, or sometimes Mrs O'Dea comes back up to the house before the children, and Simon minds them. He is very good with Bernadette, and Mrs O'Dea feels she is leaving Bernadette in very safe hands. He's wonderful with a towel, and great at slipping Bernadette's wet swimsuit off her and drying her carefully all over while bundled up in his arms.

And Bernadette loves it.

'I'm going to marry Simon when I grow up, Aunty Moll.'

'Are you now, isn't that nice?'

He kisses her on the nape of the neck and she feels shivers going up and down her spine.

So safe, so loved and so much time . . . all for her. Bernadette blossoms under his guiding hands.

He is careful. He is gentle. A little kiss goes a long way. He is happy to dry her off, to give her a hug, to have her on his lap while they look at television, and sometimes his fingers go to other places, places they most definitely ought not.

A row develops between the O'Dea girls and Bernadette.

'He's our cousin and you're taking up too much of his time.'

'He likes me most,' says Bernadette.

'He does not. He's our cousin and he likes us most.'

'Well, he kisses me and he doesn't kiss you,' says Bernadette rashly, and is overheard by Aunty Moll.

Bernadette finds herself in Aunty Moll's kitchen.

'What do you mean, he kisses you?'

'He just gave me a hug,' says Bernadette warily. She knows something has gone wrong.

'Where did he give you a kiss?'

'When we were looking at television.'

'I mean whereabouts? Was it on your forehead?'

'Yes,' lies Bernadette, sulking furiously. 'He likes me as much as he likes his cousins.'

But the toothpaste is out of the tube, and Aunty Moll is taking no chances. Bernadette is home within five minutes, and Simon is on the train back to Belfast the following day – not to be seen again.

And Bernadette is no longer quite so welcome next door.

She skulks around at home. 'No, I'm fine, Mummy,' she says to her inquiring parent. 'They're just busy next door. I think they think they're too old for me.'

'Never mind,' says Mrs O'Higgins. 'I'm glad you're spending more time here. I miss you, you know.'

But Bernadette is bruised. She feels rejected by all the O'Deas, and neither Aunty Moll nor the girls come and call for her, or ask her to join them on the beach, and she lies in the back garden and reads as the summer days die away.

'Will you walk me to school, Mummy?' she asks in September.

'Of course I will,' and Mrs O'Higgins is glad to have her daughter back, even though the terms are odd and her instincts tell her something is wrong, but she doesn't pursue it.

And Simon O'Dea went back to Belfast and got on with his life – another story for another place, but he never hurt Bernadette in the physical sense of the word. And, as it turned out in later years, Bernadette always felt that his kindness and gentleness and sexual probings with her were factors that she was able to fall back on when other things in her life got damaged.

As Bernadette is coming to the end of primary school, discussions begin in the O'Higgins' house as to where she should next go to continue her education.

'I thought we were going to send her to the local convent,' her mother protests when Dr O'Higgins unleashes his boarding school plans for Bernadette.

'I know, my dear, I know. But I feel in this day and age, not to give her the opportunities we have given the boys, not to send her to the best, will reflect badly on us later. She will see it as a rejection, that she didn't have the same value as the boys in our eyes, that we put more emphasis on them.'

'But the girls from National School will be going there, and she knows them all. It will be easier for her.'

'I'm thinking it's time we moved house,' says Dr O'Higgins. 'So she won't be going to the local convent anyway. Wherever she goes, it will be a new start for her. She's gregarious enough for it not to be a problem. And it will widen her circle of friends.'

And so Mrs O'Higgins gives in – not that she has a choice – but begs that the chosen boarding school be in Dublin so that Bernadette can come home some weekends. Dr O'Higgins, who has already chosen the school, agrees, and Bernadette is brought for her interview at St Martin's in the Fields in Dublin 2.

Bernadette is unsure who she is going to be when she gets to the school – will the O'Higgins in her come out, or will it be the mischievous O'Dea?

One look at Mother Immaculata and Bernadette plays little Miss O'Higgins, and sits with her ankles neatly crossed and a butter-won't-melt-in-my-mouth look on her face. Her fair hair is neatly plaited and her navy blue eyes look seriously at the nun. She does her assessment and scores highly.

She sits outside Mother Immaculata's office while Mrs O'Higgins and Mother Immaculata confer, and there outside the office perched on a chair is dark, curly-haired, big-smiling, large-bottomed Treasa O'Donoghue.

Bernadette eyes her cautiously, and Treasa grins. A friendship will form. It will last a lifetime – through their schooldays, through Retreats, through college and beyond. It will have its ups and downs because Bernadette will sometimes retire into herself. Initially she will suspect that Treasa may pull the rug from under her feet, but under Treasa's guiding hand, solidity and stability in friendship will be two characteristics which Bernadette will come to admire most. She will observe them in Treasa and watch how Treasa lives by them. Then she will adapt them so that she can use them in her pursuits.

That evening, back at home in the O'Higgins' house, Bernadette is telling her brothers about Mother Immaculata, and her new school uniform, and that she, too, will board like her brothers do.

'And what is this Mother Immaculata like?' asks Seamus, the elder brother.

'She is tall with a big nunny thing on her head, and she has a sharp face,' Bernadette replies.

Seamus mishears her. He thinks she says 'shark face'.

'A shark? Like a fish?' He is curious.

'No,' Bernadette answers. 'Not like a fish. Sharp, pointy, like a bird.'

'Did you like her?' he asks.

Bernadette glances to the door to make sure her parents can't hear her. She pulls a face and shakes her head.

Seamus is doing American poetry, and has joined the school drama group. He knows how to put the wind up Bernadette.

In a deep and creepy voice, he utters, 'Be careful, Bernadette – someone's tapping on your door.'

She involuntarily shivers.

'What do you mean?' she asks.

'It's the raven,' he replies. 'Rapping on your chamber door. *Though thy crest be short and shaven, thou,*' he misquotes, *'art sure some craven, Ghastly grim and ancient Raven wandering from the Nightly shore –'*

'Spooky,' says his brother. 'To be haunted by a raven.'

And so Mother Immaculata is re-christened.

Why didn't Bernadette O'Higgins like Mother Immaculata?

The reason is unclear, but later when Bernadette was older, and when she put her fine brain to good use, she thought, I felt I didn't count. I sat there, aged eleven, about to start a new phase of my life. It should have been of importance to the person into whose care I was being placed. And I felt that I, as an individual, had no import whatsoever.

'We have to get you ready for school,' says Mrs O'Higgins. 'They have a tennis court – in fact that is really the only sport on offer, so we will have to get you up to scratch!'

Bernadette, who is already a member of the local tennis club, cycles down there every afternoon after school in June, and then every morning in July. She has extra coaching, both private and in a group. She plays in the club tournaments. She likes the companionship of going for a Fanta in the clubhouse with her opponent after a match. They sit outside on the grass and other children come to join them. She prefers singles to doubles because that way you don't have to rely on anyone other than yourself. There is lots of banter outside the clubhouse and Bernadette looks forward to boarding school, where she feels it will be like this all the time – girls laughing, dressed in white, sprawling beside tennis courts, chattering and giggling, so many things to say, so much information to amass, long long sunny days.

That last summer, in August, before starting at St Martin's, Bernadette goes with two hundred other girls to Irish College, a college recommended by Mother Immaculata, and there she meets Treasa O'Donoghue again. Treasa's father too, has been prevailed upon to send his daughter up the coast north of Dublin to the school on the sea. Treasa and Bernadette recognise each other in the hallway during reception, and they stay together so as to get into the same dormitory.

They will come here for three consecutive years, their friendship will solidify, and during the third year they will meet Mary Oliver.

The late summer sea washes over the rocks, and when the tide is high the spume is in the air and you can taste the salt on your lips even when you're in your bunk.

That first summer in Irish College, Treasa and Bernadette stick determinedly to each other. Treasa's mother is dead, but she does not tell Bernadette this for nearly three weeks. Treasa sleeps on the top bunk, and when she wants to talk she leans over the side so that her head appears upside down to Bernadette, with her dark curly hair hanging down. Bernadette sometimes brushes it while Treasa hangs there like a bat.

This is friendship and it is better than the friendship that she had with the O'Dea girls. Bernadette, who has become more introverted, lets Treasa lead the way. Treasa's enthusiasm carries Bernadette out of herself. She sits with Treasa in the back row in class and they grin at each other at every possibility. In return, Bernadette imparts the Facts of Life to Treasa, as explained to her with biological precision by her doctor father.

'Are you sure?' asks Treasa in surprise. 'Every month?'

'Absolutely sure,' says Bernadette. '*And* that's when you're not fertile.'

Treasa is surprised. It's not quite the same with farm animals, she and

Vita had pooled their information and it isn't quite what Bernadette is outlining.

'Once a month is rather a lot,' says Treasa, whose information is mostly equine, with the odd bit of rabbit thrown in for good measure.

Both girls make an effort to talk Irish all the time except when they are alone together. 'The more Irish we talk, the more we'll learn,' says Treasa, 'and it'll keep us out of trouble with the teachers. And we've plenty of time alone to chat in English.'

This sounds fine to Bernadette.

'Do you have a passion?' Treasa asks her. They are sitting alone on the rocks. There are dozens of girls all around, wading, swimming, playing, but Bernadette and Treasa are out of earshot.

'How do you mean?' asks Bernadette.

'Well, I had my rabbit George,' Treasa says. 'He was the best, but he's dead now. And I love horses. My friend, Vita, who lives on the land beside our farm, she has two horses, and I get to ride one of them. Her name is Yammy. I think she is my passion.'

Bernadette thinks. She would like to have a passion, but no, she doesn't seem to have one.

'I don't have a passion,' she says. 'I always wanted a pet, but Mummy said the time was never right. One of my brothers collects stamps, and the other is mad about music, and also about drama, but I don't think I have a passion for anything.'

'You have to have a passion,' Treasa says. 'What do you like to do best?'

'I play tennis, and I quite like that. But I'm not passionate about it. I read,' Bernadette adds. 'I suppose that's what I like doing best. I'm a great reader.'

'Then that's your passion,' Treasa says happily, glad that she has that sorted.

While Bernadette is in Irish College, her parents move house, closer to town, closer to Dr O'Higgins's practice.

Ballsbridge, Dublin 4, beckons, but Bernadette will only be there during holidays. In a sense she has become uprooted. In a sense it suits her, because the agony of living next to the O'Deas' house and not having their friendship is now a thing of the past.

In later years, Bernadette will acquire apartments in different cities, so that she can move, find space, be herself. It will be a defensive mechanism, in case of a fall-out with the neighbours.

But of course she will never get that close to the neighbours.

But the Raven praying, lonely in the chapel praying, spoke only
To her God, as if her soul in each word she did outpour
Nothing further then she uttered; not a mental doubt she fluttered
Still she scarcely more than muttered: 'All Retreats have gone before
Smoothly gone from day to day, as my prayers have gone before,'
*   Feared the Raven, 'Nevermore.'*

Chapter Nine

Nun in the apse, just after dusk
Stone embracing, lying still
Shadow hovering to pounce
Saint or sinner? As you will

Mother Immaculata prayed in the Oratory while the girls were at tea on the Thursday evening. Kneeling with bowed head, eyes closed, hands joined, she asked for guidance. At seven o'clock she rose, genuflected, and with a determined expression (similar, it must be added, to her usual expression, just a shade more resolute) she headed for her study.

'Good evening, Sister,' she addressed Sister Rodriguez who was waiting for her. 'How was tea?'

'It went smoothly, Mother,' replied Sister Rodriguez. 'Kitty O'Dowd read and there was no talking.'

'Good. Now, about tomorrow,' said Mother Immaculata thoughtfully.

'That's what I wanted to ask about, Mother. What's going to happen?'

'The problem is twofold,' said Mother Immaculata. 'On the one hand, the Retreat has always lasted for five days and we have already lost one of those days which cannot be replaced next week – exam pressures etc., and anyway the priests will have their own assignments to move on to. So the question is, should we call a halt to it today and agree that this has been a very successful three-day Retreat, or shall we try and salvage tomorrow for the Retreat knowing that it will be difficult to get the girls back into the correct atmosphere?'

Sister Rodriguez looked expectantly at her superior.

'Well, any thoughts, Sister Rodriguez?'

'We should have very little problem re-focusing the girls just for the one day,' she said hesitantly.

'I'm not sure,' replied Mother Immaculata, thinking of Father McMorrow and his comments about her lack of discipline in the school. 'Don't misunderstand me. Maeve Maple has spoken to me about the younger priest . . . Father McMorrow. She wants an explanation for why he feels Kitty O'Dowd should make a confession. Is there an explanation?'

'She was misbehaving. She distracted him during Mass. Unacceptable behaviour, for which she should be truly sorry,' replied Sister Rodriguez.

'Fine. I understand the Sister Chapel will remain closed tomorrow. I have considered running the Retreat from here. But I have decided that we will have it as a day of study. The priests will come in. Mass can be said here. Confessions can be heard down in the Oratory. The girls may leave class individually and Father McMorrow has said that he will talk to any girl on a one-to-one basis who has any queries, anything that is bothering her. I want any worries about the interconnecting passageway dispelled, and I want an aura of calm to prevail again.'

'Yes, Mother, I understand.'

Thus spake the word.

'When breakfast is finished, girls,' Sister Rodriguez addressed the expectant pupils of St Martin's the following morning, 'you will go to the hall, in silence. I said in SILENCE, Kitty O'Dowd.'

Kitty raised her head in surprise as she had not spoken.

'Do you hear me?'

'Yes, Sister,' Kitty murmured. Of course I bloody well hear you, she thought. Do you think I'm deaf?

On her way to the hall, Mother Immaculata was waylaid by Miss Maple.

'Good morning, Mother Immaculata,' said Miss Maple to The Raven who fixed her with a steely stare.

'Yes, Miss Maple.'

'I'm following up on a request I made a few days ago.'

'A request, Miss Maple?'

'Yes, Mother.' Miss Maple braced herself. 'I asked why Father McMorrow had insisted that Kitty O'Dowd go to confession.'

'That is in hand, Miss Maple. There is no need for you to concern yourself.'

'Excuse me, Mother.' Miss Maple stuck to her guns – small pistols, single shots, not much use against the canons of the church. 'As Kitty's form mistress, I do need to pursue this.'

'Father McMorrow, Kitty O'Dowd and *I* will be pursuing this this very morning. Thank you for your concern. Now I am expected in the hall.' And Mother Immaculata skated past Miss Maple and headed up the corridor.

Miss Maple followed her. Her mouth was in a tight line, her frustration apparent to anyone who knew her well.

'Girls of St Martin's,' said The Raven to the silent rows of gymslipped girls, to the open faces which once knew only innocence. 'In the interests of the school, the Sister Chapel will remain closed again today. You will work in your classrooms – this will be of extra benefit to our exam students.' She eyed the Sixth Years at the back of the hall. 'Father McMorrow will come in this morning and you may apply to see him individually. Sixth Year girls only, that is. This afternoon, Father Dunbarr will see any girls from the other classes. Because this is a Retreat day with a difference, in that you will be here within these walls, you will maintain silence until this evening after tea. At which point, *if* the day has gone smoothly, you may be allowed time in the Common Room where you may communicate verbally.'

'What was she on about?' Kitty asked Bernadette as they headed for their classroom.

'I think she was saying if we behave and shut up we'll get time off this evening.'

'Oh, great. What does that mean? She'll supply us with booze and fags?'

'Boys, booze and fags, you mean,' said Treasa.

'That we should be so lucky.'

'Silence, girls,' said Miss Maple to the arriving class. 'Just get out your books and settle down.'

The door opened a few minutes later and in glided The Raven.

'Well, girls,' said Mother Immaculata to the sixth formers. 'Who of you would like an appointment with Father McMorrow this morning?'

Fifty eyes dropped down to their textbooks.

'Any takers?' asked the Maple of the silent girls.

'I see,' said Mother Immaculata. 'Fine. Then at ten o'clock Father McMorrow will see Kitty O'Dowd. And at eleven he will see Mary Oliver.'

Both girls looked up, aghast.

'Kitty, you have an apology to make to him apropos your behaviour in church on Wednesday, and then you may make confession. Mary Oliver, you have an unfinished confession to make. Father McMorrow has kindly singled you both out. Miss Maple, send the girls at the appropriate time. Thank you.' And The Raven was gone.

The class was silent.

Both girls sat still, looking at their books. The tension in St Anthony's was palpable. Downeyone caught Downeytwo's eye.

Mary Oliver looked at the mantelpiece and the statue of St Anthony watching over them. She wondered if that mark on his face could have been a tear. She had never noticed it before. She was almost sure that there was none on the statue outside the door. She wondered could a tear appear, like the stigmata. Taking the nails from her pocket, she rolled them in her palms. *Agnus Dei*, she thought. I am the Lamb of God. Surely I will be slaughtered as lambs are slaughtered. Aye, though I walk through the valley of death, I do fear evil.

Holding the nails ever tighter, one penetrated the soft flesh on her palm, but she felt no pain.

As a lamb to the slaughter, she thought. Vinegar to drink from a sponge on the last lap of the journey. Surely goodness and evil will follow me all the days of my childhood, until I reach the slaughterhouse, then God will not provide.

She tried to find the words of prayers which would comfort, which would distract her from the journey in her head. She saw no parallel with the stations of the Cross. There was no hope of salvation. Post-crucifixion, there could be no redemption for Mary Oliver.

Miss Maple sat at her desk with a feeling of irritation. She could not see how Kitty O'Dowd could handle being with Father McMorrow. Perhaps I've misunderstood, she thought. Perhaps Mother Immaculata will be there. After all, Kitty is in her care. And she did say earlier that she would be meeting both Father McMorrow and Kitty O'Dowd. And I did understand that she meant the three of them would all be present at the same time.

She glanced at her watch. Nine twenty. She wondered if she could go down with Kitty at ten o'clock and suggest being present at the interview.

Kitty O'Dowd looked at her watch. Nine twenty-two. She put her hand up.

'Yes, Kitty?'

'Please, miss, may I leave the room?'

'Yes, Kitty, you may,' replied Miss Maple, who normally did not allow the girls out to use the toilets during class.

Kitty was gone for a good ten minutes, and just as Miss Maple was about to send Bernadette O'Higgins out to look for her, she returned. She slipped back into her place and didn't look up.

At exactly nine fifty-five, the school alarm went off.

'Oh, good, a fire,' whispered Kitty with a grin to Treasa as they got up from their seats.

With that the door burst open.

'Bomb alert, Miss Maple,' said Sister Rodriguez across the throng of girls who were heading as one for the door.

'In single file, girls,' called Miss Maple.

'Head for the tennis court,' said Sister Rodriguez as she suddenly imagined the girls loose on the main road. 'Just as if it were a fire. We've done this before. You know the drill. Now go.'

'Don't run, just move quickly and keep to the left,' called Miss Maple.

At the bottom of the stairs Mother Immaculata stood as captain of the ship, last man to go down.

'This one is different,' she addressed each teacher as the class hit the main hallway. 'Move faster.'

'Man the lifeboats,' whispered Treasa to Kitty O'Dowd.

'I have a wonderful image of the school sinking,' whispered Kitty.

'Like the *Titanic*?' asked Treasa.

'Yes, just a few survivors. And I'm going to be one of them.'

'And the captain gone without a trace,' said Treasa.

''Cept for a black garment floating on the surface,'

'And a seagull perched on top!'

The girls poured out of the back door of the school, where they were herded by the nuns into the gardens.

'Now what?' Bernadette asked. 'This must be our sixth bomb scare this year. But there's something odd about this one. The nuns seem extra jumpy.'

'Is St Martin's being singled out for bomb scares?' asked Treasa suddenly.

'Nah,' replied Kitty. 'Andrew's school has had three in the last two months.'

Miss Maple joined her class. 'Keep well back from the buildings,' she addressed them.

'What's up?' asked Treasa.

'The bomb squad is on its way. Apparently a codeword has been given – this could be the real thing,' Miss Maple replied.

'Oh good,' whispered Kitty O'Dowd, letting her imagination run away with her, and forgetting that she had engineered it. 'Imagine St Martin's going straight up like a gigantic firework. Short cut to heaven for the nuns.'

'Sssssshhhh, Kitty,' said Miss Maple. 'This is no time for joking.'

'If it does go up, Miss Maple,' Bernadette O'Higgins said, 'aren't we rather ... er ... you know ... rather ... trapped here between the school and the wall?'

'Just keep as close to the wall as possible,' said Miss Maple who had already expressed concern after previous bomb scares that the tennis court might not offer the best protection for her charges should there in fact be an explosion. 'Nonsense, Miss Maple,' Mother Immaculata had replied. 'The Lord will provide.'

Downeyone eyed Downeytwo. Propitious timing, she thought.

Downeytwo nodded.

Mary Oliver, leaning against the wall, watched the school building and prayed. '*Deliver us from evil ... aye, though I walk through the valley of nuns, I fear and fear and fear ...*'

Father McMorrow was led from the Oratory by a member of the Bomb Squad, and escorted to safety on the main road.

> *In the hallway late that morning*
> *The bomb squad clearing out the school*
> *The girls as carrion on the courts*
> *But the Magpie seems the fool*

'Really,' he protested, trying to hold his ground. 'I should join the sisters and the girls at the back of the school.'

'It's not safe to go through the buildings just at the moment, Father.'

'How long will this take?' asked the priest.

'Well, Father, we're afraid it might be the real thing. A codeword was given. Not one we know, but nonetheless any code given . . . well, you know, we have to take it seriously. You know how it is. Anyway, if it is the real thing . . . well, we'll have to see how things progress. And if it's not, we'll give the all clear as soon as we can. But with a place this size, we're talking a good two, three hours . . . you know how it is.'

'I have an afternoon appointment the other side of the city,' said Father McMorrow.

'Well, Father, you won't be getting back in here this morning, so you might as well go,' said the detective.

'Jean Jacques?' whispered Anna McBride, in the corridors of her fertile mind.

'*Oui, ma petite?*'

'I hate the bomb scares.' She shivered.

'Come closer. Under my cloak.' He pulled her in against his body.

She could hear his heart beat, regular, rhythmic, safe.

'Close your eyes, my little one. They will not get you, not this time.'

'Jean Jacques,' she whispered.

'*Oui?*'

'You know what I was doing when the alarm started? I was writing my petition to the King of France. I'm appealing on my behalf to have my life returned to me.'

'I think it is to the people of France we need to appeal,' he said. 'It is the people who have risen. It is they who watch the tumbrils roll past, they who will offer assistance at the last moment. I am determined to deliver you safely.'

She sighed in his arms, her back against the wall of her prison cell, the sun shining through the small barred window lighting up her pale face.

'I am afraid of being dragged out in the tumbrils, afraid of the sound of the wheels on cobblestones – I hear them all day through the window, and the sound of the people shouting. *J'ai peur.*'

'*Ah, ma petite,*' said the manly voice of Jean Jacques Versailles. 'I will accompany you should it come to that. But it shall not. I promise you. The sound you hear is the last journey of others, *pas pour toi.*' He clasped her close and his lips touched her hair and then her throat.

'What are you dreaming about?' Bernadette's voice penetrated her thoughts.

'What?' Bridie jumped, green eyes immediately open, and found to her surprise that she was sitting on the ground, her back against the wall, beyond which lay the streets of Dublin and another world. 'Oh, I was just thinking . . . you know . . .'

'Well, I'd say it was about something romantic – that little sweet smile on your lips, a flush on your cheeks!' Bernadette teased.

Bridie, looking embarrassed, tried to brush it off. 'Oh, French stuff,' she said. 'You know. Declensions, that sort of thing.'

'Oh yeah!' Bernadette was dubious.

Jean Jacques stroked Bridie's hair.

'*Regrettes rien, ma petite,*' he said gently to her. '*Je suis ici.*'

'Sometimes,' Bernadette said to Treasa and Kitty as they moved between the walled gardens waiting for time to pass. 'Sometimes I think that I will miss this place so much.'

'Like a hole in the head,' said Kitty with a grimace.

'No, I mean it. Just stand still and listen.'

They were alone in the last garden, having wandered from the others.

'Look around,' she persisted.

The last garden was the quietest. Clematis had grown up and over the outer walls, covering them almost completely; only in places could the old

144

bricks be seen. The inner wall, which separated the gardens, had purple aubretia tumbling down it. The paving between the beds of vegetables had small white and pink flowers in the cracks and creepers grew up the netted posts. A statue of St Martin stared blindly at the girls, and in the trees the birds were singing.

'*There's a kind of hush,*' she whispered.

'Oh, I see,' laughed Kitty. 'Meet Bernadette O'Higgins, the newest of Herman's Hermits.'

Treasa smiled. 'I know what you mean,' she said. 'Yes, I will miss this corner.'

Kitty snorted. 'Jayzus,' she said. 'You two. Have you forgotten what's over that wall? It's FREEDOM!'

'Won't you miss anything, Kitty?' Treasa asked.

'Yes, I'll miss climbing out onto the roof for a fag.'

Outside, there was suddenly the sound of sirens; the noise of the city seemed to reach a crescendo, and high up in the school, soldiers searched systematically from room to room, accompanied by dogs.

'There's real life out there,' Kitty said lustfully.

'I know,' Bernadette said, but there was sadness in her voice.

That evening, Friday, Bridie received her reprieve from the King of France.

'It's come,' she said excitedly to Jean Jacques. 'This prison sentence is over.'

'*Alors, tu as ta liberté.*' Jean Jacques lifted her small face to his and they smiled lovingly and knowingly at each other, and accompanied by Mary Oliver, Bridie went home on the Saturday for the weekend.

Mary Oliver received no more Sacraments that week, nor indeed would she ever again though she was not aware of that. The reassurance she felt with the nails in her pocket gave her the courage to get through the end of the Retreat, and then it was the weekend. It was with relief that she left St Martin's with Bridie on the Saturday morning after breakfast.

Coming out of the school, Bridie said to her, 'We'll have a laugh at the party tonight.'

'What party?' Mary asked.

For a moment Bridie was pulled up short as she tried to think whether there was any way Mary might not have been told about the party, but it didn't seem likely.

'Oh, Kitty's new boyfriend,' she replied. 'He asked us all to his house this evening.'

It was clear from the blank expression on Mary Oliver's face that she had no idea that an invitation had been offered, let alone accepted.

'We can get the bus there, and my parents are going to collect us,' Bridie said. 'It'll be fun.'

'Great,' Mary said, checking her pocket for the nails and reminding herself to transfer them to whatever she would wear that evening.

'You OK?' Bridie asked, looking at Mary's pale face.

'Yes, fine. I just feel a bit queasy. It'll pass,' Mary said, as she tried to push a series of disturbing images to the back of her mind.

There was a yell from somewhere above them, and the two girls looked up to see Treasa's laughing face, with Kitty and Bernadette beside her, at their dorm window three storeys up. Treasa threw something out of the window and Bridie and Mary stood laughing on the pavement as a pair of school knickers unfolded in the air and floated down. They caught on the railing at the bottom of the steps.

'Just think,' Treasa called down. 'We only have to wear them for six more weeks!'

'But not tonight, Josephine!' Bridie called back.

Chapter Ten

Aged one and a half, Catherine O'Dowd goes missing and is found curled up with the cats in a laundry basket in the laundry room. 'Here Kitty, Kitty, Kitty,' calls Frank, her older brother, and Catherine is re-christened.

'Are you sure I'm not adopted?' Kitty asks her mother when she is thirteen.

'Quite, quite sure,' Mrs O'Dowd replies firmly. 'Why do you ask?'

'There are no photos of me until I'm four or five,' Kitty replies.

'Are you sure?' says her mother, taking the album from her and turning the pages. 'How odd. We were very busy, I suppose,' she adds by way of explanation, as she turns the pages and sees snapshot after snapshot of Kitty's brothers, Frank and Tom.

The first photo of Kitty shows her aged about four and a half with a fringe covering her forehead and little dark plaits tied with red ribbons. She is looking away from the camera and she looks scared. She is actually looking away from the photographer who was her father, and it was he whom she feared. Some six months prior to that first photograph her mother had the flu and was resting in bed when Kitty got in her father's way. Tired and irritable from running the show on his own (though how many times his wife had run the show on her own and not taken it out on one of the children is not known), he hit Kitty hard across the head for getting in his way. The blow (not the first one she had had from him) sent her across the floor where she banged the other side of her head on a table leg. Instead of leaving things at that, Mr O'Dowd got annoyed when she didn't get up and kicked her.

'What happened to your face?' Mrs O'Dowd asked in horror when she saw Kitty the following day.

Kitty shook her head. 'I don't remember,' she said truthfully. The table leg had knocked her unconscious and the dual blow to her head would in later life give her sporadic headaches.

But Mrs O'Dowd knew what had happened and she just said to Kitty, 'Keep out of your father's way.' And, as though some unspoken code had passed between the two females, Kitty understood, and after that she spent more time in the laundry room with the cats and kept out of his way.

Mrs O'Dowd bathed Kitty's poor face and put an ice pack on the lumps, even though it was fourteen or fifteen hours too late to make any difference.

'Frank, Tom,' she said tentatively to the nine- and ten-year-old boys. 'Keep an eye on Kitty, will you? Keep her out of your father's way.'

They did their best. But nearly seven years later, before finishing school and using every penny they had saved both from working in the hotel and from money left by an elderly uncle, the two boys, fed up with their father's temper and erratic behaviour, ran off to the States. Although they kept contact with their mother, they did not return.

A year later, for Kitty's protection, Mrs O'Dowd sent her, now aged twelve, to a boarding school in County Mayo.

'Sure you'll have a great time,' Mrs O'Dowd reassured the surprised Kitty.

'But why so far away?'

'It'll be a change from here.'

That was true. Out of the frying pan . . . as the saying goes.

In County Mayo the convent of St Christopher of the Ultimate Burden was built on the cliff tops with winding broken steps leading down to a tiny and very wild beach where the Atlantic crashed onto the rocks and seagulls screamed in feathered vertebrate dismay.

Dismay is the word to describe Kitty's feelings on arriving at her destination.

Later, when she first heard the word Golgotha, she thought of that edifice on the cliff's edge, and she sometimes wondered why she hadn't jumped.

'It's on the sea,' her mother said, 'like here. You're used to that. You'll like it.'

But it isn't the sea like Kitty knows the sea, with the waves washing up on the promenade in winter, and candy floss and ice cream for sale in little booths up and down the street in the summer, and lots of children digging in the sand and Bray Head rising protectively down from the hotel.

This is different.

This is desolation.

Kitty O'Dowd gets through the first term consoling herself with the thought, 'At least Dad isn't here.'

Mrs O'Dowd writes to her once a week but they are sad letters full of how she misses Frank and Tom, and how bleak the seafront is as autumn turns to winter, and bookings, which are always poor off season, are even worse that year.

At Christmas Kitty asks could she leave the convent. Asks? No, that is not the word. Kitty begs. 'It's so cold,' she says.

And cold it is. There is no one there to give solace to the lonely city girls who are used to activity on the streets.

'Will you shut up,' her father roars at her. 'There is no way we are letting you leave. Your mother and I are put to the pin of our collar to pay those fees for you, you ungrateful little—'

'Save the money,' Kitty yells back. 'Save the money and let me stay here. I'll help in the hotel . . .'

The rest of her words are lost as he hits her across the face on Christmas Eve 1967. She doesn't speak to him again for the rest of the Christmas holidays. She stays in her room, or slips out of her bedroom window and along the flat roof of the hotel kitchen, and down onto the seafront to be washed by the spray of the incoming tide.

There she meets Jeremiah Jackson (every parent's nightmare), a slim-hipped lad with drainpipe trousers and lank brown hair, who dips his handkerchief into a pool among the rocks and bathes her swollen face and gives her her first cigarette.

A little kindness goes a long way, and if Kitty had not had to go back to school in the west by train ten days after Christmas, who knows what might have happened with the seventeen-year-old Jeremiah. (But the truth is, whatever might have been with the seventeen-year-old Jeremiah, it would have been better than what Kitty O'Dowd was about to encounter.)

The holidays end and Kitty lifts her twelve-year-old face up to Jeremiah and he gives her a kiss. 'See you at Easter, sweetie,' he says, and gives her a packet of cigarettes to take back to school with her.

The train chugs out of Kingsbridge Station and Kitty O'Dowd smiles to herself as she savours the word 'sweetie' in her mind.

And there is the convent still perched precariously on the cliff top, and the waves hammering at the bottom of the cliff appear not to have shifted it one inch, despite Kitty's fervent Christmas wish. She stretches her twenty cigarettes out over the next three weeks, and she goes to confession and Communion, and she manages to stay out of trouble as puberty sets in. Easter comes, and with it a letter from her mother to say her father is ill and she can't have Kitty home for the holidays and the nuns are kind enough to say that Kitty can stay there, but she must be no trouble.

Kitty is desolate.

She has formed no friendships as such because she continually expects to be called home, to find it is all a ghastly mistake that she is locked up in this place on the west coast. And so there is no one to ask, 'Please may I come to your house for Easter?'

'You cause nothing but trouble,' says Reverend Mother. 'Now you have time for quiet contemplation in the absence of your peers.'

So home go her classmates for Easter, and Kitty O'Dowd sits alone on the forsaken beach, having climbed down the ninety-seven steps. She is wearing her gaberdine to try to protect herself from the wind which lifts the seaweed down on the rocks. And the brine in the air makes her think of home and Jeremiah Jackson leaning against a wall puffing on a fag which he holds inwards in his hand, giving him the air of 'been there, done it, seen it', which is what Kitty O'Dowd sees as maturity and aspires to.

There is little to entertain her. She watches the waves splash over and over the rocks, her mind slipping in and out of memories.

When did I last laugh? she wonders, and then a grin spreads across her heart-shaped face with her slightly pointed chin as she thinks of the school chaplain, one Father Mulrooney.

The girls are in class, Kitty in the front row having been hauled up by

Sister Beruta (Brutal to the girls) for being 'a distraction and a disgrace'. And in walks Father Mulrooney, doddery, short-sighted, hard of hearing, one of the old school of pontificators. There is a fire in the grate, and prior to the class beginning, the class captain, a country girl with bright red cheeks and a jolly-hockey-sticks approach to convent boarding life, had piled on the coal, which is sub-standard, eastern European and prone to sparking.

Father Mulrooney stands in front of the class, peering at the girls through thick horn-rimmed glasses.

'Blessed are the meek,' he says.

Jayzus, thinks Kitty O'Dowd, trying to suppress a yawn. We're going to have forty minutes of this auld fecker talking bollocks. Kitty is practising words and expressions according to Jeremiah, not Jeremiah of the Old Testament, but rather Jeremiah Jackson of Bray promenade.

'Who are the meek?' asks Father Mulrooney of the expectant class.

There is silence.

'We are the meek,' says the class captain hopefully, after a long, long pause, during which time Sister Brutal glares at the thirty-two girls and makes a thin line of her thin lips.

We are the bored, thinks Kitty O'Dowd. What will we inherit?

Father Mulrooney steps backwards towards the open fireplace, and squats slightly, with his hands in his pockets, and his black jacket lifted at the back.

A small coal explosion takes place, which the partially deaf priest doesn't hear, but he does feel the sparks which alight on his protruding backside. He leaps forward and lands on Kitty O'Dowd's desk.

'Jayzus,' shrieks Kitty O'Dowd (always one to make the most of a situation) and she jumps to her feet and into the aisle.

'Holy smoke,' shouts the priest, with clerical accuracy.

Sister Brutal picks up a French textbook from her desk and waves it behind the smoking priest, to little avail. He is leaping from one foot to the other, trying to slap himself.

'Give me that,' says Kitty O'Dowd and she grabs the book from Sister Brutal, and with an astonishingly hard swipe (All-Ireland Hurling finalist quality) she puts out the fire. Father Mulrooney plunges forward so that he is now bent over Kitty's desk, and Kitty cannot resist just one more wallop.

'You minx,' roars Sister Brutal.

'But I saved him,' Kitty protests.

Sitting on the beach, the smile, which Sister Brutal had wiped from her face, returns to hover on her lips. Sure it was a great moment in my young life, she thinks. Saving a priest from fire and damnation. Still, he wasn't very grateful either.

There had been the definite insinuation to Mother Superior that Kitty O'Dowd was responsible for the sparking coal.

Within a month of this unfortunate occurrence (unfortunate from the priest's point of view, but not from the girls', who had never enjoyed anything as much in all their young lives), the priest in question is retired from his chaplain duties and returned to his order where he pursues other activities.

Kitty on the beach is wondering how she's going to put in two weeks alone in this godforsaken place. The school is empty. Father Mulrooney is gone and his replacement is not due until the following day. Down in the village, where Kitty has slipped while the nuns are at prayer, she has bought cigarettes, and stolen one black eyeliner and two nail varnishes – one is clear for her own nails, one is bright, bright pink.

It could be worse, she thinks, on the beach. I can't imagine how, but I'm sure it could be.

She shelters from the wind at the side of the steps, and carefully applies the clear varnish to her nails. When they are dry she climbs the ninety-seven steps to the top and walks slowly back to the school.

She wanders through the empty building, notes the time: two more hours until tea. She decides to take a look in the chapel, wondering what the nuns are up to. The chapel is empty. She wanders slowly round it. And then she sees the statue of St Christopher – St Christopher of the Ultimate Burden. He is dull grey in colour, with grey clothes, grey open-toed sandals, grey hair and beard. His eyes are unseeing.

When Kitty leaves the church he has bright pink toenails, and the pupils of his eyes are black.

Back she goes and wanders the corridors, putting in time.

She heads for the refectory at teatime, to find she is alone, and there is no food. Hungry now, she goes back outside, wondering where everyone is, and she is just in time to see the sisters heading into the chapel. Following them, she wonders do they not eat when the girls are on holidays. By this stage she is ravenous.

In the chapel she discovers that this has been no ordinary day in the convent, because one of the nuns has upped and died, and not only that but she is lying in an open coffin in front of the altar.

Jayz, thinks Kitty O'Dowd, momentarily scared that whoever it is has died of shock on seeing St Christopher's toenails.

Mother Superior gestures to Kitty to come and view the body. Kitty is torn between morbid curiosity and fear, coupled with the hope that if she obliges maybe food will be shortly forthcoming.

Up she goes and peers into the coffin. What surprises her most is the greyness of the nun in the coffin, who, on further examination, turns out to be Sister Beruta (Brutal to the girls).

Kitty stands beside the coffin in complete amazement. She wonders how death could steal in like that. Last seen, Sister Brutal was living up to her name and had been in the most appalling bad temper.

Kitty contemplates a quick prayer, but then changes her mind. 'Bet she wouldn't have said one for me,' thinks Kitty, joining her hands and hoping she looks sufficiently pious in front of Mother Superior.

There is no supper that evening as the nuns appear intent on praying all night, and Kitty tries to break into the pantry to find something – anything – to eat.

She is caught. She is reprimanded. She goes to bed hungry.

On the last night of the holidays, Kitty O'Dowd runs away. She makes it to the next town by dawn, where she is picked up by the local garda and brought back to the convent.

Reverend Mother, who has received a call from the police station, is waiting for her, and after the garda leaves, Reverend Mother addresses Kitty. Every crime she has ever committed is brought out and displayed as evidence before her. 'You have been trouble since the moment you arrived, moving from one transgression to the next. The local chemist has phoned, all but accusing you of theft. The newsagents say you are their best consumer of cigarettes, you have attempted to steal food from the convent pantry, *and* you have desecrated a statue in the House of God. You will leave this place this morning, and you will put this behind you, having learned a lesson.'

'I'm being expelled?' Kitty asks.

'Yes, but with a slight difference. I have decided that although we can't keep you here, our sister convent in County Leitrim would be a good place for you to continue your education. We do not like to give up totally on our girls even when they are turning out as you are. And my advice to you is this – put this behind you. See yourself as being given a second chance and a fresh start. I've phoned Mother Magdalena in Leitrim and she is expecting you in time for lunch so we need to get you organised.'

'Does my mother know?' Kitty ventures. A train ticket home would be preferable but anything is better than staying here on this windswept cliff top.

A letter is sent to the O'Dowd parents which complains about their daughter's wilfulness and her inability to tell the truth. This is digested in the O'Dowd household with anger and animosity towards their daughter and a great deal of gratitude towards the good sisters for taking care of Kitty with such a degree of concern and arranging her transfer to County Leitrim.

And so Kitty O'Dowd's bags are packed while her classmates are at breakfast, and she is out of the convent before they know anything about it. Arriving after the start of the summer term raises questions in her new classmates' minds, and, when asked, Kitty just says that she ran away from her previous school and was expelled.

At night in bed in her new dormitory Kitty weighs up loneliness on the one hand with fear and loneliness on the other. This is a better place, she knows that, but she doesn't like it.

She has learnt several lessons though, and they are: don't trust anyone, don't bother with the truth, nobody will believe you anyway, and you're on your own so look out for yourself because no one else will.

Kitty O'Dowd comes home for the summer holidays, gets beaten by her father for the disgrace she has brought on them, works in the family hotel, and during her free time she heads down the seafront where she laughs and smokes with Jeremiah Jackson and his friends.

She lets them indulge in the odd kiss but no more than that. Kitty O'Dowd is in recovery from many of the facets of Life as she knows it.

Kitty O'Dowd returns to County Leitrim in September and puts in time. Three terms of cold and tedium, and the following summer she heads for Irish College in Cork, where she finds herself in a chalet with the blonde Downey twins who converse with each other by simply glancing at the other's face, and with Anna McBride whom Kitty christens Bridie.

She sprawls on her bunk and sends Bridie off to get her clothes from the laundry, and Bridie goes and gets her things and brings them back with a smile. And Kitty looks into her eyes and sees something in them like a reflection of herself and for a moment her heart stops and then she shrugs and her heart beats again. Kitty doesn't know what it is she has seen, she doesn't realise it for a very long time, but in that moment Kitty felt compassion and so she is kind to Bridie and to her amazement Bridie just seems to like her.

So what does Kitty learn from this?

Absolutely nothing.

She's nice to Bridie for the time they are stuck in summer camp and then she becomes the old Kitty when it is time to go home. Seven more weeks helping in the hotel before she is back on the train in the direction of Leitrim and the mooing cows, and the long wet grass and the sheer and utter loneliness and boredom at the end of the sixties in the centre of Ireland.

Back she goes with the words of 'Raindrops keep falling on my head' resounding in her ears. The pastures of Leitrim are not unlike the fields where Robert Redford and Paul Newman romp with Katharine Ross, where cycling suddenly seems like the most fun thing in the world, and Kitty O'Dowd fancies a shoot-out in Bolivia – anything rather than to be going back to the convent in Leitrim.

She is armed with a copy of *Portnoy's Complaint* by Philip Roth, a parting gift from Jeremiah Jackson. Two weeks back and there is a surprise swoop on the girls' lockers and Kitty O'Dowd loses *Portnoy's Complaint* to the nuns.

'I'd finished it anyway,' she mouths outside Mother Perpetua's door. 'Bet you won't understand it,' she hisses at the closed door and raises two fingers at the wooden panels behind which sits Mother Perpetua with her hair standing on end as she contemplates Portnoy's complaint.

Kitty O'Dowd is getting feverish.

Woodstock has been and gone and Kitty feels life is passing her by. She sneaks into Reverend Mother's room during evening chapel and takes her reading glasses and places them on the nose of the Virgin Mary in the main hall.

This is not noticed by the nuns for nearly two days. Morning prayers take place in the hall and the nuns with their backs to the statue are oblivious of its new condition. Reverend Mother has put out word that she has mislaid her reading glasses and would the girls keep an eye out for them. 'Hah,' sneers Kitty. 'She wants them so that she can get on with reading my book.' The girls stand in assembly for prayers and one by one they notice the statue with the missing spectacles. A shiver of excitement passes over them like a breeze across a field of wheat.

Day one over, Kitty is bored again.

Back she goes to Reverend Mother's room while evening chapel is on, and there in the top drawer of Reverend Mother's desk is *Portnoy's Complaint*.

Kitty looks at it. Her hand reaches out to hold it. She contemplates her foolhardiness.

Pragmatism does *not* win out.

Kitty O'Dowd takes the book from the drawer and brings it to the chapel later that night when the girls are having supper in the dining room. In the chapel there is a statue of St Francis of Assisi. He stands on a plinth, some six foot tall, in his brown robes tied with a rope at the waist and with one hand raised to wave to the birds. The thumb on the sculpted hand is the perfect distance from the index finger, and in between them Kitty O'Dowd slips the open copy of *Portnoy's Complaint*.

The first crime is considered a blasphemy and Kitty is truly sorry for herself by the time Reverend Mother has finished with her.

They've no fecking sense of humour, thinks Kitty at first when the missing spectacles are reported by the head girl after assembly the following morning. The nuns turn as one and they could not have been more horror struck if the bubonic plague had been staring them in the face.

Kitty O'Dowd apologises individually to every nun in the convent, and wonders if there is any way she can get to the chapel to remove the purloined book, as she suddenly feels she has had enough. But the opportunity does not present itself and so St Francis is discovered later in the day with his nose in page fifty-three of Philip Roth's latest novel. Following on her incident with the specs and the Virgin Mary, it is a red card – it's off the pitch for Kitty O'Dowd.

Goodbye, County Leitrim. Kitty O'Dowd is on the train back to Dublin.

Her father is convalescing after an early heart attack so Kitty's mother does the rounds of the schools in Dublin, trying to get her daughter into somewhere, any school, mid-term, with a track record that is only too obvious. The only place that will have her is the most expensive school in Ireland. Frank and Tom have sent some money home from the States and, assisted by this, Mrs O'Dowd gets the fees together and off Kitty goes to her next school – St Martin's in the (invisible) Fields.

Then methought the air grew thicker, perfumed from an unseen smoker
Inhaled by youth where bodies lie, deeply lie on carpet floor
'Enjoy,' they cry, 'our God released us – in His mercy He released us
Hallucinate and drink and smoke away the memories of yore
God forgive you and absolve you – ever from the days of yore
                              Quoth the Raven, 'Nevermore.'

Chapter Eleven

It was the Saturday on which the Retreat ended. Kitty O'Dowd climbed into the school attic, and removed a sheet of her parents' hotel stationery from her suitcase. In a very good attempt at her mother's hand she wrote to the convent requesting permission for their daughter to return to their hotel on the seafront. It was not the first time she had done this, but as it turned out it would be the last. The letter, brief and to the point, observed that although they were only two weeks into the term, her mother would like her home to help in the hotel over the weekend as they were exceptionally busy.

Mary Oliver set out for the weekend with Anna McBride (and Jean Jacques Versailles, although Mary Oliver was unaware of his existence).

Bridie, who boarded from Monday to Friday, had found the week had passed fairly smoothly and her relationship with Jean Jacques was reaching a new high as he had unribboned her bodice the previous night. At first he had unzipped it, until it had occurred to her that zips might be a post French Revolution invention. She was unsure about hooks and eyes.

Kitty O'Dowd had not been invited to anyone's house for the weekend mainly because her classmates' parents were not keen on her presence. It was not that they smelt smoke in her room after she left, because she was way too careful for that, and anyway it was the early seventies and all the parents smoked. Government warnings had not yet even appeared on advertisements. It was something to do with the way she sprawled in their armchairs and looked the fathers up and down in rather too knowing a way (was there the hint of a sneer?) and the heels on her platforms were a bit too high, and her short skirts too short, and the boys ran their hands through their hair in front of her and were as cool as they could be. And

161

there was a tension around her like an elastic band pulled too taut and about to snap.

Kitty was not bothered that she had not been invited to anyone's house because Andrew MacDonald's parents were away for the weekend, and it was his party. She intended to crash there. She reasoned that he probably would not mind and that anyway he need never know. The house was big enough with its six bedrooms for her to find a quiet corner to sleep after the party that night. He had said she could bring up to five friends but his stipulation was that she arrive in her school uniform. She had grinned when he suggested it because he always had something different going on in his head. He was only a year older than she was but he was more mature than any of the boys she knew, including her two older brothers.

Including? she thought. I mean especially my two brothers, both of whom had done a runner some five or six years earlier.

It suited Kitty O'Dowd to wear her uniform going to Andrew's house on Lansdowne Road. After all, she was expected to wear it on the train going home to the hotel.

She signed out of school at midday, carrying a small overnight bag in which she was carrying a maxi skirt, a pair of platforms and a thin, tight T-shirt.

'Be back by seven thirty tomorrow,' Sister Rodriguez snapped at her.

'Yes, Sister,' Kitty replied, reminding herself to phone her parents from Andrew's place to reduce the likelihood of their calling her at school. Not that there's much chance of that, she thought. It's out of sight, out of mind with them.

Sister Rodriguez looked at her with dislike. Kitty did not notice, and if she had she would have paid no attention.

Normally when skipping school like this she simply went to the bushes in either Merrion Square or Sutherland Square and changed her clothes, bundling her uniform into a bag. Today, to oblige Andrew, she took the bus to Ballsbridge and sauntered down Lansdowne Road, turned out in her gymslip, blouse, stockings and flat black shoes. 'We're not allowed to wear patent shoes,' she had explained to him the previous week, 'in case our underwear is reflected in them and visible to others.'

He had nearly fallen off the bench they were sitting on, initially from disbelief, and then from laughter.

'It's all right for you,' she had snapped at him. 'Scottish Presbyterian, Protestant school – sure you've got it all.'

'Tell me more,' he asked her. 'Go on.'

She had shrugged. 'No stilettos in case they mark the flooring. The school tunic must not be more than one inch above your knees – they make you kneel and they measure how high it is.'

'Then how do you get away with yours being so short?'

'I used to slouch and they sort of let it go.'

'Well, you certainly don't slouch now,' he said. 'I've never seen anyone walk like you do.'

She grinned.

Now as she looked for the right number in Lansdowne Road, unsure how far down the street she had to go, Andrew pulled in just in front of her in a Jaguar.

'Jayzus,' she said. 'You drive?'

'It's my dad's,' he replied nonchalantly. 'Give me a hand.' And he opened the boot and handed her a bag to carry. There was vodka in it, as she subsequently found out. He carried the beer. Up the steps they went.

'Nice house,' she said.

'Embassy pays for it,' he said as he let them in. 'Drawing room is off limits.' He pointed his chin in the direction of one of the front rooms. 'Mum keeps priceless things in there, or so she says. But we have the dining and living room for the party, and the folding doors open between them.'

Kitty nodded with a certain lack of interest, not knowing that folding doors were going to be her downfall in more ways than one, or she might have felt a little more curiosity.

Kitty O'Dowd lost her virginity that evening to the strains of 'Bye Bye Miss American Pie' but in her case the levee was not dry at all.

Mary Oliver came out of her shell at the party and danced until one in the morning, at which time Bridie had to prise her out of the arms of a school friend of Andrew MacDonald's.

'Time to go, Mary,' said Anna McBride. 'My dad's outside in his car, waiting.'

Mary Oliver had just had her first French kiss (she had also had her first vodka and orange) and was loath to leave, but good manners won out and she slipped out of the house with Bridie and Jean Jacques Versailles. Later in bed, hugging herself and thinking about the kiss that had sent shivers up and down her spine, she tried to masturbate for the first time in her life.

When the folding doors between the two rooms were opened, they doubled back on themselves but could be positioned in such a way that they created a hidden recess behind them. It was in one of these recesses, to the sounds of 'American Pie' playing over and over, as someone had hit the replay button on the record player, that Andrew MacDonald unzipped his black, crushed-velvet bell-bottoms and entered the very willing Kitty O'Dowd. She had not planned on that happening, but he had. It had not crossed his mind that she was a virgin. The way she carried on had given him the exact opposite message.

Despite the good quality of the carpet on the floor, her bottom burnt from the rubbing of the fibres on her skin, and to ease the burning sensation she had lifted her hips off the floor, giving him easier access, as it turned out. He thought she was very tight, but it did not occur to him that he was plucking a new cherry until the following afternoon when he closed the folding doors to return the house to its normal state before the return of his parents. Then he saw stains on the carpet which looked remarkably like blood.

Bloody hell, he thought. Oh, bloody, bloody hell.

He carefully positioned a side table so that its curved antique legs covered the marks in question, wondering how long before the carpets were due for cleaning.

She'd have said, though, wouldn't she? he thought.

She was in the kitchen eating toast and drinking tea and had promised to give him a hand as soon as she had finished. He went out to the kitchen and looked at her. She grinned at him, and when he said nothing but just stared at her, she stuck out her tongue. She was wearing a red sweater of his that almost came down to her knees, and nothing else.

'Do you want to stay tonight?' he asked. 'The parents aren't due back until tomorrow, and we could go into school together in the morning.'

She shook her head. 'Have to be in by seven thirty this evening.'

'Go on,' he said. 'I'll phone up and say I'm your father.'

'You sound as much like my father as the Pope does,' she retorted.

'I'll say I'm your uncle.'

She snorted. 'So we've just committed incest!'

'Three times,' he said.

She grinned.

'Gotta fag?' she asked.

Treasa O'Donoghue, whose bottom stuck out so that the pleats of her uniform did not hang smoothly over it, had had three vodkas and orange at the party and was on her ear within an hour. Andrew's best friend, another embassy boy from the same school, had slipped vodka into every drink he saw. In some cases there was already vodka in the drink, so those who thought they were having one or two, ended up having three or four, those who thought they were having four or five were having eight or ten, and those who thought they were drinking straight orange juice were giddy and relaxed in no time at all, and, in several cases, did not even realise that the headache they had the following morning was in fact their first hangover.

John Unwin, Andrew's closest friend, danced with everyone and then moved in on Treasa with her wild laugh and her dark curls which fell all over the place to the sounds of 'Me and Julio down by the schoolyard'. (In later years, as a Tory MP, he would slip one too many a snifter into an underage girl's drink, but that was down the road.)

Treasa, with three vodkas under her belt, ground her groin against his and would probably have given her all had not the three vodkas decided they would not remain under her belt and follow the normal path through her kidneys. She made it to the back garden where she threw up and then lay down under some unidentifiable bush and slept, to be found later by Bernadette O'Higgins who had ventured out for that strange mix of a blast of fresh air and a smoke.

Bernadette (un-plaited that evening – fair hair loose and wavy on her shoulders), having had a full week of the illustrated version of *Scrumptious Sex*, was ready for some more practical research, but Andrew and John, both of whom she fancied, were otherwise engaged with Kitty and Treasa. Or so she thought until she fell over Treasa beside the unidentifiable bush. A further search revealed that Treasa was alone, so she decided to leave her for a bit and went back inside in search of John. As she was about to re-enter the house he emerged, his hair wild, his shirt unbuttoned to his waist and staggering slightly.

'I was looking for you,' he slurred.

She momentarily contemplated pursuing her practical research with someone who was clearly blind drunk, and then decided against. 'Treasa's down there,' she said and pointed, suspecting rightly that in the state he was in, he would not only not find Treasa but would keel over before he got even halfway there.

Bernadette, who in later years would return for an annual Retreat to regularise her thought flow and assist her powers of contemplation and concentration, was feeling very 'hormonal', as she put it. She had also avoided the orange juice as she had spotted early on what John Unwin was up to. Back inside she wandered through the darkened double room, noting that 'American Pie' appeared to be stuck on the turntable. She observed the activity going on behind one of the folding doors (two pairs of feet were protruding but they gave nothing away as to their ownership), and that most people seemed to be paired off. She headed for the hallway and, glancing up and down, decided to go into Mrs MacDonald's drawing room, which contained the priceless heirlooms.

She opened the door, slipped in and closed it quietly behind her. There was a silence in the room as she looked slowly around. Moonlight shone through, giving her a reasonable view of elegant period furniture, gilt-framed paintings hanging on the walls, a plush carpet, a marble fireplace, thick expensive rugs. She moved into the centre of the room, still unaware that she was being watched.

What's that smell? she wondered.

'Hi there,' a voice drawled.

She nearly jumped out of her skin. Steadying herself and trying to appear cool, she became aware of a figure sitting in the lotus position on the floor.

So still was the person sitting that she realised that in her initial glance across the room, she had mistaken him for a piece of furniture.

'Hello,' she responded, unsure whether to retreat or to investigate.

'I'm Christopher Marlowe,' came the American drawl again. 'Come and stand in the moonlight where I can see you clearer.'

She approached the well-lit part of the room and peered at the person on the floor.

'Are you the ship that launched a thousand faces?' she quipped.

'I presume this is some quaint Irish expression designed to make a joke out of my name,' he responded. 'Very disappointing.'

She was taken aback. 'No, I was just trying to be funny,' she said, and turned to leave.

'Don't go. Sit and talk with me,' said the lotus-like Christopher Marlowe.

She slipped off her platforms and sat on the floor in front of him. She took in long, black, straight hair, a white Indian type shirt with no buttons, which hung open halfway down his chest, red or wine or plum coloured velvet trousers (it was difficult to be clear about the colour in the moonlight) and a dark velvet waistcoat that appeared to be edged in heavy gold brocade and to be studded with something that glittered.

I suppose his is a 'chiselled' face, she thought.

For his part he saw a slim girl of average height with long fair hair. She was dressed in a full-length skirt and some sort of light crinkled blouse that was loose at the neck. Sitting on the floor, she pulled her knees up in front of her and put her arms round them.

'Do you have a name?' he asked.

'Bernadette O'Higgins,' she replied.

They eyed each other in the semi-dark.

Behind the folding doors of the living room, Kitty O'Dowd was biting her lips and thinking, is this what it's supposed to be like?

Kitty was not given to in-depth thinking but she now knew that she liked being the centre of Andrew's attention, and what better way to be the centre of someone's attention than to have them more or less glued to you. His earlier concentration on her while they had got the place ready for the party had focused her totally on him, his gropings had been of a different nature to what she was used to, and later she thought of them affectionately as fondles. Bundles of fondles.

Someone changed the record, and they stayed entwined and still to the melody of 'Help me make it through the night'.

'Would you like a drink?' he asked her.

'No,' she whispered. She felt vulnerable in a way she had not felt before. She did not want him to withdraw but she could feel it happening anyway.

'I ought to go and see what's happening,' he said. 'Will you stay here and wait until I get back?'

'Yes,' she said into his ear as he kissed her neck.

She wondered if he would come back. Experience had taught her otherwise, and the very fact that they had gone all the way made her think that he would not return. However he did, and they stayed behind the folding doors for another half-hour or more. At this point Kitty started to yawn and Andrew suggested that she high-tail it up to his bedroom (top floor, back room) and that he would join her as soon as he had got rid of the rest of the party. He seemed sincere. He seemed to care. She was momentarily reminded of the Maple but she could not, for the life of her, think why.

Bernadette O'Higgins was still sitting on the drawing room carpet facing Christopher Marlowe who was explaining his embassy connection and the fact that he was in the same school as Andrew. She could not work him out. He seemed quite happy just to sit there in the half shadow, half light of the moon. He lit what she thought was a cigarette and took a drag before passing it to her. On the ground in front of him was a large cut-glass ashtray, and she saw what she assumed was the butt of a previous cigarette. She had shared the odd cigarette with Kitty or Treasa in the enclosed gardens behind the school or in the boiler room in the basement of the building and sometimes out on the roof, and that evening had bought her first packet, and so she took what she thought was a cigarette from him, and inhaled.

'Next time hold it in a little longer,' he suggested.

Her eyes widened as she coughed at the unexpected burn.

During all of this, Anna McBride was having a problem differentiating between reality and imagination. She had danced with various people and had had one drink. Having had the occasional glass of wine at home with her parents, she identified the kick that the vodka gave her without being sure what it was, but knowing that her father was going to collect her at one o'clock she finished the drink and did not have another.

'Go carefully with the booze,' she said to Mary Oliver who, having been silent for six solid days, had now, aided by the alcohol, decided to sing.

After dancing two fast sets, followed by a slow one, Bridie decided that she preferred the maturity of Jean Jacques Versailles to Andrew MacDonald's school friends. She immediately saw that this was going to create a problem, both for the evening in question and for the future. Where do you go if your fantasy is better than reality?

Two options, she decided. Either I live in my imagination or I put Jean Jacques on hold.

For the time being, at least for the night in question, she decided to spend the rest of the evening in the company of Jean Jacques and his mature fingers. She sat in a corner nursing a glass of water and watched Mary Oliver who by now was fairly pie-eyed and was locked in a slow-shuffling embrace with a lanky looking guy who appeared to be chewing her neck. Jean Jacques' kisses were slower, gentler and did not leave the marks that Mary Oliver's neck was going to display for the next six days.

Under the unidentifiable bush, Treasa O'Donoghue stirred briefly before pulling herself into a foetal position and sinking Lethe-wards as pains started shooting through her head. John Unwin, less than three feet away, lay on his back on the ground and watched the stars appear and disappear behind clouds and wondered if he had perhaps drunk a bit much.

The party drew to a close and Andrew MacDonald closed the front door before racing up the stairs to his bedroom on the second floor where he found Kitty O'Dowd asleep in her thin, tight T-shirt and a pair of bikini knickers, her skirt lying on the floor at the foot of the bed. He wondered where her shoes were. (They were behind the folding doors in the double room.) He eased her clothes off her, slipped a pillow under her hips and entered her again. This time, either because they were in the privacy of his room or because they were not being drowned out by 'American Pie' so that he could actually hear her, Kitty moaned and sighed in his arms, and afterwards when he released her from his embrace and the moon caught her face on the pillow, he wondered if there were tears on her cheeks or whether it was just a trick of the light.

Kitty curled up against him and he held her while she slept, and for the first time in her seventeen years she felt safe and secure and briefly wanted.

In the drawing room Christopher Marlowe and Bernadette O'Higgins lay on the floor, side by side, looking out through the window.

'Look how perfect each star is,' Christopher said to her.

And Bernadette, who until that evening had never heard the word 'stoned', let alone undergone the experience, looked at each star in its perfection and marvelled at how beautiful the night sky was. Each puff of cloud that wafted across the face of the moon changed and shifted the contours of the moon's face.

'He's smiling at us,' she said, and she smiled back slowly and remotely at what she thought was the moon god. 'I love the moon,' she said. 'I love the night.' Her heart filled and soared and the moonlight reflected on the gilt-edged picture frames hanging on the wall. 'Pure gold,' she said. 'Ready to be mined.' They looked at each other and smiled.

'Such perfection,' he said, as he lifted one strand of her hair and saw the fibres separate. The gold brocade on his waistcoat captured her gaze and she looked at it for a long, long time.

'It's molten,' she said, dreamily.

They looked at each other again. 'That was really good stuff,' Christopher murmured.

'Mmmmmmm,' she replied.

She thought about the sound she had just made. It made her think of a honey bee, buzzing lazily from flower to flower. No, she thought, not lazily. Maybe busily, and I am watching it lazily. Bears like honey. I like honey. Therefore I am a bear. She started to giggle.

'Do you like my fur?' she asked Christopher Marlowe.

At nine in the morning Kitty O'Dowd slithered out of bed to go in search of the loo. She stood at the window for a moment to take a look out and was surprised to see what looked like bodies in the back garden. They were two storeys up above the ground floor and the garden was at basement level, so in the early morning, with her eyes still sleepy, she was not immediately sure what it was that she could see. She blinked a few times but the apparition of legs did not disappear.

'Andrew,' she said.

He opened an eye and took her in standing naked in front of the window. 'Come back to bed,' he said, raising the quilt to encourage her back in.

'No, Andrew,' she said. 'I think you'd better come and take a look.'

He got out of bed and joined her at the window. He was about to put his arms round her when he sensed her urgency. Looking down into the garden, he let out a whistle. 'Binoculars, binoculars,' he muttered, casting an eye around the room.

She found them first. 'Jayzus,' she said. 'That has to be Treasa O'Donoghue's bottom. And who the hell is that?'

He grabbed the binoculars from her.

'Oh, no,' he said. 'It's John. He was supposed to check back into school last night.'

'So was Treasa,' said Kitty O'Dowd. 'Do you suppose they're dead? That'll give the nuns something to think about!'

'I hope not,' Andrew replied. He pulled on a pair of jeans and headed for the stairs.

They were not dead. But they were both frozen. 'Kitty, run a bath for Treasa,' Andrew instructed her.

'He needs one too.' Kitty nodded in John's direction.

'Well, either we'll put the two of them in together, or he has to wait. I'll make them coffee. We need to get them out of here fast.'

'What's the urgency?' Kitty inquired.

'Well, I don't know how the nuns handle absenteeism, but I do know that John will be for the high jump if it's discovered he's out,' he replied.

It took Treasa a full twenty minutes in a hot bath to thaw out, holding her head and moaning, 'Oh God, oh God,' which made Kitty think of how she had moaned a similar sentiment but with a different meaning several hours earlier.

'Treasa, how were you planning on getting back in?' Kitty asked.

'Usual way,' she moaned. 'I was going to get in over the back wall, and the Downey twins were going to leave a basement window unlocked.'

'Well, you can still do that if you hurry,' Kitty said.

Andrew brought coffee into the bathroom, and Treasa pulled her knees up to her chin in a vague but disinterested effort at modesty.

'I'll never make it,' she said, taking the coffee.

'Look, don't you girls usually go to Westland Row Church for ten o'clock Mass on Sundays?' Andrew asked, well acquainted with the activities of the girls of St Martin's. 'All we need do is get Treasa to the church on time, or at least before Mass ends. She can slip in at the back. No one will be any the wiser.'

'No uniform,' Treasa muttered.

'Take Kitty's,' Andrew said. 'We can get it back later.'

Before she knew it, Treasa was dressed in Kitty's too short uniform and had arrived by Jaguar down the road from the church.

'First part of the mission accomplished,' Andrew said, and then headed for his own school to drop off John.

'That was no joke,' he said to Kitty later as he eased himself back into bed beside her. 'I had to go into the school, pretending I wanted to get a textbook, and then slip down to the basement. We appear to use a similar entry and exit system to St Martin's. Then unlock the window, and encourage John who looked like death warmed up to make a run for it.'

He slipped a hand between her legs.

'You're cold,' she said.

'So warm me up!' he said.

Bernadette O'Higgins, who had genuinely hoped for some practical research the previous evening, woke on the drawing-room carpet at about ten fifteen on Sunday morning, stiff and very, very hungry. At that point Andrew, John and Treasa were already bombing towards Westland Row in Andrew's father's Jaguar, and Kitty was back in bed having finally peed. The advantage, or otherwise, of large turn-of-the-century or older houses is the thickness of the walls, and this sound-proofing had protected the sleeping Bernadette and her snoring partner in crime from being wakened. Which was unfortunate for both of them.

Christopher Marlowe's mother woke up at about ten that morning fighting off the effects of sleeping tablets and alcohol and came downstairs to find someone had broken into their residence during the night. The kitchen window lay in shards across the kitchen floor, and the back door was open.

Her husband was in London at a secret meeting not unconnected with the forthcoming defeat of McGovern the following November; the garda on duty at their front gate had not bothered to patrol the grounds during the night, a fact which of course he later denied, and Christopher, her only and most beloved son, was missing from the bedroom in which she thought she had had a conversation with him the previous evening on returning from an embassy bash. (In fact, the conversation had taken place a week earlier, but such are the effects of sleeping tablets and brandy when combined.)

After a quick survey of what might be missing and the discovery that the aforementioned beloved son had been, so she thought, kidnapped, Mrs Marlowe promptly pressed the panic button on the upper landing. The panic button was connected to the embassy and to the police, both of whom responded immediately. The embassy sent out two large and rather po-faced Marines, and contacted their security in both Dublin and Washington; the police rang the unfortunate garda on duty at the gate and sent out a squad car.

The garda (needless to say in plain clothes) rang the hall doorbell, and then raced round the back of the house to see if there was anything obvious out of place. On finding the back door open, he entered, leaping nimbly over the broken glass on the floor, and ran into the hall. Meanwhile Mrs Marlowe had retrieved her husband's automatic from his desk in the study. On hearing a sound from the kitchen, she stood in a recess in the hall, well hidden from view, released the catch on the automatic and took a pot-shot at the unfortunate garda as he entered the hallway from the rear of the house.

Brandy, sleeping tablets, a very nervous disposition on finding her son kidnapped, together with the weight of the automatic to which she was unaccustomed account for the fact that she did not actually bring the garda down, but she did hit him in the left arm.

The fact that he was shot at all was something for which he was singularly grateful, although, of course he could never admit it. But it did mean that a certain amount of sympathy flowed in his direction in the coming week, before, during and after the operation to remove the bullet.

'I'm so hungry,' Bernadette O'Higgins said to Christopher Marlowe as he stirred and looked at her with interest (not having yet seen her either in daylight or in a regular state of mind).

'Munchies,' he said. 'Me too, let's go and eat.'

He guided her to the MacDonalds' kitchen where he started pulling food out from the fridge and various cupboards. 'Toast, bacon, eggs? I'll cook. You make the coffee and pour juice,' he suggested.

Bernadette glanced at the kitchen clock and a variety of things penetrated her brain, including the fact that it looked as if it was mid-Sunday morning and that someone would be wondering where she was.

In Westland Row, Treasa O'Donoghue had slipped neatly into the back row on entering the church, and when her classmates headed for the altar to receive Communion, she queue-jumped several members of the congregation to catch up with her peers as they walked with bowed heads up the centre aisle. Downeyone turned round and raised an eyebrow at her. Treasa raised her eyes to heaven and then dropped her head to a more appropriate angle.

Back in their regular pew after a suitable interval and having made sure that the nuns were otherwise engaged, Treasa whispered to Downeyone, 'Was I missed?'

Downeyone shook her head. 'We covered for you, said you were delayed in the loo, together with Bernadette.'

Treasa nodded and rested her elbows on the back of the seat in front of her. This comment from Downeyone took several long seconds to penetrate through to her tired and shivering brain cells as the effects of the night under the unidentifiable bush were only now coming into their own. She glanced down the pew, then at the pews in front, then she swallowed uncomfortably, both because her throat was sore and because the comment was beginning to make sense.

'What do you mean, Bernadette?' she asked.

'She didn't make it back either,' whispered Downeyone.

Treasa, now sweating for several reasons, groaned out loud, bringing the beady eye of Sister Rodriguez directly on her. She buried her head in her hands and concentrated on just staying kneeling in an upright position.

'Mother of God,' Bernadette O'Higgins yelped in the MacDonalds' well-fitted kitchen. 'Oh, Mother of God.'

'Are you praying?' Christopher Marlowe drawled with interest.

'Oh my God, they'll go through me,' Bernadette moaned.

'Go through you?' asked Christopher.

'Lynch me – they'll lynch me,' she explained.

'What's the problem?' Christopher asked with increased interest. 'Why on earth will you be lynched?'

'I'm supposed to be in school. I got out through a window and I was to be back . . . well, back before dawn anyway,' moaned Bernadette as images of her secure and academically gifted future crumbled before her eyes.

Meanwhile Mrs Marlowe, having identified too late the garda from her gate, stood in the middle of her hallway waving the automatic wildly about her.

'Put it down, ma'am,' called one of the Marines from the end of the hall. Whether the American drawl reassured her or she had just had enough was unclear, but either way she took one more shot, this time hitting the chandelier which was fortunately two feet away from where she was standing. As it collapsed in thousands of tiny crystal shards on the floor, she threw the gun to one side.

The Marine, who courageously had stood his ground, covering her with his own pistol, called to his partner, 'Man down,' and went to take a look at the moaning garda who was now lying on the floor.

'We've got him, ma'am,' called the Marine by way of reassurance to Mrs Marlowe.

The garda immediately realised that he was now at risk from the Marine and started shouting out his identity to try to halt the cataclysm of disasters which seemed to be unfolding about him.

Mrs Marlowe, assuming that the Marine meant that he had found her kidnapped son, started shouting, 'Is he all right? Has he been hurt?'

The Marine, assuming she was talking about the garda whom he thought was the criminal, said, 'You've done a wonderful job, ma'am. Great shot.'

Mrs Marlowe collapsed beside the crystal chandelier.

'Don't panic,' Christopher Marlowe said to the white-faced Bernadette, showing he was more his father's son than his mother's.

'Panic?' she repeated. 'Panic? I've had it. Look at the time.'

'Steady,' he said. 'Steady does it,' which is roughly what his father said to Richard Nixon the previous evening by phone. 'Can't we sneak you back in the way you got out?'

'No,' she groaned. 'They're at church now. There is no way I'll get there before they get back. They'll have noticed by now anyway.'

'Where do you live?' he asked.

'What?' She was distracted and bothered and could not concentrate on his question.

'Well,' he said, 'if you're from Dublin, maybe we could get you home and you could say that you were so lonely or something and throw yourself on your parents' mercy rather than the nuns'.'

'But where could I say I've been?' she asked. 'Look at me, they'll know I was out on the town.'

'But you weren't out on the town,' he said. 'You were with me.'

'And you think that'll help?' she asked incredulously. (Think how much more incredulously she would have asked that if she knew that at that moment his kidnapping was being reported in Washington, and the FBI were getting into action.)

'Let me think,' he said, and popped toast into the toaster. 'Say, I'll take you home and we'll say that you met me this morning instead of going to church.'

She looked at him in disbelief. 'What good'll that do?'

'Girls' parents always like me,' he said. 'I have my father's charm,' he added wryly.

'Christopher, listen to me. If either the school or my parents find out that I was out overnight, and with a boy at that, I've had it.'

'I've got that,' he said. 'I'm saying that you were in overnight, in the school, in your dorm or wherever, and that you slipped out this morning instead of going to church. Surely that's not as bad as the other option?'

'Oh,' she moaned, as it dawned on her that he was right. 'So what'll I do now?' she asked.

'I'll take you to your parents' home. It is in Dublin, just say it is in Dublin . . .'

She nodded. 'It is in Dublin, it's round the corner on Shelbourne Road.'

'Right, I'll take you home. We'll say that we met for a walk and that you didn't feel well, so I brought you home. What's the worst they can do?' he asked.

'They'll bring me back to the convent, I'll have to face The Raven. I've had it,' she said. 'I'll never be let out again.'

'Better than expulsion?' he asked.

She grimaced. 'Probably.'

That of course was questionable.

And the Raven, never flitting, still is sitting, still is sitting
Hanging like a crucifix above my door
And our eyes bewitched, by a demon who is dreaming
And the lamplight o'er him streaming throws his shadow on our floor
And our souls from out that shadow shall be lifted shall be lifted
                              Quoth the girls, 'For ever more.'

Chapter Twelve

Three years later, sitting on Front Steps in Trinity College, soaking up pre-exam sun, Kitty O'Dowd started to laugh. 'Remember that day after Andrew's party ... the Sunday. Do you remember?'

'It wasn't funny then,' Bernadette O'Higgins said.

Treasa O'Donoghue said, 'And it isn't funny now. Sorry, guys, I still can't laugh about it. It seemed to go downhill from then on.'

Christopher Marlowe had borrowed Andrew MacDonald's car to drive Bernadette O'Higgins home. He intended to be back before Andrew discovered the car was gone, at which point he had every intention of telling Andrew what he had done. There had been no criminal intention in mind at all. Firstly he had thought the Jaguar belonged to Andrew, not his parents, and secondly it was only a question of half an hour.

On arriving at Bernadette's house, which was easily within walking distance but speed had seemed of the essence at the time, they discovered to Bernadette's relief that her parents were away.

'They've gone away for the weekend,' she said. 'I forgot.'

She got the key from under the stone in one of the garden pots and opened the front door. Now what? she wondered.

'Does this let you off the hook?' he asked. 'I mean you can say that when you left school to go to church you were feeling ill and so you took the bus home to be with your parents and then discovered they had gone away.'

'I need to think,' Bernadette said.

Salvation seemed closer to hand now than before.

'I have a spare uniform upstairs. It wasn't back from the dry cleaners when I left last weekend, and Mum said she'd drop it in to me next week.

181

Let me check that it's back.' She ran up the stairs to her room. There was no sign of the missing tunic.

'Oh bother,' she called. 'She's forgotten to collect it.'

'Would she have put it in your room?' he asked. 'Isn't there anywhere else, if she was planning on dropping it in to you in school?'

A search revealed the missing items hanging in the hall cupboard, complete with two new blouses.

'Oh, lucky day,' said Bernadette as certain fears flittered away. 'Can you drive me back into school?' she asked.

Indeed he could. And indeed he did.

'You missed Mass.' Sister Rodriguez was in the hall when Bernadette slipped in through the doors.

'Yes, Sister. I'm sorry,' she apologised. 'I took ill and I never caught up with the others.'

'What's wrong?' asked Sister Rodriguez icily.

'Bad period,' she said. Menstruation was not mentioned in front of the nuns and it seemed like a safe response to discontinue further conversation. Now that she was back in school she felt like keeling over as the events of the last hour and a half (not to mention the previous night) caught up with her.

'So where have you been?' Sister Rodriguez inquired.

'I felt so awful that I just wanted to be with my mum,' Bernadette said, putting as much misery into her voice as possible. 'And I got the bus in the direction of home, and then halfway there I remembered that my parents were away for the weekend, so I got off and waited for a bus back.'

Sister Rodriguez eyed her. There was no doubt that her face was pale, the pupils of her eyes were tiny, and she looked exhausted.

'Bernadette O'Higgins, we can't have girls just deciding to come and go at will. You've broken the rules, and that is something we just don't tolerate. You're housebound for the rest of today, and tomorrow at first break you will report to Mother Immaculata's office.'

Andrew MacDonald, rising again at midday (from his bed, that is), wandered to the front of the house and looked out onto Lansdowne Road. The absence of the Jaguar was immediately noticeable. He reported it to the police and went back to bed, to rise again on top of Kitty O'Dowd.

The police, despite, or maybe because of, their lack of modern technology, commented immediately on the fact that this was the second embassy-connected crime within three hours. Their surprise was immense when they picked up Christopher Marlowe in the stolen British Jaguar less than twenty minutes later as he was about to return it to the MacDonalds' address.

'Two for the price of one,' said Chief Inspector Foley to his men, referring to the fact that in finding the stolen car, they had also found the 'kidnapped' youth.

'A fair cop!' murmured a subordinate.

'I will never forget walking in the front door of school and seeing Rodriguez standing in the hall with that "I've got you now" look on her face,' reminisced Bernadette O'Higgins leaning back on her elbows on Front Steps three years later.

'Look, there are the Downey twins,' she said to Kitty O'Dowd who had not seen the twins in over a year and had recently asked after them. 'They used to be OK in school,' she continued. 'But now . . .' She did not bother to finish the sentence.

The Downey twins teetered across the cobblestones on incredibly high platform sandals and, on spotting their three former classmates lounging on the steps, did an about turn and headed for the library.

'That has to be a first!' Treasa laughed. 'A new way to get the student to study – let them see us.'

'What's got into them?' asked Kitty O'Dowd with surprise. 'They used to cover for us all.'

'Sex,' Treasa and Bernadette said simultaneously.

'Oh, have they got boyfriends?' asked Kitty. 'Can't imagine them ever being apart, though.'

Treasa laughed. 'Clever Kitty. They have *one* boyfriend. They share him.'

'Every man's dream, I suppose,' said Kitty.

'He looks very tired,' Bernadette said with a giggle. 'Very, very tired!'

On that infamous Sunday in 1972, Christopher Marlowe phoned his father in London.

'Hey, Dad,' he began. 'Mom shot a policeman.' It seemed a good way to get his father's attention, which in itself was an achievement. It also served to focus his father on his mother's misdeeds rather than on the fact that he had been briefly arrested for car theft, and then accused of wasting police time, apparently because he had *not* been kidnapped. The embassy did not appear to be too pleased with him either.

Andrew MacDonald had withdrawn his car theft complaint and had apologised sincerely to the gardai for taking up their time. Christopher Marlowe, on handing the car keys back to him prior to being driven home to face the chaos that his mother had caused, had murmured to Andrew, 'You better clear the drawing room.'

It was fortunate for Andrew that Christopher said this, because otherwise Andrew would never have bothered to go in there and would not have found the cut-glass ashtray complete with the five roaches; but the British Embassy de-bugging unit would have on the Monday morning when they came to do their three-monthly check-up.

Christopher Marlowe arrived home to find seven embassy personnel there, including the Ambassador, and several members of the Irish police force, and a doctor. His mother was lying on a red velvet chaise longue having tiny shards of crystal glass tweezered out of her arms by the doctor, having refused point blank to go in the ambulance to the hospital with the garda whom she had shot. The police thought she just did not want to go to hospital, not realising that she could not bear to be in any proximity to her unfortunate protector. The Ambassador, who had arrived just before Christopher, took him aside, suggesting that he phone his father. Christopher politely suggested to the Ambassador that he might prefer to make the call.

'No, son. If your father hears your voice he'll know that at least you are all right. If I call, it'll put the wind up him.'

So Christopher was forced to make the call. His father's intake of breath on hearing that his wife had actually shot someone startled Christopher at first, but then reassured him that there was little further he could say that would unnerve his old man.

'She seemed to think I had been kidnapped,' he continued. 'But I wasn't,' he added.

'Give me the Ambassador,' his father said.

The wheels of protocol, even for such bizarre situations, were already grinding into motion.

'Don't worry,' the Ambassador said. 'Diplomatic immunity. I'd be more concerned about that lovely chandelier you used have in your hall. Even as we talk the doctor is picking pieces of it out of your wife.'

Christopher Marlowe, standing behind the Ambassador during this conversation marvelled at the priorities of the adult male, and wished they would all push off because he was terribly hungry.

Treasa O'Donoghue, on that ghastly morning, tottered out of the church feeling like her head was going to explode. The combination of a hangover and the as yet unrecognised onset of a chest infection was more than she could handle. Kitty O'Dowd's tunic belt was folded in her pocket because she could not afford to put it round her waist as the uniform would then be some ten inches above her knees. She was wearing Kitty's blazer which was way too tight on her, and she was trying to slouch along, keeping her knees bent, so that the nuns would not notice her state of dress. Downeytwo walked behind her to assist in the deception, and Downeyone in front. They made it back to the school and up to the dorm, where Treasa undressed and then collapsed on the bed without remembering to tell anyone that Kitty's uniform needed to be got out to the bushes in Sutherland Square before seven that evening.

Downeyone smelled alcohol on Treasa's breath and she and Downeytwo half carried, half dragged Treasa to the bathrooms and made her clean her teeth and gargle repeatedly with glasses of toothpaste mixed with water. In her semi-conscious state, Treasa drank the glass of toothpaste water. Unknown to the girls this was an old army trick for raising one's temperature so that one could avoid midnight patrol or some other equally awful assignment, and it had the effect of raising Treasa's temperature, which may or may not have been a bad thing. It could even be argued that this saved her life because when Sister Rodriguez went looking for her at lunchtime and found her lying on her bed, she put her hand on Treasa's forehead and was startled at the heat thereon. Treasa was transferred to sickbay, and the following morning when the doctor was eventually called her temperature was so high that it was too dangerous to bring her to hospital.

Treasa, hallucinating and with a high temperature, addressed Sister Rodriguez as Beelzebub and Sister Sick as Lucifer. Neither was amused.

Her temperature subsided in less than twelve hours.

'I remember,' Kitty said, 'arriving in Sutherland Square with Andrew, and going to look in the bushes for my uniform. And it wasn't there.' She smiled. At that moment, three years earlier, she suddenly did not care, not at all. It was Andrew who was bothered. He had been fussing around her all afternoon, having been very laid back earlier. It had puzzled her then; it puzzled her now, thinking about it.

'I wonder,' she said to Treasa and Bernadette as they lolled on Front Steps, 'if we hadn't gone to that party how it would all have turned out. I mean, what would have been different.'

Treasa said with a laugh, 'You're forgetting predestination, or rather the lack of it. As the nuns would have it, we had choice but it was all already written in God's plan.'

'Load of cobblers,' said Bernadette. 'Choice but no choice. They chose to keep us penned up like that. They chose to use the strap on us. They chose to keep us ignorant about the things that count. It's a wonder any of us made it through sane.'

Kitty laughed. 'You're presupposing any of us did make it through sane,' she said.

'Well, we survived,' Treasa replied.

But at what cost? thought Bernadette to herself. 'I sometimes wonder,' she said. 'I mean I survived, but did we all? And Mary Oliver,' she continued. 'God, that wasn't even her name. It was Olivier. We let the nuns change her identity because they didn't like the French sound, or whatever it was they objected to.'

'I think it was the fact that her parents were separated that they objected to,' Treasa said. 'As bad as being illegitimate. Poor Mary.' They were all silent as they thought back to that dreadful Sunday.

Mary Oliver had slept in the spare bed in the spare bedroom in Anna McBride's house. Bridie's father, a lawyer, who had collected them from the MacDonalds' household the previous evening, had identified immediately that Mary was under the influence of alcohol. After Bridie had got Mary Oliver to bed, she had been called down to his study where he had lamented at her behaviour, at the friends she kept and the fact that Mary Oliver, inebriated, was asleep in his house. Bridie begged him to give her a chance. She kept saying that it was so out of character for Mary to have taken a drink and that maybe the drinks were spiked.

'And so how come you didn't get drunk?' he asked. Then taking a closer look at her he said, 'Did you take a drink?'

'No, Daddy,' she lied. 'I think some of the drinks were spiked and I wouldn't . . . you know . . .'

'I'll have to report Mary Oliver to the school,' he said. 'I'm responsible for her while she is staying here. And if it were you,' he added, 'I'd want to know.'

Bridie begged. Bridie pleaded. 'Mary's been ill. She had a bad week, Daddy. It wasn't her fault what happened this evening.'

Eventually he let her go to bed. She was unsure how things had been left and could only hope that he would take a different attitude in the morning. She knew better than to ask her mother to intervene. In bed she let Jean Jacques take her in his arms and hold her against his chest. She fell asleep to the regular beat of his heart – a more human heart than any she had yet encountered in her real life.

In the spare bedroom just across the landing, Mary Oliver, having masturbated, but not to orgasm (that would take her another ten and a half years), was now sleeping peacefully.

> *I try to come before I sleep*
> *And pray to God my soul to keep . . .*

On Front Steps, three years later, Kitty O'Dowd said, to no one in particular, 'I lost my virginity that night.'

'I often wondered,' said Treasa. 'You know, it was days before I recovered properly and then I was sent home for a week to recuperate and by that stage everything had blown up, but when I next saw you, you were different. And I wondered.'

'You always noticed everything, Treasa, didn't you?' Bernadette said. 'I remember you telling us that the nuns whipped themselves. And when I said I didn't believe you, you said you'd seen them. You'd have made a great spy. You knew what was going on. They did whip themselves, didn't they?' she added.

'Of course they did,' Kitty said. 'They were putting in practice.'

'I told Rodriguez I had my period that day,' Bernadette said, seated on Front Steps with the sun on her face, 'in an effort to avoid running the gauntlet. She sort of fell for it, but I said I hadn't actually got home, that I had remembered on the way that my parents were away. Such a silly mistake, because of course when The Raven spoke to my mother and my mother said that I had taken my dry-cleaned uniform from the hall cupboard, it all started to unravel.' She shuddered.

'Kitty, were you looking for trouble?' Treasa suddenly asked.

'Dunno,' said Kitty. 'Why do you ask?'

Treasa was silent for a little. 'I think I'm asking because you were home and dry that day. You were the only one of us who had got away with it and then you blew it, almost as if you wanted to.'

'It certainly reduced the heat on the rest of us,' Bernadette said, 'for which I, for one, am truly grateful.'

Kitty shrugged, that old shrug they knew so well. Back then it had meant, 'I've nothing more to say and I don't care.' It meant more or less the same now.

Andrew MacDonald had brought the car down the lane behind the school gardens, where he had assisted Kitty to climb up the wall. On her knees she had crawled along the top of the wall as far as the oak tree, and then she was over and down.

'See you next Saturday?' he had asked as they left his home in Lansdowne Road. 'We'll go to Zhivago's.'

'OK,' she said. 'If I can get a pass, that is.'

'Well, just make sure you do,' he said. 'May I phone you during the week?'

'Better not,' she said. 'The nuns don't like boys unless they're underage altar boys, priests or prospective priests.'

'Well, will you call me?' he asked.

'OK,' she said.

He leaned over to kiss her. She smiled at him. He was very direct.

Mary Oliver woke in the spare bed in the McBrides' spare bedroom. She felt well. From having been so tense, not just for the duration of the previous week but for years and years, she had this strange sense of release. She got out of bed and stood in front of the window looking down on the McBrides' swimming pool. She wondered if they would mind if she went for a swim, but she had no swimsuit. (It would be eighteen months more before she swam nude off a Greek island and then lay naked on her back to dry off and soak up the sun.)

Bridie came into the room. They greeted each other. Mary with pleasure at feeling alive, Bridie with trepidation at what she had to tell her friend.

'Could we go for a swim?' Mary asked.

Bridie hesitated. If her father saw Mary in a hale and hearty state doing lengths in the family pool he might relent, on the other hand he might get annoyed that she could be so carefree after what he seemed to think was a night of debauchery.

'Good idea,' Bridie said, putting off the dreaded moment. 'The parents are taking us to eleven o'clock Mass, so we've plenty of time.'

'I hardly remember coming here,' Mary Oliver said as she bobbed up and down the pool, wearing one of Bridie's swimsuits. The black nylon was stretched tight on her, cutting into her shoulders and her bottom, but it seemed to be loose at the waist, as if she was not filling it in the right places.

'This is brilliant,' she said. 'You are lucky.'

It was said without envy, just as a statement of fact, and Bridie acknowledged it with a nod. She did not feel lucky, not at that moment anyway. There was something not quite right with living in such a mansion, being so very isolated because her parents felt that none of the local children were good enough company for her. And her loneliness . . . it was something she never acknowledged even to herself, but she was lonely. She had peppered her childhood with imaginary friends who would talk to her and play games with her, and hold her hand at night in bed. And even now, her closest friend was an imaginary man who minded her and cared for her and brought her more comfort than any living human being.

'Lucky?' she asked Jean Jacques Versailles. 'Would you call me lucky?'

'*Oui, ma petite,*' replied the gallant Frenchman. '*Tu as la bonne chance.* You received your reprieve from ze King of France, you have been released from *la prison.* Ze people of France have let you walk from *la cellule. Oui.* You have ze luck.' Jean Jacques Versailles' accent had become more pronounced overnight.

'Mary,' she said carefully. 'I hate telling you this, but Daddy noticed the state you were in last night coming back here, and he said he was going to the school to inform the nuns.'

Mary turned her horrified face to Bridie. 'Oh, no,' she said. 'Oh, please no. I didn't have any alcohol, I really didn't. It was the juice. I wouldn't take any . . .'

Bridie whispered, 'Just swim. They're watching us out of the dining-room window.'

And the two of them swam up and down side by side.

'What'll I do?' Mary said. 'I'll be expelled,' she moaned.

Bridie turned to Jean Jacques Versailles.

'She'll have to throw herself on their mercy,' he advised.

'Whose mercy?' inquired Bridie. 'My parents or the sisters?'

'First your parents. Start there.' He smiled at her. 'It'll be all right. Just give her support. She didn't really do anything wrong, did she?'

'What'll I do?' Mary said. 'I didn't drink. Only juice. Honestly.'

When she said that later to Mr McBride, he shook his head. 'I'm inclined to believe you,' he said, 'but the fact is that you were under the influence of alcohol, and the sisters have a right to know what kind of party their girls were attending.'

'But, please,' she begged, her face white and scared.

'I'm sorry,' he said. 'I have a duty to the good sisters. Why, if you were my daughter, I'd want to know. And if you were drinking and didn't know it, the onus is on the family who owns the house and the matter will need to be brought back to them.'

Mary shuddered.

'You were due back into the convent for seven this evening,' he said to

190

his daughter and her friend. 'I'll have you back for five so that I have time to talk to Mother Immaculata. I don't want to be disturbing her in the evening. Enough said now. Time for church.'

'Bridie's dad was a shit for shopping Mary,' Kitty said as she lay back on Front Steps that early summer day three years later.

Bernadette shrugged. 'There's no one quite so hypocritical as a church-going Christian doing his duty.'

'It's funny though, isn't it,' said Treasa O'Donoghue, 'how people justify what they do. He probably really thought it was the right thing to do.'

'Well, it was liberating in a way, wasn't it?' Kitty said.

After he had brought them back to school, Bridie's father was stuck in the study with The Raven for nearly an hour, while Bridie and Mary hovered miserably at the end of the corridor. After he left, both girls were called into the study.

'Well, girls, were you drinking?' asked Mother Immaculata.

By mutual and well-planned agreement, Bridie said no, but that they suspected in hindsight that the drinks might have been spiked.

'And you, Mary Oliver?' asked Mother Immaculata.

'I wasn't aware of having a drink, Mother,' said Mary Oliver, pale-faced and fidgeting. 'I had two glasses of orange juice.'

'But Anna McBride's father says you were inebriated when he brought you home last night.'

Mary blushed and chewed her bottom lip. 'It wasn't deliberate, Mother,' she said, miserably.

'I want the name and address of the house where you attended this . . . party.' She virtually spat out the word party.

'I thought Daddy would have given you the address,' Bridie said quickly before Mary could answer.

'He gave me the address, but he has forgotten to give me the family name,' replied The Raven (as she sharpened her blade) and waved a piece of paper in front of Bridie's nose.

'O'Driscoll,' Bridie said quickly, reaching for the piece of paper. 'Yes, that's the right number on Lansdowne Road.'

Mary Oliver said nothing. She didn't think 'O'Driscoll' sounded right but she kept mum.

'Mary Oliver,' said The Raven, the blade of her knife sharpened and ready for serious gutting, 'you are due in to see me tomorrow morning for writing a letter during Retreat. I will deal with this matter at the same time. Anna McBride, watch your step. You may both leave now.'

Both girls left the study with downcast eyes.

'Why did you say O'Driscoll?' Mary Oliver asked.

'Because she's a cow and I hate her. It's enough that you and I are in trouble, but to drag Andrew MacDonald into it too, that stinks,' Bridie said, for once not asking Jean Jacques Versailles for his opinion.

That evening Mother Immaculata wrote a letter to a Mr and Mrs O'Driscoll, which was posted the following day. Dublin post being what it was in the seventies, the letter did not arrive until the following Friday. Bridie, by this stage, had filled in Kitty O'Dowd, and she in turn had phoned Andrew MacDonald. The post arrived late morning on Friday, and Andrew, who had taken both the Thursday and the Friday off school while he waited for the letter, was in the hall when the mail dropped through the letterbox. He sorted his parents' post on the letter table, popped Mother Immaculata's letter to Mr and Mrs O'Driscoll under his sweater, and headed for his room. He thought of keeping the letter as an example of self-righteous piety.

He thought of replying to it. *Dear Mother Superior*, he contemplated. *It was with the greatest sadness that my wife and I received your letter this morning. Rest assured that our son will spend the weekend in church praying for forgiveness for his sins.* No, he thought, better to take a rise out of the old bat.

Dear Mother Immaculata, my wife and I have received your letter and are truly shocked that our son supplied only vodka at this party. We hoped that we had brought him up better than that, and that there would have been a full bar on offer – whisky, gin, bourbon, wine. You name it, it should have been there. Please rest assured that in future his parties will be better stocked.

In due course he tore Mother Immaculata's letter up and burned it in the empty grate in his bedroom. He knew he would give Kitty a laugh with his proposed replies.

'Andrew thought about writing back to The Raven,' Kitty said that summer's day on Front Steps.

'But pragmatism won out,' Andrew said. They all spun round.

'How long were you there?' Treasa asked.

'Only just arrived,' he said. 'I'd hardly have known you, Kitty O'Dowd,' he added and leaned over to give her a hug.

'Long time,' she said.

They were both smiling.

'You never replied to my letters or my calls,' he said, still smiling at her.

She shrugged. That shrug that said, 'Don't know, don't care'.

'We've been doing memory lane,' Treasa said. 'Your party, Andrew.'

'And the Retreat,' Bernadette added.

'You were canon fodder,' Andrew MacDonald joked. 'Every last one of you.'

'We were arguing earlier,' Kitty said, 'about whether we survived or not.'

'Survived?' He laughed. 'It will be years before you begin to recover.'

'Still smug, I see,' said Kitty.

He laughed again. 'You always said I had it all, being Scottish and Presbyterian and abroad. I'm only beginning to dump some of the guilt that I was brought up with. You should hear our family,' he added. 'You said this!' He imitated his father's accent. 'But Dad, that was in nineteen sixty-two!'

'You trying to say you're as screwed up as we are?' Bernadette asked.

'No,' he said. 'That wouldn't be possible.'

They were joking then, teasing each other. It was twenty-five years later before they all realised the truth of these comments.

'Where's Mary Oliver?' Kitty asked, glancing around Front Square.

'She's in someone's rooms in Botany Bay,' Treasa said. 'Making up for lost time.'

They all laughed.

'She'll be along shortly. Bridie too,' Treasa added.

'What are you all up to?' Andrew MacDonald asked.

'We're having a school reunion lunch,' Bernadette said. 'Just the five of us.'

'Sounds like you're not inviting me,' he sulked, but his eyes were laughing.

'There's Mary,' Treasa said, as Mary appeared round the corner, her dark brown hair tied back, her sallow skin pale after the lack of winter sun but with a post-sexual activity flush on her high cheekbones.

'Am I late?' she asked as she greeted them all. Her baggy shirt hid her protruding hipbones, but her once hollowed stomach was now flat and she looked healthier. She had stopped sticking her fingers down her throat, except in the run-up to exams and the occasional times when someone asked her what school she had attended, and she threw up the memories together with the previous meal.

Bridie appeared on her bicycle, red hair flying, clattering across the cobblestones, having cycled down from UCD where she was reading history.

'What possessed me to go to UCD and not to Trinity?' she asked.

'Your father,' Treasa said.

'And The bleeding Raven,' added Kitty.

'I swear,' said Bridie, 'I'm going to do my Masters here. I miss you guys. And Kitty,' she said as she spotted Kitty O'Dowd sitting on the steps. 'Great to see you.'

As they were leaving, Andrew took Kitty aside. 'Free to come over to my rooms later?' he asked.

'Not really,' she said. 'I have to get back home.'

'I don't know what you're up to or anything,' he said.

She grinned.

'No, I mean it,' he continued. 'Are you free on Friday or Saturday?'

'I might be,' she said. 'Give me a buzz.'

'Still at the hotel?' he asked.

'Yes.' She looked puzzled. 'Where else would I be?'

Andrew MacDonald asked Treasa O'Donoghue later in the day what Kitty O'Dowd had meant.

'Oh, you never heard?' Treasa said. 'You remember she had two older brothers and they both went to the States. Well, they never came back. Kitty's father died last year of a heart attack, and Kitty just moved back in with her mum and took over the hotel. She's making a success of it too, by all accounts.'

'I didn't know,' he said. 'I had no idea.'

'She lives in hope that The Raven or Sister Rodriguez will come in for a drink. She says she would like to put rat poison in their glasses.'

'That'd be too quick,' he said.

'That's exactly what she said.'

Chapter Thirteen

First break on the Monday morning following the Retreat saw a queue of woeful girls sitting on the bench outside Mother Immaculata's door. Treasa O'Donoghue was in sickbay, her temperature rising by the minute but the severity of her illness not yet recognised. Kitty O'Dowd was out on the roof between the chimney stacks having a quick smoke. The sun was shining.

Nearly sunbathing time, she thought to herself between puffs, bringing up memories of the previous summer and herself and Treasa and sometimes Bernadette O'Higgins climbing up through the attic storage rooms, which is what she had just done, and out through the skylight having precariously balanced six or seven suitcases on top of each other. Then, nimbly, the girls clambered across the tiles and between the chimney pots where the slant of the roof eased a little, and there they undressed to their bras and knickers and lay back on the hot tiles to soak up the sun. They always rigged the door into the attic by piling several more cases over it, so that if some snooping nun decided to ascend, the falling cases would give them warning. What they would then do was never quite clear, but up until now the situation had not arisen.

Kitty grinned as she recalled Bernadette saying, 'Then what? Do we dance off across the rooftops like refugees from *Mary Poppins* singing "Chimchiminee"?'

She stubbed out her cigarette and instead of letting it roll into the gutter, which is what she usually did, she flicked it upwards towards the chimney pots.

'Jayzus, I should have played basketball,' she said in wonder as the fag end flipped twice and fell straight down one of the chimneys.

The cigarette butt had a clear fall right down the chimney in question and landed neatly in Mother Immaculata's cleaned out grate. Bernadette O'Higgins, standing contritely while trying not to shuffle from one foot to the other, facing The Raven's desk, saw it land in the grate. She knew immediately what it was and guessed that Kitty O'Dowd was up on the roof. She grinned.

'Take that smirk off your face, my girl,' said The Raven.

Bernadette promptly did. It had been a bad move on her part to grin, because, until that moment, The Raven had been about to abandon her line of inquiry as to why Bernadette had left the school the previous morning and not turned up in church.

'Sister Rodriguez is right,' said Mother Immaculata. 'It is totally unacceptable to have one of our girls just deciding to take off and visit her parents.'

'But I wasn't feeling well,' said Bernadette.

'And then to smirk about it – absolutely unacceptable.'

'I wasn't smirking, Mother,' said Bernadette miserably as the interview started to fall apart.

'You will do detention every afternoon this week.'

'Yes, Mother,' sighed Bernadette.

The Raven wrote a note to herself to phone Bernadette's mother and to update her as she didn't want any complaints later about the fact that Bernadette had just walked out of school and headed in the direction of home.

It was later that day, the interview long over and Bernadette sitting (bored stiff and writing lines) in detention for two hours, that Mother Immaculata dialled the O'Higgins' home.

'Mrs O'Higgins?' she asked when Bernadette's mother answered. 'Mother Immaculata here at St Martin's.' There followed several minutes of polite comments before Mother Immaculata asked, 'You were away for the weekend, Mrs O'Higgins?'

And Bernadette's mother, with no inkling of there being a problem, said, 'Yes, indeed, and I'm very glad that Bernadette dropped home and took her uniform. I was going to bring it in this week. It was just late coming back from the dry-cleaners . . .' And with every word, unwittingly, she tightened the noose on Bernadette's young and swan-like neck.

The Raven fingered her strap which was lying across the top of her desk.

Until then it had not been the worst day. Kitty O'Dowd had had her smoke up among the chimneys, and was amused to hear from Bernadette that the butt had ended up unnoticed in Mother Immaculata's grate. She decided to pull a stunt during the next class after break. It was partially designed to cheer Bernadette up, because Bernadette was moaning about the boredom of a week's worth of detention after a week of Retreat, but it was mostly designed to amuse herself.

Many of the rooms in the school buildings had interconnecting folding doors between them, and these were draped with old and very dusty brown curtains on either side of the doors to reduce the noise level between the different classes. After first break, when the girls returned to their classroom, Kitty O'Dowd went up to the front and with a wink at Bernadette O'Higgins she slipped between the dusty brown curtains and concealed herself behind them. Bernadette smiled as she took her place, and the Downey twins looked at each other and shared an impassive grin of delight.

In walked Miss Ní Ghrian (no sun shining out of her today). She stood at the top of the room and recited the pre-class prayer, before sitting and calling the roll. Down the names she went with her mind on something else, and when she called Kitty O'Dowd's name, Bernadette responded with a 'Here' and Kitty's name was duly ticked.

The class commenced. They were reading Peig Sayers.

The class was of forty minutes' duration, and everything was going fine until unfortunately, ten minutes before the end, Kitty O'Dowd, standing behind the brown curtains, sneezed.

There was silence as Miss Ní Ghrian looked over to where the sneeze appeared to have emanated from and immediately several girls in the class sneezed in an effort to distract her.

There was no distracting her. Up she got and over she went to the curtains, a puzzled look on her thin face. Kitty O'Dowd, behind the curtain, blinded by the thickness of the material, was doing all she

199

could not to sneeze again, with no idea that Grinny was approaching.

With one hand Miss Ní Ghrian swept the curtain back to reveal Kitty leaning against the folding doors with her face screwed up tightly, and at that moment Kitty sneezed again.

It is difficult to know who got the bigger fright, Miss Ní Ghrian or Kitty. Both leapt into the air with a shriek.

Mary Oliver, watching this farce, started to giggle out loud. (The rest of the class was suppressing their laughter as Miss Ní Ghrian had gone beetroot red in the face and looked as if she was about to have a fit.) Mary Oliver had been having another of those days when she was not quite sure what was happening, but she had started to get the feeling that everything was falling into place. Without any doubt Saturday night at the party had been some sort of turning point, and it was with joy that she thought of it, of dancing, of being held in someone's arms, of being kissed, of being wanted. The boy in question was not important – she knew that.

Her mind was busy assessing what it was that was important, because up until now being a good daughter had been up there at the top of her list. Being a good pupil and pursuing her religious interests – school, home, religion – these had been the facets of her life, but over the last week they had fallen apart and lost their meaning.

Mary Oliver was not at all sure what was left.

Sitting there in the classroom watching Grinny lose it with Kitty O'Dowd, she laughed and laughed until she fell off her seat onto the floor.

In Mother Immaculata's office earlier that morning Mary Oliver had had to face the combined forces of The Raven and Sister Rodriguez. She was in trouble both for getting drunk on Saturday night and for writing a letter during the Retreat, and it occurred to her as she rolled on the floor laughing that the line the nuns had taken was puzzling. First of all they had seemed to have no interest in knowing that she had not deliberately taken a drink; just the fact that she had had a drink seemed to make her a drunken sot in their eyes. 'You who took the pledge at your confirmation never to let a sip of alcohol pass your lips, Mary Oliver.'

Secondly they had no shame in reading her letter, and this seemed to her now to be an act of extreme intrusion.

'Why do you not want your sister to come here next year?' asked The Raven.

And what could she answer, she who was so well brought up, and not encouraged ever to speak up for herself? She shuffled on her chair and went, 'Er, umm.' Little sisters need to be protected, she thought. But these were not thoughts to be shared. Protected from the likes of you, her brain said, startling her with the clarity and force of the thought, but her polite impassivity prevailed.

'I'm not sure, Mother Immaculata,' she replied.

'You had not mentioned to us that you are interested in joining the order,' continued Mother Immaculata. 'And behaviour like we have seen from you this weekend would not ever be acceptable behaviour from a novice.'

Mary did not point out that as a novice she would hardly be at a party where such behaviour might take place. Nor did she point out that so much water had flown under her bridge in the course of the past seven days that in many ways she was quite a different person to the one who had written that letter the previous Tuesday night. There were so many things to think about and Mother Immaculata droned on and on about behaviour, and expectations, and suddenly Mary Oliver got the distinct impression that they were discussing her future.

Mathematics in UCD. For the life of her she could not see how they could have reached such a conclusion.

'I'm not a good maths student, Mother,' she ventured.

'But you could be,' Mother Immaculata replied.

She tried again. 'My maths marks aren't good, Mother.'

'That doesn't matter,' replied The Raven. 'If you want to study maths, maths you will study.'

Mary Oliver, looking at her, wondered if perhaps in the hallucinatory state she seemed to be almost permanently in, she might have announced her intention to study maths and not be able to remember it.

'I'm not sure if I was actually planning on going to university,' Mary Oliver said hesitantly.

'With your brains and ambition,' The Raven replied, 'university is essential. A good degree under your belt will do you no harm.'

'We can change your application form,' Sister Rodriguez said.

'I, er, um, don't actually think . . . er . . . that I've applied for university,' Mary Oliver said nervously, as she got this horrible feeling that any minute now she would wake up and find herself sitting in a lecture theatre listening to maths, of all things. Meek, demure, sitting before the nuns with her hands on her knees, Mary Oliver found it impossible to say, 'No. Don't do this to me. Of all the subjects in all the world, not maths.'

'I'll get you an application form,' Sister Rodriguez said, 'and you can fill it in and send it off. Come to my study, this afternoon after class, and you can do it then.'

'Yes, Sister,' Mary replied meekly. It was like having a stranglehold put on her.

'In the meantime,' Mother Immaculata said, 'you will do detention this afternoon. And lines. Yes, lines. And while you're doing them, think carefully about the desecration of alcohol and how you must not have it in your life. And you are not getting off so lightly, my girl,' she continued. 'On Wednesday afternoon Father McMorrow is coming in for a post-Retreat chat, and I will line up a special interview for you with him and you can talk about your vocation.'

Mary Oliver froze.

Miss Ní Ghrian hauled Kitty O'Dowd out in front of the class. Kitty could not stop sneezing. Mary Oliver could not stop laughing. Grinny turned on Mary Oliver and yelled at her to get up off the floor and to get out of the classroom. Mary Oliver, recalled to her senses by the fury in the teacher's voice, stopped laughing and apologised.

'I'm sorry,' she muttered as she got back to her feet.

What had seemed hilarious a moment ago now had no meaning for her. She stood for a moment looking at the irate Irish teacher, and then she headed for the door. There was an atmosphere of amazement inside the classroom. Firstly Mary Oliver had never been in trouble in school until the previous week when she had been caught writing the letter. Now she had been 'sent out', and added to that Kitty O'Dowd was being mauled by Miss Ní Ghrian.

Outside the door, Mary Oliver stood looking up and down the corridor and wondering if there was somewhere she could hide out. She felt she had been in enough trouble already and to be caught by The Raven outside the door was something she could not countenance.

Her luck held up for the time being as it was Miss Maple who came along the corridor.

'Were you put out?' she asked the blushing Mary Oliver, who nodded in embarrassment.

'Whatever for?'

'For laughing, Miss Maple.'

The Maple laughed. 'I can think of worse crimes,' she said as she strode on down the corridor.

Inside the classroom, Miss Ní Ghrian was beginning to piece together events.

'Were you behind that curtain right from the start?' she asked Kitty O'Dowd whom she was still holding by one arm. Kitty just sort of grunted because she could see where this was heading.

'So,' said the detective, 'who answered your name when I called roll?'

'I answered,' Kitty said with determination, and Bernadette heaved a sigh of relief.

'Right,' said Miss Ní Ghrian, abandoning her class and dragging Kitty after her. 'You're for Mother Immaculata's office.'

And so it was that Kitty O'Dowd joined Mary Oliver and Bernadette O'Higgins that afternoon in detention. With sore and aching hands, Kitty wrote, 'I must not play the fool in class,' five hundred times, while Mary Oliver wrote, 'I must not imbibe alcohol nor must I laugh,' and Bernadette O'Higgins, unaware that her mother was assisting in hanging her, wrote, 'I must not leave school without permission.'

The wheels of fate are grinding and interlocking, and one by one, like tenpin bowls, these girls are being bowled over.

When Mary Oliver turned up in Sister Rodriguez's study to fill in the form for her maths application, Sister Rodriguez was in a hurry and she sorted through a variety of forms before pulling out the one for Mary.

'Here is one for UCD,' she said. She signed it and gave it to Mary to fill in, telling her to take an envelope from the pile on the side table and giving her a stamp.

'Get that into the post this afternoon,' she said to Mary who nodded forlornly as Sister Rodriguez headed out of the study.

Mary sat down and looked at the signed form. She sighed and grimaced. She kept looking at the form and then at the floor, and a feeling of despair washed over her. Suddenly she decided to look at the other forms on the desk.

There were application forms for Trinity among them. She picked one up. She felt as if she was a different person as she read down the page. Then she carefully filled it in, putting philosophy down as her subject choice. It'll give me more insight, she thought on a conscious level. On a subconscious level the Mary from Saturday night who had danced and sung and felt like a new person, was thinking, be your own person. You don't have to go to UCD. You don't have to do maths. You're you. Be you.

She practised Sister Rodriguez's signature over and over on the back of the first form, before entering it on the Trinity College application. She folded the form and popped it into the envelope, addressed and stamped it. She took the other form with her and shredded it when she left the school on her way to the postbox on the corner. She put the torn-up paper into the bin.

I've done it, she thought. No matter what happens to me now, I'm going to get away from them. All I have to do is get through this week, and then next week, and then just a few more, and then I'm free.

Mary Oliver was shaking when she went back into the school. She felt as if the blur which had been in her brain had momentarily cleared but now it was coming back. The walls on the corridors seemed higher than usual. The statues seemed to watch her. She ran to her dormitory and up between the rows of beds until she came to her own. She threw herself face down on top of her blankets.

'What's up?' Bernadette asked her half an hour later when she went to the dorm to get a book.

Mary Oliver looked at her. 'I can't tell you what I've done,' she whispered. 'If they find out, they'll kill me.'

Kitty came in and plonked herself on the bed beside Mary's.

'What's up?' she asked. She looked thoroughly fed up but it was clear that Mary was in a much worse state.

Mary Oliver told the pair of them what the nuns had done, and to her amazement Kitty got up off her bed and came and put her arms round her.

'Good for you,' she said.

Bernadette was grinning. 'Mary, it's probably the sanest thing you've ever done. It's perfect. Philosophy is perfect for you. You'll love it, especially in Trinity. It's taught by priests in UCD. You'd have gone bonkers.'

'But they'll find out,' Mary Oliver moaned.

'So bloody what?' said Kitty. 'You're out of here in a few weeks. The Leaving Cert. and then you're done. You need never see them again. You'll be done with this malarkey – you can be you.'

'Don't you see, Mary, they can't get you. The day you walk out of here, you're finished with it. You can start again. You'll find *you*. It won't be repressive there. That's why I'm going there, and Treasa too.'

'But they wanted me to do maths,' Mary said.

'Maths?' exclaimed Bernadette and Kitty together.

'Why on earth would they want you to do Maths?' asked Bernadette. 'That makes no sense at all.'

'They think I'm going to be a nun,' Mary said, 'and they seemed to think that I'd be a great maths teacher if I were a nun.'

'They're mad,' Kitty said. 'You struggle to do honours maths. They're up to something. Pity Treasa is ill, she'd work it out.'

Although Mary Oliver was taking comfort from what they were saying, she was scared. Old habits of obedience die hard – they die slowly.

'Are you going to be a nun?' Bernadette asked in amazement as what Mary had said sank in.

'No, no, not now. You see, I did think of it, like – I really thought about it ... but things have changed,' Mary said vaguely. 'But you know how tenacious Mother Immaculata is. She says I have to talk with one of the priests, tomorrow, I think, about my vocation.'

'Oh,' said Bernadette and Kitty together.

'Why did she fill in philosophy?' Treasa asked Kitty later. The Downey twins had distracted Sister Sick so that Kitty and Bernadette could slip silently on stockinged feet into Treasa's room in sickbay.

'I don't know,' Kitty said.

'I think it was the one thing she knew they'd hate her to do – and in Trinity too,' Bernadette contributed.

The three of them laughed. It was later that evening and Treasa had started a course of antibiotics. She turned on her side in the bed, pulling the pillow closer to her neck.

'Tell me again what you did this morning Kitty,' she said. 'Everything, from the cigarette butt going down the chimney to hiding behind the curtain.'

Having felt ghastly for nearly thirty-six hours, Treasa was suddenly feeling much better – and it wasn't the antibiotics which were doing it as they hadn't had a chance to kick in yet, it was simply sharing a laugh with the others.

Bernadette said, 'You should have seen Grinny's face, Treasa. She went purple.'

'She shook me,' Kitty said with a giggle. 'She was so angry.'

'Thanks for covering for me by saying you'd responded to your own name on the roll,' Bernadette said. 'I've been in enough trouble today. And worse to come, I think.'

Mary Oliver, getting ready for bed that night, was in the bathroom with Kitty, and she had the feeling that there was something dreadful about to happen, but she couldn't for the life of her think what it might be. There was something scary just around the corner. She put some of Kitty's toothpaste on her neck to cover the love bites in case one of the nuns saw her neck while she was getting into bed.

'It looks like he chewed your neck,' Kitty said with interest.

'It does a bit,' said Mary as she touched the purple marks and dabbed on a bit more toothpaste. 'Thank goodness the collar and tie cover them,' she added.

'Was that fun?' Kitty asked, eyeing Mary in the mirror. 'Being gnawed, I mean?'

Mary smiled. She still had not got used to the idea of what had happened on Saturday night. It was a whole new feeling, letting go, dancing, feeling her hips loosen.

'Yes,' she said to Kitty. 'Yes. I felt great. Relieved, I think.'

'You know, Mary,' Kitty said, 'I haven't seen you smile like that before. You look great when you smile.'

'Do I?' Mary smiled into the mirror. 'Thank you. It wasn't the boy,' she continued, relaxing in front of Kitty who often slightly terrified her. 'I mean . . . he wasn't important. I don't particularly want to see him again, it was just that I felt good.' She shook her head. If it didn't make sense to her, how could it make sense to Kitty?

Kitty nodded. 'I know what you mean. There are boys and there are boys. And sometimes it's just a bit of fun, a bit of a giggle, nothing more, and then sometimes you think, well, this one is a bit nicer.' Kitty was thinking about Andrew MacDonald as she came out with this.

'Kitty,' Mary asked, 'why did you pull that stunt in class this morning?'

Kitty shrugged. She didn't know the words to say why. There was too much to say. It would be years before she admitted it to herself, and more years before she would tell the others.

'It was very funny,' Mary said.

Treasa, in sickbay, rolled onto her other side. She was smiling as she thought about what Kitty had done. She would have loved to have been there. She could envisage the puffs of dust coming out of that smelly old curtain, and Kitty trying not to breathe behind it. And she thrilled with joy when she thought of Grinny's shock when she pulled the curtain back and Kitty sneezed.

She fell asleep with a grin on her face.

When you suck, use lips and tongue.
The wine is blood and coloured red
A stiff white collar wears the priest
The Holy Eucharist is just bread.

Mary Oliver woke in the night. She was sitting straight up in bed. She wondered if she had been sleepwalking again. She got out of bed and checked the soles of her feet by the light of the moon. They appeared clean and dry. She looked down the row of beds at the sleeping girls, hair spread across the pillows, different shades, different textures. She thought about Lucia asleep in London.

Lucia is a Whittaker, she thought.

These were moments of clarity and she knew it.

Uncle Anthony, taking her out for lunch the previous holidays, had asked her about St Martin's, and she had the feeling he wasn't really comfortable with her reply. She knew she was going on a bit about the religion and her ambitions, and she had tried to make herself stop because she wasn't sure if her mother had put him up to taking her out to pump her. But now, thinking back, she remembered him saying something about St Martin's, and that he would have preferred it if she had stayed in school in England, if for no other reason than he could have seen her more often. He had said that her mother had insisted on St Martin's because her real father would have wanted it, and because she wasn't a Whittaker he hadn't been able to do anything about it.

At the time she had said nothing more because she wanted to be in the religious environment. It had suited her. It had tied in with the person she thought she was, but after last week . . .

Her thoughts trailed away. She only knew that she didn't want Lucia coming here. It would be bad for Lucia.

She got back into bed, and re-started her initial thought. Lucia is a Whittaker. Maybe Uncle Anthony can pull his weight and stop her being sent here.

She had hazy recollections of a dream, but she couldn't put her finger on it. Not a dream, she thought. A nightmare. Something bad. She tried to get back to sleep but it wouldn't come. It was beyond her reach. She slowly went through what had happened in Sister Rodriguez's study. She felt reassured now that she would be gone from the school before they discovered her change of plans, and there would be nothing they could do then, as Kitty had pointed out.

Long ago, Mary Oliver had taught herself to forget. She had tried to hold on to memories of her papa and Paris and the garden where he played with her, but because of the distorted way her mother had portrayed that time, she reached a point where she did not know what was real and what was not. And one day she had just let it go. It was there somewhere deep in her mind, but it was not accessible. She had done the same thing later with other memories that did not seem real. She forgot them, pushed them deep.

She had done it with what had happened in the confessional. She had done it with the strange dream she had had the previous week.

She shivered when she thought of that dream. It was a dream, she thought. Wasn't it?

And now there was something else, but she couldn't pin it down.

Back in bed she sat with her knees pulled up in front of her and her chin resting on them as her mind moved in circles. The philosophy application was right. She knew that. She knew that the relief she now felt was about having done something that was real and that was for her. She wondered how she could have wanted to become a nun for so long and suddenly to have that 'vocation' (as she had identified it) disappear almost overnight. How could that be? she asked herself. It had been so real for so long, so definite, so tied in with all her thoughts, and her prayers. So where has it gone? she wondered. Because gone it was. She knew that somewhere in the space of the last seven days it had simply evaporated.

Then to her horror she recalled what was bothering her. Father McMorrow was going to come to talk to her about her vocation. There was something about that which was unbearable, but she couldn't remember what it was.

She slid down under the covers and held them tight at her throat. She was shivering now.

Kitty O'Dowd, in her bed, was aware of Mary Oliver's nocturnal ramblings and knew that she had got up and gone to the window and that having returned to bed she had sat upright in her bed for ages, arms wrapped round her knees, obviously deep in thought. Kitty did not want to get involved. She had enough going on in her own head. Thoughts of Andrew MacDonald and his hands caressing her, finding places that were sensitive, teasing her with his fingers. She had not known that sexual arousal could be like that. She thought of Jeremiah Jackson long ago, and the other boys since with their inquisitive gropings. Her mind wandered down through the places where she had been touched, felt, probed. She felt a sense of sadness wash over her as she thought back down the years.

Life numbs us, she thought vaguely.

Kitty O'Dowd was not given to profound thought, but what was washing through her was hurting her to her bones. She felt such an ache of sadness.

You meet boys . . . Her thoughts trailed away.

She thought of Andrew getting out of his father's Jaguar, of how he looked as he lifted the boot and glanced up at her. She thought of his height, the way he stooped slightly to lift out the booze, and in her memory his eyes were laughing as he looked up at her.

Jayz, she thought. This is a load of shite.

She thought of the girls each sleeping in their beds, and the sadness which was washing through her was replaced with anger.

Why do I feel like this? she asked herself. It's as if I'm laden with guilt, and I've done effing nothing. I hate this place. I hate the nuns, I hate the statues, I hate the guilt – the endless, relentless guilt. I hate feeling like I was born with original sin on my soul . . .

Kitty O'Dowd had had enough.

Bernadette O'Higgins was finally asleep.

Hers had been a truly awful day, and she knew there was worse to come. Tomorrow morning her parents were coming in for a 'chat' with Mother Immaculata. She was still was unsure what The Raven had found out; all she knew was that after being in detention all afternoon, Sister Rodriguez had informed her that her 'day of reckoning was nigh,' and that her parents were coming in. She kept thinking of *Scrumptious Sex* and that her parents must have found out that *The Lives of the Saints, Complete and Unabridged With Emphasis on the Virgin Martyrs* was missing from their bookshelves or, worse still, that it had been denuded of its cover. She feared that her brother might have told them of the disappearance of *Scrumptious Sex*, though her logical self told her that he wouldn't have, that it had nothing to do with that, and that it had to be something to do with the weekend. But she couldn't be sure.

When she told Kitty and Treasa her fears, Kitty had said, 'Deny everything. They have to prove it. Just stick to your story.'

Treasa had said, 'Just listen. Find out first what it is they know or think they know. Don't say anything until they've told you, and then think fast.'

But Bernadette wasn't sure. She just wished she knew what was up.

Kitty O'Dowd was drifting slowly back to sleep. The balance of her thoughts had tipped over and things were beginning to make sense. The music to 'American Pie' came to mind.

She smiled as she thought of the words and how they made her feel, 'The good old boys' . . . like Andrew and his friends . . . drinking vodka and orange . . . the beat of the music . . . Andrew MacDonald's hands caressing her . . . her virginity, like a weight bearing her down, now finally gone . . . And sleep came.

Much I marvelled this stately Raven to hear discourse so plainly
Though its answer little meaning – little relevancy bore
For we cannot help agreeing that no living human being
Should be blessed with entrance through this latticed door
No child should ever enter through this or any latticed door
                    Quoth the Raven, 'Nevermore.'

Chapter Fourteen

When Kitty O'Dowd got up that Tuesday morning after the Retreat, if there were thoughts left over from the previous day, they were muted. She went through the routine of early morning preparations, of pulling up her bedclothes, tidying her cubicle and getting dressed. If she knew how momentous this day was going to be . . . well, that knowledge was buried deep in her subconscious. Suffice it to say that at that point in time there was very little on her mind, other than her ablutions, preparations and getting down on time for breakfast.

After breakfast Sister Rodriguez called her aside.

'Kitty O'Dowd, come here,' she said to her. 'The length of that skirt . . .' she hissed.

Oh, give me a break, thought Kitty.

'Kneel down this minute.'

Kitty scowled but knelt down on the wooden corridor floor just as she was told.

'That skirt is shorter than the minimum length allowed,' said Sister Rodriguez. 'It is to be the correct length by this afternoon.'

'At what time?' Kitty asked, thinking maybe she could swap gymslips with Treasa at the appropriate time.

'I,' said Sister Rodriguez with obvious dislike, her top lip lifting slightly on the left side, 'will check it personally as soon as afternoon classes are over.'

'But I'm in detention, Sister,' Kitty said, wondering how far she could push Rodriguez.

'Not today, you're not,' said Sister Rodriguez with pleasure. 'When classes end today you are to report to Mother Immaculata's study, where I will be waiting for you and I will check the length of your gymslip.'

'Mother Immaculata's study?' Kitty asked, unable to hide her curiosity.

'Yes, Mother Immaculata's study. Mother Immaculata has decided that after your appalling behaviour yesterday in Miss Ní Ghrian's class, an hour with the priest will do you good. And Father McMorrow is due in to talk to Mary about her vocation. He will see you first.'

Kitty looked at Sister Rodriguez and said nothing.

'Do you understand?'

'Yes, Sister,' Kitty replied. Oh, I understand all right, she thought.

For a moment there was silence.

'Well, what are you waiting for?' asked Sister Rodriguez. 'Move along.'

So Kitty went and fetched her books and went to class.

At the first break at ten fifty the girls trooped out to get their milk and Kitty passed Miss Ní Ghrian in the corridor. They had Irish next period. Kitty could have sworn that Miss Ní Ghrian sneered. Instead of following the other girls, Kitty slipped down the corridor and into the next house where she took the stairs, two at a time, to her dormitory. There she took another pair of black shoes from her cupboard, and carrying them behind her back she headed to the classroom.

A few minutes later Kitty went out into the gardens behind the school and approached Bernadette who was sitting on a bench.

'Bernadette.'

'Mmmm?' Bernadette said, her face raised to the morning sun.

'Bernadette, Bernadette, Bernadette, will you do me a favour?' Kitty wheedled.

'Depends,' Bernadette said, eyes closed again, and her plait hanging down her back.

'I swear I wouldn't ask you only Treasa is in sickbay and I need a favour.'

'Oh, all right,' Bernadette said. 'Ask away.'

'Will you answer my name when Ní Ghrian calls the roll next class?'

Bernadette dropped her chin, opened her navy blue eyes and looked at Kitty. 'What are you up to?'

'Nothing much,' Kitty said. 'Just this once, please.'

'We're in enough trouble,' Bernadette said. 'Correction, I'm in enough trouble.'

'Please. Just this once. I swear I'll never ask you a favour again – as long as you live,' said Kitty.

'All right,' Bernadette said. 'Just this once.'

The scene is set. Kitty's shoes are positioned carefully under the dusty brown curtain, with just the toes sticking out. The bell rings and the girls troop back into class, Kitty included. Her desk is three rows from the front against the wall with one of the Downey twins in the adjoining desk. Kitty crouches down under the desk, hidden from view by the rows of standing girls as Miss Ní Ghrian heads up the centre aisle.

'Prayer,' snaps Grinny.

As the class recites the Hail Mary, Kitty, crouching on the floor, prays in her own way. *For what we are about to receive, may the Lord make us truly thankful.*

'Sit,' Grinny snaps, and there is muted shuffling as the girls sit, recognising that Grinny is in a more irritable humour than usual.

She opens her roll, and starts calling the names. When she comes to Kitty O'Dowd's, Bernadette is unable to reply. Her voice sticks in her throat and she knows in her heart that this is too soon for Kitty to be playing one of her tricks again.

Miss Ní Ghrian looks up and sees Kitty's place is empty. Her eyes are drawn towards the curtains hanging loosely as they had done the previous day, only this time she sees the toes of the black polished shoes protruding just as inch, almost side by side, from beneath the dusty fabric.

She stares. She blinks. She looks again. She cannot believe that Kitty O'Dowd would be so stupid as to pull such a stunt two days running. Fury fills her already irritated mind, and with a roar she charges at the curtains, her right fist pulled back, and she takes an almighty swing at where she thinks Kitty is standing. Her fist slams into the door behind.

She screams, doubles over and clutches her damaged hand with her left one.

The class have watched this in total amazement. Downeyone prods Kitty's arm and Kitty sits serenely at her desk.

Meanwhile Miss Ní Ghrian, almost in a ball on the floor, is spitting fire. She is totally incomprehensible in her fury and her pain. The girls are trying to suppress their laughter, unsuccessfully, until Grinny finally stands up.

'Can you imagine what damage she would have done to Kitty had Kitty actually been there?' Bernadette said to Treasa later that day while sitting on the edge of her bed in sickbay recounting what had happened. 'I mean, she actually broke her hand. Imagine if Kitty had been there. Kidney damage? Ruptured liver?'

'And then what happened?' Treasa asked with her hoarse voice and sore throat, her eyes dancing with joy as the story unfolded.

'She remembered the shoes on the floor under the curtain, and she pulled the curtain back with her good hand, all the time cradling her right hand against her chest. She picked up one of the shoes and of course Kitty's name was in it – and that was that.'

'No,' squeaked Treasa. 'Don't say "that was that" – I want to hear every bit of what happened next and then I want to hear it all over again.'

'But I've already told you,' Bernadette said.

'I don't care,' Treasa said. 'Oh, I wish, I wish I'd been there. Tell me more.'

'She spotted Kitty sitting at her desk.'

'Go on.'

'She was so angry and in such pain that she looked like she was going to explode or implode – I don't know. Something. She screamed at Kitty, "What are you doing there?" and Kitty said, "This is my place," all wide-eyed innocence, you know. You have never ever seen anything like it.'

'You little bitch,' screams Miss Ní Ghrian, holding one of Kitty's shoes aloft. 'Do you deny this is yours?'

Kitty peers up the rows ahead of her. 'I can't be sure,' she says evenly and carefully. 'I won't deny it until I'm sure.'

'Get up here this minute.'

Kitty looks as if she doesn't think this is a very good idea, but then she seems to brace herself, and she gives Downeyone a slight push to make way for her. And up she goes to face the ranting of Miss Ní Ghrian.

'Is this yours?' she asks again.

218

Kitty takes the shoe from her and examines it carefully.

'It looks awfully like one of mine,' she says.

'It is yours. It is,' roars Miss Ní Ghrian. 'Your name is in it.'

'Couldn't Kitty have denied putting it there?' Treasa asked.

'I suppose she could have, but she didn't,' Bernadette said.

'Why did Kitty want you to answer her name at roll call?'

'I think Kitty's plan was that it would happen later in the class, not right away. But as it turned out it wouldn't have made any difference. I mean, if Kitty wanted to reduce Grinny to her true state, well, then that is what she succeeded in doing.'

'What happened then?' Treasa said.

'Grinny suddenly threw the shoe at Kitty and headed for the door. We all sat there. We'd stopped laughing by the time Kitty was identified as the culprit and there was this horrible feeling that everything was out of hand. Kitty went back to her place, taking both shoes with her. After about five minutes an ambulance arrived at the school – we heard it coming up the street and we all went to the window to take a look, and sure enough Grinny was taken off in it.'

'What did Kitty say?'

'She didn't say anything. She just sat there at her desk beside the wall. I looked over and she was the only one who wasn't participating. The rest of us nearly knocked each other over to get a view out the window.'

'And then?'

'Then ... then Mother Immaculata arrived at the door and we charged back to our places. You know what it's like. She glided up the aisle, fixing different girls with the old gimlet eye – and then she spotted Kitty.'

'A word with you, Kitty O'Dowd,' she says. 'NOW.'

Kitty looks at her – and later Bernadette thinks that she saw Kitty bracing herself again, which of course is not unreasonable.

'Yes, Mother,' Kitty says.

'Outside,' says The Raven.

Kitty stands up again, and Downeyone lets her pass. Mother Immaculata heads for the door and Kitty follows her. Just as they go out, Kitty turns back and looks at Bernadette.

She smiles at her, and then she waves.

Kitty O'Dowd has done a runner
Packed her make-up, had her fill
Her friends stand silent at the window
And the Raven's fit to kill

'She raised one hand at me – it was really like a farewell wave,' Bernadette said.

'And then?' Treasa demanded. 'What then?'

'You may have broken Miss Ní Ghrian's hand,' Mother Immaculata says to Kitty O'Dowd.

Kitty shrugs. 'I didn't touch her.'

'You have given nothing but trouble, Kitty O'Dowd, since the day you came to this school. And you were lucky to be let in with your track record. You have six weeks until your Leaving Certificate. Can you think of any single reason why you should not be expelled?'

Kitty looks at her. It is a long, slow Kitty-look. She wants to say, 'I quit.' She's seen that in a film about a guy who was about to be fired. But somehow under the gaze from The Raven, she can't get the words out.

'I'm phoning your parents,' Mother Immaculata says. 'They can collect you this afternoon. Go and pack your things.'

Kitty says nothing. She turns and leaves the room and goes to her dorm where she takes off her school clothes and puts on her maxi skirt, T-shirt and platforms. She packs her make-up, and that is all she takes with her. She leaves everything else lying on her bed.

She goes downstairs, opens the main door and lets herself out. And down the steps she goes without looking back.

Two floors up, in the Sixth Year classroom, Downeytwo looking out the window sees Kitty O'Dowd walk briskly away from the school.

'And she didn't come back?' Treasa said sadly.

Bernadette shook her head.

'What was it like in the classroom after she left with The Raven?'

'We were all very quiet. We just sat there. She was obviously in big trouble.'

'I see.'

'When Downeytwo said she could see her on the street, we rushed over, but she didn't look back. She just walked down the street, head high – you know, the Kitty walk. We stood there watching her. Long after she'd disappeared we still stood there. Then while I was still at the window, my mother arrived, and I was hauled out. And I thought it was going to be dreadful because The Raven was going to be in such a fury. But in fact she was totally distracted. I had been caught out about not going to the house on Sunday. I'd lied – it had seemed the right thing at the time. You know. Anyway, suddenly it all seemed very trivial. The Raven skirted around it, and eventually said, "One expulsion is enough." Which was when it was clear that Kitty was gone. It had looked to me as if I was for the high jump. I'd been going on about how I hadn't wanted to get into trouble and having realised on the bus that my parents were away – oh, it was all so boring. I thought it would never end.'

'How did your mother take it?'

'She tried to cover for me. I think she felt that she had landed me in it, and then suddenly the inquisition and the lecture were over, and the executioner's chopping block, which I could so clearly visualise, was removed, and I was sent back to class. That was when Mr and Mrs O'Dowd arrived – I suppose to be told that Kitty had scarpered.'

Treasa lay back and thought about it all. 'Why did Kitty pull that stunt today? I mean, today of all days? She must have known that Grinny would go mad.'

'I know,' Bernadette said. 'I've been thinking about it. I think she wanted Grinny to go mad.'

'What's the news on the Grinny front anyway?' asked Treasa.

'No news, other than that we're getting a substitute teacher for the next two weeks at least. Which I suppose means that Grinny is as damaged as she appeared to be. The Maple said she'll be in plaster for weeks.'

'Small blessing,' Treasa said. 'I wonder where Kitty is.' She leaned her head back on the pillows and was swamped with sadness over Kitty's departure, and concern over where Kitty might go. Black Tuesday, she thought. So near to the end of school – and yet so far. Poor Kitty. I wonder why she did it. She was nearly at the finishing line.

Bernadette was relieved that she had escaped The Raven's knife. During prep she wrote and thanked her mother for sticking up for her, and

221

apologised for the bother she had caused. But her heart was heavy when she thought about Kitty's departure. Such a waste, she thought. She's survived so much, and to throw it all away at the end. She wondered if Kitty might sit her Leaving Certificate somewhere else, but she knew that was not a reality, and she sighed and returned to her own studies.

Anna McBride (Bridie to her friends) slipped out after tea and phoned Andrew MacDonald.

Bridie, two feet on the ground when it counted, despite her fantastic fantasy life, rang Andrew because she cared so much for Kitty. And Andrew came to the phone.

'No need to worry, Anna,' he said. 'I can't tell you where Kitty is because she doesn't want anyone to know. But she is safe.'

'Do you promise?' Bridie asked.

'I promise,' he replied. 'And I'll tell her you were concerned. But just keep it to yourself that you contacted me. I promise that she is safe.'

Bridie slept easier that night, but couldn't tell any of the others.

And Mary Oliver had her hour's vocation conversation with the priest and emerged white-faced and shaken, and never took Communion again.

'In September you can come in as a novice,' said The Raven, waiting outside the door for her, 'and commute from here to UCD. It's within pleasant walking distance.'

And Mary looked at her and thought, what am I going to do? Because Mary didn't have the courage to say, 'Not only am I not going to UCD, I am not joining your order or any other one.'

Mary Oliver bit her nails for the rest of the term, and on the afternoon of their last Leaving Cert. exam, when the girls were getting their cases down from the attic, Mary Oliver looked up at the skylight. Through the tiny panes of glass, the blue sky beckoned. Then she climbed up on the precariously placed cases, which Kitty O'Dowd arranged so carefully every term. And with a twist of her wrist Mary opened the skylight and climbed through, out onto the rooftops where the others had so often climbed to sunbathe or to smoke.

> *On the parapet near the chimneys*
> *Statue-like above the ground*

Mary Oliver's looking down
At last an answer she has found

She looked across the roofs and at the skyline of chimneys and down across the city at the carefully positioned and well-proportioned squares, and her spirit, which had sunk within her, damaged and repressed, suddenly lifted.

'Goodbye, goodbye,' Mary Oliver hummed to herself as she pulled herself out onto the roof, climbing across the hot dry tiles.

Heedlessly, she headed across the tiles between the chimneys and then down the slope of the roof of one of the middle buildings to the edge, where she sat with her thighs across the gutter and her legs dangling over the side to the street four floors below.

And all the girls came to say goodbye
Because that's what they do when you die

A few minutes later, Treasa entered the attic and, looking up at the open skylight, she thought to herself, one last smoke for old times' sake, and for Kitty.

So she, too, clambered up the staircase of suitcases and pulled herself up through the opening onto the roof, and there to her horror she saw Mary Oliver sitting on the edge with her legs dangling down.

'Mary,' she called gently, terrified of giving Mary a fright, because she could see that any sudden movement and Mary would be gone over the edge.

'Hey, Mary,' she called a little louder. 'What are you up to?'

Mary Oliver turned and looked at her and then said, 'Go away.'

'Bernadette,' Treasa hissed down through the open skylight. 'There's a problem out here – I'm going out to take a look.'

And Treasa headed across the roof to Mary, while Bernadette put her head through the open skylight and looked in dismay at the drama unfolding in front of her eyes.

'Mary, come up here and have a smoke with me,' Treasa said invitingly as she eased herself between the stacks higher up the roof.

223

'No,' said Mary Oliver. 'I'm not going back. Not for anything.'

'No, no,' called Treasa, as casually as she could. 'I meant just climb up here to the chimneys and we'll have a smoke and think about Kitty. I wonder what she's up to. It's weeks now since we heard anything about her. Not since that day when she walked out.'

'She was expelled,' said Mary Oliver. 'They expelled her. I wish they'd expelled me.'

'Come on back up here,' Treasa said. 'It's comfy enough sitting with your back to the chimneys.'

Mary shook her head and went silent.

Treasa tried everything she could think of to encourage Mary away from the edge, and Bernadette, ever practical, hearing the strangeness of Mary's voice and the nervous quaver and the strain in Treasa's, climbed down and went to phone the fire brigade.

Treasa, looking down towards the gutter and imagining the sheer drop below, forced herself to stay as cool as she could, and eased herself carefully down to join Mary at the edge.

'What's the plan, Mary?' she asked.

'I don't have a plan,' Mary said. 'But I'm not going back in there.'

I don't think we'd get back in there, Treasa thought to herself, looking over her shoulder. The skylight looked too far away, and the roof looked so steep from this angle. She could not imagine what to do next.

'What would you like to happen?' she asked. She could hear her voice quivering. She had never really thought about heights before. In the past, it had just been a lark to climb out here, but from this angle at the edge, the chimneys looked too high up, and the skylight seemed inaccessible and the drop to the street looked endless.

'Don't know,' Mary said. Her voice had taken on a childish quality.

In the windows across the street, office workers had gathered and were watching the two girls on the edge.

Treasa forced herself to stop looking downwards and to concentrate on Mary.

'You must have some idea,' she said.

'I want my papa,' Mary said, in her new baby voice. 'I want my papa,' and her bottom lip quivered, just as Treasa's voice had.

'What would you say to him?' Treasa said, wondering where Bernadette had gone.

'I want him to come and find me. I want my papa back,' Mary Oliver said, as her mind journeyed backwards and she was two years old again – a little girl with a smiling face playing in a garden in Paris. 'Papa, Papa,' she called.

And she heard him respond, *'Viens ici, ma petite.'*

Treasa heard the fire engines before she saw them. She was afraid to look down now, afraid of falling, afraid of Mary being distracted. She felt that as long as she could keep Mary occupied, perhaps it would be all right.

Down below, gigantic sheeting was being stretched out in case one of the girls fell. Inside the school, two firemen were making their way up the stairs, two at a time, towards the attic and the open skylight.

'Hello, girls,' one of them called as he put his head out.

'Keep away,' Mary Oliver screamed. 'Keep away,' and she clung to Treasa who started to see her life flash by.

'What started this?' the fireman whispered to Bernadette just beneath him.

'I don't know. Mary, that's Mary Oliver, she was out there when Treasa climbed out, and Treasa felt there was something wrong. I don't know.'

Negotiations began.

The fireman was afraid to go any further as he could feel the tension out on the roof, and as he said to the psychologist who was shortly called to assist, 'I think this might be more your ball game.'

It escalated. In forty minutes there were two fire engines, their crew, a police psychologist, television cameras, every nun in the building, office workers from the surrounding buildings, passers-by and every policeman who was on duty in the area that afternoon.

'Post-exam tension?' asked the psychologist of Bernadette O'Higgins and Anna McBride.

They shook their heads.

'May I go out?' Bridie asked. 'Let me go out and ask what she wants.'

'It's too dangerous. It's bad enough that the other girl is there too.'

'Treasa is probably the reason Mary hasn't jumped yet,' Bernadette snapped.

'Let me at least call to Treasa,' Bridie said.

When asked, Treasa called back, 'Mary Olivier wants her father.'

Treasa was surprised to hear herself call Mary by her real surname; surprised, too, that it didn't sound wrong to her ears.

And Mary Olivier called in her baby voice, 'Papa, Papa.' It sounded so very French, and Mary Olivier looked so helpless, with her neat brown hair cut in a bob, and her hands on her too-thin wrists holding the gutter on which she was seated several storeys above street level, her white-socked slim legs and narrow knees hanging over the edge.

'Papa, Papa,' she called out across the street with a slightly glazed look in her brown eyes.

The television cameras were positioned in a top-floor room in the opposite building, where the excited office staff moved unwillingly from the window to accommodate them.

As the six o'clock news began on television, the drama moved live to the small screen and was reported on the BBC. At the close of an evening meeting in the French Embassy in London, a secretary said to the diplomat, Jean Jacques Olivier, 'You don't have a daughter in school in Ireland, do you?'

'No, why?' he answered, gathering his papers together.

'I just heard on the news that a girl called Mary Olivier is out on a rooftop and is calling for her father.'

Time stood still for Monsieur Olivier.

'What? Where? Show me,' he said.

And he raced to the next room where the television was showing two girls very high up on top of a building. They were both dressed alike, in a green gymslip, white blouse, green tie with a tiny crest, which appeared in a larger version on the gymslip. The cameras picked up the words 'Humanitas et Virtus'. The smaller girl, olive-skinned with her hair cut in a neat bob which outlined the delicate bones in her neck, was staring down towards the street, her eyes wide in disbelief. The other, bigger girl, with dark tousled hair, was shouting about the duty of the religious orders to eradicate themselves.

'You think there is something rotten in the state of Denmark?' called Treasa, addressing the television crew in the building across the street.

'Dream on. The very core of this system is rotten. Karl Marx says that it is the duty of the bourgeoisie to commit suicide as a class. Well, he got it wrong. It is the duty of the religious orders to commit suicide en masse to obliterate all traces of religion in Ireland.'

'She is articulate, isn't she?' said the admiring assistant in the French Embassy in London.

'Get me the Irish Embassy at once,' M. Olivier said. He had no doubt – no doubt at all – who the smaller girl was.

Mary Oliver, looking down four storeys to the ground, was fascinated by the circle of dark-clothed people. Her mind was drawn to her dream several weeks earlier, when she looked up in the Sister Chapel from her work with the crucifix, and thought she was surrounded by nuns in their dark habits. What she now saw was a circle of tense firemen who were waiting for her to fall, but this did not penetrate her mind. It appeared to her as a circle which was complete. Either she would be caught within it for ever, unable to break ranks, or the alternative, which was equally unbearable.

Anna McBride, with a rope round her waist, eased herself across the roof towards Treasa and Mary, where Treasa, in an effort to keep her own spirits up, was repeating her diatribe on the religious orders in Ireland. Then she became aware of Bridie's approach with ropes for her and Mary.

'Mary,' she said. 'Mary, listen to me. Mary, we're going to get down from here and we're going to walk away from this. And if anyone asks what we were doing, we came out here for a smoke. Do you hear me?'

Mary pulled her eyes away from the scene on the street below. Pale and puzzled, she looked at Treasa.

'What?' she asked.

'Listen to me, Mary. Can you hear me?' Treasa repeated. 'We came out here for a smoke and you slipped and that's why we ended up here at the edge.'

'I'm not going back inside,' Mary said.

'We're going back together.'

'I'm not going back inside,' Mary said clearly.

'We came out for a smoke and you slipped,' Treasa said. 'That's all. That's what happened. Have you got that? Do you hear me?'

'I hear you,' Mary said, her voice a little steadier. 'We came out for a smoke and I slipped.'

'That's right. Now Bridie is going to pass us ropes and we can put them round us, and then we will be safe.'

'We're not safe in there,' Mary said.

'No, but once we've gone inside we can then go downstairs and walk out,' Treasa said.

'They won't let us,' Mary replied. 'I'm not going in there. They'll never let me go.'

'They will,' Treasa said. 'I promise. I'll stay beside you and we'll just walk away. We're finished with St Martin's. You need never go inside the buildings again. It's over.'

'But they want me to become a nun. They'll never let me walk away.'

'They will,' Treasa said. 'They fecking well will.'

Bridie called to them, 'I'm going to pass these ropes to you. Mary, Mary, I've been told to tell you that your father has been in touch. He's on his way.'

Mary started, thinking she heard Bridie say, 'Father has been in touch.'

'What? What?' she said, sheer panic in her voice.

'Your father – they said, your father, Jean Jacques Olivier . . .'

Mary heard that all right, but she had already jerked in shock, and just as Treasa was putting the first rope round her own waist, Mary lost her balance on the edge. She clawed furiously at Treasa who, fumbling with the rope, did all she could to grasp her, but she slipped through her hands and disappeared over the parapet.

Presently my soul grew stronger; hesitating then no longer,
'Jesus,' said I, 'God our Father, true forgiveness I implore;
But the fact is I was napping; and so gently you came rapping
And so faintly you came tapping, tapping on my chamber door
That I scarce was sure I'd heard you,' – here I opened wide the door
                                        Darkness there and nothing more.

Chapter Fifteen

Take a group of girls, now young women, and give them freedom. It is summertime in the year of Our Lord nineteen hundred and seventy-five. Third Year exams are over and it is party time. The girls have gone to Greece.

It is four in the morning and several bottles of retsina have been consumed over the previous six hours. Lack of sleep at both appropriate and inappropriate times is part of this holiday.

Mary Olivier (once known as Mary Oliver), the Downey twins, Bernadette O'Higgins (with navy blue eyes) and Anna McBride (still Bridie to her friends) are assisted from a small boat onto a passenger ferry. They are laden with rucksacks and sleeping bags and they drag themselves up the tiny ladder. As they pass the rows of yawning people who are waiting to climb down into the tiny boat, Mary Olivier suddenly says, 'Hey, look, it's Andrew MacDonald.'

And so it is.

Leaning against the railing, dressed in cut-off jeans, T-shirt, sweatshirt and sandals, Andrew MacDonald is waiting patiently to disembark and to head for Santorini.

The girls waken up. 'Hey, Andrew.'

'Where are you all off to?' he asks. He seems way less surprised than they are, but then Kitty had told him that they were 'doing' the Greek islands, so it is rather less of a coincidence for him.

'Paros,' they reply.

But there is no time for further conversation. The passengers behind are piling up and they are herded along the deck of the boat, calling back to him to enjoy himself and to keep his sleeping bag tightly closed at night.

'I'll find you,' he calls to them.

He disappears down the ladder and they are left on deck to watch the tiny boat heading for shore.

'Was he with anyone?' Bernadette asks. But it was difficult to tell in the dark.

They huddle together under a lifeboat and try to keep warm as they wait for sunrise. They sing 'I am sailing . . .' Linking arms and moving with the rhythm of the ferry, they cross the sea.

Mary Olivier leads them from the port to a sandy beach where the Mediterranean laps gently on the shore. There they lie on golden sand, marvelling at how shampoo will not lather in salt water, relaxing in each other's company, frisking as dolphins in the water, drinking in the harbour bars in the evening.

'Who has the most buoyant breasts?' asks Mary Olivier of her peers.

They're in the sea, and she and the Downey twins are topless.

'For God's sake, Mary,' says Bernadette, 'sometimes I think you are more interested in biology than I am.'

They laugh, and Bridie says, 'Well, mine are too small to count,' and she swims away.

'Mine are staying in their bikini,' says Bernadette, 'so you'll just have to leave me out of your equation.'

'How did you find this place and when did you first come here?' Bridie asks Mary the following morning.

'Papa took me here that summer when we had done our Leaving,' Mary replies. 'And I've come back every summer since. This is my fourth time.'

'You didn't sleep on the beach when you came with your father?' asks Bridie in surprise.

Mary smiles. 'Yes we did. He said it was the kind of thing we would have done when he was younger and it would make up for the missing years.'

Bridie ponders this. 'How wonderful,' she says. She is lying on her back on the sand, clothed in a bikini, her feet in the water, eyes closed.

The Downey twins have disappeared. They headed off mid-morning, having silently communicated with each other but forgetting to fill the others in on their plans.

Bernadette is further up the beach. She is draping the sleeping bags out on the bushes to air them. Her plaited hair is clipped on top of her head. Her shorts are baggy, and she has cut the sleeves off a shirt, and with just two buttons done up, she has tied the tails under her breasts.

Beside Bridie, Mary Olivier, wearing the bottom half of her bikini, is lying on her stomach, resting on her elbows, feet trailing in the water.

'I like your dad's name,' Bridie says.

'What, Jean Jacques?' Mary asks.

'Mmmm,' replies Bridie, still amazed several years after meeting Mary's father that not only is the name the same as her fantasy lover, but that in the interim years her Jean Jacques now looks remarkably like Jean Jacques Olivier.

Mary Olivier's breasts are dangling down, her nipples just above the sand, touching it occasionally as she half turns towards Bridie and then turns back.

'Well, I'm meeting him in Athens in ten days' time,' says Mary. 'You're welcome to join us. Nice hotel. Lots of hot water, clean hair,' she teases.

'Aaargh,' Bridie moans. 'Like, clean hair? Like, no salt in it making it sticky?'

They both giggle.

They have sailed such stormy waters to find freedom.

And that is what Andrew MacDonald sees as he strides along the beach a few days later, rucksack on his back, sweat sticking his T-shirt to his skin. He glances down, looking for the girls who were once of St Martin's but not really hopeful of finding them. From the top of the sand where he stands, he sees two figures lying on the shoreline, their feet in the sea.

Anna McBride he recognises immediately, her dark red hair like a flame in the sunlight. Then his eyes are drawn to the other girl who is lying on her stomach, propped up on her elbows, her breasts swinging from side to side as she exchanges comments with Anna McBride.

At first he doesn't recognise her. She has filled out and looks healthy and it is only as he approaches that it dawns on him that this is Mary Olivier.

'What were you laughing about?' he asks Mary later.

'I don't know,' she says.

And she doesn't. It was just another day on the beach. Another day in another year. One more laugh.

Bridie it was who rolled over and yelled, 'Andrew, Andrew.' And she got up and ran up the beach to hurl herself into his arms.

Mary, whose life was built on her fragility (not a good foundation for anyone, as time will tell) looked up lazily and smiled at him. He lowered his backpack onto the sand and hugged Bridie, his eyes caught by Mary's free-swinging breasts.

'Mmmm,' he says into Bridie's hair.

'Don't say a word,' she says. 'I know it doesn't smell of apple or peaches!'

But he doesn't hear her. He is watching Mary who sits up and languidly waves.

And later that night, he and Mary move their sleeping bags a little down the beach from the others.

'So, where do you go to my lovely, when you're alone in your sleeping bag?'

'Get in and find out,' says Mary Olivier. They zip their bags together and she lets him caress those same breasts which had swung earlier before his eyes.

'Mmmm,' he says again, this time into her ear. 'How does that feel?' he asks.

'Lovely,' she lies. Mary Olivier (once Mary Oliver) feels nothing.

Bernadette O'Higgins, draping sleeping bags on bushes as she does every morning, looks up and sees Andrew MacDonald from behind and he reminds her of someone. It takes her some five years to realise that he reminded her of himself. At that moment when she sees him standing with his back to her looking at the shoreline, she thinks of her tutor in college. He also lectures, and a perfect image presents itself before her eyes. He is standing at the board with his back to the lecture theatre, and he is pointing at something he has transcribed. In her mind's eye she watches his stance and the spread of his shoulders, the broadness of his back as it narrows to neat hips, and she feels a twinge of desire.

In due course Andrew comes and greets her, but her mind is a thousand miles away and she wonders what Dr Denyll is doing right that moment.

Later, when she is married to Dr Denyll for three years, four months and twenty-two days, she remembers that moment on the beach in Paros. Then she realises that if her three plus years with him are anything to go by, he was probably pulling some other undergraduate and taking her from behind, over the arm of his study sofa. Oh, one was so hopeful and full of optimism in one's early twenties, she thinks as she packs her bags and moves out of their home. 'I don't need this s***,' she writes to him. 'I put some value on me, which is just as well, as you value nothing except yourself and your prick.'

The Downey twins are found sitting outside a bar in the little fishing village, drinking espresso. As the others approach, each twin pats one pocket in her shorts and, glancing at each other, they smile. They each still carry one of Mary Olivier's nails. Mary, noticing their furtive hand movement but not knowing the contents of their pockets, promptly checks her own pocket for the reassurance of the two nails she took from the glaziers' toolbox in the Sister Chapel porch.

She has never been inside a church since her tumble from St Martin's roof, and indeed does not consciously think of the images which once haunted her. She no longer connects those nails with anything; they are simply a talisman, hers for safekeeping.

In the not so distant future Andrew MacDonald will ask her the meaning of the nails, and she will look distinctly puzzled for a moment before replying, 'They're terribly handy. You never know if you might want to hang a picture or . . . Look,' she takes a nail in each hand and crosses them, holding them out in front of her, 'you can ward off evil spirits with them.'

'How about a clove of garlic?' he asks, and they both laugh.

'Treasa has arrived,' says Downeyone.

'Already? She wasn't due for another day or so, was she?' says Mary.

'She was on the same boat as me,' says Andrew MacDonald, languidly resting his left foot on his right knee. 'With a friend – Vita.'

'Who?' asks Mary. 'Do we know her?'

'Well, you will shortly,' says Downeyone. 'They've gone to check into the hotel.'

'No beach and sleeping bag for Treasa?' queries Bernadette. 'That's not like her.'

235

'I think Vita likes her comforts,' Downeytwo responds, and they look over at the hotel, and there hanging out of the first-floor window is Treasa O'Donoghue, waving cheerily.

'Now we're only missing Kitty and we could have a St Martin's reunion,' says Bernadette.

'We'd need The Raven and Rodriguez for that.'

'Not to mention Grinny.'

'Wonder where they all are now.'

'Last thing I heard of them,' says Bernadette, 'was when the convent was sold. Do you remember? Those pictures in the papers . . .'

They all smile as they think of the picture of the four adjoining houses, and the shot of Treasa and Mary perched on the gutter on the roof, and then the wonderful snap of Mary in full flight as she fell to the waiting firemen, her school knickers showing but her socks neatly pulled to her knees. 'A memorable moment in the history of St Martin's,' the caption read.

'Grinny got married,' says Downeyone.

'What? How do you know?' They are all agog.

'Miss Maple told Kitty, and Kitty told Treasa and Treasa told us,' says Downeytwo, in one of the longest sentences she has ever uttered.

They have pulled up chairs and are sitting around the little bar table with various expressions of amazement and amusement on their faces.

'Kitty said to Treasa that she probably punishes him for being late in, gives him detention, and beats him black and blue. Bet she took her strap with her – *something old . . .*'

'*Nothing new, something borrowed . . .*'

'Bet she borrowed The Raven's!'

'*Something blue . . .* That'd be the bruises.'

They laugh.

'Yes, that's exactly what Kitty said,' says Treasa as she joins them and introduces the blonde-haired, blue-eyed, slight, neat Vita, who smiles happily at them all and expresses her pleasure in finally getting to meet them.

And when they sit, Vita's right hand touches Treasa's arm for a moment too long; long enough to make it clear that it was no accident, and as they go on talking about Grinny, and asking after Kitty, all their eyes are drawn to that hand. The prolonged touch seems to hover in the air long after Vita has taken her hand away, but they are all now aware of the gentleness of the look which Vita bestows on Treasa, and the proprietorial way in which Treasa checks with Vita what she will drink.

'Well, well, well,' says Bernadette to Bridie later. 'I didn't see that coming.'

'I don't suppose I did either,' says Bridie. 'They do seem awfully well-suited, don't they? Like chalk and chalk, or cheese and cheese. In a way I envy them,' she continues. 'I've always wanted to find my soul mate.'

'Time enough,' says Bernadette, thinking of Dr Denyll in his lab.

'Time enough indeed,' replies Bridie, thinking of Jean Jacques Olivier who will shortly be flying into Athens.

And time there is. In due course Mary Olivier and Anna McBride will head for Athens to meet up with Jean Jacques, and Mary will slip out after dinner to meet Andrew who has followed her to the capital.

And Anna McBride (always Bridie to her schoolmates) will look shyly across the table at Mary's father and he will be smitten by the girl-woman who has carried a torch for him since the age of twelve.

'But what do you mean?' he asks her in his French accent. 'Explain to me, please. I don't understand.'

And she blushes and looks down at her coffee, and tells him something of her secret life. He smiles gently at her, captivated by the images she conjures.

And she, who was just cringing at the first confession she has made to him, or indeed to anyone, about her fantasy life, suddenly finds it easier to let more of her story unfold . . . and unfold . . . and unfold.

Downeyone and Downeytwo are sitting drinking. They are, like Siamese twins, undergoing separation surgery, in the process of disentangling themselves from each other. Their thoughts, ideas and plans flicker over and through each other.

'I'm thinking of not finishing in Trinity.'

'I know. But I think you should. One more year and you have your degree.'

'Should we give Mary back the nails?'

'No. She has already replaced them.'

'We shouldn't have sex with the same person again.'

'Not at the same time anyway.'

'You're right.'

'It's not helping.'

'I know.'

'How do you know she has replaced the nails?'

'She replaced them years ago. I don't know how I know. I just do.'

'Why do you keep yours?'

They are drifting apart, have been drifting for some time, no longer sure of the other's thoughts.

'Safety. They're for luck.'

'Yes. After we got them, that day, at the confessional. We were safe after that. Weren't we?'

'Yes. Almost. Nearly. Warding off the devil.'

'*Deliver us from evil . . .*'

'*Amen.*'

'Finish your year. We're going different ways. Finish it out.'

'You sticking with law?'

'Yes. You?'

'I want journalism.'

'You'll get it better with a law degree – it'll always stand for you.'

'I know . . .'

'So, we'll keep our nails?'

'Yes. Yes. They've brought us luck.'

'*Et in secula seculorum?*'

'*Amen.*'

Kyrie Eleison, Christe Eleison . . .

The singing comes from the local church. The girls, dressed in shorts and T-shirts, tanned and healthy, stand stock still on the little pathway at the side of the building.

Kyrie-ey-ey-ey . . .

The sound is dragged out, a male voice extending the vowels over and over. Mary Olivier (once Oliver) slips her hands into the pocket of her short and rolls the nails in her palm.

'Should we go to church?' asks Bernadette. It's Sunday. They will be leaving the island in twos and threes over the next few days.

'You can,' says Mary Olivier. 'I'm going for coffee.'

'I think Bernadette was joking,' Treasa interjects.

'Well . . .' Bernadette hesitates. 'I wasn't really. It was just a thought. To see what it was like. The singing reminded me . . .' she finished lamely.

'Count me out,' say the Downey twins as one.

'And me,' says Mary Olivier.

'I'll go with you,' says Bridie helpfully.

So Bernadette and Bridie slip into the church and while they are kneeling, deep in thought, a male voice whispers into Bernadette's ear, 'I know you.'

Long-haired, bearded, denim jeans cut off on the thigh, leather thongs round his neck with a peace symbol on one and a crucifix on the other, a leather thong round his forehead, blue eyes sleepily smiling at her when she turns, Christopher Marlowe, last seen spaced out in Dublin 4, is now sitting spaced out in a church on Paros.

'Hi, honey,' he says clearly, and the congregation turns as one to see who has interrupted the proceedings.

Down in the dock in the café which is now their regular haunt, Andrew MacDonald and Bernadette O'Higgins are sitting laughing with Christopher Marlowe.

'This really is like a reunion of everyone we knew in seventy-two. More and more people turning up every day,' Bernadette says. 'How did you find us, Christopher?'

'I didn't find you,' he replies dreamily. 'You found me. I was sitting in the church.'

'Don't tease her, Christopher,' laughs Andrew MacDonald, turning to Bernadette. 'Christopher is joining us in Trinity in October. He's taking a year out from Princeton.'

Christopher smiles his sleepy smile, his fingers busy rolling a cigarette.
'A disagreement between my dad and me,' he says.

'Oh, call it an agreement, Christopher,' Andrew says.

'Because it sounds better?' Christopher laughs.

Andrew smiles too, but doesn't say anything more. He knows of the battle which has taken place in the Marlowe household. Bernadette, intuitively, drops the subject for now but brings it up later with Andrew.

'So what's the story?' she asks him. They're drinking retsina on the beach, waiting for the others to join them.

'With Christopher Marlowe?'

'Yes.'

'Daddy Marlowe is running for Congress. I gather there was a mutual agreement that he would stand a better chance if Christopher were elsewhere!'

'Why, what did Christopher do?'

'It's what he didn't do,' Andrew laughed. 'Didn't get his exams. Didn't study.'

'A blot on the parental horizon?'

'Something like that. Fancy him?'

Bernadette shook her head on her swan-like neck and thought of Dr Denyll, and drank a little more wine. 'Nope.'

Late that night, Mary Olivier stirs alone in her now double sleeping bag and sits bolt upright. The sky is filled with thousands of sparkling stars, and in that moment of waking, startled from her slumber, from some terrible nightmare, Mary thinks the sky is full of lighting candles, and she imagines the sound of music wafting in above the lapping of the water. Can someone hear me? she wonders. Can anyone hear me?

'You OK?' Andrew asks her as he approaches silently over the sand.

I am dying, for ever crying . . . The words of a song haunt her.

'Who are you?' she whispers.

In the starlight he can just make out the terror on her face and the cold damp sweat on her forehead, and he clambers in and holds her.

'What are they?' she whispers, pointing upwards to the sky, to the candles in the sky.

Puzzled, he looks up. 'Meteors, the Milky Way, eternity, which do you mean?'

'The lights,' she says. 'The lights in the sky.'

'They're stars,' he reassures her as it dawns on him that she is asleep.

'Falling stars, and stationary stars. Stars for ever and ever.' He is holding her tightly now and her eyes close and she goes tumbling back down into the darkness where crucifixes move on the walls of her mind, where virgins weep tears of blood, and nuns flagellate themselves and each other.

'Do you want to bed Christopher Marlowe?' asks Downeyone of Downeytwo. 'Do you?'

They are both silent. They have agreed not to sleep with the same person again.

'I do if you don't,' says Downeyone.

They are having a pee behind the bushes at the top of the beach.

'He might be a bit out of it,' says Downeytwo, standing up and looking down the beach where the others are sitting.

'Well, if at first I don't succeed . . .' says Downeyone.

'Then give up, as Andrew MacDonald would say,' replies Downeytwo with a wry smile. 'And I'll take over.'

The beach is flat, hardly sloping at all until the waterline. The sound of laughter rises above the gentle lapping of the sea. They join the others. Downeyone sits beside Christopher Marlowe who passes her a joint.

Bridie watches with curiousity. She is the cautious one. She doesn't smoke or drink. Her virginity is intact, although in her fantasy world she has been ravished – often.

Bernadette is leaning back on her elbows looking at the night sky. Vita and Treasa are both sitting cross-legged, Treasa's left knee just touching Vita's right. Andrew has rejoined them, having left the sleeping Mary safely tucked in their conjoined sleeping bags.

A little up the beach, Mary Olivier jolts upright again and stares down the beach at the circle. She can really only see shapes, the outlines of people in a circle, and her mind fumbles frantically as she tries to identify what she is seeing.

'No,' she screams. 'No. Don't let them get me.'

They all come running as one.

'Something in that that doesn't agree with her,' Andrew says to Christopher, pointing to the roach between his fingers.

'It's not affecting anyone else. Has she ever smoked before?'

No one seems to know.

'It's us,' Treasa says to Mary. 'Your friends. It's just us.' She holds the terrified Mary in her arms.

But Mary Olivier (once Oliver) is walking in the Garden of Eden, and around the trunk of every tree a snake with glinting red eyes is watching her, the dead skin on his body peeling back like a foreskin. And in her mind she starts to run, frantically pushing aside the branches of the trees with their heavy foliage and their crop of outsize apples. She comes upon a small open place and there stands the Virgin Mother, white-robed, blue-gowned, hands outstretched.

'Save me,' she cries aloud.

'Bad trip,' Christopher Marlowe says.

But the Virgin Mary, seeing her approach, retreats back through the trees and disappears, and Mary Olivier knows true abandonment. The apples fall from the trees, and the closest snake smiles at her.

There is no escape.

Bridie watches as Andrew slips off his T-shirt and gets back into the sleeping bag with Mary. She wonders what it is like, to be held by someone for real.

When they go back to where they were sitting, she takes the joint from Downeytwo when it is passed her way and takes her first puff.

'I smoked the other day,' Anna McBride tells Jean Jacques Olivier outside the Parthenon. 'A joint. Well, a couple of puffs really.'

'And what was that like?' he asks.

'I don't know,' she says. 'I felt lonely. I thought it would make me feel more like the others.'

'In what way?' He talks to her gently.

'They're all older than me. I've never really fitted in.'

'They include you, though, don't they?'

'Yes, but that's because of Kitty – Kitty O'Dowd. They include me because she did. I always feel like I'm trying to catch up.' She is unafraid of being a child with him.

'You must have been very young when you finished school,' he says, thinking back to that June evening when he watched the girls of St Martin's on the roof of the convent.

'I was fourteen,' Bridie says. 'I'd just turned fourteen.'

He nods. He remembers clearly watching her climb from the skylight dragging the ropes behind her. His eyes were glued to the television in the Embassy, one hand holding the phone, hardly able to breathe.

'What did you miss the other night that made you feel left out?' He is unafraid of probing.

'It's silly,' Anna says. 'I wanted to be cuddled by someone.'

Jean Jacques slips his arm round her shoulder. 'Like this?'

'Yes,' she whispers. 'Just like this.'

'I'm too old for you,' he says, as he strokes her hair.

'No, no,' she protests. 'No, you're not. Please don't stop.'

And he doesn't stop. He kisses the virginal lips and touches the virginal throat with lips that caress her skin and Anna McBride melts in his arms. The French Revolution is abandoned in favour of 1975 in the Acropolis.

'No, don't stop,' she moans.

'What would you like me to do?' he asks her.

'Everything, everything,' she says. 'Everything. Please, I want to make up for lost time.'

'Only when you tell me each thing you want me to do will I do it,' he teases her gently. 'Much more exciting. Much more pleasurable.'

And the years slip back and forth as she revisits the gentle fingers of Jean Jacques Versailles and gently, cautiously, head bowed with shyness, she tells Jean Jacques Olivier how to proceed.

'What happened?' asks Downeytwo of Downeyone who is looking out to sea.

Downeytwo is sitting on the sand beside her sister. From the rear, perched on the beach, they are identical, down to the way they sit, knees pulled up, right arm resting on one knee. In the heat they have their hair scraped back into a ponytail. Facially there are tiny differences.

243

Downeyone's nose might be just a fraction shorter, and she raises her eyebrows higher on the rare occasions when she expresses surprise.

'Nothing happened. Nothing at all.' She gazes impassively at the horizon. 'He just wasn't interested.'

'My turn?'

'Yes. Your turn.'

Later in the day, Downeytwo goes to meet Treasa and Vita for coffee, bread and honey.

'Do you have scissors with you?' she asks them.

They do.

'Will you cut my hair for me? Short.' She wants to look different from her sister when she makes her move on Christopher Marlowe.

However, by one of those strange quirks of fate, Downeyone, with Bernadette for support, goes to a little barber's on a back street, and she too has her hair cropped, at around the same time.

We're doomed, thinks Downeyone. Her mind runs through the past, herself reflected in her sister, every action, every thought. What I do, she does, and what is done to her is done to me. We are as one.

However, Christopher Marlowe doesn't seem to think they are as one; he had no sexual interest in Downeyone but he is turned on by Downeytwo. We may be created from the same mould, thinks Downeytwo, and branded with the same number, but we are different.

'I didn't know,' Anna McBride says to her lover in his Athens hotel room.

'Didn't know what?'

'I had no idea it could be like that.'

'Better than in your fantasies?' He smiles. 'Am I as good as Monsieur Versailles?'

She blushes. She covers her small breasts with her hands. 'Better, better,' she says.

And when they kiss again, she murmurs insistently, 'More, more.'

He takes her wrists and lifts her hands away.

In the same hotel, in another room, Andrew McDonald sleeps with Mary Olivier in his arms. Once more she dreams the dream of the damned.

She is Daniel in the lions' den, but unlike the biblical Daniel she has no resources.

'*Agnus Dei*,' she says in her sleep. '*Danielus Dei.*'

Chapter Sixteen

Yes the memories taunt and twist
They torment and tease and bite
Round the corners of your mind
They are seldom far from sight.

Back in Trinity that October, some of them are heading into their last year. Anna McBride has completed her BA in UCD and heads down Grafton Street to Trinity to start her Masters. Jean Jacques Olivier flies into Dublin once a month for the weekend. Mary Olivier gets to choose the venue and the day or days for their meetings. If she takes the Friday, he invites Anna out on the Saturday, and vice versa. Sometimes Mary wants both evenings with him – and she gets them. Jean Jacques doesn't mind. He will for ever be making up for lost time with Mary, and he wants Anna to have some time to grow up.

'You're very young,' he said to her in Rome on their journey home from Greece.

'But I know what I want,' Anna protests, shaking her dark red hair back off her shoulders. 'I really do.'

'Listen to me,' Jean Jacques says. 'I want you too. But we have time. Let's not rush this.'

This is like conversing with Jean Jacques Versailles, she thinks to herself. 'But I want to be with you,' she persists.

'Do your Masters. Take your time.' He runs his hand through his dark straight hair. 'We have time. I'm not going anywhere. You see, I know how to wait. I can put in time. You're worth waiting for.' He can be persistent too. 'You need to date, to be with boys your own age,' he says.

'But I want to be with you,' she says again.

In the end she agrees to return to Dublin, to continue on the course she has marked out for herself, and to see him once a month.

'But wouldn't you mind if I dated other boys?' she asks.

'I will mind terribly,' he murmurs into her neck.

Then there is Mary Olivier, back in Trinity. She has changed her course. Philosophy has been abandoned in favour of history of art. With her nails in her pockets and the Greek sun still warming her blood, she sits in Sutherland Square with Andrew MacDonald who is going into his final year of political science.

'What does this place mean to you?' he asks, because she often suggests to him that they go and sit there.

'It's everything that school was not,' she says obliquely. 'It's where Kitty came to get away while the rest of us were locked up ...' Her voice trails away.

'What was it like?' he asks. He's intrigued by the different memories the girls all have.

'I don't remember,' she says. And she doesn't.

Kitty O'Dowd is busy in her hotel.

Brrrrr. Brrrrr. The phone rings at reception where Kitty is sorting keys.

'Good afternoon,' she says into the mouthpiece.

'Good afternoon to you,' is the reply in a Scottish lilt.

'Andrew.' She's surprised. She knows from the others that he's involved with Mary Olivier.

'I'm coming out your way this evening,' he says. 'Can I take you out for dinner?'

'I'm a bit busy,' she says.

'Well, a drink, and if you can fit it in, then dinner too?'

After she has put the phone down and sorted the afternoon post, Kitty O'Dowd heads for her apartment and decides to take a quick shower. Only because I need one, she tells herself. Not because I'm meeting Andrew for dinner.

Bernadette O'Higgins returns to college, and the final year of her science degree.

248

'Dr Denyll,' she calls down the pathway as she spots the broad shoulders and the neat hips of her tutor just ahead of her at the cricket pitch.

He spins round and he sees her – fair hair bleached further by the summer sun, the corners of her mouth turned up in a happy smile, dark blue eyes looking straight into his.

'Well, well, well, if it isn't my best student,' he says. 'You look like you had a good summer.'

'Mmmm.' She nods, thinking about the great winter she is planning.

'So where did we go?' he asks. 'We look like we've overdosed on clean living.'

She laughs. 'Very scruffy living,' she replies. 'We hitched across Europe and then went island-hopping in Greece. Sleeping on the beach,' she adds, in the hope of stirring his imagination.

She succeeds.

'Oh, really. Did you? How many of you?'

'Oh, it varied,' she replies vaguely. 'You know. A lot of us from here. We'd meet up, spend a few days together, and then move on . . . you know.'

'I don't,' he says. 'Come and tell me about it over coffee.'

She does.

Christopher Marlowe says to Andrew MacDonald, 'Is it true that you've lost your roommate?'

Andrew hesitates. 'Yes, yes it is. He's suddenly decided to take a year out to pursue a Swedish girl he met in the Grand Canyon.'

'Well, man,' says Christopher Marlowe endearingly, 'that means you've got a spare bed, doesn't it?'

'Possibly,' Andrew says. 'But they do know about John in Admissions, that he's taking the year out. The room is probably already filled.'

'Mind if I go and check?' asks Christopher Marlowe.

'No,' says Andrew. And he doesn't really mind. He's sorry in a way that John and he won't have rooms together, but Christopher is possibly a better option than someone he doesn't know.

'I'm planning on doing well in my finals,' he warns Christopher.

'Don't worry,' says Christopher. 'My studying won't disturb you!' (And indeed it won't, because he won't be doing any.)

249

And Christopher Marlowe gets the other bed in the other room. He's easy enough, more interested in smoking and lying in bed than in serious partying, but he does have his moments.

'I missed you, Kitty O'Dowd,' says Andrew MacDonald over a pint of Guinness.

She smiles. Kitty O'Dowd is no fool.

'In your sleeping bag, do you mean?' she asks.

He grins. 'We haven't slept together in a sleeping bag – not yet anyway, though we've tried most other places, haven't we?' he teases.

She sips her drink and eyes him over the top of the glass. 'Are you trying to flirt with me?' she inquires, her eyes taking in again how brown he is, and she thinks of what it is like to run her fingers through his curly hair.

'No, not trying. I am flirting with you.'

'Andrew, you're involved with Mary, aren't you?' Kitty wants everything clear so that she knows where she stands.

'In a way, yes.'

Kitty picks up the menu and looks at it.

'We're not sleeping together if that's what you mean,' he says casually.

'That's not what I heard,' Kitty says to the menu.

'Not in the biblical sense.'

'I don't want details,' Kitty says, trying to keep her voice neutral.

'I'll order for us both, shall I?' he asks, watching her carefully.

She almost nods. She has always liked the way he does that, but not this time.

It's Saturday night and in the Buttery are Bernadette O'Higgins, Anna McBride, Treasa O'Donoghue, Vita Grennit, and the Downey twins. Mary Olivier is out for dinner with her papa, and Andrew MacDonald has disappeared – in fact he's out in Dalkey wining and dining (and trying to woo) Kitty O'Dowd.

They all have rooms in Trinity, except for Vita who is staying the night with Treasa.

'It's awfully quiet, isn't it?' Bernadette moans.

'Christopher said to come up later,' says Downeyone. 'He has a surprise lined up.'

Bernadette looks around in the vague hope of seeing Dr Denyll, but for some reason the place is nearly deserted. There is no Dr Denyll. Indeed, there is hardly anyone.

In the Saddle Room in the Shelbourne Hotel, Jean Jacques Olivier asks his daughter about her rooms.

'Mmmmm,' she says as she picks at her food. 'I like my room. You'll see it later. It looks out on New Square. I'd have preferred Front Square but I was lucky to get a room at all.'

'You're not eating much, are you?' he asks.

'I'm not very hungry tonight,' she says, shaking her head. 'Sorry. I know I chose here. Sorry.' She shrugs.

'So, what'll we do for Christmas?' he asks.

She smiles. She loves him asking her this. He has asked it every year since he found her, and although it was far too late, it still gave her a feeling of belonging somewhere.

Kitty O'Dowd is in a stroppy mood and doesn't feel like listening. Kitty O'Dowd's biggest problem is that she doesn't think enough.

'What we have always had is special,' Andrew says to her.

'Ah, it was all right, I suppose,' she says.

'Don't be like that.'

'Don't be like what?' she says peevishly. 'Don't be irritated because I thought you and I were going out together again but it transpires you were screwing Mary Oliver on the beach in Greece? And then when you got back you didn't bother to call or anything.' She can hear herself and she doesn't like the sound of it at all, but she can't stop.

'OK,' he says, running his hand through his hair. 'Look, maybe I shouldn't have slept in the same bag as Mary, but we didn't have sex. She was out of it, either sozzled or stoned most of the time, and it was only a bit of fun, comfort, something like that – and, for the record, I only got back a few days ago. I had to go home to the parents in Scotland before heading back here.'

But Kitty can't stop. Her pent-up anger is running loose, and so is her jealousy that they all had their time abroad while she was stuck in Bray, and her usual nonchalance falls asunder.

'Don't give me that shit,' she says.

On his way back to town, Andrew MacDonald reasons that she could only be that annoyed if she had real feelings for him, but that Kitty O'Dowd in a huff is more than he wants to handle. As he crosses O'Connell Bridge, a light breeze coming up the Liffey from the sea lifts his hair. It also lifts his spirits and by the time he has stridden through Front Gate and is on the cobblestones, his scowl is gone.

He takes the stairs two at a time and stands on the silent landing, three floors up, hands in his pockets, looking out of the window at the tennis courts, and wonders where Christopher is.

Behind the door there is almost complete silence. The girls sit in various positions on the floor or on the sofa. In front of them is a large screen, and the whirr of a projector sounds in the background. The picture is still, pausing on hold. None of the girls move.

When Andrew MacDonald opens the door, the first thing he is aware of is the projector and the screen – and he halts in utter amazement.

He wonders where on earth the projector and screen came from. Then he momentarily wonders if he is in the wrong room. The silence, the stillness, the noise of the projector, the darkness lit by the screen. Then he takes in the girls, sprawled on furniture and on the floor. He shakes his head as he absorbs the scene. He looks again in surprise at the silent girls and then at the screen. He turns his head sideways to take in the still – it is a quivering picture of a man and a woman. It is explicit. He looks back at the girls and he sees the joint being circulated. He sniffs the air and grins.

They smile at him languidly.

'Hello, Andrew,' is the chorus.

'What's going on?' he asks. 'Where is Christopher?'

'He'll be back in a minute. He's gone to the loo.'

Andrew sits on the floor. Christopher returns and presses the button on the projector and to Andrew's amazement the man on the screen dismounts from the woman and the pair of them proceed to tear their clothes back on. There are no other words to describe their action.

'We're watching it in reverse,' Christopher informs him. 'This is the best bit.'

The girls are cracking up on the floor. Anna McBride is almost sick with laughter. Bernadette O'Higgins is rolling on the carpet clutching her stomach. Treasa and Vita and the Downey twins are almost in hysterics.

'May I inquire why you are watching it in reverse?'

'We've watched it the normal way,' Bernadette tells him, between gasps of laughter. 'Twice, in fact. We'd never seen a dirty film before. But it does get quite boring, so Christopher said we should try it this way.'

'It's so funny,' says Downeyone. 'The sex is sort of the same, but it's the other bits which are so hilarious.'

With that the couple on the screen reverse out of the door, now fully clothed, and the door closes. They go down the stairs backwards, climb backwards into two cars and reverse in different directions down the street.

'That was brilliant,' is the common sentiment.

'If you got really bored with your partner,' Bernadette opines, 'you could try having sex that way – starting at the end and doing everything backwards, and ending up with your clothes on.'

'Climaxing before you start?' Andrew inquires. 'I think you'd better pass me that joint so that I can catch up with the lot of you.'

On her way back to her rooms, Bernadette O'Higgins is still smiling when she hears a voice calling her.

'Miss O'Higgins!' It's Dr Denyll.

'Hello, Dr Denyll,' she giggles.

'I was looking for you in the Buttery,' he says. 'I thought you might be there. Do you have rooms?'

'Yes,' she laughs. 'I have rooms.'

'And do you serve coffee there late at night?' he asks.

And Bernadette suddenly has a vision of her room on the third floor in Number 7, her narrow bed, her two armchairs, the barred gas fire, her desk at the window, her own small paradise. But the flaw is that she has heard her nextdoor neighbour grunting and the sound of the neighbour's bed springs, and although she wants Dr Denyll, or maybe because she wants him, she cannot bear the thought of someone hearing them on her creaky bed.

She hesitates.

'Why don't we have coffee in my rooms?' he asks quickly, sensing some inhibition.

They repair to his study with its squishy sofa, and, when coffee is over, he guides her to the arm of the sofa, thinking she will bend compliantly for him so that he can take her from behind, just as he has taken dozens of others before her, and will in due course take dozens of others after.

Dr Denyll got this one wrong.

Bernadette O'Higgins, standing beside the arm of his sofa, turns her dark blue eyes on him and smiles.

'Maybe another coffee?' she suggests.

> *Yes, the sex is very good*
> *Even when we're stoned and weak*
> *It makes up for the lost years*
> *And drowns those memories ever bleak.*

Kitty O'Dowd walks purposefully from the bus stop back to the hotel. Nodding at the girl in reception, she goes into the small lounge and bar where five or six guests sit having a late-night drink. She clears one of the tables and takes the empty glasses to the bar. She chats briefly to the barman. He is about to take three drinks to the window table. She does it for him.

'Oh, you're the girl who checked us in this morning,' says one of the guests, a good-looking young man with a northern accent.

She smiles as she places their drinks on the table.

When she returns to the bar, he follows.

'Can I buy you a drink? Or is that not allowed while you're on duty?' he asks.

Kitty O'Dowd is momentarily tempted. He looks nice and she thinks for a moment that maybe that is what she needs. Someone she doesn't know to follow her to her apartment, to her bed.

But Kitty O'Dowd is too streetwise and knows never to mix business with pleasure.

She shakes her head. 'Sorry, not allowed,' she says, not adding that this is her hotel and that if she wants, anything is allowed.

She gets herself a large gin at the bar and disappears through the service door. She goes to her rooms, runs a bath, pushing away the memory of the man's disappointed face, and with it she tries to push away the memory of Andrew MacDonald kissing her lightly on the cheek and saying. ''Bye, Kitty. Take care.'

She has finished the gin by the time the bath is ready, and so, naked, she goes into her tiny kitchen, picks up a bottle of gin and brings it with her.

Lowering herself in under the foam in the bath, the thoughts and memories rise again.

We're tied, she thinks. Tied to the past. To all the different things that bring us to where we are today.

A profound thought indeed for Kitty O'Dowd, but then she does not want to let Andrew MacDonald go. She, too, is sailing stormy waters, but the water seems to be carrying her away from him. Sitting upright in the bath, she pulls her knees up and rests her chin on them. She pines for him. She knows that if he were there, his fingers would move slowly but surely up and down her long elegant spine; that he would lift the hair at the back of her neck so that he could kiss her there, just under her hairline.

She opens her throat and pours the gin from the bottle straight down.

Treasa O'Donoghue and Vita Grennit are lying on Treasa's bed in Number 32, a floor above Mary Olivier's rooms. There is a string with a small pebble carefully tied to it hanging from Treasa's window straight down to Mary's. When Treasa wants to contact Mary and doesn't feel like going down the stairs, she simply pulls the string up and attaches a note to it. When she lets it drop out of the window, the pebble taps on Mary's window – and Mary reaches for her message.

When Mary wishes to contact Treasa, she ties a note to the bottom of the string and yanks gently. Another pebble, carefully positioned at the top, then taps on Treasa's window.

These girls are resourceful.

'Treasa?'

'Mmmmmm?'

'I'm going to miss you,' says Vita, blue-eyed, blonde-haired, long-legged, perfectly tanned.

'Mmmmmm,' replies Treasa.

'Miss me?'

'Mmmmmm,' murmurs Treasa again.

'Christmas?'

'Mmmmmm.' Sleep is calling Treasa. And indecision. There is no rule that says she must decide about Christmas right there and then.

Her eyelids are heavy.

And Treasa is asleep.

Tap, tap, tap.

'I'll get it,' says Andrew MacDonald, standing up and going to open the door.

Christopher Marlowe is lying on the sofa with Downeytwo in his arms. Anna McBride (still Bridie to her friends) and Downeyone are sitting on the floor on either side of Andrew's legs, until the knock on the door.

Mary Olivier smiles at him through half-closed eyes when he opens the door to her. Stepping out onto the landing, he opens his arms to her and she lifts her face to his lips.

'Is that you, Mary?' Anna McBride calls to the half-open door.

'Er, ummmmm,' responds Mary Olivier.

'Time for me to hit bed,' Anna McBride says to the darkened room, and she gets up to go.

'I know where she's gone,' says Downeyone to no one in particular.

Downeytwo giggles.

'Where has she gone?' asks Christopher Marlowe as he languidly runs his fingers through his twin's hair.

'She's gone to Mary's papa,' replies Downeytwo.

'What?' says Andrew MacDonald.

'Don't be ridiculous!' says Mary Olivier.

'Bet you she has, though,' says Downeyone.

'Who cares?' says Christopher Marlowe.

Neither of the Downey twins answers.

'Does it matter?' Christopher asks with a rare degree of curiosity.

It matters to Anna McBride.

She rolls on her back and looks at the ceiling. She wishes Jean Jacques

256

Olivier would stay the night. But he won't. He doesn't want Mary, whose room is above Anna's, to know what he is doing directly below her.

Mary Olivier, who espied the projector and screen the moment she entered Andrew and Christopher's rooms, insists on watching the porn film.

When it is over, she sits on the floor leaning against Andrew's legs, knowing that her cheeks are bright red. She swallows. She has no idea what to say.

'Dull, isn't it?' says Downeytwo.

'Mmmmmm,' responds Mary, trying to work out what the earlier consensus was.

'Christopher, play it in reverse for Mary,' says Downeytwo. 'This is so funny, Mary. You'll love it.'

These are good guidelines for behaviour, and so Mary laughs with the others as the film reverses. But she is squirming inside. She has managed to portray the image of the liberated student to the others, frolicking in rooms when she should have been at lectures, appearing rosy-cheeked with languid eyes an hour or so later, but the truth is Mary Olivier is virga intacta.

'God bless America,' sings Christopher Marlowe to the room.

'Well, that's questionable,' responds Andrew, 'both as to whether he'd want to, and as to whether it would be appropriate.'

'Wouldn't it be nice to be able to go to the cinema for once without a bomb scare?' Downeyone asks. 'I've seen so many films these last years where we've been booted out halfway through, and it's so boring having to watch the first half again when you go back.'

'Maybe you should ask them to simply play the whole film in reverse and you can leave when they get to the part you've already seen. You can tell them how successful other films are when shown backwards!'

This suggestion is met with howls of laughter.

'There's a late night film showing in the Academy, why don't we go there?' Christopher asks.

He ends up going with Downeytwo. Downeyone heads for her room, while Andrew and Mary stay where they are.

In the hotel in Bray, the man with the northern accent approaches the barman and asks about Kitty O'Dowd. He is informed that she is the proprietor and the manager, and the man waits until the barman's back is turned then slips through the door where he saw Kitty O'Dowd disappearing some twenty minutes earlier.

Kitty is in her bath, supine, and dreaming. Her phone rings. She opens her eyes.

It's got to be Andrew, she thinks. She half rises from the bath, then sinks back down into it. Let him stew, she thinks.

As it happens, it is a wrong number, and in due course the caller rings off.

A moment later, the man with the northern accent reaches the door of her apartment and knocks.

Convinced that it is Andrew, and thinking now that he must have been inside the hotel when he rang, she reaches for her towel and scrambles out. Suddenly the thought of being in bed with him is all-consuming, and dripping foam and water, with the towel partially covering her, she hastens to the door and opens it.

Later she said to Treasa, 'It was a bit like that day I hid behind the curtain and sneezed. I know you weren't there, but there was the same element of surprise. I don't know which of us got the bigger shock!'

'What happened then?' Treasa asked.

'I started to giggle.'

'And he, the man, what did he do?'

'He laughed and laughed.'

'For goodness' sake. What did you do?'

'What do you think I did?' Kitty said with a grin. 'I asked him in of course. I'd been drinking, I was a little woozy and very giggly.'

'Well, go on. You can't leave me in suspense,' Treasa pushed.

'Well, in he came. I'd been holding the towel in front of me, and so when I turned to lead the way inside . . . well, you know!'

'No, I don't know,' Treasa said. 'You're being very coy!'

'I think he thought that too. He got a full view from behind, which wasn't deliberate. It really wasn't.'

The man lets out a gasp of both surprise and appreciation, because there is no doubt that Kitty O'Dowd's body is very beautiful. It is both lean and gently curvy, long and supple, and she looks back over her shoulder to see why he has gasped and then she realises that he is getting a full dorsal view.

There is no point in trying to cover her bottom, because in doing so she will simply reveal more, so she shrugs Kitty-style and goes on in ahead of him.

'I'm just going to put something on,' she says. 'I'll be right back.'

'Don't,' he answers her. His voice is suddenly low and heavy. 'Don't. Stay like that. Please.'

Maybe it is something in his voice, or perhaps it is Kitty reacting to not having lolled topless on Greek beaches, but either way she smiles and sits.

They face each other on chairs. Both are quite still as they take in the other.

Kitty, a little the worse for gin, feels both wanton and wanted.

And he, the nameless man with the northern accent and the handsome face, watches her, taking in again the high cheekbones he had noticed earlier, and her slim neck, the clarity of her collar bones and the angles of her shoulders.

It is like a moment cut out of time and woven into tapestry.

He lifts his head slightly and in doing so somehow indicates that he would like her to let the towel drop.

And Kitty O'Dowd does.

'You did not!' said Treasa O'Donoghue.

'Yes, I did. Why not?' asked Kitty defensively. 'Why shouldn't I? I work really hard. I'm careful and sensible and all the things I never wanted to be. Why shouldn't I have?'

'I'm sorry,' Treasa said, with a sudden insight into what Kitty's life was like now. A routine of early rising and late to bed, covering up for missing staff, frugal, careful living, with little time for herself. 'You're dead right,' Treasa continued. 'Why shouldn't you have fun. I just meant, weren't you scared? I mean, you didn't even know his name.'

'I don't know,' Kitty replied. 'There was something about him. He seemed nice ... no, I wasn't scared. And anyway, I'd already had rather a lot of gin.'

They both smiled.

'And was it good?' Treasa asked.

'Was what good?' Kitty was going to make Treasa pay for her momentary surprised disapproval.

'The sex,' Treasa said. 'You know – *one, two, three, four, who's that knocking at my door; five, six, seven, eight, slip in quick before it's too late.* The missionary position or whatever you got up to.'

Kitty laughed. 'Not telling,' she said.

And so they have affairs. Some are secret, some are not. They curl up with their lovers and share whispered thoughts. They laugh with each other and share anecdotes, and pry, sometimes gently, sometimes ruthlessly, into each other's lives.

The sun doesn't rise as high, and the shadows it casts are longer and darker as autumn moves to winter and the girls cast off the past.

'But we are tied to the past,' Kitty had said to herself in her bath. 'We can't escape it. It is the link between birth and now.'

Gin-sodden thoughts that washed down the drain when Kitty pulled the plug.

Through the bustling days of childhood, bustling tragic days of childhood
Days that thrilled her, days that filled her with terror never felt before
So that now, to still the beating of her heart, she stood repeating:
"'Tis some visitor entreating entrance at my chamber door—
Some late visitor entreating entrance at my chamber door;
                    This it is and nothing more.'

Chapter Seventeen

It is early summer after the turn of the century, the year of Our Lord two thousand. Kitty O'Dowd, blonde streaks in her well-cut hair, is drinking coffee in the conservatory attached to her office behind the hotel. She is checking orders, ticking off items, page after page. The intercom buzzes and the receptionist at the front desk calls through on the line, 'Miss Maple is here to see you.'

'Send her through,' Kitty says. 'And have some more coffee sent in, thank you.'

She ticks off two more items, and then puts her pen down just before there is a knock on the inner door.

'Come in,' she calls, getting up and going through to greet her old teacher.

'Kitty, my dear.'

'Miss Maple, how nice.'

'Maeve. I always tell you to call me Maeve.'

They meet fairly regularly as Maeve Maple still lives within a mile of the hotel.

'Old habits die hard, Maeve,' says Kitty. 'Come and sit. Coffee is on its way.'

'Have you seen the paper?' Maeve Maple asks.

Kitty shakes her head. 'Not yet. It's often evening by the time I get to it. Why?'

Maeve passes her the newspaper she has folded under her arm. 'It was on the news this morning,' she says. 'But I take it you didn't hear that either.'

Kitty takes the paper from her and shakes it out so that she can read the headlines.

'Jayzus,' she says. She puts the paper on the table by the window and sits down and reads the article carefully.

'Jayzus,' she repeats. She looks up and she and Maeve Maple gaze at each other.

In Edinburgh, on that same morning, Andrew MacDonald has just finished dressing after showering. Bernadette O'Higgins rolls onto her back and says, 'I really better get up.'

'Stay where you are,' he says. 'I'll go and get the papers and some croissants and I'll come back. I don't have to be anywhere until twelve.'

'I'll shower while you're gone,' she says, sitting up among the crumpled bedclothes. 'And I'll put coffee on. Will you get me the *Irish Times*?' she adds.

'Old habits,' he says, at about the same time as Kitty O'Dowd uses the very same term.

'There could be a review of my book – although I don't think it's likely. I don't think it'll be until Saturday. No, that's just an excuse. You're right. Old habits . . .'

'It's much more likely there'll be a review in one of the papers here after the reception last night,' he says. 'I'll check while I'm out and buy whatever.'

'Don't worry,' she says, swinging her legs out of the bed and stretching naked in front of him, her arms straight above her head, her back arched. 'My agent will pick up whatever there is.'

'Nonchalant, aren't we?' he says. He reaches out and very deliberately takes hold of her right nipple which he grips between his thumb and forefinger and, looking into her eyes, tweaks it.

She runs her tongue slowly over her top lip. Neither says anything. Their eyes are locked. He removes his hand and guides her gently backwards towards the bed before unzipping his trousers.

Anna Olivier (née McBride) stirs in Jean Jacques' arms in their bed in their apartment in Washington. Jean Jacques Olivier holds her in his sleep, aware that a tremor has gone through her, knowing that her old nightmare is troubling her. She wakens in his arms and forces herself to open her eyes to shake it off, to escape the clutches of the torment which occasionally penetrates her sleep. She gets out of bed and goes to the kitchen where she puts on the kettle. She will drink tea and read for half an hour before going back to bed. By then she will have distanced herself from the dream and will sleep again safely spooned against Jean Jacques' back, until the alarm goes off at half past six – or so she supposes. But she has got that wrong because this is no ordinary night.

Andrew MacDonald returns to the apartment which Bernadette rents, complete with the *Financial Times*, the *Irish Times*, and *The Scotsman*. 'There's a photo of you in *The Scotsman*,' he says and places the papers on the table. 'And there's been an attempted crucifixion in Dublin,' he adds.

'Sounds gruesome,' says Bernadette, reaching for *The Scotsman*. As she slithers the paper out from under the *Irish Times*, her eye is caught by the photo of a priest on the front page of her home paper. She picks the paper up and stares into the face of Father Michael McMorrow. She shakes her head as she reads the article.

'Did you read it?' she asks.

Andrew is watching her. 'Do you know him?' he asks.

She nods. Her face has paled.

'What is it?' he asks.

She shakes her head again. 'Just a priest we knew at school. Someone . . . well, someone mustn't have liked him very much. It's very odd,' she says. 'Look.' And she hands him the paper.

'Couldn't have happened to a nicer fecker,' Kitty O'Dowd says drily to Maeve Maple. They are sipping coffee from a silver coffee pot in china cups. 'I didn't like him,' she adds, in case Maeve hasn't picked that up.

'So I gather,' Maeve Maple says. 'I hadn't realised. I was quite shocked when I heard it on the news this morning, and when I saw the photo of him I had no doubt that it was him, and I was shocked for him. But why didn't you like him? Goodness, I remember, you had a run-in with him, didn't you? During the Retreat.'

Kitty O'Dowd shrugs. 'It's history,' she says. 'It's nothing to do with now and I don't want to be reminded of it. I actually think crucifixion or whatever you would call this is too good for him. I'm glad he didn't die.'

Maeve Maple is startled. She has never seen Kitty so angry or so bitter. 'I didn't mean to upset you,' she says. 'I was coming down to you anyway to see if you'd like dinner this Friday or Saturday.'

'I'd love it,' Kitty says, tearing her eyes away from the paper. 'That would be lovely.'

Andrew MacDonald checks his mobile while Bernadette pours the coffee.

'Ooops,' he says. 'I have to call the office urgently. Start without me.'

Bernadette puts the croissants in a tiny wicker basket and places jam and butter on the table. She can hear his side of the conversation and from the first few words she knows something is up.

'Hello, Ian,' Andrew says. 'What?'

He sits down.

'Repeat that? You can't be serious . . .' He reaches for the *Irish Times* and looks at the picture. 'Get me on the next flight for Dublin. Call me back on the mobile – I'll leave it on.'

He disconnects.

'What's happened?' Bernadette says. 'Just tell me.'

'Mary has been arrested,' he says. 'In Dublin, for that . . .' he nods towards the paper. 'My wife, Mary,' he adds, in case Bernadette is in any doubt as to which Mary he means.

Bernadette sits staring at him as she tries to make sense of what he's saying.

'It must be a mistake,' he says. 'She couldn't have . . .'

Bernadette's eyes are closed now. She's thinking, no, this can't be. And her brain, clear-thinking and logical, is overriding her emotional response and is saying, yes, this is it. This has really happened.

'I'm coming with you,' she says. 'I'll transfer my ticket – as soon as you know which flight Ian has got you on. I'll ring in. I'll be with you.' Her mind is leaping backwards to long ago, and forwards to now and the practicalities of the present. Time enough later, she thinks, to remember and to understand.

'What about Olivia?' she asks Andrew about his seventeen-year-old daughter.

'What do you mean?' he asks.

'Where is she?'

'At school. She's a boarder.'

'Don't tell me she's a boarder in Ireland?'

'No,' he replied. 'She's here, in Scotland.'

'Well, you need to protect her. Either you get on to the school and you talk to her, or you get Ian or a relative over there now. She has to hear about this from family, not from the papers. It'll be on the evening news if not the lunchtime one.'

'Yes, yes,' he says. 'May I use your phone? I need to keep my line clear.'

'Of course,' she says.

Within the next half-hour he and Bernadette have afternoon flights lined up for Dublin. His sister is on her way to the school to talk to Olivia. Ian has arranged a lawyer in Dublin.

In Washington it's six in the morning and the phone rings. Jean Jacques Olivier reaches out a hand and picks it up.

'Hello, Andrew,' he says.

Anna Olivier (née McBride, once upon a time Bridie to her friends) opens an eye and looks at her husband. She wonders why he is being called at such a time.

Jean Jacques listens. He makes various gasping sounds as he takes in what he is hearing.

'Mary,' he says. 'Mary. My daughter. Our Mary?' His disbelief is almost tangible.

Anna sits up beside him in the bed. Her hand holds his bare shoulder. She can feel how frantic he is.

'We'll be on the first flight,' he says.

And they are.

Treasa O'Donoghue on the farm in Wexford hears on the lunchtime news that Mary MacDonald (née Olivier) has been arrested for the attempted murder of Father Michael McMorrow. She sits down when she hears it. She puts her elbows on the table and rests her head in her hands.

'Oh, God,' she says. 'Oh my God.' Over and over.

Vita Grennit, her partner, comes into the room, and comes and puts her arms round her.

'On the news,' Treasa says. 'I heard on the news . . . that my uncle, you know, Uncle Mick . . . Someone . . .' She can't finish the sentence. She sits there, trying to let the details of what she just heard sink in.

Vita sits beside her and waits.

'You remember,' Treasa starts again. 'You remember Mary Olivier who married Andrew MacDonald . . .'

'Of course I do,' Vita said. 'And Anna McBride married Mary's father one month later. I was there. It was all such fun. It's all right, I know who you're talking about. You're obviously shocked, Treasa. What's happened? Mary was coming here to stay, remember. She was due yesterday. Now, what's happened?'

'Well, Mary has been arrested for the attempted crucifixion of Uncle Mick. At least, that's what they said on the news.'

When it has sunk in, Treasa goes to the phone and calls Kitty O'Dowd.

'Kitty, is that you? Did you hear the news?'

Kitty only knows what she has read in the *Irish Times*. The bit about Mary MacDonald, née Olivier, is news to her. She had been standing at her desk when the phone rang; she sits down suddenly when Treasa tells her about Mary.

'Do you suppose Andrew knows?' Treasa asks.

'Of course he must,' Kitty says. 'I wonder is he here in Dublin?'

'I don't think so,' Treasa said. 'Mary was coming to stay with us for a few days, and when she didn't arrive last night . . . well, I just thought she'd come today. She was going to do some shopping in Dublin and then come on down . . . She said Andrew was busy in Edinburgh . . .' Her voice trails away as none of these things now seems important.

Kitty is silent. She is thinking.

'Shouldn't we do something?' Treasa asks.

'Andrew will make contact,' Kitty says. 'As soon as he arrives. We still meet up for the occasional drink whenever he's over. Bridie and Jean Jacques will come over no doubt, but they'll probably want to stay in the city. It'd make more sense.'

'Can I come up and stay with you?' Treasa says. 'I feel very cut off down here in Wexford.'

'Hold on until we hear more. It could be a mistake,' Kitty says, but her voice is doubtful. She doesn't think it's a mistake.

Andrew and Bernadette arrive late afternoon, and are immediately ensconced with Mary's legal team.

'Why did they arrest her?' is Andrew's first question.

'She walked into Pearse Street garda station and gave herself up.'

'And what had she done? Or rather what did she say she did?' Andrew asks.

'She said that she saw him in a video camera in a shopping centre and, quote, "I decided to crucify him," unquote. She followed him and when he went into the oratory of a small church, he was alone. She left him.' The lawyer consults his notes. 'She went and bought a hammer, and a wreath of flowers because the flower shop didn't carry wreaths of thorns. That's a quote, by the way. She went to an outdoor sports shop and purchased an item, which could only be described as a spear, and then she returned to the oratory. There was no sign of him, and so she sat down and waited.'

'And does any of this tie in with what subsequently happened?' Bernadette asks.

The team of four nod as one.

'Why a hammer?' Bernadette queries.

'Apparently she had nails in her bag,' is the reply.

'That would be right,' Andrew says. 'She always carried nails.'

'She what?'

'Oh, long story,' he says.

'No, it could be important. Why did she carry nails?'

'I always thought it was supposed to be . . . I don't know, some kind of satire on people who carry rosary beads. I mean, she wasn't a Roman Catholic – she'd left the church long ago. In fact it was difficult to get her ever to go into one. I think she went once for something – a confirmation maybe, something like that. She didn't like churches. She objected to the icons in the church – said they belonged to the Dark Ages and smacked of witchcraft.'

'Can we see her?' Bernadette asks.

'Not this evening. She's appearing in court in the morning. I imagine a psychiatric evaluation will be the next step.'

'For God's sake,' says Bernadette. 'I mean she's mad. If she did it then she must be barking mad – they can't send her to prison if she did it.'

'What exactly did she do?' Andrew finally gets the words out.

'What exactly did she do?' Kitty asks. She is sitting in the bar of the hotel where Anna and Jean Jacques Olivier are staying. Jean Jacques and Andrew are with Mary waiting for the psychiatric evaluation to start.

Kitty, Treasa, Anna and Bernadette are sitting drinking coffee. They are all in various stages of shock.

'I mean, you can't believe half of what is in the papers.'

'I think in this case you can,' Bernadette says. 'Unfortunately.'

'But what does it mean?' Treasa asks. 'I mean, why, why would she put a spear through his side?'

'I think she meant to kill him,' Anna replies. 'She hit him with the hammer first – presumably to incapacitate him. Then she speared him. She put the wreath of flowers on his head – she says she couldn't get a crown of thorns – and she placed a nail in each of his hands.'

'But she didn't hammer the nails in or anything, did she?' Treasa says.

'No . . . no, she didn't.'

'So it wasn't really a crucifixion at all, was it?' Treasa is being very persistent.

'No. It wasn't,' Bernadette says. 'It's more like a parody of a crucifixion – more like she was making a point . . . though maybe we shouldn't pursue that line, it makes her sound very sane.'

'And sanity won't do,' Kitty says wryly. 'Sanity won't do at all. Well, I, for one, am delighted McMorrow is down and nearly out.'

'Why?' Bernadette asks.

'Why what?'

'Why are you delighted?'

Kitty doesn't answer. 'We need more coffee,' she says, and she raises her hand to attract the waiter's attention.

*   *   *

270

Anna Olivier (née McBride) is sitting with Jean Jacques in their suite. He is pale and tired.

'I just don't understand why she did it,' he says.

Anna says nothing for a moment. She is trying so hard to keep the shutters down around her memory. She doesn't want to open that segment of her life.

'It's all right,' she says comfortingly to him. 'It will be all right. It'll all fall into place – I'm sure.'

'Why would she do that?' Andrew MacDonald asks Bernadette. 'If you know something, would you please, please tell me.'

Bernadette bites her lip.

'What did he ever do to her that she would do something like that?'

'Kitty says that she's really glad McMorrow is down if not out,' Bernadette ventures. 'Though she is sorry that it was Mary who did it,' she adds hurriedly.

'And how do you feel about it?' Andrew asks.

'How do I feel about what?'

'About Father McMorrow.'

Bernadette gets up and goes to the window. They are in her apartment.

'I'm glad he didn't die,' she says.

'What kind of a reply is that? What do you mean you're glad he didn't die?'

'Because I want him to suffer and I don't believe in an afterlife and neither does Mary – and that's why she didn't kill him,' Bernadette says. Her voice is very quiet. Very tired.

Andrew says nothing for a few minutes as he digests this. 'Are you going to tell me what this is all about?' he asks.

Bernadette shakes her head. 'No.'

'For Mary's sake, if not for mine, will you tell me?'

'I don't know Mary's story,' Bernadette says. 'I only know my own. And because of that I'm glad she did this mock crucifixion on him.'

'Well, will you tell me your story?' Andrew asks.

Bernadette shakes her head again. 'It's not relevant. Not now. If it

271

becomes relevant, I'll tell you. Do you know something – another irony in this story? When I started school, one of my brothers gave Mother Immaculata the nickname The Raven. He teased me, saying that she would come tapping on my chamber door. He frightened me, actually.' Bernadette pauses for a moment before continuing. 'And it was a long time later that I realised it would have been a more appropriate name for Father McMorrow.'

> *See that priest with rosary beads,*
> *He makes her shiver, then she cries,*
> *A snake and balls has The Magpie*
> *And he will show her paradise*

'I think one of the girls called him The Magpie, and that was appropriate too,' she adds vaguely.

Bernadette O'Higgins is fourteen years old. She is in Irish College with Treasa O'Donoghue, in a large school building at the edge of the sea some sixty miles north of Dublin. She has her period and so she isn't swimming. Treasa is leaping up and down in the waves with dozens of other girls. She looks occasionally at the rocks and waves at Bernadette.

Bernadette is dressed in yellow shorts and a pale primrose T-shirt. She has plimsolls on her feet and her bare legs are brown. Her fair hair is plaited – neatly braided by Treasa. They often do each other's hair. Treasa's is more difficult to do as it is a mass of long black curls and is difficult to tame. Bernadette has a bit of a pain in her stomach.

It's a colder day and there is quite a breeze – hence the waves. The next time Treasa waves to her, Bernadette gestures that she is returning to the school, that she is cold.

She climbs back over the rocks and onto the little winding path that leads back up to the grassy playing fields beside the school. She moves along nimbly on the narrow path.

'Hello there.' It's the priest who's attached to the school for the summer. 'Where do you think you're going? Aren't you supposed to be down on the beach with the others?'

'I was feeling cold, Father,' the fourteen-year-old Bernadette replies politely. 'I'm coming back up for a jumper.'

'Well, I'll accompany you,' he says. 'What's your name?'

Bernadette shudders. She opens her eyes and she is in the living room of her apartment and Andrew MacDonald is still sitting on the sofa opposite her. He doesn't say anything. He just watches her.

'Can I sleep here tonight?' he asks.

She nods. 'I assumed you would. You're always welcome. I think I'll have a bath,' she says.

'You look like you could do with a drink rather than a bath.'

'Will you pour me one? And bring it in to me?'

He nods.

He sits with her in the bathroom, holding the glass of brandy to her lips whenever she looks for a sip. She is lying full length in the bath, her hair is pinned up on top of her head. Her nipples point upwards out of the water. Andrew takes a sponge and caresses her with it under the water.

'Hold this,' he says.

She looked down in disbelief. She's seen one before – more than once; after all, she has brothers, but not like this, not stiff, not protruding from a man's trousers. Not this. Not like this.

She is frozen.

'Hold it like this,' he says.

'You're crying,' Andrew says.

'It's just the steam from the bath.' But there are tears slowly rolling down her cheeks.

'It's all right,' he says to her. He takes the flannel and he wipes her face. He pulls the plug and helps her to her feet and wraps her in a towel.

'It's all right,' he says as he unpins her hair and brushes it out. He dries her carefully and she slips between the sheets.

'Don't leave me,' she says.

'I have a call to make, then I'll be right back.'

'That was Andrew on the phone,' Kitty says to Treasa. 'I'm seeing him in the morning.'

They, too, are sipping brandy.

There are so many unsaid things. So many things they have never asked each other – or when they did, the other accepted the throwaway response.

But Treasa knows.

And so does Kitty.

Treasa O'Donoghue is nearly eleven. Her mother has just been buried in the local cemetery. Her Uncle Mick is the priest presiding over the funeral rites. Treasa has a grubby hankie balled up in one hand. With her other hand she is holding on tightly to one of her siblings' hands. Years later she doesn't know which sibling it is. The face of the person beside her is white; so is Treasa's. Her eyes are red-rimmed. Her father bends down and takes a small handful of soil from the ground. He carefully picks a stone out from the earth and drops the stone on the ground. He looks at the soil in his hand and he lets it sieve through his fingers into the hole. There is a light thud and rustle as it lands on the coffin. Treasa feels as if she cannot breathe.

They go back to the house. Uncle Mick pours whiskeys and Treasa goes outside to the big oak tree. Vita is there. She wasn't at the funeral because the Grennits are Protestants and wouldn't have felt welcome in the little village church. Treasa and Vita are about to climb the tree when Uncle Mick appears.

'I need to talk to my niece,' he says to Vita.

'I'll come back later,' Vita says, 'if I'm allowed. Otherwise tomorrow.'

Treasa wishes Vita doesn't have to leave.

''Bye Vita,' she says.

Vita goes to get her pony and heads across the fields back home.

Treasa stands at the foot of the little wooden ladder and Uncle Mick says, 'Hold this for me.'

Treasa looks at Kitty over her brandy.

'How old were you?'

Kitty scowls. 'How old was I what?'

'Don't, Kitty. Not now. Please. How old were you? I was eleven. It was the day they buried my mother.'

Kitty stands up, picks up her cigarettes and goes out through the conservatory to the garden. She lights one and looks up at the starry sky. She can smell the salt on the sea breeze.

Treasa appears beside her.

'We live in a wonderful world,' Kitty says. 'Childhood is gone, and we can be us. I am NOT going back down that road. Not for anything.'

'Not even for Mary?'

Kitty doesn't answer.

'Hold this for me. That's right. No, tighter. Now loosen your grip. Now tighter. Kneel down, my child, and bring it to your mouth.'

'I can't,' Kitty says. 'I won't. I won't. Now I wish Mary had hammered him to death. I wish . . .'

Treasa says nothing. She stands there in the garden looking at the movement of the trees, feeling the warmth of the summer night, tasting the slight saltiness in the breeze. She folds her arms across her chest and holds herself tightly.

'I remember once,' she begins, 'in Trinity, sitting on the steps . . . Do you remember? We were meeting for lunch and we were talking about school and someone said, "Sure, we all survived." Was that you? Could it have been you who said that? And I thought, "Yes, she's right. We did. We all survived." But I don't think so. I don't think so now.' There are tears coursing down Treasa's face.

'Oh, Kitty. I feel sorry. Sorry for all of us. For you and me and Mary – and for all the others – there will have been others, I'm sure. Kitty, I want to survive – I want to walk away from here and never look back. But life's not like that. I don't want Mary to go to prison for what's she's done. Assuming that she did do it. I don't see why she should go to prison for it. And I'm going to do whatever I can to help her. No matter what.'

Kitty looks at her and stubs out her cigarette. 'I can't.'

'The more of us there are, the stronger we will be,' Treasa says.

'I don't want to tell anyone. I don't want . . .' Kitty's voice breaks. 'I can't. I don't want to remember.'

It's the following morning. Kitty is back in the garden, this time with Andrew. They're drinking coffee. Kitty is smoking, one cigarette after the other. She has asked how Mary is.

'She's appearing in court this afternoon. I don't have long. I have to get back into the Four Courts.'

'So what's up, Andrew?'

'Tell me what happened that made Mary try and murder Father McMorrow.'

Kitty stubs out her cigarette. 'I can't. I knew that was why you were coming. And I can't. All I can suggest is that you talk to Treasa.'

'You're as bad as Bernadette.'

'Bernadette?' Kitty sounds really surprised. 'Bernadette ...' There is silence as Kitty digests this. 'Not Bernadette too,' she says eventually. 'Oh, God, not Bernadette too.'

'Give me Treasa's number,' Andrew says briskly, taking out his diary.

'She's inside. She's staying here.'

'Then get her, please go and get her. I need to know. It's the only way I can help Mary.'

Kitty sighs and then she stands up and goes inside.

And as she reaches her office door, she suddenly finds herself thinking of Anna McBride and that summer when she first met her. She remembers looking at Anna and thinking why did they stick such a child into our chalet, and then she got to know Anna, and there was something about her that made her want to help her.

Her hand is motionless on her office door handle. She feels a chill going through her. She knows suddenly why she felt that empathy. She knows ...

God, Anna, she thinks. Little Bridie ... But she couldn't have known McMorrow. She couldn't. He would have been in the West of Ireland then. And she hadn't started at the convent. Or maybe she had, maybe she had just started ... but before that she didn't even go to school. She didn't start school until ... until when? Maybe I'm wrong. Maybe ... it could have been with someone else. It can't have been McMorrow. McMorrow didn't turn up in St Martin's until our last year.

She hesitates. She almost goes back to tell Andrew, then changes her mind. What right have I to talk about Anna, when I won't even talk about myself?

She fetches Treasa.

'You said you would help Mary, Treasa,' she says. 'Andrew is in the garden and he would like to talk to you. And I'm sorry, but no, I haven't told him what happened to me. I can't. But if you can tell him about you, that might help.'

Treasa nods.

She is wearing navy blue trousers and a light blue shirt with the top buttons open.

'You look very well,' he says to her. 'Reassuringly the same.'

And she does. She looks healthy, her dark curly hair still tousled, she still has a large bottom, but her shirt hangs neatly over it now. They kiss lightly.

'I missed you yesterday,' she says. 'Though I was there.'

'I don't have much time,' he says. 'Please, will you fill me in? It's like a book, not just with pages missing but with whole chapters left out.'

'I've promised myself to help Mary,' she replies. 'If what I tell you is not relevant, will you promise me that you will simply forget it?'

He agrees.

'A long time ago . . .' Treasa begins. It's difficult to find the words. There is this fear that by saying them, she is opening something that won't close.

'A long time ago,' she repeats, 'Father McMorrow . . . he is my uncle, by the way . . . He . . . he abused me. I'm sure there is some legal term for it, but I don't know what it is. He orally raped me.'

Andrew sits looking at her.

'I was eleven,' she adds.

He doesn't say anything for a long time. He feels waves and waves of shock wash over him. He feels like Kitty felt ten minutes earlier when her hand was on her office doorknob and it was as if the numbers in a combination lock suddenly clicked into place.

'I'm so so sorry,' he says. 'I don't know what to say. I'm so sorry.'

She sits on her chair, her legs crossed, her handsome face lifted so that he can see her clean-cut features, her lovely dark eyes, and he looks through what is there before him, and he sees a little girl.

He puts his hand to his head. 'Oh, God. I'm so sorry.'

'You don't have a lot of time,' Treasa reminds him. 'Ask what you need to know and then you should get back into town. The traffic . . .'

'Thank you,' he says. 'Did Mary? Was Mary? Did she . . . ?'

'I don't know. I think so. Several things happened in our last two months of school. And Father McMorrow was there. Mary fainted ... I don't know why. And then she started acting very strangely. There was always something slightly off balance about her back then, but later ... after the incident on the roof, she seemed fine then. She really did. Her father turned up that night after she had fallen from the roof. And their wonderful meeting. Mary seemed reborn. And then Trinity – and, you remember, Mary was the life and soul of the place.'

'It would tie in,' he says. He is thoughtful. His mind is running up and down the years, trying to piece things together.

'Nails,' he says. 'What are the significance of the nails?'

'I don't know. What nails?'

'She always carries nails with her. She said they were to remind her.'

Treasa shakes her head. 'I don't know. It doesn't mean anything to me.'

They are silent.

'Treasa,' he says. 'I'm grateful to you.'

'What happened to me may not be connected,' she tries hopefully. 'But if it is, I'm here and I'll stand by her.'

'Why did you decide to tell me when neither Kitty nor Bernadette would?'

'Bernadette?' Treasa is truly shocked. 'Not Bernadette ... oh, no, not Bernadette ...'

'The thing is,' Andrew continues, 'you are *not* alone. This is probably way bigger than you think. If, just like that, there are already four of you, you'll find there are way more. And if it is connected with what Mary has done, and I think it has to be, then the more of you we can find who will talk, the better.'

'I wonder what sparked it off with Mary,' Treasa says. 'I mean why now, what made her do it now?'

'Apparently she saw him, on a video screen, standing behind her outside some shop. I don't know if that is enough to explain it. Maybe there is something else. I just don't know. Look, I have to go. I'll be in touch.'

He stands up and they embrace.

'Kitty and I are coming too,' Treasa says. 'We want to be there.'

'If you can get her or Bernadette to talk ... well, that would help.'

'I'll try,' Treasa says.

Chapter Eighteen

M ary MacDonald (née Olivier) is charged with attempted murder and is released on bail into her father's custody at his request.

'What about Andrew?' Kitty O'Dowd asks Anna Olivier (once McBride, Bridie to her friends).

'How do you mean?' replies Bridie. 'Because Mary's not in Andrew's custody?'

'Yes, I suppose that's what I meant,' Kitty responds.

'Their marriage is long washed up,' Bernadette says with inside knowledge. 'They've done their own thing for years, just stuck together because of Olivia.'

'How is Olivia?' asks Treasa.

'Fine,' says Bernadette. 'Andrew is great with her. So is Mary, but obviously not at the moment.'

They leave the court, Mary surrounded by her family and friends. She is dressed in her olive green trouser suit and a contrasting top which usually accentuate her foreign good looks and her sallow skin, but which now make her look wan and ill.

Jean Jacques Olivier has his arm round her, supporting her, and Andrew moves ahead with the police, making a way through the crowd until they reach the cars. Mary and the other four women slip into Kitty's BMW and go to Bernadette's apartment, while Jean Jacques goes with Andrew to organise an apartment through a letting agency as they will have to stay in Dublin in the interim.

Kitty puts on coffee, and Bernadette organises Mary with fresh towels and clean clothes.

Anna Olivier gets the cups and saucers. Treasa pours milk into a jug.

As soon as they have done their designated task, they move into the living room and in due course are joined by Bernadette, Kitty and the coffee.

There is little, if any, talk between them. They each appear to take on certain duties, and occupy themselves with fulfilling them.

Mary has showered by this stage, and emerges looking clean if a little pale from the bathroom.

'I smell normal again,' she says. 'That was awful. Awful. I don't want to spend another night in custody or prison or anywhere locked up ever again.'

'And you won't,' Treasa says fiercely. 'You won't.'

'Would she have diplomatic immunity or anything?' Kitty asks hopefully. 'I mean with her father being in Washington, and Andrew being in the Scottish Parliament.'

Anna shakes her head. 'It doesn't arise,' she says.

'Wishful thinking on my part,' says Kitty.

'Thank you all for being here,' Mary says. 'Thank you for . . . I don't know . . . rallying around.'

'Do you know what I'm reminded of?' Bernadette says suddenly. 'I keep thinking about the Three Graces – we are like them, only we're the Five Graces. Coming together to support each other, giving each other help, when help is needed.'

'I don't know that you can do much to help me, though,' Mary says, tying the belt of Bernadette's dressing gown round her and sitting down.

'What are the Three Graces?' Treasa asks.

'It's a statue, marble, one piece – of three women, the Graces—'

'That's the one in Edinburgh,' Mary interjects. 'Picasso did one as well – stunning in its own way. Their names are Euphrosyne, Aglaia and Thalia.'

'It was the Edinburgh one I meant,' Bernadette says. 'I forgot you did art history, Mary, or I'd never have tried to show off my little knowledge. I always think of you doing philosophy. I forgot you transferred.'

They laugh.

'*These three on men all gracious gifts bestow, Which deck the body or adorn the mind* . . .' Mary quotes. 'And the point of the Three Graces was not that they gave each other support. Isn't it funny how you remember some things and forget others?'

'What do you mean?' Anna asks.

'I had forgotten so much,' Mary says. 'And yet I forget nothing about art or things that are beautiful.' She looks at the coffee cup in her hands. 'I'd forgotten the things that I shouldn't have forgotten,' she says sadly.

'That's what we do to survive,' Anna reassures her. 'We can't carry all the bad or painful things with us – it would hurt too much. So we bury them. Is that what you're talking about?'

Mary nods her head.

'I did that,' Anna says. 'As well as I could . . .'

There is silence.

'I didn't,' Treasa says. 'I wasn't able to forget, all I could do was push it away.'

Kitty gets up and starts topping up everyone's coffee.

'Sit down, Kitty,' Treasa says. 'Please. It's like Bernadette said. The Three Graces, only we're five. But in our case it is support we can offer each other. And I think, I'm almost sure, we're all in the same boat. Five of us can work better than just Mary and me on our own.'

There is silence again.

'I've thought about this nonstop for two days,' Anna says. 'I don't want to go into the bad place in my mind. I don't want to remember, but if it will help Mary and Jean Jacques . . . for them I will go down this road. Treasa is right. Five of us can work better together.'

'Well, now we're three,' Treasa says.

No one looks at Kitty and Bernadette.

Bernadette swallows. 'I don't want to do this. I don't want my pain shown to the world. It'll be in the papers. I can't bear the type of publicity it means. Although the irony is that I live off publicity. But the truth is, we're going to be in the papers and on the news anyway. They'll dredge up everything. We're all going to be on the news this evening, coming out of court with Mary, pushing our way through the crowds. And the reality is I will be here with Mary for the duration, and I need to be able to live with myself. So if my telling my story is likely to help Mary, then I will. Count me in.'

'Then there were four,' Treasa says.

'I need more time to think,' Kitty says. 'I have to have more time.'

'That's OK,' Anna says.

'I was eleven,' Treasa says to no one in particular.

'I was fourteen,' Bernadette says.

'I was eight,' Anna says.

'I was sixteen,' Mary says. 'But I didn't remember. I remembered nothing until last week. I'd gone for hypnosis because I have claustrophobia and it came out during the hypnosis. I've been trying to deal with it . . . with the memories . . . for just over a week. They were fragmented . . . the memories, I mean . . . just bits, horrible bits . . . things he'd said in confession . . . dirty things . . . and something to do with the Sacristy . . . I don't know how I got there . . . I think he brought me . . . he made me do things in there . . . and every time he saw me alone, he'd come up and say things, suggest things. I don't know how many times he got me that week . . . you know what I mean . . . got me . . . did me . . . forced me . . . I don't know. Then I saw him. I just saw him standing there and everything came back. All of it. How he kept appearing in the school. And then there was that awful day in Mother Immaculata's office – the day you were expelled Kitty. How I envied you. God, how I envied you. I was paralysed. He paralysed me . . .'

Anna gets up and comes and sits beside Mary. She puts her arms round her. 'It'll be all right now. I know it will be. I just know it.'

'Oh, God,' Mary says. 'You're my stepmother. That in itself has always stunned me. You're younger than I am. And now I discover that you went through the same thing . . . and you were only eight. For God's sake. You were eight. It's unbearable. How do you live with it? How do you live with the memory? How do you live with the bits that keep coming up to the surface and won't go away?'

'You get used to it,' Kitty interjects suddenly. 'You get used to it.' Her voice is angry and bitter.

Mary is crying now. She looks over at Kitty and shakes her head. 'I don't know how to,' she says.

'We'll help,' Bernadette says. 'We'll all help. We'll talk about it. We'll support you. We'll do this all together.'

'I wish I'd stuck that spear in him,' Kitty says. 'I wish I'd thought of banging him on the head with a hammer. And the floral wreath on his head, Mary. I loved that.'

'They didn't have one of thorns,' Mary says sadly.

And suddenly they are laughing.

'Did you really try to buy a crown of thorns?'

'Yes, but the assistant in the shop said it was the wrong time of year. Holly wreaths only at Christmas, she said.'

And they crack up. These women in their forties, in a plush apartment overlooking the city, are suddenly laughing so hard that there are tears pouring down their cheeks.

'A crown of thorns,' Kitty says. 'Oh, Mary, how did you think of it?'

'I made him kneel before I hit him with the hammer,' Mary adds.

'God, Mary, you didn't?'

'I did too,' she says. 'Just like he made me kneel.'

'Good for you,' Kitty says.

'And the spear? What about the spear?'

'Oh, it was more a harpoon, for deep sea fishing, you know,' Mary says.

And yet again the four of them shriek with laughter, and this time Mary laughs too.

'This is how you're going to live with it,' Bernadette says. 'This is how we're all going to live with it. Somehow we are laughing – can you believe that? Somehow we are laughing about it all. And when this is over, someday when this is over,' she repeats, 'when we come out the other side of this, the five of us, and whoever else out there, we will laugh again.'

'I have such a wonderful image of that unholy fecker on his knees and you bipping him with the hammer,' Kitty says. '*Oh, Mary had a hammer,*' she hums. '*And she hammered in the morning . . .*'

'If he doesn't recover, it'll be a murder charge,' Mary says. 'And I wasn't trying to kill him anyway. If I had been, he'd be dead. Believe me.'

'I refuse to ask how he is,' Kitty says. 'But, will he recover?'

'Probably. The bastard is on the critical list, but his order says "they are hopeful".'

'Hah,' Kitty cries. 'Hopeful! They won't be quite so hopeful when we tell the world our stories.'

'He may be crippled,' Mary adds.

'Good. Crippled is good,' Kitty says. 'He crippled us. He destroyed part of our lives, why shouldn't he be crippled?'

'What happened to Christian forgiveness, Kitty?' Bernadette asks teasingly.

'What happened to Christianity?' Kitty replies. 'What happened to *suffer the little children* . . . ? What happened to the myth of compassion and love and . . .' Her voice gives way, and she makes a sort of silent gulping sobbing sound. She rests her head in her hands for a few minutes. Then she looks up and it is as if she has braced herself. Bernadette is reminded of that look on her face on her last day in school. A decision made, Bernadette thinks.

'Kitty,' she says aloud. 'That last morning in school, when you put the shoes behind the curtain, you wanted to be expelled, didn't you?'

'Yes,' replies Kitty. 'The Raven had lined up an appointment for me with McMorrow – and there was no way I was going to meet him.'

They watch her as the pieces of the jigsaw fall into place.

'By the way, where were you all when it happened to you?' asks Kitty suddenly, assuredly, of the others. 'I was in a convent in Mayo.'

They look at her as they realise she has joined them. Bernadette smiles at her. It is like a team being picked, or lines being drawn, and they are all on the same side.

'I was in St Martin's, as you probably know,' Mary says.

'I was in Irish College in County Louth,' says Bernadette.

'I had just come home from my mother's funeral in Wexford,' Treasa says.

'I was at home. He came to the house to prepare me for my First Communion,' says Anna. 'He said, "Now you are a true bride of Christ."'

'Bride of Christ,' says Kitty O'Dowd. 'The bastard.'

'He got around, didn't he?' Bernadette says thoughtfully. 'Bridie was eight when . . .' Her voice trails off. 'And then Bridie was fourteen when he got Mary . . . so in the space of six years he was in five different places that we know of. Isn't that odd? Surely that is odd. Aren't priests put in one place and stay there for a number of years?'

'Are you saying . . . are you suggesting . . . do you mean that he was moved deliberately?' Treasa asks.

'Well, I've never heard of a priest getting around like that,' Bernadette replies.

'But that means either someone knew and was shifting him on or ... or what? What else can it mean?' Anna says.

'Oh, they knew all right,' Kitty says.

'What do you mean?' Bernadette and Anna ask together.

'I told them,' Kitty replies. 'I told them.'

There is silence as the other four look at her.

'Told them?' Bernadette says. '*Told them?*' she repeats. There is disbelief in her voice. 'Who did you tell?'

Kitty clenches her hands. I can do this, she thinks, as she opens the windows of her memory. I can do this. I can walk into the memory, take it out, share it, and then put it away for ever.

There is silence. The other four are looking at her, expectantly, nervously, hopefully.

'It was Easter,' Kitty says. 'My father was ill, and I'd been left in the convent for the holidays.'

At first her voice is low and quiet as she searches for the words to tell her tale – the story she has kept secret and silent since that fortnight.

When Father Mulrooney leaves the parish and the convent situated on the darkest edge of Europe, and returns to Dublin, having set fire to his backside during class, he is replaced by a young curate fresh from a wealthy suburb in South County Dublin, rosy-cheeked, small greedy eyes, blond curly hair (main interest: girls, pre-pubescent, pubescent, post-pubescent – he isn't fussy.)

He arrives during the Easter holidays, when there is only one girl in the school.

'Good morning, Father,' says Kitty O'Dowd when she sees him outside the convent on Easter Saturday as she heads for the beach to smoke a cigarette which she has bought for herself with the money her mother has sent her to make up for not going home during the holidays.

'Good morning,' he says with interest as he eyes the pubescent Kitty whose legs are lengthening by the day, and whose little breasts are budding under her gymslip.

Two weeks later Kitty O'Dowd goes down to the meadow beyond the north wing of the school, and there she takes off all her clothes. She grits her teeth and lies down on the tall nettles (Easter is late this year and the nettles are plentiful) and she forces herself to roll over and over on them.

Afterwards she crawls back to her clothes and with shaking screaming fingers she re-dresses herself and crawls back in the direction of the convent. Sister Christopher and Sister John, wimple-clad, with ruddy, round faces, find her as she knees her way onto the gravel.

'God Almighty,' says Sister John in total shock at what she sees. They carry Kitty, who by now has swollen almost beyond recognition, her face blotched and raw, her eyes closed, into sickbay. The kindly Sister Jude, whom Kitty has not yet met, undresses her with care and calls the doctor immediately.

'Never seen anything like it,' he says. 'Almost like millions of nettle stings. Extraordinary.' He leaves calamine lotion to be spread on Kitty, and gives her an injection to deal with the pain, and promises to call back in the morning. After the injection Kitty stops shaking and lies totally still, clasping Sister Jude's hand and refusing to let it go, even when Sister Jude whispers, 'You poor sweet child, let me put the lotion on.'

Kitty, whose neck is swollen, cannot even shake her head, but her eyes speak of her anguish and distress, and Sister Jude postpones treating her with the calamine lotion and sits and holds her hand and whispers comforting words.

'I don't know,' says the doctor in the morning to the kindly Sister Jude. 'It's like allergy on top of allergy. It's easing a little, I think, but she is in great distress. Call me if there is any change.'

And Sister Jude sits with Kitty until the school chaplain arrives.

'Leave me alone with her, Sister,' he says to Sister Jude.

Kitty moans and moans and reaches for the kind nun's hand.

'I think I ought to stay, Father,' says Sister Jude, all crisp white in her nursing garments and a small neat wimple on her head.

'I'd like to hear her confession,' says the priest as the distressed Kitty tries to hold on to the nun.

'I'll just be outside, Kitty,' says Sister Jude. 'I'll be back the moment Father is finished with you.'

Kitty shaken, Kitty white, Kitty raw ... Kitty opens her mouth and screams.

Later that day, after another injection, safe with Sister Jude, Kitty whispers, 'Don't leave me alone with Father McMorrow, please don't, Sister Jude.'

286

And Sister Jude suddenly stiffens as if an icy hand has crawled over her skin, and she says to the troubled feverish child in the bed, 'Why not, Kitty?' She swallows nervously, because Sister Jude is afraid of the answer. 'Why not, Kitty?' she repeats.

And Kitty, just like most girls of her age, doesn't have the words to say why not, cannot explain properly, and she whispers, 'Bad man,' and she points vaguely to her sore mouth and makes a vague gesture which looks as if she is miming holding an ice pop.

Sister Jude says, 'It's all right now. It's all right. Sleep now. I'll mind you.' Finally Kitty sleeps and she starts to get better.

'Reverend Mother.' Sister Jude is standing in Reverend Mother's room, a white room with large windows and a crucifix on the wall. She looks to the crucifix for courage, her heart is pounding.

'Mother,' she repeats. 'I have a problem and I need your help.'

The rain pounds on the window, the sea is crashing beyond the walls, even the seagulls have hidden. It could be the end of the world – but it isn't.

'The child is lying,' says Reverend Mother. 'How dare she.' There is a pause while Reverend Mother considers the situation. 'Though perhaps her fever caused her to hallucinate. I wonder . . . How is she today?'

'She slept through the night and there has been a definite improvement this morning. Her temperature is nearly normal and the allergy has abated somewhat,' says the nervous but kindly Sister Jude.

'Not a word of this to anyone, Sister. I will handle this when she is better. Another day or two, do you think?'

Sister Jude nods.

Reverend Mother sweeps into sickbay the following day to take a look at the patient, and then sweeps out again. Sister Jude holds Kitty's hand and she is afraid for the thirteen-year-old whose skin is fast returning to normal.

Kitty recovers and returns to her dormitory two days later. The following morning she is called to Reverend Mother's room where she is hit with the strap repeatedly for lying.

'But I'm not lying, Reverend Mother,' says Kitty steadfastly. 'I told Sister Jude the truth. I did.'

Kitty is a pragmatist but she is also stubborn. She holds out.

'I'm not lying,' she sobs some time later. 'He did . . . he did those things. He did.'

'I put it to you,' says Reverend Mother (also a pragmatist), 'that you just think these filthy things happened because you dreamt them up while you were ill.'

Kitty doesn't answer. She stands there looking at Reverend Mother with tears pouring down her face and a cold and frightening fury building up in her heart. There is silence and Reverend Mother chooses to take this silence for assent.

'You are a wicked, wicked girl, Kitty O'Dowd,' says Reverend Mother. 'And I am going to have to deal with you severely. But first I want you to go to confession and then report back here to me. Father is down in the chapel waiting.'

Kitty O'Dowd backs out of the room. She is shaking. She is distressed. She feels a multitude of emotions as she tries to work out what to do. She cannot . . . She will not . . . He must not . . . This is aloneness. This is isolation. This is terror. She feels that she has had it. There is no one to help her. She trusted Sister Jude and now she feels betrayed. And there is no one else. There is nothing. She thinks of the cliff edge – if only she had jumped that day, that first day last September. She thinks of running there now, but Reverend Mother is beside her and the long walk to the chapel has begun, where he, her tormentor, is waiting.

Kitty O'Dowd thinks long and hard. He is not going to touch her again, she would prefer to be dead. But how can she stop him?

'Reverend Mother,' she says in a small voice.

'Yes,' snaps Reverend Mother as they progress down the corridor.

'Please, Reverend Mother, will you wait while I'm doing confession?' says Kitty as her mind furiously works to find a way to survive.

'I most certainly will,' says Reverend Mother. 'I still haven't decided what to do with you. I will be right outside the door of the box, my girl.'

If he touches me I'll scream, thinks Kitty to herself.

Of course he can't touch her in the confessional. The bars between where he is and where she is keep them apart. He slides back the tiny door so she can see his profile, and then he turns his eyes on her and they look at each other.

She drops hers. She is afraid. She has no armour. She starts to see that her

288

only weapon is never to be alone with him, but she cannot see how she can safely ensure that when he calls all the shots.

Outside the confessional, Reverend Mother listens to the silence, and she prays for guidance.

That night Kitty O'Dowd runs away. She makes it to the next town by dawn, where she is picked up by the local garda and brought back to the convent.

Reverend Mother, who has received a call from the police station, is waiting for her, and after the garda leaves, Reverend Mother addresses Kitty. Every crime she has ever committed is brought out and displayed as evidence before her.

'You have been trouble since the moment you arrived. You are a thief and a liar – most of all a liar,' says Reverend Mother. 'Under the circumstances, and bearing in mind your recent illness which brought about hallucinations of the worst kind – clearly the hand of the devil at work I feel that we cannot keep you here. There is no place for a liar in our midst. You will leave this place this morning, and you will put this behind you, having learned a lesson.'

'I'm being expelled?' Kitty asks.

'Yes, but with a slight difference. I have decided that although we can't keep you here, our sister convent in County Leitrim would be a good place for you to continue your education. I've phoned Mother Magdalena in Leitrim and she is expecting you in time for lunch so we need to get you organised.'

'Does my mother know?' Kitty ventures. A train ticket home would be preferable but anything is better than staying here on this windswept cliff top with that chaplain wandering the corridors and grounds of the convent at his pleasure.

A letter is sent to the O'Dowd parents which complains about their daughter's lies and her wilfulness. This is digested in the O'Dowd household with anger and animosity towards their daughter and a great deal of gratitude towards the good sisters for taking care of Kitty with such a degree of concern and arranging her transfer to County Leitrim.

And so Kitty O'Dowd's bags are packed while her classmates are at breakfast, and she is out of the convent before they know anything about it. Arriving after the start of the summer term raises questions in her new classmates' minds and, when asked, Kitty just says that she ran away from her previous school and was expelled. She knows no one would believe her if she told them what had really happened.

She trades a kiss for a fag and that's as far as it goes that summer. Kitty knows what's behind the zipper. Her innocence has been destroyed, her natural curiosity deadened and she's not going to make out with anyone, not even Jeremiah Jackson, until she is well and truly ready. So, despite the fact that she gives the impression of having been there and done that, in actual fact she hasn't been there, but she has had that done to her. She's cynical now. She sneers at the parish priests when they come into the hotel for tea and scones. She looks at them with a slightly raised eyebrow and her head held just marginally too high.

'That girl is trouble,' they say to each other . . .

'Golgotha,' says Kitty O'Dowd, as she finishes her story. 'I called that place in County Mayo Golgotha. On the very first day I stood on the cliff edge and I thought about jumping. I've wasted years of my life knowing that it would have been better if I had jumped.'

Anna Olivier (still Bridie to her friends) is sitting back in her armchair, her eyes are closed and tears are pouring down her face.

'Poor Kitty,' she says over and over. 'Poor, poor Kitty.'

'Poor me?' asks Kitty, looking up and around at the others.

'Yes, poor you,' says Bernadette. 'And poor all of us.'

Kitty gets up and goes to Anna. 'Little Bridie,' she says. 'Don't pity me. You were only eight years old. For God's sake . . . eight years old.'

Treasa brushes the tears off her cheeks with the back of her hand. She cannot speak. She too stands up and comes over to Kitty and Anna and she holds them both.

They reach round and hold their arms out to Mary and Bernadette.

'Recently,' Anna says with a small smile coming through her tears. 'I had a dream.'

Holding her in their circle, they listen.

'I dreamt I was in the garden with my bear – I had a bear called Grizzle – and these friends . . . imaginary friends I used to play with. And two of them, Tom and Mary I think . . . two of them were swinging a skipping rope and singing a skipping song. And the song went

First it's soft and then it's hard
I won't think about my God
He wouldn't do such a thing to me
Hop, skip, jump . . . would he?

I can skip and I can hop
But I can't ask the priest to stop
White on black, and black on white
He can get me day and night.

A bride of Christ and very good
I always do what I should
Kneel when I'm told before my God
First it's soft and then it's hard.

'That's it. That's all I could remember.'

'That's a nice song for the playground,' Kitty says, the irony heavy in her voice.

'That was our playground,' Mary MacDonald responds.

'Mother!' said I, 'God of evil! – Mother, Father, bird or devil! –
Whether sent by God, or whether tempest tossed thee here ashore,
Desolate, yet all undaunted on this island cliff enchanted –
In this place by horror haunted, – tell me truly, I implore –
Is there hope and love and truth – tell me, tell me I implore!'
                    Quoth the Raven, 'Nevermore.'

Chapter Nineteen

Bernadette O'Higgins goes to visit her mother. Mrs O'Higgins is sitting in a comfortable armchair in her room in the nursing home. She is wearing a blue dress with a thin white cardigan around her shoulders. She manages to look both frail and elegant as she sits beside the window. Her hair has a rinse in it, which adds to the silver greyness of it. It is softly permed.

'Hello, Mummy,' Bernadette says, a smile on her face as she approaches her ageing parent to kiss her. There is the gentle fragrance of flowers and perfume. It's subtle. It suits.

'Oh, Bernadette,' says Mrs O'Higgins, lifting her face to greet her only daughter. 'Why, I saw you on the television last night!'

'Oh?' says Bernadette carefully.

'That looks like it was a very successful book launch,' says her mother.

'Mmmmm,' says Bernadette noncommittally.

'Everyone wanted your autograph,' says her mother.

Interesting perspective, Bernadette thinks to herself as it dawns on her that her mother saw the news with herself and the others pushing through the crowds outside the Four Courts.

'You're such a high-achiever, as they say nowadays. I'm very proud of you,' her mother says.

'Oh, no, no,' Bernadette says. 'I just do my best. Isn't that all any of us can do?'

'Well, you've done well.'

Bernadette did not know what she had been expecting, but it certainly wasn't this. She pulls up a chair and sits on the other side of the window where she can see her mother and look out over the garden.

'Which book was it?' her mother asks.

'You have my latest one,' she replies obscurely. 'Would you like to sit out in the garden?'

'No, I'm fine here, thank you. It's warm with the sun coming in the window and I'd have to wear a warmer cardigan if I went out.'

They talk around things, food, the weather, personal items which her mother might want Bernadette to bring for her. It is an easy conversation between mother and daughter, although Bernadette knows that her mother's mind is slowly becoming less stable, that if she says she would like more talcum powder, or a new slip, she may in fact not need or want either at all. There will be less and less time to ask pertinent questions.

'Mummy,' she says. 'May I ask you something? It's something that sometimes puzzles me.'

'Yes, darling. Ask me anything.'

'Why did you send me to St Martin's?'

Her mother sighs. 'Well, I thought the local convent would be more . . . convenient, I suppose. But your father wanted the best for you, like the boys got the best. And St Martin's was that. It offered everything. Not great on sport, I know. But it had everything else. Good teaching. And you were safe there. That was one of the things I liked about it.'

Bernadette thinks about this. Do you really believe what you are saying? she wonders to herself. Presumably. And yet you too are a product of the convent system. She is puzzled. 'But, Mummy, you only know in hindsight that the teaching was good. And not everyone did as well as I did.'

'You fulfilled your potential – *that* was what counted. The nuns always gave a good education. Your father said that would happen there.'

'But what about the other things? The safety, for example. Why do you think I was safe?'

'The nuns, darling. The nuns – they offered that kind of secure environment.'

Bernadette, who has been looking out of the window at two elderly men walking down the garden, now looks over at her mother. You believe that, don't you? she thinks. 'But you read things in the papers,' she says to her mother. 'You know, you must have seen things about, well, about abuse, for example.'

'Oh yes, darling. I have read that kind of thing. But that wouldn't happen to people like us. Dublin Four? Safest area to live in. People like that wouldn't come near there. They'd stand out a mile. And your convent, it was the best – it was the best!'

Bernadette nods. There is no point in pursuing this. No point in distressing an elderly lady who thinks her daughter's latest book was launched on television the previous evening. 'Has Daddy been in?' she asks.

'I'm not planning on seeing him again,' her mother says, after a moment's pause.

'Why ever not?' Bernadette asks.

And then to Bernadette's consternation, she sees tears in her mother's faded eyes. She looks more closely at her.

'He was the one who insisted you went to that school,' her mother says again. 'He said it was the best place.'

The two old men, who have now reached the end of the garden, turn and start their slow walk back. Bernadette watches them. One points at the flowers with his walking stick, and she can see that they are chatting. What's the point? she thinks. What is the point? My mother knows. She knows only too well. What is the point?

She looks back at her mother who is fumbling for a handkerchief. Bernadette gets up and fetches her a freshly laundered one from her wardrobe.

'Slightly watery eye,' her mother murmurs.

Bernadette leans over and hugs her. She knows that they are tears, and not slightly watery eyes.

'That's all right, Mummy,' she says. 'You were a good mother, you know that, don't you?'

'I did my best,' her mother replies. 'It wasn't always right, but it was my best.'

'I know,' Bernadette says. 'I do know that.'

Her mother's tears are flowing faster now, and suddenly Bernadette knows that her mother is only too aware what she saw on the news the previous evening.

There is a gentleness between them.

Bernadette wants to say, 'You should see Daddy again. It wasn't his fault either. It was no one's fault. It was the times that were in it. It was the Church not taking responsibility. It was the power of male over female. And just as we were manipulated by the nuns and Kitty was outmanoeuvred by them, so did they have their strings pulled by the male hierarchy.' But she knows it is not the right time to say anything. She smiles instead at her mother and picks up the book she is reading and asks her about it.

'Everything is all right, Mummy,' she says gently. 'There is nothing to worry about or to be angry about.' Later, she thinks. Later, I will tell her it really is all right. That she should see Daddy again. They did their best. I know that. In so many ways, so many people did their best. It's just unfortunate that their best was not good enough.

She thinks about Sister Jude in the convent in Mayo. And she knows in her heart that Sister Jude did not let Kitty down, no matter what Kitty may say. That Sister Jude epitomises so many of the good and decent nuns they knew over the years. That Father Michael McMorrow, although one of many, is not representative of the whole.

'Tell me something,' Treasa says to Kitty O'Dowd. They are sitting in Bernadette's apartment. 'Tell me something that has always puzzled me. What did you do that day you were expelled? It's always been on my mind. I lay there in bed in sickbay, and I was feeling better until you scarpered. I remember lying back on the pillows after Bernadette left the room, and all I could think was, "Where are you, Kitty? What are you doing?" And I was so upset for you. I could imagine you walking around the streets and I was so upset.'

Kitty O'Dowd shrugs.

'No, go on, Kitty. In the spirit in which we are all sharing and coming to terms with things, please tell me.'

'OK,' Kitty says. 'OK. I left the building. I remember walking down the steps and being glad it was a warm day because I had no sweater or jacket with me. I had nothing. No money. Nothing. And I wasn't going to wait in the school for my father to arrive. I mean to say, out of the frying pan, etc.' She pauses. She can remember clearly that feeling of having escaped as she set off resolutely down the road, unsure of where to go or what to do, but knowing she had to put some distance between herself and St Martin's.

'I went to Sutherland Square, thinking maybe Andrew would be there, and I sat down and had a smoke, and then it dawned on me that it was only late morning and there was no reason to think Andrew would turn up there at all. I mean, why would he? I'd said I'd phone him during the week, we had no plans.' She smiles. 'Isn't it funny how, when you think you are free, you actually are not. You need your friends. Like now, I mean.'

'So what did you do?'

'I walked to his home on Lansdowne Road and I found a coin on the ground outside his gate. I pocketed it and then I knocked on the door. A maid or someone answered, and said, quote, "Young Master Andrew is not at home." So I went and bought a bar of chocolate in the kiosk at the top of the road and I sat down on a seat that used to be there and I ate it. And I waited and waited. God, I must have waited for hours.'

She remembers the day getting hotter and hotter, and all she wanted was a glass of water and then suddenly she saw him. He got off a bus and she couldn't believe her relief on seeing him.

'I nearly got knocked over running across the road. I think I was afraid he was a mirage. And a car horn blared at me and I nearly burst into tears. Can you imagine?'

'You bursting into tears? No,' says Treasa. 'Not really.'

'I suddenly felt really vulnerable. Anyway, Andrew took me back to his house and I had something to drink and a sandwich, I think. Something like that. Then he phoned Christopher Marlowe. Remember him? Well, he phoned him and we went round to his place.

'There had been quite a lot of activity in the Marlowes' over the previous day or so. On the way, Andrew filled me in. It appeared that Christopher's mother had had a breakdown of some sort, booze related, I think, and she had suddenly left for the States for some kind of a detox unit. And there was a staff problem in the house, to do with her erratic behaviour, so Christopher ensconced me in the servants' quarters.' Kitty laughs at the memory. 'I was the live-in maid, and Mr Marlowe, when he got in from whatever he did, was delighted they had finally got someone to live in.'

'How on earth did you get away with it? I wouldn't have known what to do.'

'That bit was easy enough. You've forgotten I was brought up in a hotel. I had no problem with cleaning floors and scrubbing loos. And they had a cook who came in daily. It worked perfectly. Admittedly it wasn't what I'd planned, but it did work perfectly. While you were all doing your Leaving Cert. I was shining the front doorknob and dusting the bookcases. Actually, I'm exaggerating. I put in about two hours a day and the rest of the time was mine. There was just Christopher and his dad around, and his dad was hardly there. I kept that up all summer, and in September I got the job of my dreams.'

'What was that?' Treasa asks.

'I wanted to be a model in the College of Art – I really, really wanted to do that. Dreadfully paid, I know, but that wasn't the point, and what with the Marlowes paying me anyway, it didn't matter. I wanted to be able to say to The Raven, if I ever saw her again, that I had fulfilled my dreams! Think how much that would have annoyed her. Anyway, I stayed in the Marlowes' and did their housework around my few hours in the college.'

'I'm impressed,' Treasa says. 'Real survival instincts at work there, Kitty. Did Mrs Marlowe return from the States?'

'She did,' Kitty replies. 'And do you know something funny? She really liked me. I think she was quite vulnerable when she returned home. I don't know what had gone down before she left, but I think it was pretty dramatic whatever it was, because when I arrived there that Tuesday, there were a couple of guys replastering the walls and there were some very strange holes in them – the walls, I mean! Anyway, Mrs Marlowe liked me. She would come and drink coffee in the kitchen with me and she was just really nice to me.'

'And Christopher? Where did he fit into all of this?'

'Well, he was busy with his Leaving Certificate at first. Then he was out and about. I was still seeing Andrew. Then in October Christopher went to college, Stateside, as they say. And Andrew had gone into Trinity with you lot, and I sort of lost touch.'

'And your parents?'

'Oh, I got in touch with my mother. I sent her a postcard saying I was alive and well and living in the lap of luxury – which was sort of true. And in due course I increased the contact and we met, and I'm so glad about that. Really glad about that. Because the year after, my father had the big heart attack – remember?'

Treasa nods. 'Yes, I remember. That was when we got in touch again.'

'And the rest is history. I went back to the hotel and helped my mother. She died the following year and it was suddenly mine – and that was wonderful. It was like being given another chance.' She looks down at her hands. 'I've always been given another chance. I really was lucky and I know that. That's why I don't want to blow things now.'

The charges against Mary MacDonald are reduced to common assault.

'Is this good or bad?' Anna Olivier asks her husband who has aged considerably in recent weeks.

'It's good,' he says. 'Come here, Anna.'

She curls up in his arms on their sofa in their rented apartment in Dublin.

'I'm torn apart,' he says. 'With guilt that I wasn't there when Mary was a child. That I wasn't there for you when you were a child. That when Mary fell from the roof in St Martin's, we didn't pursue it then. That we didn't pursue why she was out there in the first place. It suited me to think she had gone for a cigarette. I didn't want to think what is now so clearly apparent.'

'But what could you have done?' Anna asks him gently. 'It wasn't your fault that you weren't there in those early years. You looked for Mary. And even if you had found her, then what? She might still have ended up in St Martin's. She might still have been on that Retreat in nineteen seventy-two, and Father McMorrow would still have been the priest. She might still have ended up climbing out onto the edge of the roof. What happened might still have happened. And you wouldn't have been able to change that. And we covered up. We, as girls, covered it all up so carefully – a mechanism for dealing with it. You can't beat yourself up over that. And I truly believe that Mary forgot what happened. After she fell from the roof, it was a form of escape for her. That's what the psychiatrist said. She just blotted it out. And your coming back into her life at that point, well, that was everything she needed. It stabilised her. Remember, by October she was in great form, and she went into Trinity and took it by storm.'

'What would I do without you?' he asks.

'It works two ways,' Anna replies. 'What would I do without you? That night in seventy-two, when we met in the hospital, when they were checking Mary and you arrived ... remember, Treasa and I were sitting in the corridor in the hospital and you appeared ...' Her voice trails away. 'I've told you this before. I know you don't really remember me from that night, but I remember you. I've told you about your name and how you were the man in my dreams, you know all that. You know what you mean to me.' She smiles at him. 'When we met in Greece a few years later ... well, not every girl gets to live her fantasy life. Now, enough of that. Tell me about the reduction of the charges to common assault and the implications.'

'It's unclear,' he says. He, too, is smiling. He knows every intimate detail of her fantasies and how he brought those fantasies to life. He is just shocked at the things she hadn't told him. He strokes her hair. 'It appears that either Father McMorrow or his order is behind it. It's a much lesser charge. But the defence stays the same. The testimony of you girls is everything.'

Anna smiles. He always refers to her and the others as 'girls', and it pleases her.

'Afterwards,' he says, 'we'll take Mary back to Washington with us. She needs a long rest and a lot of care, and I don't think returning to Scotland is a good idea.'

'Does she know?'

'Yes, both she and Andrew have agreed. She needs help. She'll leave him now and come with us and we'll get her that help in the States.'

'But she's not mad, or anything,' Anna ventures.

'Mad?' He thinks about the word. 'No. Not mad. But I don't think anyone could argue that what she did was totally sane.'

'I think it was. So do the others. I think it was about the sanest thing Mary ever did. And since then she seems ... different, more in control, more focused. She's identified what has been bothering her for years, and she knows she's not alone.'

He nods. 'I know, *ma petite*, but I'm insistent that she gets help. And this time I'm going to see that she does. She didn't slip that day on the roof at St Martin's, did she?'

Anna thinks about this. 'I don't know. I really don't know.' She thinks about the crucifix being dismantled in the Sister Chapel, and how Treasa thought that Mary had done that. She wonders if she should tell Jean Jacques. She usually tells him everything, just as she once told the fictitious Jean Jacques while she was at school. Time enough, she thought. If we get Mary back to the States and she goes into therapy – time enough then. If she did do that, then it is one more thing to lay to rest.

'What about Olivia?' she asks.

'She'll stay in Scotland. Andrew will look after her. Mary needs a rest from all those things – the ties, the worries, her daughter – everything.'

'It's funny. If she hadn't had the hypnotherapy for her claustrophobia, none of this would have happened,' Anna says.

'You mean what she did to McMorrow? It would have been something else. The psychiatrist said it would have been something else. The memory was waiting to be triggered.'

'What's bothering you?' Anna asks. 'I can feel it. Tell me what it is.'

He sighs. 'The problem is that the prosecution will undoubtedly produce some psychologist who will argue that this is false memory syndrome, that the hypnotherapist suggested the "memory" to Mary and that she was never in fact sexually abused by McMorrow.'

'But she was,' Anna says. 'There is no doubt about it. We all were, and she now remembers it.'

'Yes, but it is arguable – false memory syndrome, I mean. There are proven cases where the so-called memory, which emerges at the time of hypnotherapy, is in fact not a memory at all. All the prosecution need do is produce a few such accounts and when they cross-examine Mary . . . well, she is so fragile, I suppose our barristers don't think she'll hold up. The problem is that if they argue that her testimony is faulty, you will never get as far as the witness box, and then there are no extenuating circumstances to explain why she assaulted him.'

Anna looks at him aghast. 'You can't be serious?'

'I am. That's what our barrister says will happen, and that even if your testimony has gone in and been heard, it could be disallowed.'

'But this is awful,' Anna says. 'This isn't possible. This is an insult to the rest of us. It happened to us. Let no one deny or doubt that. It happened to us. And what Mary has recalled is identical to what happened to us. This isn't possible. No. No.' Her voice trembles in her distress. 'Why would someone say that? No one can deny what happened to us. It happened. What are we going to do?'

'It's all right,' he says. 'It's all right. I don't want you to distress yourself any more.'

'But we're going public. We're only doing that to help Mary. They can't do that. They can't listen to us and then disallow it. They can't.'

'Gently,' he says. 'Gently. There are a number of options. It will be all right. Don't worry.'

But he is worried. And she can see that.

The four women are sitting in a restaurant in Temple Bar early in the morning. Since their initial greeting and placing orders for coffee, juice and toast, there has been little conversation between them. They are smartly dressed, well made-up, their hair styled and perfectly in place. They are all paler than usual, and the tension at the table is palpable.

At one point, Bernadette's hand seems to shake as she reaches for the coffee pot.

'I'll do that,' Treasa says, taking the pot and pouring.

'All for one,' Anna says, the smallest and the youngest, with her neat oval face, red hair and green eyes. Her voice is not quite steady. Although she appears not to be addressing any one of the others in particular, she does half look at Kitty, who nods her head.

Kitty's skin suddenly seems stretched across her fine high cheekbones. Her cropped hair has blonde streaks in it. As she looks at Anna, her eyes suddenly seem clearer, and the determination, which has been lacking in her over the last few days, is suddenly evident.

'And one for all,' she says with a smile.

'Here's Andrew,' Bernadette says, observing the tall, dark-haired man coming in the door.

His face is serious until he reaches them, and then he smiles. He is formally dressed in a dark suit, white shirt and tie.

'Everyone all right?' he asks, pulling up a chair and signalling the waiter for another cup.

'Everything is fine,' Anna says. 'Where's Mary?'

'Her father is taking her. She preferred to go directly to the courts. We'll meet there.' As ever, Andrew has everything under control. 'Let me take you through it once more. When we arrive, we will ignore the media. Try to avoid any eye contact; that will make it easier. You will be taken to a separate room where you will wait until you are called. Anna first, then Bernadette, followed by Treasa. And last of all Kitty.'

'Will it take long? Will we be waiting long?' Kitty asks.

'I shouldn't think so,' he replies. 'The prosecution is only calling two witnesses. The florist and the sales assistant from the sports shop.'

'Why on earth are they witnesses?' asks Treasa.

'They both will identify Mary as being the customer who bought the wreath and the harpoon. Their testimony can't take longer than five minutes. We've been told that, barring any surprises, the cross-examination, if there is any, will only be a formality.'

'And then me?' Anna asks.

He nods.

Her face is very pale. 'My mouth will go dry, I know it will.'

'There'll be water. If you need anything, you just ask for it. It will be all right. There is nothing to be afraid of.'

'I am afraid,' she says. 'I can't help it.'

Treasa reaches out and holds her hand. 'We're all together,' she says. Her dark curly hair looks tousled and she runs her hand through it. She is suddenly the Treasa she was twenty something years earlier, her eyes kind and intense, her leadership qualities evident now as they were then. 'We are all in this together.'

Anna swallows nervously. 'I know,' she says. 'I know. I'm just afraid of the cross-examination – afraid of them making me feel stupid, afraid of how it will appear later in the papers. What people will say . . .'

'We've said these things before,' Kitty says. 'Don't unnerve me, please. I was the one who held out the longest because those are the very things I'm afraid of.'

'Stop now,' Treasa says. 'We're in this together. And if at any point we have doubts, that's what we have to remember.'

'The Five Graces,' Bernadette says.

They smile.

'It will be all right,' Andrew says again. 'The car is outside. It's time to go.'

Chapter Twenty

'T he case has been dropped.'

Andrew and Jean Jacques approach the waiting women. Jean Jacques' arm is round Mary's shoulders. She looks angry.

'What do you mean?' Bernadette is aghast. She is looking at Andrew. 'For God's sake. What do you mean?'

'Just that. The charges have been withdrawn. The case is dropped.'

'Can they do this? Does this make sense? Where does it leave things?' Their questions fall over each other.

'They can do it. And they have. *Nolle pro sequi.* The powers that be have pulled the strings and there is no case,' Andrew says.

'It's not a bad thing. It's the best option.' Jean Jacques says.

'I wanted my day in court.' Mary is aggrieved.

'We've been over this,' Jean Jacques says to her. 'This is the better option. You're off free and the others don't have to testify.'

'But I wanted to tell,' Mary says. 'I wanted them to listen. I wanted to tell them what I remembered.'

'But, darling,' Andrew says, 'you know what they would say.'

'Don't darling me,' Mary says, pulling away from him. 'Don't you darling me. Just because they would have called in some two-bit psychologist with twopence worth of shit to say I had dreamed the whole thing up. I didn't. I DIDN'T dream it up. All you have to do is listen to the others. Each of them – each of them. Look at Bridie, she was eight, for God's sake. And Bernadette, and Kitty . . . for God's sake, look at Kitty. And Treasa, he got her on the day they buried her mother. Don't you talk to me about false memory syndrome. Don't any of you talk such shit to me.'

'Steady, Mary,' Andrew says. 'No one is doubting—'

'Don't you fucking touch me,' his wife says. 'Don't you fucking come near me. I don't want anything to do with you. I want . . . I want . . . I don't know what I want.' She is sobbing now. 'But I don't want this. I'm worth more than this. I don't want the ignominy of someone saying I bloody dreamed it up, but I am entitled to shout it out. I'm entitled to tell what happened and have that dirty priest hang his head in shame. For God's sake, I'd have finished him off if I'd thought this would happen. I'm entitled to my day in court. I'm entitled to that. And the others, my friends, they all came out to back me up. I want my day to tell it. I want it. I want . . . I want . . .' her voice trails away. 'I want my nails back. I need my nails.'

There is silence as they look at her.

'I left my nails in his hands. I want my nails.'

'It's all right,' Jean Jacques says to his daughter as he enfolds her in his arms. 'It's all right. I'm here now. I'm going to make this all right.' He looks at Andrew. 'We need to get out of here.'

Andrew nods. 'There is a police escort waiting. None of us will say anything to anyone. Just keep your heads up and go straight to the cars. It's over,' he says. 'We'll head for Bernadette's. OK?' he asks her.

Bernadette nods.

At the cars, with microphones still being thrust at them, and journalists trying to make contact, Mary looks up and recognises a face in the jostling crowd. A card is thrust into her hand. She glances down and sees that a nail is threaded through the card like a needle. She holds it tightly. Looking around for the person she recognised, she sees nothing now except a sea of faces and people pushing.

Mary refuses to get into the car with Andrew. She will only travel with Treasa and Anna.

Jean Jacques, Andrew, Kitty and Bernadette are in one car.

'It *is* the best option,' Andrew repeats. 'It saves you all, and it saves Mary, but she can't see that.'

'Mary doesn't want to be saved,' Bernadette says. 'Mary is too raw, she's too hurt. She doesn't want salvation. She wants to talk. She needs to talk.'

'We're taking the first flight out in the morning,' Jean Jacques says. 'Anna, Mary and me, back to Washington.'

Kitty looks at Andrew. 'You OK with that?' she asks.

'Yes,' he says. 'Yes. Mary and I ... our marriage has long been over. My only concern is that she is well again.'

'You're not denying what happened?' Kitty asks hotly.

'No,' he replies gently. 'No, I'm not. I'm only trying to protect her now. That's all. She's been hurt enough by the clergy. And unfortunately the power is still there. To have this case against her dropped says it all. They're protecting their own. But for Mary's sake it is as well the charges have been dropped. Get her into court and she will be destroyed. They have enough psychologists in their pockets. And for all the good ones, like the one who has helped Mary these last few weeks, there are those who will say that the hypnosis brought this up, that it isn't real. They would have torn her apart in court, and her memory is unreliable. Bits of what happened have come back, maybe all of it but then again maybe not. She's just too vulnerable. You can imagine how it would have gone. It's all so, I don't know, so obvious. Like a script already written.'

'And Mary doesn't need this,' her father interjects. 'She needs a safe place where Anna and I will mind her, and she can be outside this environment and get proper help. It's already arranged, the help at the other end, I mean. First flight out in the morning, and by tomorrow evening she'll be on the road to recovery.'

'And us?' Kitty asks Bernadette. 'What about us? Where does this leave us?'

Bernadette makes a face. 'I don't know.'

'And everything that's been churned up in the last few weeks?' Kitty continues. 'All the foul and filthy memories I've been forced to dig out so as to assist Mary? What happens to them? I go back to my hotel and I smile at the people, serve them breakfast, have lunch with Miss Maple every few weeks, and I tell myself to forget?' Her voice is very bitter.

'I, for one, am strengthened by the knowledge that the five of us went there, that we were all in that terrible place that you, Kitty, referred to as Golgotha. I am the stronger for knowing that I am not alone,' Bernadette says. 'Even though when I walk out that door, I am alone. I am *not* alone. That is what I have from these few weeks. That and the knowledge that if I am ever needed by any of you, I will be there for you. And you will be there for me. Do you know, for years and years I have read the crime reports in the papers wondering if one day I will read something that I know intimately – that I would find out that someone else out there was got by the same man. And I used to dream that I would go and give that person the support they needed. I dreamed that I would stand up in court and say that I could back every ghastly detail that had come out. It almost happened today. But it didn't. It wasn't meant to. Not now. Not this time. The important thing now is that Mary is safe, and we all have each other.' Bernadette stops suddenly. 'Longest speech I've made in a while,' she laughs.

'Having agreed to give support in court, having agreed to come out and tell it all,' Kitty says, 'I feel badly done by.'

No one speaks.

In the apartment where Mary is staying with Jean Jacques and Anna, the three have headed for bed, exhausted from the day that is now behind them.

Mary takes the card with the nail from her pocket. She pulls the nail free and rolls it in her palm. She feels its familiarity, and she wonders where the other one is. She has no doubt it is one of the pair that she was holding that day in confession during the Retreat. My last confession, she thinks. But I want to confess again. I want to say out loud – not behind a tiny curtain in a wooden box – I want to say, 'God damn you, Father, for you have sinned . . .'

She looks at the card and reads it. She walks to the window and lifts back the curtain to look out at Sutherland Square.

For a moment she can smell the incense, hear the voices of the girls in the gallery: '*Tantum ergo, Sacramentum* . . .' She sees the monstrance raised high on the altar in the priest's hands. Bars of gold rising from the Host in the centre.

I was the lamb of God, she thinks. The nuns led me to the slaughter. They sacrificed me to that evil man. Pray for me, pray for us, someone, somewhere pray, because I don't know how to any more.

She looks again at the card in her hand, then she lets the curtain fall.

310

She gently lifts the phone in her bedroom and dials the number on the journalist's card.

'Hello, this is Mary MacDonald. Yes. Yes. *That* Mary MacDonald. Yes, all right . . . Mary Oliver . . . Yes, of course I recognised you . . . I'm just calling to say that I'll be in Dublin Airport in the morning. I'm leaving on an early flight. Yes. I would be happy to give that interview you were looking for . . . yes . . . Eight fifteen would be fine . . . What? A press conference? . . . Oh, I see . . . Yes. Yes, I'll be there – in the airport. Yes . . . I'll give you all the details. May I suggest that in the meantime you look up all the postings of Father Michael McMorrow. I can shed light on some of his activities between nineteen sixty-six and nineteen seventy-two . . .'

Downeytwo hangs up the phone. She stares at it for a while before dialling her twin.

'It's me,' she says.

'I know.'

'Mary Oliver just called. You know the case against her was dropped this morning?'

'Yes. I saw it on the news.'

'She wants me to meet her in the airport in the morning. She's going to spill the beans.'

'So?'

'You know. Don't say "so". You know. It's all about to come out. All of it. She's going to be gone, out of the country. I'm going to call four other papers so that there is maximum coverage. He did us the same time as he got Mary Oliver . . . at the Retreat. She says she can give details of others starting in nineteen sixty-six.'

'So?'

'The case has been dropped, which means that Mary cannot have her say, cannot give an explanation.'

There is silence from the other end of the phone.

'She wants to tell her story,' continues Downeytwo.

'What's the point?'

'If what she has to say appears in the papers, and the rest of us come out with our stories, the state will have to investigate. The question is, are there enough of us who are strong enough to stand up and be counted?'

'Don't count on me,' says Downeyone.

'The future of our children, your children, their safety, their innocence – all that lies in our hands.'

'I don't want to hear this.' Downeyone hangs up. She is shaking.

She goes into her daughters' bedroom and looks at her sleeping twins. Standing in the doorway, she leans against the doorjamb for some twenty minutes. The sleeping girls lie in adjacent beds, facing each other. The room smells clean and fresh, their gentle breathing soft on the darkened air.

She pats her pocket and feels the nail against her thigh. She takes it out and looks at it, then rolls it in her palm.

'Maybe it is time to give Mary back her nail. Maybe it is time to open the door and shovel out the dirt . . . Maybe it is time . . .'

She goes to the phone and calls her sister back.

'Count me in.'

Tell these souls with sorrow laden, each one born a friendly maiden
They shall survive, they will walk forth, pure and white as virgin snow,
Leave no black plume as a token of the sin thy soul has spoken
You will go back into the storm, retreating to Golgotha's shore
Take thy beak from out my heart, and take thy form from off my door.
                    Quoth the Children, 'Nevermore.'

Now you can buy any of these other bestselling Headline books from your bookshop or *direct from the publisher*.

FREE P&P AND UK DELIVERY
(Overseas and Ireland £3.50 per book)

Backpack	Emily Barr	£5.99
Icebox	Mark Bastable	£5.99
Killing Helen	Sarah Challis	£6.99
Broken	Martina Cole	£6.99
Redemption Blues	Tim Griggs	£5.99
Relative Strangers	Val Hopkirk	£5.99
Homegrown	Gareth Joseph	£5.99
Everything is not Enough	Bernardine Kennedy	£5.99
High on a Cliff	Colin Shindler	£5.99
Winning Through	Marcia Willett	£5.99

TO ORDER SIMPLY CALL THIS NUMBER

01235 400 414

or e-mail <u>orders@bookpoint.co.uk</u>

Prices and availability subject to change without notice.